NIGHT WATCH

NIGHT WATCH

a novel by
JACK OLSEN

Times
BOOKS

Published by TIMES BOOKS, a division
of Quadrangle/The New York Times Book Co., Inc.
Three Park Avenue, New York, N. Y. 10016

Published simultaneously in Canada by
Fitzhenry & Whiteside, Ltd., Toronto.

Library of Congress Cataloging in Publication Data

Olsen, Jack.
Night watch.
I. Title.
PZ4.04985Ni   1979   [PS3565.L77]   813'.5'4   79-12011
ISBN 0-8129-0829-5

Manufactured in the United States of America

For Su and Sara

Scobie said sharply, "Don't talk nonsense, dear. We'd forgive most things if we knew the facts." He smiled unwillingly at Wilson. "A policeman should be the most forgiving person in the world if he gets the facts straight."

—Graham Greene
The Heart of the Matter

I wake and feel the fell of dark, not day.
What hours, O what black hours we have spent
This night.

—Gerard Manley Hopkins
Carrion Comfort

NIGHT WATCH

1

He gripped the fake telegram with quivering fingers that smelled of dishwasher soap and walked up the uneven old staircase as though he lived in the place. He was relieved to see that no light gleamed from under her apartment door. Right now she should be miles away, boarding the dark-green bus marked "Stanton Park."

He sucked air in a quick spasm, half breath and half gulp, and knocked with a single knuckle. If a stranger answered, he would hold up the telegram blank and offer apologies for his mistake. "Isn't this the Swansons'?" He'd be speeding away in the car before they stopped to think that Western Union sent most of its messages by phone these days, and seldom at midnight.

Sweat leaked down his forehead and into his eyes. His handkerchief was soaked, useless. The hottest night of the year: typical lousy luck.

He patted his other pockets. The flat flask, wrapped in a woman's blue nylon knee stocking, gave him slight comfort.

He knocked again, tilted his head.

Silence.

Glossy black plastic bags of trash sagged against each other in front of the next apartment. In the other direction, a peeling brown door was dark and still behind a pair of empty wine bottles. He had the feeling it would swing open and a tub-bellied red-faced man would come out and level a .45 at him. God, he was getting irrational, paranoid. He told himself to relax. He was the dangerous one, not the fools asleep in this dumpy boardinghouse. The dead air was sour. Catpiss. He knew that smell.

He wiped his moist hands on his jeans and shoved a knife blade into the door crack. The latch yielded, and he bit his lip and turned the worn wooden knob. His heart fluttered in his chest like a bird; he felt at once exhilarated and scared. Would there be another lock, a chain, maybe a whole series of locks?

The old door opened inward to his push.

He spun inside, eased the creaky door shut, and began to breathe again in shallow puffs. He thumbed his Pen-lite and saw that he was in a ratty kitchenette apartment. So this was how the bossy bitch lived! The Queen of the May, strutting around the restaurant, telling him what to do. . . .

One room, just as he'd figured.

A simple job. Where would she run?

He looked for the bed, decided it must be hidden in the worn forest-green corduroy sofa with the purple crocheted napkins on the back and the Hawaiian-flowered pillows. He checked out the kitchen, a few steps away from the couch. In an alcove a yard deep, he saw a two-burner hot plate, a deep laundry sink full of stained dishes, a single overhead cabinet decorated in faded daisies, and a chipped turquoise refrigerator that chattered as it fought the heat. On the stained Formica counter a broad-tip marker pen lay alongside a pink note pad. He saw the word "Tampons" scrawled in big black letters. She had the rag on, for the last time. . . .

On the far side of the room, a door was open a few inches. A closet? He could wait in there. One-room apartments didn't offer many hiding places. Or maybe he'd hide in the bathroom and come shrieking out at her. No, no, she'd blow her mind, she'd scream her stupid head off. Exactly what he didn't want. He needed time, he couldn't be rushed. It had to be done—with style.

He brushed at his eyes, felt the sweat lubricate his fingers. A tatter-winged moth flitted through the narrow cone of overhead light and did a series of slow rolls till it disappeared behind the couch. He swallowed hard; his throat was parched from mouth-breathing. He reminded himself to be relentless, methodical. He was inside now, the danger was over, unless—unless she came home with a friend. His heart pumped hard till he remembered that she didn't bring men home; the tease was her play.

Her spiteful words jumped into his head: "Get lost, creep!" God, it was like a kick in the stomach, just remembering. Not only the words, but the way she'd said them, with such cold contempt, such a look of disgust, as though he were—a bug, a snail. Something you step on and wince. All those months of watching, dreaming about her, fantasizing, and when he finally asked her to acknowledge his existence, when he finally made the tiniest plea for her to admit he existed—why, she said—she—she told him to . . .

He wouldn't repeat those words. Not even to himself.

What did he do to deserve that?

Nothing.

And what did he do to deserve all the other kicks in the face? Why was he still washing dishes in the steaming kitchen and running his legs off when two other helpers had already been promoted to busboy over him? Had he ever been late? Broken a dish? Hassled the cook? Hassled *any* of them?

What had he done?

It was his face. . . .

He wiped a sleeve across his eyes and blinked. Don't think about it, he reminded himself. Jimmy Doremus, you damn jerk, relax!

She'll look up with those wide green eyes full of tears. *Too late! Too late, Betty! Don't bother apologizing.* He'd make her open that Kewpie-bow mouth with the cinnamon-red lipstick, that street slut's mouth that teased and cursed, and he'd say, "Here! Drink! That's it, whore, *drink!*"

Just like the dreams . . .

He stepped into the bathroom and poked his wavering light around. A mildewed shower stall looked like a coffin set on end. A wooden toilet seat showed a lacy pattern of cracks in the enamel. On a narrow shelf of pale-green glass his flash picked out a white jar of skin cream, a small brown makeup box flecked with loose mascara, a wrinkled, uncapped tube of toothpaste and a yellow plastic drinking glass with white smears around the rim. She must have been in a rush this morning. He remembered that she'd punched in late as usual. But then certain employees had special privileges. . . .

The oppressiveness of her place made him jittery. Top-floor apartments were ovens anyway. A scarred tan air conditioner hung from the single window. Silent. Or broken. Probably the landlady sneaked in and tampered with it during the day. The way the super did at his place.

He tried to anticipate the arrival scene. She'd strut across the room in that wriggling stride of hers and flick the air conditioner on and shake out that impudent blond mane and start yanking off her clothes. Let's see, what had she worn today? A light-blue flowered skirt that weighed maybe an ounce and a dark-blue jersey that clung to her nipples like spray paint. He'd watched as she pranced across the street on her lunch break, tight little backside twitching as she stepped off the curb in her high-heeled wedgies, skirt swirling like a Latin dancer's as she rounded the corner. Men turned to stare at her, and she knew it. The slut actually dressed for it! Tried to make men hot, then jacked them around. He knew about women like that. "C.T.s," they were called. Cock teasers. Lived to tease and torment. . . .

Damn woman talked like a ten-dollar whore, too. "Shit." "Piss." Every day the words spilled out like an overflowing septic tank. Last Monday she giggled and gave the head busboy the finger and whispered "Motherfucker" while the chef acted amused. Cute. *Cute!*

James J. Doremus would give her "motherfucker," all right. He'd give her all the filth she could handle. In liquid form. He checked his watch. Her belly-dance class was supposed to finish thirty minutes ago. Counting the walk and the bus ride, she was about due. He leaned against the blistered wallpaper of the bathroom and slipped his Pen-lite into his pocket, hearing it clink against the knife. He snapped the blade out and tested it against his cheek. Short and sharp, double-edged, honed for hours on his Arkansas whetstone.

Oh, lordie, just wait! He'd grab her by that long hair, bend her to her knees, and shove the cold blade against her throat. Then he'd slam her down and jump on her and uncap the flask. *Drink! Drink, sewermouth! "Get lost," huh? Isn't that what you told me to do? Huh? HUH? What's the matter, you can't talk now? Is something the matter with—*

A rumbling noise snapped his head around and almost made his knees crumple.

The street. A couple of souped-up cars racing. All night long, crazy kids dragged this street, waking people up. Well, tonight the noise might help. She could cry out and nobody'd pay attention. He'd pry her mouth open, make her beg and plead, and then he'd pour it in. Slowly, *slowly* . . .

There'd be one less foul-mouthed C.T. in the world.

Why'd she have to say a thing like that to him? *Why?* He jerked his head abruptly when he heard the footsteps downstairs. . . .

One two three four five six steps, then clip-clop across the landing to the second-floor staircase, then one two three four five six steps again, across the next landing. . . .

His right hand gripped the bone handle of the knife and his wet shirt clung to his skin as he pressed backward against the bathroom wall.

A key scratched at the lock.

The room glowed for an instant and then went black as the door shut.

She was alone, humming a tune.

When the overhead light clicked on, he stepped from the bathroom and said, "P-p-please, d-d-don't make a m-m-m-move."

2

The night watch commander's shaggy head twisted sideways and one sea-blue eye squeezed almost shut as he tried to comprehend the arrest report on his desk. What the Christ was Patrolman Willie Bethea trying to get across? It was becoming a nightly chore, deciphering these scribblings and fixing them up. Sure, he could leave Willie B's report in its original pidgin English, but that would reflect against the whole station. He knew what the desk jockeys at headquarters thought of Precinct Nine already: they called it Lower Slobbovia and treated it like a land-fill project. Every time they flopped a detective for incompetence, they sent him to the Ninth. Every time some troublemaking harness bull wrote a letter to the editor, they exiled him to Lower Slobbovia.

Then Lieutenant Sverre J. "Packer" Lind, commander, third watch, would begin another of his patented salvage projects. First, a friendly chat in his office. "I know what you've heard about the Ninth, Officer, and it's cowshit. We got a solid bunch of troops, you'll fit right in." A suggestion here, a compliment there, a light kick in the ass, and always the personal touch. A watch commander had to care about his men, and it couldn't be faked, at least not for long. So Packer Lind struggled over Willie Bethea's arrest report. He would *not* allow Willie to look stupid. That's just what those pencil pushers uptown wanted to think, and the captain of the precinct, too, for that matter, and they were dead wrong.

The night lieutenant adjusted his sweaty backside to his imitation Naugahyde desk chair and stared at Willie B's inked letters again:

Suspect No. 1 stated this was going to be their last Escaped, himself and Suspect No. 2 would never steal another car wheather R.O. and Partner arrested them now or not.

He rubbed his damp forehead, his crabbed and twisted little finger worrying the pale-pinkish rut that bisected his left eyebrow. Chrisakes, what was a "last Escaped"? It was too damn hot for this kind of duty.

He got up and circumnavigated the rack of three dark-green lockers, one for the commander of each watch, and tried to separate his clothes from his skin with a sinuous wriggle. He opened his locker door and toyed with the idea of changing into a dry monkeysuit. The plastic nameplate read "Lt. Sverre Jon Lind," but it had been a long time since he had been called any of those names. It had been "Packer" ever since a moonlighting job humping sides of beef, and he preferred it. Through high school and the Marines, they'd all pronounced his name "Severe." Who needed a name like that?

The W.C. looked at the fresh uniform hanging at attention in his locker and shut the tinny door. Of course he wouldn't change: not with dry cleaning so expensive and him and Amnee saving every cent. He shuffled back to his desk and sat heavily. Willie B's report hadn't gone away.

Maybe I should break the sentences down element by element, he advised himself, try to get a clue to the meaning.

Okay. "Suspect No. 1"—that was the driver of the stolen car. "Suspect No. 2"—that was the passenger. "R.O. and Partner" referred to the reporting officer, W. R. Bethea, and his partner, Rollie Beemer. When the unit made an arrest, why didn't Beemer write the report? At least he was familiar with simple English, whereas that turkey Bethea—what was it he wrote after the riots? "I ordered the woman to disperse." Now how the Christ could you order one person to disperse?

He rubbed the smart-ass smile from his face, even though there was no one in his office to witness his disloyalty. It was flat stupid to make remarks about Willie B's command of English and it was flat inaccurate to call him a turkey. Matter of fact, he would take Willie for backup in preference to a couple of hundred so-called police officers he could think of, including most of his other eighteen men and his two sergeants. On a searing summer night like this one he'd seen Willie disarm a psycho waving a razor and threatening to impale his own infant on a picket fence. Willie ran right up, choke-held the guy with one arm and threw him down so hard he bounced twice and handcuffed him behind his back, all in about five seconds flat. A new rodeo record for bulldogging an armed lunatic. Willie Bethea was a skilled cop. Very skilled and very cool. And God knew the city needed good black officers. There was a new estrangement of blacks and whites, especially in the poor sections, and it was widening every day. The watch commander wasn't sure why, but he suspected it had something to do with humans relabeling humans, stigmatizing them by race. In Vietnam, he remembered, nobody killed people, they "wasted Congs." And throughout the city, policemen didn't arrest blacks or Negroes; they busted spooks, jigs, spades, niggers. Arrested them and sometimes roughed them up and once in a while shot one. But police officers never killed. Killing was what the bad guys did. The men in blue dusted, dumped, burned, smoked, or dropped their targets, or blew them away. The slang words made the killing less painful.

Packer Lind sighed at the imponderability of it all. He was suspicious of glib politicians with easy answers, but he had no answers of his own. Most police officers were an improvement over a few years back, he knew that, but they still had a long way to go. A *long* way . . . And now that the taxpayers had taken a meat ax to the city budget, he didn't see how they would ever get there.

By God, he said to himself, the heat's softening my brain. My mind's wandering, just when I was beginning to get some work done. He adjusted his futile little desk fan and clapped a damp hand against a damp forehead. Why, Jesus Christ, he intoned under his breath, I'm turning into a do-gooder, a regular social worker. In the police lexicon, there was no bigger insult.

A train rumbled down one of the nine tracks that ran on the main line, carrying industrial products and raw lumber and winos out of town and returning with lettuce and oranges and a fresh supply of winos. The fading, tinted picture of His Honor Mayor Donald Coulbourn rattled against the cracked and mottled wall. Freights always made the picture rattle, high-speed passenger trains jiggled it lightly, and switch engines herding boxcars made the picture bump and sometimes slip sideways.

He hefted one of his size thirteen orthopedic shoes atop the cheap desk and tilted backward in his undersized chair. When his curly gray-black hair touched the wall, he felt the warmth that the afternoon sun had broiled into the building. "It hit ninety-five today," the second watch commander had said when Packer relieved him. "You're lucky you work nights." Yeah, lucky. Now it was pushing midnight and the thermometer had dropped all the way to eighty-six. He could feel the sweat mushing around in the all-wool irregular socks that he had picked up at the Army-Navy. Soon he'd have to find an excuse to get out on the street, create a refreshing breeze with his unmarked olive Fury. He made a mental note to feed the mutt before he left. A tramp dog of mixed furs and colors had stopped by the station long enough to give birth a week ago, and now the family was residing in an improvised chicken-wire enclosure behind the parking lot in back. We don't have enough problems, he said to himself, the place is turning into a kennel. All the men gooing and cooing while she licks her pups. If they love dogs so much, why the Christ don't they help feed her?

Once again he picked up the arrest report and read slowly. " . . . going to be the last Escaped . . ." Had Willie meant to write "last escape"? But the computer print-out showed the suspect had no rap sheet, none whatever. Why would he promise a "last escape" if he'd never been in jail before?

For a second the lieutenant toyed with the idea of using his portable radio and asking Willie B directly what the report meant. But that would be an unnecessary embarrassment to a hard-working officer and also a waste of street time, the only time that counted to a watch commander. What good was a supervisor who couldn't understand his own men? Maybe if he sounded it out, syllable by syllable, the way kids did in remedial reading classes . . .

SUS-PECT NUM-BER ONE STAT-ED THIS WAS GO-ING TO BE THEIR LAST ES-CA-PED . . .

Es-ca-ped . . .

Escapade! He should have known.

Hunching his wide shoulders over the desk till his eyes were inches from the paper, he corrected the spelling, straining to simulate Willie B's colorful printing with its random mix of capital and small letters. Then he erased the "a" in "wheather" and applied his seal of approval at the bottom: "Lt. S. Lind, 3d Watch, Pct. 9." Pleased with his accomplishment, he slid the report into a cracked wooden box bearing the word "OUT" on a crinkling strip of paper pasted at one end, and reached for the phone.

Nope, he wouldn't call her this late. He withdrew his big hand and yanked open a balky desk drawer instead. Lately the baby had been troubled by prickly heat, and he didn't want to risk waking the child out of a deep sleep and forcing his wife to walk the floor again. Poor Amnee, she had responsibilities these days, too. It wasn't like the old days when he could call home at any hour of the watch and wisecrack in his Marlon Brando voice and she would laugh and joke right back and say how much she missed his ugly face and tease him about what they'd do when he got home.

Well, nobody promised that life would never change, did they? That was half the fun, keeping up with the changes, meeting the challenges.

Last Escaped . . .

He smiled and glanced at his gold-filled Elgin watch, purchased out of pawn when he was a burglary dick. The plastic band was rimed with white: the residue of sweat. 11:15 P.M. He looked upward. Would it rain? Ever? *Please?* If only there was a window in this dungeon. He lifted himself to his six feet four, writhed like a disco dancer till his shorts released his balls, and walked.

The open area around the station's admitting desk turned out to be as parched and stifling as his own office, despite a propped front door that admitted occasional noxious puffs from trucks rolling toward the loading docks uptown. "Here, Lieutenant," Patrolman Gerald Yount mumbled, handing over an unopened roll of toilet paper.

"Thanks, I already been," Packer said.

"Oriental woman brought it in," Yount explained in his tight compressed voice, as though begrudging every word. "Said this is for the, uh, crap we been handing them."

Packer wished the deskman would speak up instead of swallowing his words, and stop covering his mouth like a man with new teeth. "We been rousting any Orientals I don't know about?"

Yount mumbled an answer.

"Hmmm don't *hmmm?"* Packer asked sharply.

"I don't know," Yount repeated, slightly louder. Chrisakes, the poor guy sounded a hundred years old. So—defeated. At twenty-four. And two years ago you had to chain him down to keep him from making warrant arrests at three in the morning.

"She was probably pissed about a ticket," Packer said, handing back the roll.

"Right, Lieutenant"—Yount's favorite expression. Packer wished the guy would learn another one, it was getting tiresome. *Right, Lieutenant. Sure, Lieutenant. Right . . .* "City Hall turned into cream cheese last night, Gerry." *Right, Lieutenant.* "Chicago blew up today, Gerry." *Sure, Lieutenant. . . .* How could you have a conversation with a guy who didn't respond?

Packer had a reputation for patience, but Gerald Yount was testing it. He took a long look at the deskman, slumped in his chair, shirt mussed up, collar unbuttoned. A police officer who's supposed to meet the public. Just *look* at him! Sunken cheeks, the flesh tones of a clam, the skin around his dark eyes all puffy and pink. From crying? Packer doubted it. The men often gossiped about his case, and they all agreed. Yount didn't cry; he'd be better off if he did.

For almost two months now, Packer had gone out of his way to be helpful, but how could you help a brother officer who loved to suffer?

And over what? The no-fault divorce was going through without contest, far as anybody knew: no problem, no fuss, no messy testimony. There were no kids to pull apart and mourn over, and as for losing Darlene Yount—well, it couldn't be that big a loss. Packer remembered a heavy, poorly proportioned woman: wide in the seat, flat in the bust, with a face that might have been pretty if it hadn't been so puffy.

Certainly not worth having a nervous breakdown over—

Wait! What a stupid thing to say! Christ, he was becoming judgmental again. Just like the captain. He figured it must be the heat. Who knew what poor Yount was losing, or *thought* he was losing? What business was it of anybody else's? Darlene Yount seemed as fascinating as a fire hydrant, sure, but maybe some of the men felt that way about Amnee, too. Himself, he had always tried not to question other men's tastes and other men's feelings. There was a Latin expression about taste, *de gustibus* something something something; he had failed to memorize it in the two weeks before dropping the class.

Well, everybody in Precinct Nine had a graveyard theory about the strange behavior of Gerald Yount; one more wouldn't hurt. Captain J. Singletary, with typical charity, said, "Certain types, they burn out quick, like cheap motors." A nice easy analogy, a little too nice and easy for the watch commander to buy it. Gerry Yount was deeper than that, more complex. He had been a highly motivated young officer, headed for the detective bureau as soon as he put in the minimum time and passed a few tests. Then overnight he'd become a physical and mental wreck. Why, he must have dropped twenty, twenty-five pounds in two months! His uniform hung like a bloodhound's pelt; he had tics and blinks and spasmodic body movements like an advanced alky, and the guy wasn't even a drinker. Never touched it.

Packer felt frustrated, helpless. "Gerry, you feeling okay, pal?" he asked, knowing the answer already.

"Sure, Lieutenant."

"Anything I can do, kid? Anything at all?"

The deskman shook his head, once. Packer turned toward his office. What could he do? The desk job was the customary rest haven for overstressed men. But Yount hadn't wanted it, he'd wanted to stay on the street, and the street was the worst place in the world for a troubled policeman. The lieutenant had noticed the deterioration long before Yount's partner, Billy Mains, came in and asked to be switched to another car. "Fucking guy don't talk, he don't eat, don't respond, he just sets there," Mains had complained. "It's wigging me out, Lieutenant." Packer had detailed Yount to the desk, but now he was wondering if he shouldn't have sent the poor soul to the hospital instead. A little force-feeding, maybe, the way they did some of the gooks—some of the Vietnamese prisoners, he corrected himself. A month of rest with no responsibilities whatever. And then—maybe a few more weeks on the desk, under the W.C.'s watchful eye, and the long healing process would begin. He's one of ours, we can't give up on him, he reminded himself. We can't . . .

Yount stared at Packer's left shoulder and held up the roll of toilet paper. "What should I do with this, Lieutenant?"

"File it!" He was annoyed at the deskman and doubly annoyed at himself for raising his voice.

"Under what?"

He managed an apologetic smile. "I dunno, Gerry. Community relations."

"Right, Lieutenant."

Packer returned to the solitary confinement of his office, away from the deskman's defeated look and manner. No, by God, he could *never* excuse a lack of pride in *any* officer for *any* reason. He wanted to go back and grab Gerry Yount by the lapels and scream at him, "Chrisakes, man, at least show a little respect for your uniform!"

But instead he drummed his long fingers on his desk, cracked his walnut-sized knuckles, then took a deep breath and blew out a sibilant stream. *Pride.* After twelve years on the force, he had strong feelings on the subject. Back in his first few years, before the scandals and the trials and the general housecleaning, he'd known plenty of policemen who were ashamed of their uniforms and ashamed of their jobs. And almost always they developed into the worst thieves and grafters. He thought he understood. Lacking pride, they went for the money; it became their only satisfaction. He cringed when he remembered how it had been almost routine for cops to shake down drunks and strip the wallets from D.B.s. And if the cop didn't lift the cash off the dead body, the crew of the meat wagon did.

Those days were gone, thank Christ, but a new disease was spreading fast, and there was no cure in sight. The taxpayers' revolt had cost the city three hundred men from a force that was already thin. Efficiency was falling off, and public complaints were way up—complaints from the same citizens and taxpayers who created the overwork problem in the first place. And the top brass—he cringed when he thought about the chief and his three deputies. Once good men, now they played the politicians' game. Ran around busily pointing the finger of blame downward at individual cops instead of upward at the city bosses and the shortsighted taxpayers. The troops felt abandoned, dumped on, and goddamn it, they were right! Look at that bike man in the Eleventh last month. Chain-whipped by a kid gang while the dispatcher called for help. Backup was thin and late, and now the bike man was a vegetable. Messages like that weren't lost on the force. Some men drove scared, flinching at shadows. Some sucked pills or booze to get through the watch. Some gritted their teeth and tore compulsively into their work and let their personal lives go up in smoke. And some—

Aw, Christ, he didn't want to think about it. His critics were right; he wasted too much energy worrying about the problems of the whole P.D.; there was enough trouble right here in Precinct Nine, and a lot of it was his own fault. He identified too much with his cops. He wasn't a patrolman anymore, hadn't been for six years, hadn't been a sergeant for two. He was a patrol lieutenant, a watch commander, a man of authority, and why the hell didn't he exercise it once in a while? "Jesus Jones!" Captain Singletary had griped at him. "Half the precinct calls you by your first name! What kind of leadership is that? You got to back off, Packer, establish some distance. You're not running for Miss Congeniality, you're the ramrod on a night watch. Now get out there and act like it!"

Well, by God, he would. Yes, sir, just watch. Heads would roll at Precinct Nine.

How many times had he made that promise to himself? But this time he meant business. Damn right he did! Already made a start at roll call tonight, didn't he, when he got on Zebra Seven's case? What a couple of losers! Car Zebra Seven was manned by two uninspired old survivors, and all they did was cruise right past an on-view complainant the night before. Citizen comes running out on the sidewalk screaming that his burglar alarm's going off, and those two dummies drive by like a couple of old ladies in a funeral procession. Windows sealed so their air conditioner would work better. Came right out and admitted it! Probably listening to Stay-up Sam the record man, too, even though they'd never cop to that. At roll call he'd delivered a short sermon entitled "Insulated Officers in Insulated Cars," rattling a few of the station's grimy old windows in the process. He doubted if anybody in Precinct Nine would be driving in sealed-up cars tonight. No, not tonight. It would take them a shift or two to slip back to their old ways. . . .

He shook his head as he remembered their excuses. "Jeez, Pack, it was hot!" "Yeah! Musta been ninety-fucking-five out there." Luckily the burglar alarm turned out to be a short circuit instead of some coked-up gunsel inside the house, or a couple of cops' asses would be up before a review board.

Well, it was a fact that the car air conditioners didn't work right with the windows open, but that problem didn't seem important to the night watch commander as he sat in the only police station in town that wasn't refrigerated and felt the dark stains ooze wider in the armholes of his uniform. The simple idiots! Anybody wants comfort, why don't they apply in Juneau?

3

Sergeant Zoltan "Turk" Molnar, floating in the David sector of Precinct Nine, eased his shiny green-and-white into the parking lot alongside the empty patrol car. Under a window sign that said "Special—Cod Filets, $4.55 lb.," he made out the familiar forms of Patrolmen Endicott Wry and Sam Demaris at the checkout stand, interviewing the suspects: females, two of them; they looked to Molnar like Indians or what he thought of as "high yellows." A pile of groceries lay on the counter; he figured it must be the evidence. Christ, where had they concealed all that shit? The two women were wearing just about enough to cover a bat's snatch. Stuffed the loot in their handbags, he guessed. All the amateur shoplifters carried handbags, or else they had raincoats over their arms, or umbrellas. Dead giveaway, they might as well wear T-shirts that said "SHOPLIFTER."

Well, he'd step inside, make himself available for consultation. He thought of his job as "teachin' and preachin'." Sergeants weren't required to screen misdemeanor arrests, but for a change nothing heavy was happening in the rest of David sector and the store was air-cooled and Turk Molnar was already giving off steam like a spent dray horse. The heat was upsetting his stomach and his dinner was repeating; periodically he could taste the thick borscht that had been garnished with chewy little rafts of dark bread topped with sour cream.

He cut the engine and burped a tiny tribute to his present wife, Thelma Krazowski Molnar. What a choice he'd made, what a fine piece of work! After his divorce, he'd spent a year alternately dating Thelma the police matron and her cousin Helena Guminska, the clerk in the motor pool, till one night over boilermakers his partner advised him, "Turk my boy, sooner or later you got to stop vacillating between those two Poles." Molnar was glad he had chosen Thelma. She was heavier than Helena by some fifty pounds, "the huge economy size" as he was fond of saying. He was also fond of saying, "Good things come in big packages." No one could convince him that this wasn't the correct wording.

The easygoing sergeant winced as he stepped onto the hot surface of the parking lot. Heat rays were still floating up from the soft asphalt three hours after sunset. There were times when he wished he had never left his native Bessemer, Alabama. At least they anticipated the summer back home, dressed for it; their patrol cops wore loose-woven short-sleeve shirts open at the collar and they were allowed to roll up their car windows so their air conditioners would work.

That was certainly one subject the lieutenant was bug-fuck over. "Keep those car windows *down!*" he'd hollered at roll call tonight. "All the way down!" Shit oh dear, he was *loud!* Nobody could remember Packer Lind blowing his cool like that. "Get out there and talk to people!" he'd shouted, gimping up and down the ranks like—Turk Molnar stroked his flowing blue-black mustache and tried to remember the name. Oh, yeah. Sergeant Queeg in the old movie.

Nobody had talked back, not even Patrolman Artie Siegl, and Artie usually had a wise-ass comment for everybody. Molnar had kept his own face shut, too, nodding grimly as the lieutenant jutted his heavy jaw into the gleaming faces up and down the line. The old sergeant reckoned he had already heard more than his fair share of Gettysburg Addresses by watch commanders. They had become routine to him: six of one and a dozen of the other, as he liked to say: neither flesh nor fowl. The W.C.s made their speeches and the troops drove off and did as they pleased: a block from the station they were King Shit again.

Well, Packer Lind had made himself understood in no uncertain words, the sergeant said to himself as he walked toward the door of the all-night grocery. Come to think of it, Packer Lind always seemed to make himself understood, even when he whispered. At the academy they called that "command presence." Himself, Turk Molnar had been born without it. That was why he hadn't made rank till he was forty-five and ignored the lieutenant's test for the last ten years. As he often asked himself, what was the use of shoveling coal against the tide? Sector sergeant wasn't a bad job anyway, plenty of jacking around and laughs and a brew or two with the boys when the watch was over, and then Thelma to go home to. Two hundred and five pounds, and every one of them jiggling just for him. A good dancer, too.

He smiled contentedly and followed his protruding stomach into the store, inhaling his first breath of refrigerated air with relief. Patrolman Endicott Wry was pressing hard in his ticket book with the triple carbons while Sam Demaris stood to one side and called out the evidence. Both men straightened up when they saw their supervisor. A pimply young clerk who looked to Molnar like a spic strolled over to make friends with his stripes, but the sergeant held up a palm that resembled an undercooked turkey pie, trying to convey the message that he wasn't here to interfere, his men were on top of the situation, let's you and me butt out.

"Two packages ribs, six pounds," Demaris resumed in a professionally bored voice. "One bottle of rib sauce. A bag of rice, two pounds. One two three four five six seven eight nine packs of Kool-Aid."

The sergeant caught the bloodshot eye of one of the suspects and shook his head disappointedly at her. She stopped popping her gum and moved her lips in a silent curse. He figured she was maybe twenty, a spook with a touch of white blood. Somebody must have changed his luck a few generations ago. The fat one with the brown cigarette dangling from thick purple lips had to be an Indian or a half-breed. She stared at the grid of lights embedded in the plastic ceiling and hummed softly. Probably strung out on pills or grass. What kind of dummies would caper at midnight, when there was nobody else in the store to distract the clerks and the watchmen behind their one-way mirrors? The poor and the drunk, that's what kind of dummies, and everybody knows shit runs uphill. They even stole poor. Imagine going to the trouble of shoplifting ribs: a buck sixty a pound and 90 percent of it bones. Rice and Kool-Aid, can you believe it? Why, there was shrimp in the back, butterfish filets; there were chuck steaks an inch thick, stuffed anchovies and ripe olives and plump knackwurst that popped when you bit into them. Why go to court for a bunch of ribs and rice?

Because that's all they know, he answered himself. The poor cunts, they probably never seen a lobster or a knackwurst except on the tube. Well, he wouldn't feel sorry for them, standing there sulky and mean, trying to stare a hole in the linoleum. He wouldn't go soft. He knew better than to make *that* mistake, hadn't made it since his rookie years in Bessemer. You start sympathizing with this type, you turn around and find a blade up your ass. Yeah, he knew about rehabilitation, but you couldn't rehabilitate this type any more than you could rehabilitate a cockroach into a june bug.

Patrolman Endicott Wry, short and wiry and born to wear bow ties, laid a slip of thin yellow paper on the counter in front of the black perpetrator and said in a singsong voice, "Okay, Brenda, this is a citation for shoplifting the listed items below. Your signature's required right—there. Just like the statement reads, Brenda, it's not an admission of guilt, it's just your promise that you'll obey those instructions on your copy of the citation. Now this is a mandatory court for shoplifting, Brenda. Okay?"

"Shit on you, man. I didn't take nothing."

Their cussing was as simple-minded as they were. *Shit on you.* Molnar shook his head. What were minorities coming to?

"Sign right here and you can go home. Okay, Brenda? That's it. Thank you very much."

Sam Demaris handed a yellow slip to the other subject and made the same speech almost word for word. The Indian woman signed without comment, ashes spilling from her lip-soaked cigarette as she squinted over the ticket slip.

"Okay, ladies, thanks," Demaris said in a tone of false courtesy.

"Be seeing you," said Wry, closing his evidence case with a snap.

"No you won't," Brenda responded.

"Shits," the Indian woman muttered.

"Okay, ladies, thanks again," Demaris said, his face twitching. Molnar wondered what the two men would be saying if he hadn't dropped in to observe. "And have a nice evening," Demaris added through clenched teeth.

"Fuck off, Four Eyes," one of the women said. The sergeant couldn't be sure which; he was already following his men out of the store.

"Police brutality if ever I seen it," he said, leaning into the window of David Seven. "Rousting fine upstanding citizens like that. Don't you guys know them girls are Junior League? What're y'all, on a misdemeanor quota?"

"Might as well be," Demaris said, sliding his portable radio into the console. "Sometimes I feel like a goddamn hall monitor."

"Well, don't take on about it, Sam," Molnar said, laying his thick hand on the driver's forearm. "Sometimes you act like one, too."

Demaris grunted, and Wry gave out a phony laugh, the special kind for supervisors. "You men eat yet?" Molnar asked.

"No, and we won't be," Demaris said. His face flushed pink in the light from the market's sign. "Not till we finish our paper work."

"Paper work? What paper work? You just done it when you wrote that ticket."

"He means a buncha other crap we handled," Wry said, talking across his partner. "An impound. A missing kid. A four-nine-one. The usual."

"Buncha goddamn accountants," Demaris said, tapping the black imitation-leather case on his lap. The sergeant knew what he meant. Inside the case were two dozen different kinds of forms, ranging from major-crime report blanks to gas log sheets. Scratching a hairy ear, he remembered the old line about a lot of justice at the end of a nightstick. Well, how much was at the end of a ballpoint pen?

"Hey," the oven-bellied sergeant shouted at the departing green-and-white, "y'all keep them windows down, hear?"

"Huh?" Wry called back. He made an elaborate show of rolling up his window and pressing his clown face against the glass.

"Very funny, son. I'll mention it to the lieutenant. He likes a good laugh hisself."

The patrol car eased toward the exit, then stopped and backed up jerkily. "Hey, Sarge," Wry asked, the trace of a leer on his face, "you heard anything tonight about Mains and his, uh, partner?"

"Should I of?"

"Well, uh—"

"You boys just mind your own bidness," Molnar said, harsher than he intended. "Billy'll be all right. And so'll the broad—the lady—the *woman*."

"Yes, *sir!*" Wry said with exaggerated respect.

"And don't call me 'sir,'" Molnar barked. "A simple 'your highness' is okay." They left him in a cloud of exhaust gas.

The whole goddamned precinct must be checking on Mains and his new partner, he said to himself. Packer took a hell of a chance, assigning the new broad to David Three. She was shaped like a piece of a jigsaw puzzle, and she was already driving some of the troops into the cold shower. No one knew her exact bra size, but the sergeant had thirty-six-C in the pool, and he only wished he had drawn a thirty-eight, a thirty-nine. She could be trouble, too. The captain was right. A few nights ago in the Slammer bar, the old man had revealed his true feelings on the subject of female patrol officers. "Any woman that rides in a police car," the precinct commander had said in a rare burst of frankness, "they're gonna make waves, bet on it. But it's not the broads' fault, it's the yay-hoos in the station. They give 'em so much attention they start to think their piss is Cold Duck. Overnight they're Cleopatra Queen of the Nile. It's an artificial self-esteem they pick up, and based on what? Based on the ordinary hot pants of the ordinary cop."

Steering his patrol car along Bertram Boulevard, the sergeant started to make a run at a blue Galaxie that failed to signal a lane change, but he dropped back when he noticed the bumper sticker "Support Your Local Police." A nice guy, he realized. Probably *did* signal, and I just missed it.

Yes, sir, for a change their head poncho was right. Well, the new assignments would answer one burning question. Could Patrolwoman Mary Rob Maki hold off a horny cop like Mains from eight at night till four in the morning? A cop whose going-away gift when he was flopped for making a pass at a lady judge had been a dozen ribbed black cundrums? Could *any* policewoman handle a stud like that?

Turk Molnar feared the worst and secretly wished for it; he told himself hopefully it was 99 to 100 there'd be trouble. The tip-off had come the night before, when Mains had announced in the locker room, "It's my honest opinion that women shouldn't patrol with men, but I'm willing to be the guinea pig. Say, any you guys got a French tickler?"

Nobody'll ever reform snatch-hounds like Billy Mains, the old cop mused as he slowed to check a few front doors. He couldn't remember a precinct without its share, running around with their tongues hanging out like chow-dogs. Some of them even managed to do a good job, at least for a time. There'd been a time when Billy Mains was a balls-out charger, made about forty felony busts a year piloting an undercover car out of Central. He was still a handy man to have around when you needed a door kicked in, or a woolly head cracked.

The senior sergeant hung a lazy right at Prospect Avenue and headed for Kap'n Klam's. Tonight he would eat lightly, out of respect for Thelma's dinner. He'd order—let's see, maybe a dozen oysters, a bowl of shrimp—no, make that two; it was irresistible the way the Kap'n steamed them in beer—a couple cups of coffee, and the usual slab of key lime pie a la mode. Molnar burped in anticipation, and smiled again at the staying power of borscht.

He wondered if he should pick something up for the station's dog. Maude, they'd named her, she might be craving a midnight lunch; she was nursing four hungry pups. Their father must have been a Great Dane, by the looks of things. He wondered if dogs liked shrimp. Probably not. Maude had already turned her nose up at the raw fish Patrolman Sol Nakamura brought in, and who could blame her? Nakamura claimed the stuff was fresh albacore, six bucks a pound, the Japs called it "stashimi" or some such name. Well, the dog didn't go for it. Call it all the fancy names you want, raw fish was raw fish.

He had just touched his front wheels to Kap'n Klam's drive-in entrance when the radio interrupted his plans.

4

Cursing the stubborn heat, Packer Lind shoved his fifty-watt gooseneck lamp toward his office wall. The light bounced off the faded municipal-green plaster and returned a bilious glow. F-2, the radio channel for Precinct Nine, emitted background noise that sounded like paper ripping. The watch commander turned up the volume and converted the static into a waterfall, closed his eyes and imagined himself standing under it in shower clogs, his gray-black curly hair plastered to his head. He cut the volume abruptly when a loud voice broke in over the splashing waters: "David Seven clear on the Oh-Six-Four."

Packer thought back to the original shoplifting call less than an hour ago. Who was David Seven tonight? Wry and Demaris, as usual. Good cops. Not the kind who would use a simple shoplift as an excuse for a couple hours downtime. They were back on patrol already. That was the way it had to be done these days: a quick response to calls and a quick return to the street. You didn't have to go to command school to learn that.

He listened as David Three called in to announce a thirty-minute 934—out of service. Billy Mains. The lieutenant recognized the raspy side-of-the-mouth delivery. That's a long time for a leak, he was thinking as Radio acknowledged the message.

He thumbed the button on his own portable RCA to drop a hint that Mains and his new partner, Mary Rob Maki, cut it short, but he decided not to bother. The precinct had been overworked in the hot spell; everybody needed a breather. Packer remembered tonight's calls: the shoplift, serve three or four warrants, a runaway, direct traffic at a couple of minor accidents, investigate report of an on-view lily waver in front of a boys' school, return a senile man to his daughter's home, a juvenile brawl, two burglary investigations. . . . Chippy stuff for a change. The only case that might cost time in court was the lily waver, and that was bound to be a walkaway, cut and dried, six months suspended, see the court-appointed psychiatrist and quit pulling your pud in public. Or at least have the decency to do it in front of a *girls'* school, for God's sake. Packer laughed at his own joke. Then he looked up at the ceiling and murmured, "Just this one night, let it stay quiet." There wasn't enough air moving to raise the feathers on a canary's ass. It was *no* night to be fussy about lengthy 934's, the watch commander reminded himself. Let Billy enjoy his leak, or was it Mary Rob's turn? Well, that might justify the whole thirty minutes, by the time she peeled off her Sam Browne belt and her slacks and her pink panties and all. . . .

Order in the court! Lieutenant Packer Lind, judge, jury, and executioner, indicted himself on charges of sexism and found himself guilty as charged. By God, he'd have to do better. A good supervisor didn't think of patrolwomen in terms of underpants any more than he thought of patrolmen in terms of jock straps. Hadn't there been endless seminars and bulletins on the subject?

[21]

SEXIST BEHAVIOR MUST GO! a memo from the chief's office had insisted. And what was sexist behavior? It was assigning women to low-crime districts because of their presumed physical weakness. It was shoveling paper work at policewomen because females were supposed to be better at detail. It was Sergeant Turk Molnar kidding a tired patrolwoman, "Whatta you got, your monthlies?" And it was Officer Billy Mains meeting Mary Rob Maki: "Nice to know ya, hon. Say, you on the pill?" Every officer in the precinct had been ordered again and again to avoid the sexist remarks, but Billy Mains was famous for disobeying orders. Infamous!

Packer had come close to furloughing the veteran cop for a few days, but instead he'd had a brainstorm. Why not face the problem directly? Why not show the whole P.D. that sex or lust or whatever you called it didn't have to interfere with patrol work? If Mains and that hot-looking Maki could work together in a car, then *any* team could work together, and the precinct could forget the boy-meets-girl stuff. Pleased with his own idea, he'd ordered Sergeant Molnar to put the two of them in David Three. The move brought hoots and gasps at roll call.

Packer wasn't worried. What the hell, the integration of other females in other precincts had gone smoothly, on the whole. No, *no,* he warned himself, don't use that phrase! Chrisakes, a man had to watch every word! If he ever bragged at roll call that women cops were working out "on the whole," some of his troops would die of the smirks. Artie Siegl for sure, and Mains. Turk Molnar, if he caught the double meaning, which wasn't always certain. The other sergeant, Richard Not Dick Jellico, would continue to stand at parade rest, cap pulled down to the tops of his rimless glasses, his praying-mantis face a mask as always.

A passing car shook the office walls with an exhaust like a high-school trombone section. He figured the driver was turning at least fifty in the twenty-five-mile zone. Calm down, Junior, he murmured; you're a big boy now, you don't have to prove you got nuts. Silly game of chicken the kids played, racing past the police station in their chopped and remodeled come-mobiles with headers and side pipes and mag wheels and laid-back girl friends popping gum. Did they expect the deskman to run out and lob a book of tickets at them? They didn't know this deskman. Gerald Yount was far too busy staring into space to write a speeder.

The whirring little desk fan barely stirred his papers, Packer noticed. He gave it a quarter twist toward his face and glanced at the R-C Cola thermometer on the wall. Eighty-five. Down another degree. A regular cold front. By the end of the watch, it'd be all the way down to eighty-four, eighty-three. His damp salty shorts squeezed at his crotch, and he detected a light oily smell in the air. Sometimes the old station sweated like a living thing, giving off a faint, familiar odor from its sagging walls, each at its own individual cant. The captain was always griping that the whole house stank, but the old man was delirious on the subject of dirt and smells; he'd probably spend his last days in a mental home, swiping at bugs and flies that nobody else could see, in a building made of plastic and acoustical tiles and soft recessed lights like the new Federal Center. Places for—automatons. Packer preferred the smell of the rundown old station. And a damn good thing I like it, he said to himself. There's not a penny in the city budget for a new one. . . .

11:30 P.M. Pretty soon he'd use up a few gallons of the mayor's gasoline. Anything but shuffling papers inside this mausoleum. With great effort he dug into a manila envelope marked "Confidential, S. J. Lind" and withdrew a memo on blue precinct stationery. He started to read, then shoved the page aside. If it was too late to call Amnee, it was too late to reread the captain's newest outburst. He wondered what caused good men to get the red-ass in their old age. Was it insecurity? Hardening of the arteries? Tired blood? He had known Singletary first as a popular young sergeant, later as a nervous lieutenant, and now as a finicky captain, forty-seven years old and deteriorating fast, mostly in the personality. The W.C. found it hard to believe that the old man had once been known as "Brassballs" for the arrests he made. Maybe he was having trouble with Agate, his wife. There were rumors about her; Packer had refused to dignify them, both for the captain's sake and the precinct's. But this hazing of a good cop like Artie Siegl—well, it was so goddamn petty.

"Subject: Station Etiquette," he began to read against his better judgment. "To: All personnel. Fm: Julius Singletary, Capt., Cmdg."

He wouldn't read another word. Not—one—more . . .

Okay, he'd just scan it, the way he picked at scabs as a kid. His tongue clucked softly as he read:

> For some period of time it has been acceptable in Pct. 9 for various supervisors to refer to the precinct commander as "Skipper" or "Skip" as well as the more standard "Captain." Please be advised, however, that it is definitely not "okay" for any personnel below the supervisor level to avail themselves of this "nickname." Patrolmen will refer to myself as "Captain," never "Skip" or "Cap" or any other nickname. However, "sir" is always acceptable to use.

He slid the paper back into its envelope and slammed the desk drawer shut. A grown man! Everybody in the station knew the memo had nothing to do with "All personnel," it had to do with Patrolman Artie Siegl, period. And what terrible offense had Artie committed? He had bumped into the captain leaving a pornie movie and remarked, "Hey, Skip! How's your hammer hanging?"

Well, Chrisakes, wasn't there a kidder in every precinct station? Artie was—he frowned as he groped for the right word. "Irrepressible," that was it. Artie was also slightly goofy from twenty-six amateur bouts as a featherweight, including a split-decision loss in the finals of the 1960 Olympic trials, and every once in a while he was a minor problem, too, but you accepted it from Artie because you knew he was just an insecure kid underneath. Not a nasty cell in his body.

The watch commander tilted his chair back and stared at the ceiling with its network of cracks. Funny about some men. Rubbed each other raw, and who could figure why? Chemistry, probably. Years ago, he'd seen Julius Singletary go to bat for cops who'd stolen, cops who'd knocked up teen-agers, cops who'd become chronic liars and drinkers and fuck-offs, but now he was feuding with a good man like Artie Siegl. "That punchy yay-hoo has one more chance with me, one more!" the old man had barked. "The next time he screws up, it's—it's—" Wattles shaking, face crimson, the precinct commander couldn't finish his sentence.

Packer glanced at the roster and reassured himself that Artie was at work in David Four district; the station was depending on him to turn up a Driver of the Month nominee. Packer grunted. As if his men weren't already snowed, they had to waste time finding candidates for the mayor's good-driver award, the latest P.R. brainstorm from City Hall.

He scanned a few more reports and then sneaked another peek at the clock: 11:55 P.M. He'd correct exactly two more papers and then drive. He picked up the burglary clipboard and began to read the preschool printing of Patrolman Ernie Smoliss: "Subject stated she had went to bed and was all most alseep, and after 15 minutes had gone passed, she heard . . ."

He dipped his heavy head as though in prayer and ran the remaining two joints of his right ring finger up and down his reconstructed ear. He reached under his limp size-seventeen collar and brought up enough sweat to make a visible spatter on the worn wooden floor. Lord, Lord . . . Would this long night ever go passed?

Outside, another train rumbled down the line, and just as he reached out to increase the volume on his radio, he heard the three alerter tones that warned of an important transmission, followed by a female dispatcher: "David One, see the woman, Five Six Four Meredith Avenue. Possible Zero One Zero and Zero Two Zero."

The basso voice of Patrolman Willie Bethea acknowledged "David One received" as calmly as though he handled hot felony calls every night before dinner. Cool, man, cool. Good old Willie B. . . .

Packer grabbed his service cap and his portable radio and lurched past the immobile Gerald Yount and out the back door to his unmarked olive Fury. He slotted the slim gray two-way radio with a *thunk,* noted that the red "charging" light blinked on, grabbed the mike with one big hand and turned the ignition key with the other. "Two Two Three responding to Meredith Avenue," he said crisply.

"Two Two Three responding," the dispatcher echoed.

There'll be a hell of a lot more than 223 responding if that report is verified, he realized as he whipped the car out of the back lot and onto the empty street. There'll be a couple 700s from the downtown dicks: there'll be Charlie Ocean 6, the coroner's meat wagon, and Charlie Lincoln 2, the portable crime lab, and half a dozen reporters and cameramen who'll roll out of their sacks when they hear the same alerter beeps on their radios at home. Every ghoul with a scanner knew what 010 and 020 meant without even opening the code book.

Pity the poor woman, Packer thought as he flicked on his roof lights and switched his siren selector to "howl." I hope she didn't suffer.

5

Patrolman Gerald Yount made a labored entry in the station log, then continued to peer into the polished glass globe of the gumball machine on the counter. As though from miles away he heard the lieutenant's heavy footsteps clomping down the hall and a few seconds later the clear voice on the radio, "Two Two Three responding," but the deskman took little notice. The watch commander came and went as he pleased. At night, he was the law south of the canal and north of the county line. Didn't even have to answer to the captain, since Singletary worked nine to five and almost never came in off-shift. Bankers' hours. Sometimes Yount had trouble remembering what the precinct commander looked like.

A week ago the test for detective cadet had been given city-wide; the deskman hadn't applied. Several of his ex-partners were working their way up the sergeants' list, but the young officer now sat alone in the station staring into the spheres of penny gum so intently that the blacks and yellows and reds and greens seemed to bleed into one another, like a child's watercolors left out in the rain.

He wished he could get some sleep. His eyes burned, and a headache hummed like a quivering ax blade in his skull. He blinked hard and clawed his fingers along the gray metal desk till the sound made him realize he had ripped a nail.

He hadn't slept the day before, or the day before that. He was uncertain about the previous days, but he seldom slept more than an hour or two anymore—wrenching, writhing catnaps filled with nightmares. A few times he dreamed of his father's death, and awoke lathered in sweat, remembering clearly what he had perceived only dimly at the age of four: the hysteria in the crowded house, the older children drawn with grief, his father's heavy gray face as he lay on the satin, wisps of white cotton peeking from his nose; the sickly perfumed smell, a different after-shave, not his father's at all, when his mother held him up to kiss the waxen cheek. But most of all he dreamed about the whispered voices in the house afterward, the weeks of dullness and lifelessness and the long nights alone in his bunk bed aching with loss. Why was this coming back now? Was it because Darlene had left? But that was only temporary. *She would be back.* Oh, please, Lord, let her come back, he whispered to himself. I promise, God, I'll be—nicer to her. . . .

He shut his dark poached eyes and tried to understand what was happening to him. Every night he would stagger into the old station house and his brother officers would smile and offer sympathy. Burned-out cops, even at twenty-four, were an old story to them. "Get any sleep today, Gerry?" one would ask.

"No."

"Just a few hours, huh?"

"No. None."

They thrust their suggestions at him like spears. "Why don't you get laid, kid? It'll relax you." He would mutter his thanks and try to look busy. "Gerry, baby," Willie Bethea had told him, "you got to lighten up. Take a drink. Ain't nothing a snootful of Bombay gin won't heal." Johnny McClung had grinned his lopsided Irish grin and slipped a fat red capsule into his hand. "Here, son. This'll give you some rest." The first chance he had, he flushed the jumbo Seconal down the toilet. He had hardened his mind: he would not chase women or smoke dope or gobble pills or swill whiskey or use any crutch of any kind. They were for the weak. He would wait for her to come back. Till then, he would act like a man.

The idea made him laugh derisively and look nervously around the

station. A man! What a man he was! Suddenly he realized the lieutenant was gone and he was completely alone. He began to panic. *Alone!* He turned the switch on the scanner to bring in all channels, even the fire dispatcher; he needed human voices to help fill the hollow in his stomach. He prayed under his breath: Dear Father in Heaven, don't—let—me—be *alone!* Let the door swing wide and someone walk in. Anyone, Lord. *Anyone* . . .

His insides felt light, insubstantial, filled with bubbles. He imagined himself floating away and not being able to return to earth. He gasped and opened his dry eyes. He wanted to cry, but he couldn't. It was high on a list of things he refused to do, would never do. His mother had always trained him not to cry; when a sad scene appeared on their living-room television, he would raise a comic book over his face, or run into the bathroom. And soon the reflex of tears was lost. Now he sat at the front desk in Precinct Nine, scared and alone, but he wouldn't cry.

He jumped up and rushed to the open front door. The streets were silent, empty; no trucks rumbled along toward the warehouses a few blocks away; no train was in sight. He was—*alone.* At the thought, the blood rushed to his sunken cheeks; his face caught fire.

He ran back to the desk and slumped dazedly and stretched his skin down over his temples. The lieutenant's words sounded in his head: "Anything I can do, kid? Anything at all?" He swallowed hard, as close to tears as he could manage. They all tried to help, oh yes, they all tried. He had wanted to answer, "Yes, please, Lieutenant, take me off the desk. Don't put me on display. Let me go where nobody can watch me." He had wanted to say, "Please, Lieutenant, if Billy won't ride with me, give me a one-man car." He had wanted to say, "Just let me do my job. *Please, won't anybody listen?*" No, nobody would. They streamed past his desk, looked into his haggard face, and tried to jack him up. "Getting any, kid?" "Hey, how's the split coming along? You'll feel better than ever, pal." "Coming for a drink later, Ger?" They knew he didn't drink, but they invited him anyway, night after night. "Lots of broads, kid. Gonna get down and get dirty." Half the watch met at the Slammer, after they were relieved at four in the morning. He'd been in the dark-brown place once, with Darlene, and he'd had to drag her out at dawn, still protesting that she'd dance by herself if he insisted on being such a pill. . . .

Let me off this desk! He wanted to fall on his knees and beg the watch commander. But he wouldn't beg. He knew how to take orders. "I want you where I can watch you," Packer Lind had said when he made the reassignment. "I'm worried about you, Gerry." Trying to be nice. Weren't they all? "How about checking in with the shrink?" the lieutenant had added. "Then we'll see about putting you back on the street." The department psychologist! Stupid idea. Gerald Yount wasn't crazy. He—was—not—crazy.

But he *was* alone. His heartbeat nudged at his soggy shirt. Veins and tendons wriggled like worms on the backs of his bony hands as he clenched and unclenched and clenched them again.

"Let's talk about it," the lieutenant had suggested, but he'd never been open with men. *Gerald Yount didn't want to talk about it.* Couldn't they see that? He didn't want their sympathy. He needed them as—friends. Warm bodies. Acquaintances. He couldn't afford to lose a single one, not even Billy Mains.

His stomach contracted. He ground his fists into his midsection and pressed inward till he almost felt his backbone. He couldn't throw up, couldn't lose control; someone might walk in. He looked at the ceiling and flinched; for a second it had started to descend on him.

Another close call. Since Darlene left there'd been many. A bus had nearly hit him this morning, but after he jumped back on the curb the bus was gone, out of sight, the street completely empty, and yet he had seen the big-wheeled shape bearing down, smelled its fumes, heard its roar, watched the passengers reading their papers as the dull-green body hurtled by. . . .

He peered at the gumballs, the muscles around his thin lips flexing. "The time is twenty-four hundred hours," Radio announced on all channels. Four to go. Then he would drive home and beat on the walls, shout and babble and flail about. Jump in his old T-Bird and speed to the beach, looking for people, approaching groups and then slipping away when someone began to watch him too closely. And always trying to dissolve the pictures from his brain.

Why couldn't he blot out the pictures? Time was supposed to muffle things, but each day he saw her more clearly, heard her voice, smelled her smell. In the apartment, he talked out loud to her. One second she would be there, and the next she'd be gone, like the bus. *When would she be home to stay?*

Sleep . . . Maybe today he would sleep. Every two or three days he would drift off, sleep for an hour or ten hours, he was never sure, then get up and stumble around and fall down and find himself sprawled by the refrigerator or twisted around the coffee table or slumped against the toilet bowl where he had gone to turn his stomach inside out. "Darlene?" he would call out. *"Darlene!* Are you home?" Later, back at the station, somebody would ask "How you feeling, Gerry?" and he would hear it as "How you feeling feeling feeling feeling?" and he

[28]

would answer "Fine" and hear it as "Fine fine fine fine. . . ."

How could he tell them what was happening when he didn't understand it himself? "Look, Gerry, we all got our family troubles," Packer Lind had told him when she first left.

"I know," he said. "I know." He turned from those intense blue eyes.

"Look, Gerry, you and Darlene are separated, kid. Everybody in the station knows. Why try to keep it to yourself? Chrisakes, man, we been friends—two years."

"She's just—on a trip." He started to walk off.

"Whenever you want to talk—"

"Right, Lieutenant. Right . . ."

How could he express his unease about the desk job without seeming ungrateful? How could he tell the W.C. that he really wanted to lose himself in his car, push the green-and-white a couple of hundred miles a night through the familiar darkened streets of his district, just let the black shadows wash over him till morning? In a one-man car, he would think things out, he would go over the old ground, he would be surrounded by familiar scenes as he patrolled his district alone. It wouldn't be the way it was when he drove with his partner; Billy Mains had wanted to stop every fifteen minutes: talk to a snitch, drink coffee, flirt with a woman, make a phone call, anything but drive. The partners began to snipe at each other, and then—bang!—the lieutenant split them up and dumped him on the desk. Penal servitude, broken only occasionally by routine jobs: log a prisoner and send him downtown for booking, give a Breathalyzer test, brew a new pot of coffee for the watch and drink most of it himself. And bite his nails till they bled and inhale two packs a night down to his toes. Camels, the real thing, not the phony filters that people smoked so they'd live longer, as though it was up to man, not God Almighty, when they died.

The deskman snapped off his scanner and monitored F-2, the precinct's channel. Just this once, when he needed to hear voices, it was quiet. He looked back at the gumball machine. The lieutenant should be returning from—what was that call? He'd forgotten already. He checked the desk log. Possible 010 and 020. Rape and homicide. Did anybody verify? He hadn't heard.

Seeking comfort, he tried to remember himself as a young officer, cruising the streets in his gleaming green-and-white, the last few beads of water from the police car wash rolling up the windshield. He saw the storekeepers waving at him, elderly ladies offering him cold lemonade on summer days, younger women offering something stronger while he laughed them off, clouds of tiny black hands reaching through the window to touch his uniform whenever he parked at the settlement house:

"What's 'at?"

"A revolver."

"What's *'at?'*"

"That's my holster."

"Kin Ah have it?"

"No."

"What's them things there?"

"Pouches. For my bullets."

"Kin Ah have one?"

"No. Too dangerous."

"Jes' one?"

"Just none."

"You got handcuffs?"

"Yep."

"Kin Ah have 'em?"

"No."

"Ax you sumpin'?"

"Sure."

"Why you be a peeg?" The broad toothy smile of the innocent.

"Hey, listen, I gotta be going now. I'll do the howler one more time, okay?"

"Aw *right* . . . Whoo-ee! . . . Onc't again? Jes' one more time? Kin Ah do it . . .?"

Gerald Yount shook his head and looked up at the clock: 1:15 A.M. Impossible! A few seconds ago Radio announced "twenty-four hundred hours." It couldn't be 1:15 now. The clock must be broken.

He looked at his watch.

1:15. What . . .?

With shaking hands he grabbed the clipboard and checked the log entries.

"0018, drunk caller, hung up."

"0031. Barking dog, referred to 911."

"0105. Citizen turned in noninjury accident report."

The entries were in the same left-handed slant he'd been taught in grammar school. But he couldn't remember making a single one.

He dug his knuckles into his sore brown-black eyes and rubbed hard. Another scene was coming on, he could feel it moving from back to front in his skull, the way they always did, till the awful pictures would erupt square in front of him and he could see her clearly, watch every filthy movement, hear every disgusting sound. . . .

Oh, please Lord, not this time! Please stop the pictures. Please . . . Let—me—rest! No, no, no, *no, I don't want to see her doing—that!*

Think of something else, Gerry. Don't give the pictures room to come in. Crowd them out with other pictures, Gerry. Concentrate, *concentrate!*

Flowers . . . Orchids and roses and wildflowers: daisies and dandelions, descending fields in every direction, yellow and white and green in the sunlight, out to the horizon. See them, Gerry, see them. . . .

But it didn't work. He began to see her instead, and *him;* he began to see *them.* He crammed a knuckle into his mouth and bit till he drew blood.

But he would not cry.

6

The address was only a short hop from the station, and Packer realized he might beat the district car there. He didn't want to embarrass two good men, but rape and/or homicide left no time for professional courtesy.

He came out of the straightaway on the belt parkway doing seventy-five and braked quickly to avoid a senior citizen in a Cadillac Seville who swerved left instead of right when he heard the howler. You never knew what they'd do. Some cut left, some right, some hit the brakes, some just panicked and veered all over the road. "The bull horrors," policemen called it: the same uneasy feeling that made a driver slow to a crawl when a green-and-white showed up in his rearview mirror, or sit forever at a four-way stop, too intimidated to make the first move. The worst problem was the hard of hearing, or kids listening to their stereos. That was why most of the men kept moving the selector from "siren" to "wail" to "yelp" to "hi-lo" when they were chasing in traffic. Some ears picked out one type of sound better than another.

The air poured through his open windows, cooling him for the first time all night. As he sped along, a row of lighted storefronts appeared as colored blobs in his peripheral vision. He turned ninety degrees and skittered half out of control across the tracks at High Street and careened by the tire warehouse with its rotating white and amber lights inside to keep the pigeons from roosting. He'd reported the flickering glow as a fire years ago and so had almost every other newcomer to the precinct.

Then he was speeding up the hill toward Stanton Park, jerking the

Fury into a smoky four-wheel drift at Meredith and smoothly applying throttle to help guide the lurching car onto the wide avenue bordered by decaying trees and tired old mansions long since converted into boardinghouses and settlement houses and cottage industries. He knew the signs by heart: "Sewing Old-fashion Style," "Mrs. Mom's Pies Baked Daily," "Jesus Saves and Sanctifies." His own bungalow was on the other edge of Stanton Park, less than a mile away, and Packer knew these people well. He had walked their streets as a rookie, intruded on their personal disasters as a crew-cut young detective, met them again as a sector sergeant in a green-and-white, had even broken in some of their sons on the force. Rollie Beemer was one, and Don Reichert was raised right around the corner on Welling Avenue. Good people: steady, solid, hard workers. Uncomplicated tastes and pleasures. A balanced meal in Stanton Park was a double order of clams and fries and a couple cans of ale. The local dreamwagon was a pastel Continental five years old. The goal in life was to be able to gather the whole family in front of a paid-up color TV in an unmortgaged house in a neighborhood where prowlers didn't prowl by day and muggers didn't mug by night. And where 010 and 020 were Bingo numbers at St. Timothy's. Pumping the worn brake pedal, he asked himself how come there were so few rapes and murders in rich neighborhoods? An old police axiom came to mind: only the rich murder the rich. Everybody murders the poor.

There it was. 564. A box-shaped apartment building faced with worn sandstone and set behind a dying strip of coarse Bermuda grass maybe three feet wide, dotted with dog crap. There was more architectural style and originality in the places he used to put on Park Place and Boardwalk. An unshielded white light burned above the buckled two-step entranceway. Welcome to the fuzz: our nighttime friends and daytime enemies.

He needn't have worried about David One. Bethea and Beemer were already yanking on the knurled wooden door knob, calling out, "Police!" Their car was double-parked, light bar still rotating and turning their hatless heads blue every three fifths of a second, making them look like a pair of bouncers at a disco joint. That's three different no-no's, he said to himself, but who keeps track on a hot felony call? Sergeant Jellico, maybe, but Richard Not Dick was working in Zebra sector, the other half of the precinct, driving his car in a military manner, the only living human who sat at attention. Sergeant Turk Molnar would screen this report, when it was finally written, and then Schoolmaster Packer Lind would translate the combined effort into an approximation of police English.

"Two Two Three arrived," he said into his microphone. He slid his portable transceiver from its slot and hooked it into his belt-holster. The door rattled as he reached the sagging porch and exchanged nods with the two officers.

"Took ya long enough," a female with a scratchy voice said as she opened the door, and he thought, Yeah, we always take a long time, lady, it must have been three minutes since we got the call. Well, we stopped to get a blow job and collect a couple payoffs. You know how it is with cops, lady. He stood back to let the assigned unit enter first.

The faded middle-aged woman wore a shortie bathrobe and talked in a parakeet cackle as she led them up the well-worn stairs. "Heard it myself. Midnight, straight up. Thought it was a bad dream, but then it come again. A high scream, ya know?" The backs of her spindly legs reminded him of a road map of California. "I jumped outa bed and opened my door. I'm on the third floor, see, right next to Betty. Betty Evans, that's her name. Cute little thing, works downtown in the, uh, Copper Kettle. Thought I heard a noise from her place, so I holler, 'You okay, kid?' I always call her kid. I figure she's got to be dreaming, hot night and all, and then her door flies open and I see a guy with a blue nylon stocking over his face. He's moving so fast I can't even duck outa the way, but he just says, he says, 'W-w-watch out!' and he goes down the stairs three or four steps at a time."

'Didja get a make on the guy?" the slow-talking Rollie Beemer asked.

"A what?"

"Did you see what he looked like?" Packer translated. "Could you identify him?"

"Naw. Moving too fast. Medium height, wearing a stocking, that's about it."

A door opened noiselessly as the delegation clomped across the second-floor landing, the watch commander bringing up the rear, and a wizened turtle head poked out. "It's nothing, Wilbur," the woman said in a surprisingly gentle voice. "Go back to sleep." The head retracted. Men in uniform can't be much of a novelty on this staircase, Packer figured.

"So I didn't know what to do," the briny woman continued between excited inhalations as they started up the final flight. "Maybe he had a friend still inside her place, ya know? A girl's never safe in a dump like this. Then I heard the front door slam, and I run over anyway. The door's open, like it is now, and she's on the floor. There. Look! Jesus, she hasn't moved."

The woman stepped to one side and began dabbing at her wan face with the collar of her worn bathrobe. Willie Bethea squeezed by impatiently and flopped to the floor, his left hand behind him beckoning for silence. A good cop with a good cop's instincts, Packer said to himself. This wasn't an 010 or an 020 till the fire department's aid car got here and verified. Till then it was strictly a "possible," a "woman down," and the officers had a responsibility to the victim that wouldn't end till the aidman arrived and bullied the body to life or looked at his watch and barked out a time to whoever was writing.

"Nothing," Bethea said, squirming to press his ear tighter against the woman's dark-blue jersey. He came up batting his eyelids and sniffing hard. Was the imperturbable Willie B upset? Packer couldn't believe it.

In the dull amber light from the hall he made out the stretched form of a woman, legs pathetically bare, a thin skirt ripped almost its full length. There was a sharp smell in the air. Semen? No. Too heavy. The poor girl must have cleaned her apartment today, and used a strong disinfectant, maybe even a fumigant. Well, some of these Stanton Park rooming houses did have a mustiness about them. People had died in these rooms, babies had been born, drunks had vomited into the floor cracks, cooks had let pots boil over, toddlers had crapped their training pants, toilets had erupted. . . . And now a young woman lived here and tried to make the grubby old place respectable.

For a male visitor, maybe? That would explain the strong disinfectant. A losing battle . . . Smelled like . . . He inhaled again. A little like lye, a little like rotten eggs. Too bad she didn't know the captain. He'd have put her onto Pine-Sol, the good clean aroma of the high mountains. How the men hated it.

He backed to the door and felt for a light switch, found one, and flicked it with his fingernail to preserve any prints. A bandbox apartment jumped into view, decorated in floral colors and bold designs: Woolworth Modern. A bed had been pulled from the sofa, and there were fresh smears of blood on the pillow.

The victim lay on the floor at the end of the bed, as though she had fallen off or been shoved. She was young, a few years younger than Amnee. A child. The word "slut" was inscribed across her abdomen in blue-black letters. Block printing, Packer noticed. The common denominator of printing styles, no character, no individuality. The hardest of all writing to identify. The rotten no-good son of a bitch knew what he was doing when he used block printing.

"She been cut," Willie said quietly, leaning over the body. The smell seemed stronger. Rollie Beemer stood to one side and spoke softly into his radio. Packer grabbed a hand mirror off a cheap dresser. "Anything?" he asked, and Willie B shook his head slowly. Packer thrust the mirror into the kneeling policeman's hand, and Willie held it to the victim's open lips, almost touching, and then examined it in the light.

"Goddamn," he said. "She bubbling." He pinched his flared Arabic nose and turned away sharply.

"Where's the cut?" Parker asked, dropping on his haunches as a pair of huffing paramedics rushed in with their kits and apparatus.

"We got it," one of them said, elbowing a path through the policemen. Within seconds they had begun forcing oxygen into the girl's lungs with a plastic mask and a tank. One of them raised her right hand, speckled with scarlet. A few swipes with a medicated cloth revealed a deep slash across the palm. Packer thought he could see twin blue-black discolorations on either side of the Adam's apple: the signature of a strangler. Squeeze right there for a minute or two and the victim is unconscious. Squeeze a little too hard or a little too long and the larynx is crushed and the victim is beyond help.

A familiar loud voice called from the hallway. "Whatta we got?" Sergeant Turk Molnar walked in, displaying his gypsy smile. "Oh, hello, Lieutenant. I was taking my Nine Three Two. How's it look?"

"So far it's attempt rape, attempt homicide," Packer whispered. "You got it now?"

"I got it. Hey, what's 'at smell?" Whatever the situation, Molnar always spoke as though he was at the circus.

The little room was already overcrowded, and more cars were en route. On his way out Packer slapped Willie B on the ass and said, "Nice moves, turkey," nodded amiably to Rollie Beemer and headed down the stairs. "It's nothing, Wilbur," he said to the aging head protruding from a door on the second floor, and once again the head vanished.

Out in the sultry night, he slipped behind the wheel of David One, still parked in the street with its light bar on, and eased it into a place by a hydrant. He spotted the aid truck on the next-door lawn, nosed into a hedge. Those fire department paramedics would knock you down and walk on your face to save a life; they weren't too fussy about where they parked.

He walked back to his own cruiser and slotted his radio and told the hand mike, "Two Two Three returning," rearranging his shorts while the dispatcher acknowledged. As he leaned back in the seat, the upholstery warmed his skin like a masseur's hot towel. Someday a merciful inventor would devise a police car with a built-in shower. Make a fortune.

In the middle of the U-turn, he remembered the huddled form of the young victim and shoved it out of his mind. Every time he went on a call like this he had to struggle against becoming personally involved, against feeling angry or upset or vengeful or sad, and each time that he won the struggle he felt a little less human. After twelve years on the force, his hide had gradually thickened until now he could look at a violated human being like the girl in the apartment and feel only the slightest pull on his emotions. Was that good? Maybe not, but it was necessary. He thought back. Three years. Yep, it had been three years since he cried on a call, and that was when the little blond-haired boy got hooked on a car's bumper and dragged half a mile and, worst of all, survived. He sneaked a look at himself in the mirror as he drove along Meredith. Was he damaged emotionally? Was he coarsened beyond help? Something else to worry about. Of all the damn fool things . . .

The station was still three blocks away when he heard the radio.

"David One." Beemer's voice.

The same female dispatcher answered, "David One." She would stay with the case all night.

"Make this an Oh-One-Oh."

"Verified?"

"Affirmative."

So the aidmen had lost a patient for a change. Her windpipe must have been crushed. The poor girl, Packer said to himself. The poor— child. He thought of Amnee and Emily sleeping at home, considered turning around and cruising the bungalow. But no killer was stupid enough to hit twice on the same night in the same part of town.

That was the trouble with loving too much. You worried about everything. You took a bomb scare in the next county and built it into a threat to your family. He couldn't allow that weakness: not in himself, not in his men. Home was home and work was work. When you broke through an armed criminal's door, you did it as a professional policeman, not as a husband and father. You did it balls-out, and you ignored the danger. You didn't stop to figure if the insurance was paid up, or if you'd remembered to kiss the baby good-bye. . . .

Maybe cops should all be single, he said to himself as he pulled into the station. Certified free of emotional entanglements. God, how he loved those two at home! Amnee and Emmy . . . If anything ever threatened them . . .

No, not again. He'd had his share, paid his dues, whatever the expression was. He sealed his mind tight, climbed out of the car, and heard a whimper. He walked over to the tramp dog's chicken-wire enclosure. Four small shadows lay in the dust outside the doghouse. The mother dipped jerkily from one to another, nuzzling and pawing, whining as she looked up. Packer did a deep knee bend to see.

The pups didn't move. Their heads were curiously flat. Then he realized. They were dead.

He reached out instinctively and patted the mother, looking imploringly at him through chocolate-brown eyes as though he had the power to revive her young. Bereaved citizens had looked at him the same way. He touched the satiny stomach of one of the pups. Warm. The crime was minutes old.

He felt his skin grow hot. He jumped up and peered into the darkness behind the old station, and saw exactly what he had expected to see: a black tangle of weeds and brambles on the vacant lot. He cupped an ear and heard only the distant hiss of traffic on the freeway and the faint metallic hammering of a switch engine pounding down the line.

Kids . . . It had to be kids. Sociopathic, that was the word. No capacity for feeling. "You can't put the blame on them," the visiting professor had explained at command school. "They're the worst victims themselves."

No, he mimicked, you can't put the blame on them. I'd like to have some of those little punks here right now. I'd blame their goddamn nuts off. . . .

He lifted one of the bodies by the back of the neck. The crushed head wobbled loosely, like a dead bird's. A rat ran into the clearing, sniffed, and slid into shadow as though on wheels.

No, you can't blame the poor little underprivileged kiddies for something like this, but it would feel good to slap the crap out of one just the same. . . .

He swiped at his eyes. He thought he had seen every kind of violence, but these were his first puppy victims. Oh, Christ, he thought, what's the use? What's the use?

He found Gerald Yount sitting at the desk, staring into the gumball machine. "Ger, did you hear anything out back while I was gone?" he asked.

"No, Lieutenant."

Packer looked down. "Somebody stomped the puppies to death," he said. "A few of the guys come in, have 'em dig a little grave, will ya?"

The deskman's dark hollow eyes flickered across the watch commander's face, then back to the machine. A series of furrows appeared on his cadaverous forehead; for an instant he looked even more pained than usual.

"Right, Lieutenant," he said.

7

Patrolman Arthur Siegl, former plainclothesman, had heard the 010 and 020 calls as he cruised Ninth Avenue at patrol speed, five miles per hour over the posted limit, searching the night with his puffy ex-featherweight's eyes. Two of his gnarled fingers curled loosely around the wheel as he steered in and out of the scattered post-midnight traffic, while the other hand propped up the open window frame.

Even at this speed, he was itchy with sweat. He reached out to turn on the car's air conditioner, but thought better. With the open windows admitting twin blasts of warm air, the unit's pump could easily break down from the strain, and then he'd have another beef to clear with the captain. Enough already! He could close the windows, but the lieutenant had gone bug-fuck on the subject, and who could blame him? How could *patrol* officers do a *patrol* job behind safety glass? He had known Packer Lind for ten years now, and when the guy got pissed, there was usually a reason.

As pilot and crew of one-man car David Four, Artie Siegl spent most of each watch rehearsing his comic routines out loud, preparing impromptu remarks and sharpening up his verbal counterpunches. Tonight he was working on what to say the next time he ran across the deputy chief who had rudely put him back in uniform. "Yes, sir, Chief, your record proves one thing," he would start out. "Yes, sir, Chief," he'd repeat in a loud voice, to get everyone's attention. "If a monkey climbs high enough, he'll expose his ass."

Guffaws, thigh slaps, and general hysteria. That would be the last time that guy flopped a good plainclothesman.

Up ahead, two black men in pimp threads were strutting past a storeroom window: "Worldwide Furniture Mart, Buy at Discount." Artie lifted his size six elevator boot from the gas pedal and drifted in behind them, engine idling almost noiselessly. They bobbed as though on springs, with universal connections at every joint. He knew what the blacks called it: styling. Sometimes they styled so energetically they seemed to be moving sideways, or backwards. "That's their fuck-you walk," he remarked to his invisible partner. "No, their fuck-you *Whitey* walk." He goosed the car past in a burst of noise, the official police department fart-in-the-face, and when he looked in the mirror the black dudes seemed to be dancing contemptuously a foot or so above the shimmering sidewalk. He grumbled aloud, "How the hell can they stand all those clothes in this heat? Probably racked up on coke. No sweat off my ass." They could snort all they wanted, as long as they didn't caper on his beat.

As a Jew in a police station, he tried hard to be unprejudiced. "Don't act, you know, uh, *pushy,*" his first watch commander had advised him tactfully. "You'll work out okay." Translation: keep your Yid mouth shut, stick to the program, be grateful to all those wonderful Gentiles who made your job possible. "Mind your own damned business, Lieutenant, I'll just do it *my* way." No, he hadn't said that, but it sounded good as he turned into Alhambra Avenue. He *should* have said it. And he would, the next time some creep supervisor told him not to act—you know, uh, *pushy.*

Artie Siegl admired cops who went their own way. Cops who spoke up, who didn't piss their pants every time they were threatened by some two-bit politician. He smiled as he remembered the discussion between Billy Mains and the new patrolperson, Mary Rob Maki, at a short coffee meet earlier. "Say, my partner here's a double minority in the Ninth," Billy had said, laying on his dime-store charm. He was one of several men in the precinct who seldom talked to Artie about anything but racial matters, as though his Jewishness was all that defined him. "She's Finnish and female," Mains said, smirking at his own cleverness.

"Isn't that amazing?" the broad had shot back. "Finnish descent and I speak English. Me very smart for a woman." You tell 'em, baby! *Me very smart for a woman.* That was a good one.

Artie wondered how Mains was making out with the chick, he hadn't heard David Three on the radio in a long time. "Keep it in your pants, Mains," he said as though the precinct's star cocksman was sitting alongside. "A squad car's no place to play hide-the-eel, even with a broad that's a thirty-eight D-cup." At least he hoped she was a thirty-eight-D. He stood to pick up eighteen dollars.

Something troubled him as he rolled past the Shell station on East Marshall, babbling to himself. He was supposed to do . . . what?

The Driver of the Month!

Holy balls, he'd nearly forgotten. He spun a doughnut across the double-yellow and eased the Fury into the shadows of the closed gas station. In the thick night air the scents of gasoline and grease made his nostrils twitch. Jeez, there must be a better place to watch traffic. No, this was Packer's suggestion. . . .

He turned off ignition and lights and lit a cigar to clear the air. "If the lieutenant says this is the best lookout, then this is the best lookout," he observed aloud. Of all the police brass, Packer Lind was the only one he obeyed without thinking. The watch commander had a street cop's instincts. "Unfuckingcanny," Artie said as he expelled purplish fumes into the foul air. You'd drive with the W.C. and he'd say "Make a right!" and just as you turned the corner a burglar would slip off a fire escape with a portable TV dangling from his belt. That was one subject they didn't teach at the academy: instinct. There were police officers who swore that Packer could hear a burglar alarm before it went off.

"Too bad that stupid captain's working the guy to death," Artie said to the nearest gas pump. He spat out the window to emphasize his opinion of the precinct commander. "Our watch does three quarters of the work for the whole precinct, then Packer has to come in and bail Singletary out of all his dumb jams, and still he hits the street every night two, three hours." Too much pressure. Nobody could keep up that pace, not even Packer Lind. "Someday the whole thing'll go up in smoke," Artie said. "Oh, yes it will!" he exclaimed, as though a gas pump had disagreed. "I seen it before." There'd be a divorce, or— something. And another burnt-out supervisor would be walking the streets. "Wasn't Packer divorced already?" he asked. "No," he answered. "His first wife died in childbirth. Hemorrhage, I think it was. Yeah. On a camping trip. Lost the kid, too. They said he was a wreck for a long time after. . . ."

Through the slats of an uneven wooden fence, he could see a full half mile down East Marshall, but no Driver of the Month candidate came into sight. A Chevy van appeared and ran the stop sign at Scadlock, busted the red at Fulton, and paid homage to the yield sign at Turner by cutting off a Day-Glo-orange Porsche. Probably not your ideal nominee, he said to himself. Then what about the Porsche? Nope. That turkey had already gunned to fifty in the twenty-five zone. "Nobody'll cut off *his* ass for a while," he said, snickering. Everyone on the watch knew that foreign-car drivers never won the good driver award, no matter how lavish the reports you wrote on them. Too un-American, all those Datsun and VW and Volvo owners. They want an award, let 'em buy American; that's the way the thinking went up at headquarters. How well he knew, how well he knew. . . .

He sucked on his panetela and waited, thin gray eyes squinting into the night. The situation made him force a laugh. A homicide going down in Stanton Park and him parked in a gas station trying to catch a good driver. Well, if they needed him, they'd send a carrier pigeon. *Ha-ha* . . .

An Olds 98 white-over-blue observed two stop signs and the red light and then ruined its chances by bumping across a center island and into a driveway. A Thrift-rite truck crawled along the street, the driver busily shifting in and out of his compound gears. Artie snorted and looked away. "Damned if I'll do any favors for those rip-off artists, not since they raised the price on sirloin again." A Nu-Drug truck was disqualified for similar reasons. "A buck ninety-eight for a bottle of suppositories and I use to pay two cents apiece and lucky to have my business. I'll use my fingers first."

The retired pugilist dragged deeply on his soggy cigar—thirty-five cents apiece, another consumer rip-off, except that he got them "on the tin," and who was he to deny Lopez Custom Tobacconists the privilege of doing a little something for the boys in blue? Technically it was against the rules to accept even a cup of coffee; it was graft and payoff and corruption. Suppose someday he had to bust Lopez for ax murder or assassination or overtime parking; how could he carry out the assignment with all those free cheroots on his breath?

"Very easy, very easy," he said to his steering wheel. Rules were meshuga, rules were for brasshats like Sergeant Jellico and Packer. No, not the lieutenant. He used a little common sense, he wasn't married to the manuals. But Jellico . . . Artie was glad he'd transferred into Turk Molnar's sector. He appreciated his new sergeant more every day. The Hunky didn't act like his asshole was made of crepe paper, he could take a joke and dish one out. That second night in David sector, Artie had glued a sigh, "Hunky Mercedes," on the bumper of Molnar's 1965 Falcon, and the old sergeant laughed louder than anybody, and the sticker was still there, the simple guy was actually proud of it. . . .

Artie's practiced eye picked up the Malibu three intersections away. Some kid had lavished a lot of attention on that bright herring-scale finish. Probably used the car to drag and pick up gash. He certainly wasn't dragging now. Artie squinted and tried to guess the Chevy's speed. At least five miles below the limit.

"He's staying in the slow lane where he belongs," Artie whispered, as though to keep the potential Driver of the Month candidate from hearing. "My God, he made a full stop at Scadlock and signaled with his hand?" He couldn't remember the last time he'd seen a driver use a hand stop signal. Must be Albert Schweitzer on his way home from the clinic. Can't he see there's nobody on the street to signal to?

Reflexes, maybe. The reflexes of a *good driver*.

He twisted the key and slipped his green-and-white into "drive" as the Malibu cruised past. His police instincts made him note that the car was a 1974 model, green over yellow, wide-track whitewalls, left headlight just a pubic hair out of line, giving it a slight wall-eyed effect, but not nearly enough for a violation. Lone occupant a W-M, age indeterminate, his head turned slightly away.

The gleaming blue car swerved as it came abreast of David Four.

"The bull horrors!" Artie said. "Shit! He must of made me down the street. That explains the careful driving. Now I'll have to sit here for another hour playing with my dick."

No, wait, that was impossible. A bald eagle couldn't have spotted him through the fence at that range. Artie eased across the center line and began a pace. "Hey, what's this?" he asked his dashboard. "The guy's rabbiting on me!"

Nope, wait, he's slowed down, not more than ten, twelve miles an hour. Showing respect. *Yes, sir, Mr. Officer, I always keep it eight or ten below the limit. Just a habit, ya know? Where can I pick up my statuette?* The games drivers played. Even good drivers, like this one. He guessed the dude had spotted him, instinctively hit the gas, and then realized he was making a bad mistake and slowed to a crawl. "Exactly what I'd of done myself," he said, "if some crazy copper started tailing me in the middle of the night trying to fill out his ticket quota."

Up ahead, the Malibu was sliding to the curb. Talk about good citizenship! Artie hadn't even turned on the light. Did the dude have a guilty conscience? From what? His driving had been grade-A perfecto. Artie was already composing the report in his head, piling praise on praise. No one could remember when a Precinct Nine nominee had won the Driver of the Month award, mostly because the reports usually consisted of vague, ungrammatical statements, but he was ready to make a fight for this guy and his herring-scale beauty. "Highest traditions of good driving," he would write. ". . . Despite relative sparcity of traffic, obeyed every rule to the letter. . . . Never in my years on the force . . ."

He pulled up behind the parked car, adjusted his cap, and punched the button on his hand mike. "David Four at Willow and Marshall. Request a warrant check. Victor George Ivy Three Four One." He spoke in his usual singsong broadcasting voice; a supervisor at Radio once told him he sounded like a chink. Jealous! The female dispatchers ate up on it. "A nineteen seventy-four Malibu two-door," he continued in his mellifluous voice. "That's a ninetee-yun seven four Chevrolet Ma-li-boooo. . . ." And in a final outburst of showmanship, he reported the color: "Avocado over lemon."

"David Four received," a businesslike female voice came back. "Warrant check Victor George Ivy Three Four One, a seventy-four Malibu *green over yellow*. Stand by." They all knew good old Artie. Avocado over lemon. What a joker. Of course the whole idea of running warrants on Driver of the Month candidates was a big enough joke by itself. They had Patrolman Ernie Smoliss to thank for the new procedure. His last nominee turned out to have $1,100 in warrants for such offenses as driving the wrong way on the interstate and mistaking a telephone pole for the center line.

When the dispatcher reported "No wants or warrants," Artie sang, "*Reeee*-ceived!" He could just see the chickie at Radio smiling at his style. He'd made her night. Now he'd make the Malibu driver's.

As he walked toward the car in his light ex-boxer's stride, he felt more and more pleased with his selection. The guy probably broke some chickenshit rule a few miles back and couldn't wait to sign the ticket. This was the kind of citizen who said, "Thank you, officer, and have a nice day" when you stuck it up his ass for thirty in a twenty-five.

The blue car shot forward just as he reached its rear bumper. Too late, he realized that its engine had been idling all the time. He spun and ran back to the squad car and grabbed the microphone. "David Four," he told Radio as he gunned the engine. "He took off on me. Westbound on Marshall." He was glad he'd followed procedure: the dispatcher already had license number, description, and location.

Now it didn't matter why he'd stopped the car. "Caught him dirty!" he shouted to himself as he sped away from the curb. "That explains the careful driving. Probably has a trunkful of grass, or maybe heroin hidden in the rocker panels, like that guy in *The French Connection*. Maybe a body in the back. . . ." He let out a howl of glee as the Fury responded to his foot.

The rabbit had a one-block lead. "No problem," Artie assured himself. He flipped on his Visibar and spun the siren switch to "manual." Now he could touch his horn ring and squirt a little siren noise across each intersection, or whenever it became necessary. Suddenly it became necessary: an aged Concord lurched into his path from a side street. He spun the wheel and missed the junker by inches. "God*damn!*" he hollered in frustration as an acrid cloud of rubber fumes poured into his open window.

He had lost ground. Maybe the two drivers were working together, trying to avoid winning that ugly statuette. He chortled and polished the line for later use at the Slammer. "Son of a bitch had a close call," he would say. "Almost won the Driver of the Month award. But he got away from me."

He floored the pedal and watched the speedometer needle climb. Sixty-five, seventy, seventy-five . . . Too fast, even for this hour. The overextended Fury swayed on its worn shocks like a spavined horse. He was enjoying himself, but daytime chasing was better for the health. At night, it took only one dumb bastard like that Concord back there. At night, people drove sloppy and loose. They'd had a few belts or just finished getting their ashes hauled, or they were coming home from the second shift and were bone tired or half asleep already. He could see the deadline:

HERO COP KILLED CHASING GOOD-DRIVER CANDIDATE

He began to close the gap. The book said to make your chase short and sweet: better to drive sixty in a quick spurt than forty halfway across town. He remembered why that advice had been put in. Two traffic officers had been pacing a speeder for several miles; just before they finally decided to pull him over, the speeder drove through a crosswalk and killed two old men.

He felt the air jetting through his open windows. "Air conditioning, the hard way!" he said, then stood on the brake pedal as a black boy of twelve or thirteen coasted into the next intersection on a bicycle, Look, Mom, no hands, while the bucking Plymouth screamed to a stop on the divider. "Where do they *come* from?" he yelped.

He re-started the Fury with a weary sigh and the engine jumped. He shoved the automatic shift lever to "D" and felt the transmission grind through its two gear changes, wasting horsepower each time. If he had his way, patrol cars would have stick shifts instead of these soggy automatics. "But if we had sticks," he said aloud, "the captain couldn't drive. He's a public menace already. Needs a set of training wheels on his Buick." He laughed and leered and mashed the accelerator.

Now he was a block behind and closing fast. The blue Chevy seemed to be fishtailing and laying smoke. "Westbound on Marshall at Pendleton," he said matter-of-factly into his mike.

"David Four westbound on Marshall at Pendleton," Radio echoed. "Any unit to back David Four?"

"Zebra Four'll go that way!" He recognized the excited voice of Tennyson Mills. The rook still handled every call as though he was on TV.

"David Five headed in from West Market Street." Smoliss! For God's sake, lay back, Ernie, Artie said to himself. Don't fuck me up. Being helped by Ernie Smoliss was like being hugged by a porcupine.

"The state's setting a block at the freeway," another voice put in.

"*Ree*-ceived."

"Two Victor en route from Federal and South Park." The precise tones of Sergeant Richard Not Dick Jellico. The pursuit had taken the two cars into Jellico's Zebra sector. Artie wouldn't be surprised if Packer Lind joined in, too; he liked chases. Especially after midnight when the paper work was caught up.

"Two Victor received," the dispatcher droned.

Chaser and chasee careened downhill toward the river. "Approaching the bridge on Marshall," Artie advised, keeping his head low as he nearly bumped the Malibu's tail. At eighty mph, he drafted on the blue car for a block, then dropped back a few lengths and waited for the dude to wise up. But the Driver of the Month spurted forward as though on afterburner, and the two cars whined across the bridge and into a long wooded stretch that Artie knew would soon change to a two-lane and finally become an on-ramp for the freeway.

"Smarten up and pull over, asshole!" he shouted in frustration. "This is getting ridiculous. *Pull over now!*"

The Malibu sped on as he rehearsed his lines for the final showdown. "Hey, grabba chunka curb, mister! You're going downtown, learn some manners. . . ."

They approached Vega Drive, a major intersection. "He's coming on a red light at Vega," he radioed as they neared the crossing bumper to bumper at eighty-five.

"Still westbound on Marshall," the dispatcher said in a monotone. "Coming on a red light at Vega."

The Chevy never slowed, but Artie had to watch for cross traffic and gave up another fifty yards. "He busted the light, headed for the interstate," he called in.

"Through the light, still westbound on Marshall. Headed for the interstate at Crestview on-ramp. Any unit to intercept?"

Several voices competed. As far as Artie could tell, a one-car roadblock was almost in place. He didn't want a goddamn roadblock, he wanted to catch the son of a bitch bastard asshole rabbit himself and wring his goddamn neck before any witnesses showed up. He wanted to give the cocksucker his rights—with a palm sap. *Whap!* Run from Artie Siegl, eh? *Whack!* You got a right to remain silent. *Zap!* If you give up the right—*bam!*—anything that you say can and will be used—*crack!*—against you. Just once he'd like to handle a rabbit the way he'd handled Jimmy Kid Thomas that night in Pensacola. But he knew he never would. It was fantasyland. Funny how fast the steam went out of you after a chase. There was almost an official profanity code: when a rabbit first took off and you had to start risking your life to catch up, he was a stone cocksucker. When you finally shut him down, he turned into an asshole. And back in the station, the former cocksucker and asshole now became something else: a citizen, with more rights than a teen-age mugger.

Artie's foot danced back and forth from accelerator to brake as the two cars roared up the stretch toward the on-ramp. "Approaching the interstate," he reported. "I'm right on his, eh, bumper."

"We're starting a lot of help," the state dispatcher put in. "The block's in place at Crestview. Ambulance standing by."

Clumps of trees and dark thick brush streamed by as his straining green-and-white cracked ninety. Suddenly the left-front end dipped and he had a momentary feeling that the Fury was airborne. The wheel spun sharply in his hand and the car slid into the high curb as though on ice. While he hauled frantically at the wheel, the Plymouth skidded across to the other side of the road, lurched broadside for two or three seconds, and then skated along the center line on two wheels before stopping in a cloud of steam and smoke. He stomped the gas pedal to the floor and the engine snarled and spat, but the car moved only inches, crawling on its belly like a dog with broken legs.

"*Shit!*—and two makes four!" Artie snapped. He took a deep breath and flexed his joints one by one. No pain. The disagreeable smell of toasted rubber mixed with the warm woodsy air. On both sides, the trees were silent. The Malibu's twinkling red taillights were fading fast a quarter mile up the hill. His own engine coughed and died. His squad car was a dark useless hulk straddling both lanes.

A lone cricket broke the silence. "Fuck your ass!" Artie called out his window. A frog gave a tentative croak and was offered the same advice.

He grabbed the mike to tell Radio that he had lost the rabbit, but there was too much cross-chatter and bullshit. Trained police officers, for God's sake! They were supposed to keep the channel clear for the primary pursuit vehicle. At a momentary break in the confusion, he managed to blurt into his radio, "David Four. I'm disabled north of the freeway."

He had to repeat twice; he realized he must be nearly out of radio range. He had just replaced the mike when he saw the wall-eyed headlights bobbing down the slope toward him.

"Holy fuck!" he said. His watery eyes opened wide through the scar tissue. "He musta seen the block at the top of the hill and done a three-sixty." He punched the mike button hard. "He's coming back, he's coming back."

He grabbed the door handle to jump clear, but the speeding Malibu was too close. Behind it came blue and red lights whirling and howlers tearing up the night.

He covered his mouth to protect his latest investment in credit dentistry as the speeding Driver of the Month tried to squeeze between David Four and the curb. His head was snapped back as the Malibu glanced off his trunk, spun like a toe dancer in the two-lane road, then groaned down the hill with both rear wheels wobbling off center and one of them shooting sparks like a Roman candle.

"You're finished, cocksucker, I got you now!" Artie was shouting gleefully when a skidding state police cruiser careened into David Four and rolled it up and over on its roof.

He sat on the headliner and fumbled at the door handle. He felt giddy and disoriented, but still no pain. Who gets hurt in bumper cars?

Then a green-and-white crunched into the state police cruiser and neatly shoved Artie's car another quarter turn on its side. "Hey, cut the shit!" he heard himself crying. "A joke's a joke. *Hey, you guys . . . !*"

He unslotted his radio and snaked his skinny body through the open window on the driver's side. He shook himself free of glass pellets, spat a few out, and touched a nasty knot forming on his forehead.

Thank God, no blood. . . . He would live, at least long enough to catch one shit-eating rabbit. . . .

From the tract-house neighborhood below the woods, a dog unpealed a tragic howl and another responded with a series of sympathetic yips. Artie spoke with unaccustomed seriousness into his portable radio: "David Four half mile north of the freeway. We have vehicles in collision."

"David Four," the dispatcher replied. "Backup's almost at the location. Can you stand by?"

"Backup's already here," he answered sharply. "Backup's all over the place."

"Can you *please* stand by?" Radio sounded irritated.

"Negative," he snarled into the unit. He could see an ambulance speeding down the hill toward the scene. "Log me on foot for a while."

He unholstered his .38 service revolver with the 200-grain hot loads and began running in his elevator boots down the dark road.

One rabbit's ass was about to be grass.

8

Sergeant Richard Not Dick Jellico dashed from mangled car to mangled car to see if anybody was hurt. Except for bumps and scratches, the officers seemed whole. There were two state troopers and his own man, the rookie Mills. Where was . . . ?

He slid his dry hands down his sharply creased trousers and inspected David Four, balanced on its side. He scratched his crew cut and said, "Well, I'll be." He was proud of the fact that he had completely purified his vocabulary in response to a general memo from headquarters about foul language. "Where's Siegl?" he asked loudly.

Tennyson Mills, in his irritable schoolkid's squeak, said, "Gee, Sarge, I don't know."

"Well, find out!" Jellico snapped, as though Mills was responsible for such things. Sometimes it was wise to instill a touch of guilt in your men, especially the rookies. It made them feel ashamed, culpable, as though they'd let down the whole department. They shaped up better the next time.

A chunky state trooper hustled over, the seams in his uniform under severe strain. "Looking for your man?" he asked. "Ran down the road. Thataway." He pointed toward a pink wisp of taillight twinkling weakly in the night.

The patrol manual strongly advised against allowing ordinary patrolmen to move about entirely unsupervised. "Two Victor to David Four," the sergeant enunciated precisely into his portable radio.

"Go," Artie Siegl's hushed voice came back.

"Your location, please."

"I'm—I'm—" The radio went silent.

"Location, please!"

A young state trooper headed down the hill on foot. "He's probably at the car now, Sergeant. Might need backup." Jellico didn't approve or disapprove out loud; he refused to be held responsible for the trooper's actions. The idea of backing up Artie Siegl hadn't entered his own mind.

"Two Victor to David Four," he said in measured cadence. "State—your—location!"

A long hiss came out of the miniature speaker, *"Sssssshhhh,"* followed by a croaked "Get off the air!"

The sergeant squeezed hard on the transmitting button, then released it. No telling what that irresponsible Siegl might blurt out. They could settle this before the lieutenant.

A siren sounded in the distance, then another. Ambulances, squad cars, other supervisors, all were imploding on the scene. Unnecessary and excessive, Jellico said to himself as he pushed his rimless glasses up his straight-line nose. He couldn't imagine why Radio had put out a Triple Three Emergency. What had really happened here? A bunch of Keystone Kops crashed into each other in a dumbhead chain-reaction pile-up. And who started the whole goof-up? *Who else?*

Well, it wouldn't be long before Siegl's retirement, forced or otherwise. Sergeant Jellico had discussed it with the captain, or listened, anyway, while the angry precinct commander ranted about "the Israeli." Richard Not Dick would never call Artie Siegl an Israeli or any other racial epithet; racism was grounds for departmental censure or punishment. The problem wasn't that Siegl was a—a Jewish person; the problem was that he was an incompetent, a nebbish, if that was the right expression. When he wasn't talking out of turn, he was blowing assignments, embarrassing his supervisors, disgracing his uniform. Until tonight, he had been Molnar's problem and the W.C.'s, but now he had crossed into Zebra sector and caused one of Jellico's men to pile up his car. . . .

The sergeant worriedly reviewed his own actions since the first call about the fleeing Malibu. He decided that he had handled himself with customary discretion, nothing to be concerned about. He had responded to the intercept promptly, had yielded the air to the primary pursuit vehicle, and had proceeded down the hill after the fleeing blue Malibu at a safe and prudent speed, unlike those other clowns. Look at the mess they'd caused: David Four totaled, a state cruiser's front end squashed, and the rookie's corrugated Zebra Four leaking vital fluids all over the road.

A bell clanged from the direction of the freeway. The fire department. A wonder the dispatcher hadn't summoned the National Guard and a bomber strike. Meanwhile the suspect was getting away. He wished he knew the original offense. Probably some heinous crime like spitting on the sidewalk, if he knew the men of David sector. They had the judgment and discretion of stampeding cattle, and what else could you expect, when their leader was a man who had flubbed the sergeant's test nine times before he made rank?

". . . Gone," a voice crackled. "The Malibu's empty."

The sergeant whipped out his radio and order, "Repeat!"

"David Four," the featherweight's sullen voice came back. "The car's empty. Our rabbit's doing the heel and toe."

Jellico acknowledged the call and pondered this development. He stood as straight as a flagpole; in this chaos *somebody* had to imitate a police officer. He was all too aware that certain of the men called him "The Mantis" and mocked his erect posture and his stiff military strut. "You know how he walks?" Artie Siegl had said one day as Jellico listened from behind the door. "He walks like somebody that just come out of the crapper, see, and all of a sudden he remembers he forgot to wipe. *He forgot to wipe!*" There'd be a day. . . .

He whipped off his rimless glasses and stared into the dense screen of maples sealing off the woods on both sides. He knew there was a tract-house development a quarter mile down the black hillside along a county road. The suspect could be down there endangering the householders, or he could have gone the other way, up the hill toward—what was up the hill on the ridge road? An abandoned gas station, he remembered. Some single-story commercial buildings. An asphalt plant and a dump. A junkyard farther along. How to find somebody in a mess like that? The manual gave the precise answer.

Section 31: "Pursuit." Sub-section C: "On Foot."

"Two Victor," he said into his transmitter.

"Two Victor," Radio responded.

"Request a dog."

He could imagine the derisive laughter in the dispatcher's bullpen. Before the citizens' tax revolt, the department had maintained a whole K-9 kennel; five or six shepherds and a couple of bloodhounds with handlers around the clock. Now the K-9 division, as it was still called, was down to a single elderly shepherd and a fifty-five-year-old handler, both with flea collars.

"Stand by," Radio answered.

A minute later he was informed that the handler was at rest in his north suburban home and it would take at least two hours to get the dog to the scene.

"Request a chopper," Jellico said. Sub-section C, Paragraph 4.

"Stand by." The dispatchers were probably falling off their chairs with amusement. So what? Richard Not Dick Jellico knew procedure. If a review board played these radio tapes back later, they would find he had obeyed the rules exactly. *Exactly!*

The dispatcher reported that the helicopter was laid up for a valve job. Maybe by afternoon . . .

"Disregard," the sergeant said. Vehicles were arriving from both directions, sirens winding down like cats in heat, lights playing across the tangled frieze of cars. "Two Victor to David Four," the sergeant called. Time to restore order and discipline; the lieutenant would be along any minute. "Your location, please?"

"In the woods, I dunno," Artie Siegl answered disconsolately. "Just off the road—someplace."

"Can you see anything?" Jellico spaced his words as though talking to a two-year-old.

"Affirmative," the wise guy answered. "My—hand—in—front—of—my—face. That is all."

Ridiculous. Pursuit in these woods was out of the question, except maybe by dogs. You could pass within a few inches of the subject and never spot him. There were no stars, no moon, just a thick layer of heavy hot air suitable for a Turkish bath. He pursed his thin supervisory lips in aggravation. He shared with Captain Singletary a hatred of disorder, of wheel-spinning; it was unnecessary and unprofessional, and here he was deeply involved in it. Why couldn't Molnar's morons keep their—their ball-ups in their own sector?

"Two Victor," the dispatcher's voice intruded.

"Two Victor."

"We woke up the registered owner, Sarge. The Malibu's stolen. Guy didn't know it himself."

"Received," Jellico said, trying to conceal his surprise. How had a pigeon-brain like Siegl known the car was stolen before it was put on the hot sheet?

With anxious eyes, he saw the unmarked olive Fury arrive and the massive form of Packer Lind materialize in the night. "Anybody know why Artie was chasing the guy?" the watch commander asked without returning his salute.

"A T.V., I think," he answered.

"The guy rabbited for a traffic violation?"

"That's all I know, Lieutenant. I wasn't in on it. Started in David sector. That's why I'm not—"

"Get Siegl back here, quick."

The ex-featherweight ambled up in a few minutes, his uniform marked with leaf stains and dirt, his right sleeve torn at the elbow. Nothing unusual for Molnar's squad, Jellico thought in disgust. Discipline began with the uniform, but the sloppy Hungarian who ran David sector didn't seem to understand fundamental police science. What kind of supervisor would report for duty with his whole dinner menu on his tie and his breath?

"Pardon my drag," Siegl said to the W.C. "My tux didn't get back from the cleaners."

"The lieutenant wants to know how this thing got started," Jellico said brusquely.

Siegl seemed to hesitate, then began in a defensive tone. "A piss-ant traffic stop, that's all. I walk up to his car. *Zip!* He rabbits." The sawed-off patrolman slapped one palm across the other in demonstration. "Woulda had the cocksucker, but I blew a tire or something. Terrific equipment we got, Packer. Why don't we switch to skateboards?"

The sergeant frowned on behalf of his watch commander. There was a right time and a wrong time for light humor. And you never called a supervisor by his first name on the street. But Lind was smiling. How could the man expect his personnel to learn procedure when he didn't follow procedure himself?

"You okay, Artie?" the watch commander asked, patting the disheveled officer on the epaulet.

"Never laid a glove on me," Siegl said. "I'll squeeze this bump on my forehead if it ever gets a head on it. Oh, here." He pulled a woman's flimsy knee stocking out of his pocket.

The lieutenant lowered the blue nylon into the glow of a cracked headlight as Siegl said, "Found it on his floorboards."

Jellico watched in surprise as the W.C. yanked his own radio from its holster and said, "Two Two Three to all units in the search area. Be aware there is an R factor. Repeat, there—is—a—*verified*—R—factor."

As Radio repeated the warning for incoming units, a puzzled-looking Artie Siegl asked, "What's the risk factor, Packer? You think maybe the dude's on our want list?"

The watch commander sniffed the night air as though he could smell the fleeing rabbit. "You stopped tonight's sex killer, Artie," he said in a low voice.

"Huh?" Siegl said as Jellico edged closer to hear.

The lieutenant held up the blue stocking. "Guy wore this over his face when he left the apartment. That's why he—"

"Rabbited," Siegl finished up, nodding his head vigorously.

The sergeant sniffed. That stupid Siegl had chased all the way into Zebra sector to lose a killer. Fine police work! And what an injustice! Imagine: Siegl was on Molnar's roster; the screw-up was David sector's all the way, and now he, Sergeant Richard Not Dick Jellico, would have to write a report; he, Sergeant Richard Not Dick Jellico, was in a position where he had to explain an embarrassing sequence of errors by another supervisor's man. And the irony was that he'd been hoping and praying for a spectacular crime or a challenging case to show the promotion board that he could do more than pass tests.

But not this, for God's sakes. Not this—this—no-win situation. If he wrote the truth, he'd be condemned around the station for showing up Siegl as an idiot. But if he covered up, he would run the risk of being caught in a lie and facing an angry review board instead of an angry precinct station. A fine choice. Just—fine.

Well, he'd write a report, they could bet their backsides on that. He'd find a way out; hadn't he always? The chips must fall.

But not on himself.

9

An hour after dawn, James Doremus emerged from his hiding place deep in a box hedge bordering a small brown Tudor house. Somewhere nearby, accelerating traffic snapped and spat in the morning warmth; he homed on the sound through a backyard littered with play domes and swings and outdoor toys and clawed his way over a wooden fence. He scuttled on all fours across a vacant lot with parched weeds and emerged at a stop sign on a country road. He stuck out his thumb and a battered Dodge pickup pulled over.

The yawning driver in the yellow hard hat didn't want to converse, and neither did Doremus. As they approached town, streams of traffic merged into a jam. The morning rush; no cop would stop him now. He was just another worker headed into the city.

The driver dropped him off six blocks from his apartment. A police car turned the corner as he hurried down his street. It didn't even slow down. He smiled to himself. Let me get inside my place, and I'll be just another . . .

Statistic. . . .

I'll be just another . . .

He thought of all the words. Corpse. Cadaver. Stiff. Dead body. Funny he couldn't think of more.

Well, dead was dead, whatever you called it. And a deal was a deal. This was the deal he had made with himself. Just once he had struck back. Just once . . .

Enough for a lifetime. . . .

He turned into his alley, kicked an empty beer can, and opened his door. A gray tiger cat brushed against his jeans. He picked her up and kissed her prickly whiskers. "See ya, Maureen," he said, and slid the animal into the morning sunshine.

Inside, everything was ready. He'd visited three doctors, and now he had more than enough. He'd conned those doctors good.

"Can't sleep, d-d-d-doc. I need some k-k-kinda sedatives."

"Ever used barbiturates?"

"B-b-b-barbiturates? Uh, om, uh, yeah, a few years ago. The family d-d-d-doctor, back in Cleveland? G-g-gave me some—Nembutal, I think it was."

"Any problems with it?"

"N-n-no. Slept good."

"I'll prescribe a dozen. Take one a night. If they don't do the job, we'll have another look at you."

Now he grabbed a plastic container off the table. "One capsule as directed," he read. "Nembutal, ¾ gr." Twelve tiny yellow cylinders. Chintzy bugger.

Another container said, "Seconal, 1½ gr." More like it. There were twenty reds inside. The third container was his prize. The old pill pusher in the shopping center had awarded him fifty hits of Dalmane, thirty mgs., pretty little capsules of two colors: the red of clotted blood and the creamy hue of skin. He held one between thumb and index finger and admired it in the light. Thanks, Doc. You're a decent old sucker to help me like this. When I need it.

He mixed his collection in an empty jar, then poured the capsules from one hand to the other. When he tired of the game, he carried his pharmacopoeia into a small bathroom and began gulping the capsules three and four at a time with tepid water. Stomach full to bursting, he stretched on his lumpy bed and waited.

He felt giddy, almost excited. His visit to the apartment hadn't gone exactly the way he'd intended, but close enough. He hadn't meant to strangle her right off, but he couldn't get the bitch's mouth open. He hadn't intended to leave a message on her stomach, either, but the felt-tip pen lay next to her shopping list, and he wanted the world to know what she was.

. . . Called me a creep. . . .

He felt a rush of energy, started to jump from the bed, then reeled back.

Light-headed already.

He looked at his watch. Eight minutes had gone by. Eight minutes? Or was it eighteen?

He didn't understand why he felt good. Better than good. He felt *great:* strong and full of life. Just a little—wobbly.

He didn't feel sorry for himself or the girl. For once he had done the right thing.

He realized he was prone again and his eyes were closed. He opened them with effort, then let them fall shut. He saw her in the backs of his eyelids, clear, her bluish-white throat exposed as she received his thumbs, her dark-pink tongue twisted and hanging out the side of her mouth, like a mongrel dog on a chase. *Wasn't that what she was?*

Then why had he wanted her so much? Wanted—Betsy? Betty. That was it.

Oh, how typical, how stupid. He forgot to leave a note for his father. *Stupid!*

He struggled to get up again, desperate this time, but found he could barely move his head. Soon he gave up trying. . . .

What's the use? Let him read about it. . . . Not that important anyway. . . .

No, not to Dad . . .

Oh, gee, I forgot to leave . . . a note. . . .

Dad! Hey, Dad! I made an inpimp . . .

Made—an—impin . . .

An imp . . .

Daddy, Jimmy made—

An imprint . . .

10

In jerks and spurts, Captain Julius Singletary backed his midnight-blue Buick Riviera out his suburban driveway toward Cul-de-sac Lane. His radio-operated garage door refused to cooperate, and he had to squeeze from behind the velour seat and pull it down by hand. Son of a bitch works fine when the planes fly over, he muttered to himself.

Cheap piece of crap. A real contractor's special. Does anything work right nowadays? Certainly not those yay-hoos at the precinct. *My* precinct, he reminded himself, personalizing his domain as usual. All totally useless: my precinct, my officers, my patrol cars, my wife—

No, he wouldn't call Agate his wife.

Not after last night. She lived under the same roof, but as a wife she was . . . As a wife she'd make . . .

Words failed him. Goddamn stubborn woman . . . Acted like her twat was spun from glass, some kind of rare ancient treasure. Ought to get it insured at Lloyd's, goddamn thing's so goddamn valuable. . . .

Maybe he should start playing around. It was in style. That sausage-shaped sergeant in Juvenile had been after his own sausage shape for ten years now, like unto like. Why, she eye-raped him every time he came near her desk! Didn't she? Maybe . . .

No, he—would—*not*. He was no plaster saint, but chippying was out. He wasn't even tempted. Agate was—what?—thirty-nine now, and still a fine-looking specimen. Others might see her as an aging woman with sagging bazooms; to him she was the Venus with arms. And lately just as warm and affectionate. . . .

He hauled on the wheel and looked back at the home of his discontent. The new cat was batting something around in the pachysandra. He squinted. It was a mouse, a terminal case. Good, he said to himself. Every family needs one pussy that works.

Halfway down the block he lowered his window and shouted, "Watchit, yay-hoo!" at a silver-gray Fiat Strada that pulled in front of him. After twenty-four years of riding in police cars, he believed in his heart that all traffic should veer to the curb when his Buick showed up, lights should automatically turn green at his approach, and the general population should treat his private car as though it were the star vehicle in a presidential motorcade.

He tried to figure when she had last—cooperated. Monday a week? Or was it on her birthday? Nope, not *that* night. He'd bought her a genuine simulated marten stole and taken her to a faggoty ballet downtown and still managed to strike out, he remembered clearly. Said she had "the curse." The eighth day.

Jesus Jones, he couldn't list all her excuses. Diarrhea. Sick headache. The misery of gas. Hemorrhoids. Leprosy was coming up any day now. . . . When he did get lucky, it was only after hours of tickling and massaging and cooing in her ear, and then she responded like a traffic victim.

He heard a faint crackling noise and realized he had forgotten to turn up the Buick's scanner. "David Four, a D.B. at Six Three Nine Drexel."

"David Four received."

[55]

A dead body for the first watch. Maybe it was Agate. No, she was still sleeping. What in the name of God did it take to bring the woman off? She used to go for it, didn't she? Came like the great geyser at Yellowstone, or was she faking it? No, his first wife had been the great pretender; that Georgeanne belonged on the legitimate stage. But Agate used to *love* it, couldn't get enough, provided you knew what buttons to push.

Driving along with a fist in his lap and his toes clenched tightly, he recalled the motel at Disneyworld, when he was thirty-seven and Agate was—let's see—not quite twenty-nine. He'd poured just the right number of rum Cokes into her. Too few and she wouldn't put out, too many and she'd want to dance your ass off. That was a night. . . . Screwed, blewed, and tattooed, as they said in the Navy—a "trip around the world," except for the tattoo, his first and last. . . .

He made a sweeping left turn onto Rolling Vista Drive and moaned aloud for the past. He'd weighed 175 then, lean and light on his feet and sharply dressed in his three-piece color-coordinated Botany suits and reddish-brown chukka boots from French, Shriner & Urner. He still tried to maintain the same mental picture of himself, but there was a full-length mirror in the precinct's locker room; he'd had to avoid it ever since the day it tried to show him someone he didn't recognize: a softening hulk of 215 pounds. The mirror seemed to reflect a head built up with successive layers of congealed grease, the watery hazel eyes set in loose pouches of flesh above a bulbous nose. Not only that, but the goddamn mirror had tried to show him a pair of grayish-yellow eyebrows with wild tendrils whirling about, and on top of his scalp the biggest lie of all: a reddish-brown hairpiece that looked as realistic as a plastic dog turd. The mirror sucked. More than he could say for Agate. . . .

A tank truck bore down on him as he started to enter the freeway, and he swerved out of the way. "I'll get your license, yay-hoo!" he snarled, but by the time he caught the Peterbilt his mind was back on his marital miseries. He'd given her 236 strokes the last time, and that was counting in and out as one stroke, not two, the way some guys counted. And what response did he get from the snow queen? Nothing. Zero! No, no, she *had* given him a response, come to think of it. "Stop now, Jules," she'd whined. "You're chafing me." Chafing her? What did she have down there, a fresh wound? Why, any other woman would be shooting sparks out her ass after 236 strokes. . . .

Ten minutes to the station. Headquarters must be nuts, calling him in this early. He sped along in the lane marked "buses only."

"David Six headed in on paper," a voice said on F-2, the precinct's channel.

Whole damn station does nothing but write reports, he said to himself. Ought to trade in our revolvers for typewriters. From what I heard, we'll be writing our fingers off the next three shifts. He swung off the freeway and jammed on his power brakes to avoid running up the back of an Alfa-Romeo slavishly obeying the exit speed. Goddamn wop cars, they ought to be banned. . . .

What had made her change? He thought back across the whole twenty-one years, back to when he called her privates "Betsy" and she called his "down there." And they actually held hands when they walked. She had always been touchy about words. Christ, he had to talk like an altar boy the last year or so, or she'd go dead. "I'm coming, I'm coming!" he'd bellow, and she'd pull away and leave him spouting at the ceiling.

"Don't use that word," she'd insist. "I just *hate* it."

The word "orgasm" was permissible, but lately she'd been using it in a way that puzzled him. "Jules," she would complain at a crucial time, "didn't you orgasm *yet?"*

"Didn't I what?" he would say, losing his stroke count.

"Didn't you orgasm?"

What had the woman been reading? You couldn't use the word that way, for God's sake, Why, you might as well say you had to airplane to Pittsburgh, or you had to steamship to Paris. *Say, I'm going out and beer a couple brews. . . .*

Reaching the station driveway, he poked at his violet-tinted unlined bifocals and overspun the wheel, missing a delivery van by inches. "Watchit!" he shouted, steering the bucking Buick into a place stenciled "Pct. Cmdr." behind the grimy building.

Goddamn! There was a whole new set of tire marks from the night before. How many times had he told the supervisors: it was *not* repeat *not* necessary for the men to lay rubber every time they left the parking lot. It made ugly black parentheses and commas all over the pavement, and the trusties couldn't get them out. Didn't everybody know that he hated stains, dirt, unclean vehicles, overflowing ashtrays, half-empty pop bottles, cigar butts, and flies, dead or alive?

No, they didn't know, that was the sad truth. Not this bunch of yay-hoos. . . . By God, he had the worst misfits on the whole P.D. He ticked off some of the choicer specimens: a flap-mouth ex-fighter, three or four flopped dicks, a matched pair of falling-down drunks, a brooding useless deskman, a hunky sergeant who couldn't find his dick in the dark with both hands, three spooks just out of the watermelon patch, and now the last straw—a red-headed broad with a college diploma and tits like fixed bayonets. Probably a feminist or some other kind of radical.

Okay, everybody had to be stationed somewhere. He'd ride their beefs and whip them into shape and try to produce a rated precinct. *But first the place had to be clean!* Couldn't these yay-hoos get that through their skulls? Appearances counted. There were pea-brained inspectors who would mark down his whole operation if they found one cigarette butt in a urinal. The silliest thing was his men didn't even have to do the cleanup themselves; there were trusties to do it. And still the station resembled a latrine in the Ethiopian Army.

Well, they were getting a poorer grade of trusty lately: hypes and winos and degenerates. And you couldn't raise your voice to them. Back in the good old days . . .

Back in the good old days I could get my ashes hauled, too, the captain mumbled as he squeezed his blocky body out of the driver's seat. He rolled his eyes at the hot silver-blue sky as he remembered the night he'd screwed her with his cowboy boots on. "Wa-hoo!" he'd hollered, carrying out the theme. "Ride 'em, cowboy!" Then for a few memorable years he said things like "Right up the old turnpike!" as he rammed it home, and snorted hoarse instructions: "Spread! *Spread!* Raise your hips! Higher! *Higher!* Now shove back. Shove! S . . . h . . . o . . . v . . . e!" Man, she'd loved it. *Loved it!*

Where had the romance gone? Jesus Jones, he was only forty-seven. The doc had warned him, "Use it or lose it." Oh, God . . .

A dried-up patch of ivy looked about to break off the brick wall as he yanked at the back door of the station. The place smelled like booze and piss; somebody must have processed a drunk. A curl of vomit in the shape of a scimitar decorated the worn stone step. He would order a trusty out with Pine-Sol right away. Goddamn drunks, they slimed up the station every night; he wished the last watch would stop arresting them. He'd even dropped a hint to Packer Lind, but the big yay-hoo was too dense to get it. The first watch had orders to have the place shipshape and sprayed with commercial-strength deodorant by the time the precinct commander checked in at 9 A.M., but this morning he was ahead of schedule. He looked at his watch: 7:35. And already blisters were bubbling up in the asphalt. He should be home in his cool bed, sleeping off an orgy, his spent wife still breathing her tribute in his ears. . . .

"Bring me the reports," he called to Barker, the first-watch commander. He didn't have to specify what reports he had in mind.

"And get that puke off the steps! *Phnfff!*" He often sniffed sharply for emphasis.

The reports were almost enough to take his mind off Agate. The homicide was ugly, and that idiot Siegl had let the perpetrator walk. God, what a mess! This definitely wasn't one of your hot-blooded boy-meets-cock-teasing-girl rapes, or your two-drunks-wrestling-in-the-front-seat rapes, or your typical Saturday-night spook rapes with a razor or Mexican rapes with a machete or the old standard rape where the father comes busting in on the young lovers and the girl turns state's evidence on the spot.

No, this was a nut murder, cold-blooded, the kind of homicide that gave sex crimes a bad name. He clucked loudly at each detail. *"Strangled . . . Hand cut, evidently result of struggle. . . . Perpetrator wrote S-L-U-T across victim's abbominal area in apparent felt-tip pen. . . ."* Oh, Christ, he lamented to himself. The kinkiest kind of homicide. The guy not only kills, he writes on the victim after he gets his rocks off. That—is—*sick.* That—is—*trouble.* . . . He penciled a note for Packer Lind: "Let's watch spelling." Damned supervisors, none of them could handle detail.

For the next half hour the unhappy precinct commander creaked back and forth in his office chair with the leaky stuffing and caught up on the sordid record of the third watch. An atrocious performance, even for that wrecking crew. A sex killer lost and two cars wrecked, three if you counted the state's. And they let some whacko juveniles come in and kill the pups. Well, at least there'd be a little less dog crap around the station. He'd never wanted the pregnant mongrel in the first place, that was the Animal Shelter's job, but some of his men were like children. "Oh, Captain, sir, we'll take good care of her. *Promise!*" "Captain, *please?*" You had to humor them. And the puppies were cute enough, when they weren't peeing on your shoeshine. . . .

Jesus Jones, Internal Affairs would swarm into the precinct like a school of piranhas, there wouldn't be enough trucks in the city fleet to cart off the forms and reports he'd have to write.

Well, the wrecked patrol cars were the state's fault, I.A.U. couldn't help but see that. "Car No. 2 driven by State Trooper O.W. Klycynski broadsided R.O.'s vehicle, Car No. 1," Loudmouth Siegl's report observed, "and Ptn. Tennyson Mills in Car No. 3 was unable to avoid the two disabled vehicles blocking the right-of-way and completed the demolition derby. See diagram." *Demolition derby!* Smart little bastard. What did he think this was, a joke? Punch-drunk idiot, somebody ought to transfer his ass to the Hebrew commandos.

The report on the manhunt, written by Sergeant R. W. Jellico and screened by Lieutenant S. J. Lind, told how the available officers had been frustrated by the thick woods and darkness and had been ordered into quadrants to await daybreak. A few men were still out there beating the brush, but plainly it was a waste of time.

Where else but my precinct? he asked himself sarcastically, pursing his leathery lips. The guy pulls off a juicy 010 and drives away in a stolen car and then Officer Friendly stops him for a chat and off they drag at ninety miles an hour till the dumb bull spins out and takes two more police cars to the junkyard with him while the killer does a Houdini act in front of half the precinct. If crime was that easy in Precinct Nine, maybe the yay-hoo would try to stick up the station house today, in between a couple more stranglings and a bank job. He broke off two pencil points scribbling a reminder to himself:

1. A. Siegl is *furloughed*. No discussion.
2. Ask Lind: why no dogs? No chopper??? Standard search procedure.

Then he slapped the button on his intercom. "Sam?" he said. "How many killings we got this month?"

"I'll get the stats, Skip," the first-watch commander replied.

The precinct's homicide clipboard showed three earlier murders for August: two black and one black-on-white. A small number for a hot summer month. And no apparent connection with this sex killing.

"The extra dicks show yet?" the captain asked.

"What, and interrupt their sleep?" Lieutenant Sam Barker answered. "Detective bureau's as shorthanded as we are. I'm not expecting any more dicks around here till ten, eleven o'clock."

"Internal Affairs call about the wrecked cars?"

"Long time ago."

"Bastards never sleep. *Phnfff.*"

"Not when they can pound our ass."

"Well, give 'em anything they want. This time we're in the clear." Maybe if he repeated it often enough, it would come true. Nine months till retirement . . . Nine lousy months . . . He lit a cigar and laid down a bluish smokescreen. "They got any special questions, tell 'em check with—"

"Packer Lind."

"Right. Uh, what about the dogs?"

"What about 'em, Skip?"

"Did you bury 'em, or what?"

"Already buried when we come on. Back in the brambles." Barker put on a long face.

"Good and deep? Where they won't, uh, smell?"

"I guess. Packer said his men dug the graves themselves, wouldn't leave the job for the trusties. They had a little, om, er, service."

The captain bit back a caustic remark; Barker already looked downcast enough. Jesus Jones, the man was digging his boot into the buckled wooden floor like a shy schoolkid. "Eh—Cap," the W.C. said, then coughed and turned his head.

"You got a hernia problem?"

"There was a call first thing this morning," Barker said quickly. "Friend of mine at Radio. Says a complainant phoned Nine One One around midnight, reported two, uh, gays loving it up at Twelfth and Pomander." The day watch commander stopped and looked sideways.

The captain snorted. Was there one goddamn problem in Precinct Nine that could be handled below the command level? Two fruits at Twelfth and Pomander! "So what?" he snapped.

"My friend says they were, uh, well, eh, my friend says the individuals were, uh, officers."

The captain looked up. "Police officers?" he asked.

"In uniform."

"In—*uniform?*"

"In a squad car."

"In—*a squad car?*"

"Right, Skipper." Barker was sounding less sympathetic, as though to emphasize this wasn't his problem. Well, it wasn't. He was boss of the first watch, 4 A.M. to noon, and it had been two or three weeks since Internal Affairs had caught any of his monkeys in a mis-, mal-, or non-feasance. But poor Julius Singletary, Ninth Precinct commander, had to bear the responsibility for every one of the station's sixty-four stupid yay-hoos, including the misbegotten third watch presided over by Packer Lind.

"Crank complaint," he blurted out. "Musta been. *Phnfff.*"

"Possible," Barker said soothingly. "Complainant ran off at the mouth, said the P.D. should never of hired fruits, everybody knew it'd come to this, lousy example to the kids. The usual garbage."

"The guy get any badge numbers? Car numbers?"

"No. Said he was just driving by, noticed one officer, uh, uh, *mounting* the other in the front seat. Said he was too shook to stop. A few blocks farther he got up some Dutch courage and went back, but the green-and-white was gone. So he called Nine One One to gripe and—"

"Did you say Twelfth and Pomander?"

"Yeah. Square in the middle of David sector."

"That's—"

"Molnar's."

"What's your friend think?"

"My friend?"

"At Radio."

"Oh, yeah. Says they all got a big, uh, laugh. One of the dispatchers said . . ." The day-watch commander looked reluctant to continue.

"Said what?"

"Anything can happen in the Ninth, and usually does."

The captain felt his face redden. Goddamn it, that was a personal insult. "Oh, how cute!" he said with heavy sarcasm. "That's just too goddamn *clever!*" He stabbed his cigar in Barker's direction and sputtered, "Well, you tell your, your friend at Radio"—he stopped and coughed to avoid choking on his own phlegm—"you tell him there's, uh, there's, uh, two things everybody's got one of: an opinion and an asshole. *Phnfff!*"

"Right, Cap. I'll tell her."

Barker was backing toward the door when the precinct commander remembered a crucial matter. "The outside stairs. Did you—"

"Trusty's working on 'em now, Skip."

"Use plenty of Pine-Sol."

"Yes, sir."

The captain lifted his gaping nostrils into the warming air. The station still reeked. "You got a D.W.I. in there?" he asked, motioning toward the one-cell lockup.

"No, sir. It's the new trusty."

"The new trusty?"

"Pissed himself when they brought him down from the central lockup this morning."

The captain's head shook, setting his jowls into motion. "The jail sent down a sick trusty?" he said in tones of disbelief. "You got a sick trusty cleaning *my* steps?"

"Well, uh, yeah—"

"Goddamn it, Barker, forget the steps and wash the trusty! Hose him down good, hear?"

"Skip, the book says—"

"HOSE HIS ASS GOOD!"

"Will do, Skip. Yes, *sir.*"

"Pine-Sol. Plenty of it. *Phnfff!*"

After the W.C. left to carry out his assignments, the captain emitted an angry grunt. Eight more hours to go, a psycho strangler on the loose in the precinct, three cars wrecked, and two of his men doing the Greek in a squad car. Who could the yay-hoos be? He ran a thickening finger down the roster of the third watch. Smoliss, maybe, he was dumb enough. But dumb and queer were different, some of your queers had high I.Q.s, and anyway Smoliss was married with six kids. Reichert? Hell, no. He was just a bitter survivor. That Billy Mains, he'd screw a rattlesnake he could get his dick in it. But it had to be a *female* rattlesnake, the guy wasn't queer. . . .

He threw up his hands. Packer Lind could handle this one. The third-watch commander was always bragging what a great crew he had, they never did a damned thing wrong, just a bunch of Explorer Scouts and novitiates serving mankind. Let him explain this one away. Two sissy cops getting it on in a patrol car. . . . Jesus Jones, what next?

The jangle of the phone answered his question. "Singletary!" he announced. He never used his title on the phone. Everybody knew he was *Captain* Singletary, didn't they? Besides, "Singletary!" sounded more businesslike, as though he were swamped with work and needed to conserve every second. A technique he'd learned from his first-watch commander, now chief, the same master of appearances who taught him to say "Yale!" instead of "Yeah!" on the grounds that "Yale!" sounded abrupt and professional.

"Morning, sir," a pleasant female voice said. Thank God. Just what he needed. "One moment please for Captain Antonelli. Internal Affairs."

He slid the phone off his ear and rolled his eyes at the flaking ceiling. As he tried to summon his strength, the events of the long disgusting night flickered through his mind like a runaway newsreel, and he was reminded once again of the truth of an ancient proverb, taught to him by a counselor when he was phasing out his first wife:

When trouble begins, it begins in bed.

11

While the baby clacked toys in her playpen, Amnee Lind tiptoed into the shade-drawn bedroom where Packer slept. She tilted her slender body over their second-hand poster bed and looked with mingled love and pity at the face that always reminded her of a ruined sculpture. The pink channel that bisected his bushy left eyebrow was fading, but the scar was still naked of hair, despite all the vitamins she had rubbed into it. ("Chrisakes, Amnee, who wants an eyebrow smells like fish?") Now he had a permanent reminder to stay clear of Latin gang fights at midnight. "Nobody can tell your husband nothing," Turk Molnar had bawled when he called her from the emergency room. "Should of been back in the station on paper. But you know him."

She knew him, all right. The surgeon had saved his savaged eye, but somehow made it rounder than the other, with a lazy lid that seemed to function according to the phase of the moon. She resisted a temptation to run her finger down the bridge of his straight rebuilt nose, the result of a chase back in the old Twelfth, when two green-and-whites had collided at an icy intersection and left him with a splinter of steel permanently seated a half inch away from his spinal cord. Progressive degenerative nerve damage had set in and now his left leg was a full inch short; he wore a lift to lessen his limp. That accident was before his first wife, Rosalind, had died. Amnee had been—she tilted her small head back like a sparrow as she tried to figure how old she had been. Right. Ten. Probably playing hopscotch while Packer was on the operating table. Oh, God, she'd rather not think about it. . . .

Abruptly the big form rolled over. A sniff, a snort, a half sneeze. Sleeping lightly, as always. Solving personnel problems in his sleep, or tearing along Canal Street at ninety miles an hour.

Now she could see the dotted-line scar where the ear lobe had been repaired, the result of every cop's most-hated call: 241, family disturbance. No, second most-hated. She would never get these things straight! The most-hated call was 293, barricaded subject with a gun, but 241 was close. Packer had once told her why: "The husband and wife, they can be fighting like tigers, see, and she's covered with her own blood, but if you try to lay *one finger* on her old man, she'll tear you to shreds." Or, in this case, nip off your ear lobe.

Amnee felt an urge to kiss one of his adorable scars and make it well, the way she did with Emily, but the dear hassled man needed his sleep. He had wobbled in at 6 A.M., murmured something about a three-car collision, not Artie's fault, the poor *poor* little pups, Singletary'll blow his cork, he'll tell her about it later. . . .

Lieutenant Packer Lind, watch commander. Her—husband. After nearly three years of marriage, she could still hardly believe it. The luck of it! The absolute, weird, strange, beautiful *luck!* She had known exactly what she had wanted from the age of sixteen, *exactly,* but who ever expected him to turn up on the stage of a women's college, delivering a lecture on crime prevention? A police sergeant, of all things! An *older* man. But otherwise—perfect. And now a lieutenant, slightly shopworn, but still—perfect. She leaned over the bed. His wide mouth slanted slightly downward from left to right as she looked at him. That face, she said to herself; it looks like something put together from a kit. Where have I seen that imbalance? In a Picasso drawing, that's it. Or was it a Dalí?

She sighed and straightened up, but something caught her flecked green eyes. Just below the sleeper's flat midsection a miniature pup tent was making an appearance under the covers. She brushed the apex lightly with her middle finger, and the pyramid quivered. Now who could the rotten beast be dreaming about? *It better be Amnee Lind!*

Wait! she told herself. Why not make sure? Wives whose husbands worked the third watch had to be resourceful.

She checked to see that peace reigned in the living-room playpen, then kicked her thonged sandals halfway across the room. Her embroidered Mexican *camisa* fluttered over her head like a large dove, revealing small upturned breasts and tanned shoulders. Waves of prickles began sizzling across her freckled skin. A shower, a shower, that was what she needed. It had already been two hours since the last one, and he loved the smell of her lemon verbena soap.

Blue jeans fell in a crumpled heap and left her naked. She looked down. In a moment of abandon, he had told her she had legs "that won't quit." She had always wondered, Won't quit what?

As she reached in and turned on the spray, she remembered how squirrelly he'd acted when he was transferred to the third watch, eight at night till four in the morning, six days on and two days off, till the end of time, or maybe longer. Their previous lovemaking had flourished in darkness, but with the shift change he would seldom be home at night. Three chaste days went by, then a fourth. . . . He hung around the house leering at her. She realized with a chill that he was waiting for his nights off. *The poor thing did it only at night. . . .*

She couldn't help asking, "Is it a violation before dark?"

Well, yes, he seemed to think so. Even now, six months later, he still preferred the cover of night, but she was slowly retraining him. He always acted surprised when she tantalized him before sundown; he would suffer attacks of shyness and modesty before getting into the action. "Where's baby?" he'd ask, blue eyes darting about. "She okay? What if somebody knocks?" She knew it was his farmboy background, the Methodist Episcopal Church, the Boy Scouts of America, all those subversive organizations. Her own generation had learned directness.

She stepped out of the shower and slipped her glowing body into a new taupe chiffon peignoir, $29.95 at Murphrey's, marked down from $49.95. Her unblemished skin erupted in bumps, the way it always did when she was aroused. She opened the bathroom door a few inches and listened. Stay quiet, Baby Emily! Play on, little angel! She looked at the bed. The pup tent was still there, but it was subsiding. *Damn!* What she had in mind was something more like—Ringling Brothers. She giggled silently and ducked back into the bathroom.

The nightgown tugged lightly at her slim thighs. Some people thought that small backsides were sexy. Her husband, for one, unless he was an awful liar. In school one of the Gamma Alphas had accused her of being "built like a boy," and it was the awful truth, and she was afraid she hadn't changed much in the three years since then, even as a nursing mother. God knew her face was unspectacular and her hair was just a limp swatch of wheat; she wasn't even sure what color to call it. *"He* likes it," she'd answered back, and now *he* liked it, too—that big wreck of a thirty-seven-year-old cop lying under the covers and making a tent with his—cock.

She shivered at the word. Sometimes it sounded dirty, filthy, vulgar; sometimes it sounded—stimulating, hot, the *right* word. She would have to buy more sex manuals and study up. Her hardening nipples brushed against the chiffon, and a glow radiated from her breasts. If they could see her now. . . . All those friendly advisers, with their conventional straight-faced warnings. . . . Her mother: "Remember, dear, you marry the uniform, but you have to live with the man." Her Aunt Flo: "He seems strong, and, uh, virile now, but what about when you're thirty-five and he's, uh, fifty-one?" Her big sister Karen: "And when you're forty-five and he's—*sixty*-one?"

She had remained indifferent to their warnings and bawled out her tired father in short Anglo-Saxon words for refusing to back her up. From the beginning, Packer never knew what hit him. She had loved him before he had loved her, she was sure of that, although he now politely professed that it had been instant love, rewriting history the way men did, "but you seemed like such a kid, hon. I didn't dare let myself feel it, see what I mean?" So what if he was sixteen years older? The way he took care of himself, didn't smoke, worked out in the police gym, watched his diet, took his daily vitamins with only minor squawking when she thrust them on him—why, he was good for another fifty years, provided that shard of steel didn't pierce his spinal cord. And by then she'd be a little old lady herself, beyond sex, with happy memories to warm her bed at night. More than most married women could say. . . .

Who am I trying to convince? she asked herself, but she already knew. She stepped from the bathroom and approached the bed. She lowered herself gently on the far side and reached out to touch his stomach. The circus had left town; the tent was a memory. She kissed him lightly on the lips. He squirmed and sat up—

Damn! She should have known better.

"Time's it?" he asked fuzzily, wiping his hand against his mouth as though a snail had walked across. "Where's Emmy? *Huh?*" She should *never* have kissed him. Now she'd spooked the poor straight-laced soul. . . .

She shoved her small hands against his heavy chest, backing him down. "Rest," she said soothingly. "It's nine. She's playing. I just—"

"*Nine?*" He sat up again and yawned, showing his strong white rebuilt smile. "Cripes, Amnee, I got a million things to do." He blinked his light-blue eyes hard; one lid descended and one tried and failed. "Hey, what're you doing in your peejays?"

Trust him to call her fifty-dollar peignoir "peejays." Sometimes he had the keen sensitivity of a, of a—cop. "You like?" she asked, hating her own arch tone.

"Yop. But hon, I gotta—"

"You gotta lie down."

"I can't, honey. Hey, did the day watch call yet?"

She gulped. He had an instinct for plunging to the heart of things. "I don't know." She averted her eyes. "I've been outside most of the morning, uh, talking to om, uh—Mrs. Robbins."

"You turned the phone off again," he said in an annoyed voice.

"No, I didn't, Packer!" Damn his insights! "Honest, I didn't. I really didn't, sweetheart."

"Honest, you did. You really did." He looked at her accusingly. "Amnee, how many times have I begged you, hon? A supervisor can't turn his phone off."

There it was again. The job. The damned job. Priority Number One, *always.* "You looked so tired when I got up," she said. "You still look tired, sweetheart. Don't they have other supervisors?"

He climbed wearily to his feet and pulled on his blue-checked boxer shorts. In the pale morning light he looked like a slightly overage Olympian about to work out with discus or javelin. But then he spoiled the image by trudging toward the bathroom in his flatfooted way, wrenching each foot upward as though pulling it from mud. The farmboy walk: you could tell it a mile off, with or without the foreshortened leg. Forever skirting around cowpies and gopher holes. City boys cruised straight ahead, never looking down. They *knew* the sidewalk would be smooth underfoot. Farmboys clomped. This city girl thought it was cute.

"Yop," he called from behind the closed bathroom door. "They have other supervisors, but—" His voice broke off. He never talked when he peed. Just didn't feel right about it, he'd explained when they were first married.

The toilet flushed prematurely, to muffle the sinful sound of spattering urine. What a repressed generation!

"Had a busy night, honey," he began again. "You catch any of it on the scanner?"

"Uh—no."

How could she tell him? She never listened to their police radio. She didn't savor excitement and she didn't enjoy tension. For the same reasons, she never went to horror pictures or stayed up to watch scary movies on TV. Some of the other wives felt the same way; at their last gathering the women of Precinct Nine had talked about the increasing stresses on policemen and their families, and how to avoid biting the wallpaper, and the consensus was that rules one, two, and three were to take an ax to all scanners in the home. She had found the discussion refreshing, for a change. Usually the station wives talked about their husbands' bravery, their husbands' sacrifices on behalf of an ungrateful community, their husbands' chances for promotion and/or number of years to retirement, their husbands' skill with weapons, and their husbands' horrifying adventures. Sometimes the heavy emphasis on husbands annoyed Amnee, not that she didn't adore her own. It made by-products of the wives, as though they would cease to exist if those important men didn't lend substance to their lives. The husband as thickening agent. God, she could remember discussions that had absolutely nauseated her. The boring, noxious details! A couple of meetings back, Linda Wry happened to mention that her husband, Endicott, almost fainted from tension after he emptied his gun at an escaped prisoner, and for one hour and thirty squirmy minutes the wives of Precinct Nine gabbled about shootings they had neither participated in, thank God, nor witnessed, thank God again. Thelma Molnar ended the marathon of war stories by telling how Turk had exchanged shots with a robber back in Alabama and didn't realize he'd fired till he saw the man holding in his intestines. *Ugh!*

Personally, Amnee wished they would declare a moratorium on shoptalk, especially the grisly variety, but the only time she ever dared to broach the idea, Genna Jocelyn had made her feel like an ingrate. "Oh, Amnee," the reedy-voiced widow had said, "you just can't bury your head. God knows the job's scary, but that's the vocation, isn't it? What do you tell the lieutenant? Not to bring home his stories? I did that with Eddie, and for a week we hardly spoke. Then one morning we started talking about his work, and it was fun again, all the old griping and the crazy arrests and the work load and the funny things that happened at the station." Genna sighed. "One week later—" She turned away.

"I know, Genna, I know," Amnee said gently, putting her hand on the tiny woman's arm. Patrolman Eddie Jocelyn had been directing traffic at a mill fire when a wall fell on him. That was eighteen months ago, but his widow still came to the wives' meetings, still sent birthday cards and fresh-baked cakes and presents to her husband's old watch-mates, still lived in the same apartment in David sector and gave police parties on the slightest pretext. Sometimes Amnee wondered why Genna didn't date and remarry, but why bother? She was already married. To a whole precinct. To Amnee it all seemed strange, maybe a little sick, but there were different ways of coping with grief, and who was she to judge? If a wall ever fell on Packer . . . And it could happen tonight. *It could happen tonight. . . .*

Despite the warm morning air she felt a chill and pulled the sheet around her bare shoulders. She couldn't imagine life without that big backward klutz. She was twenty-one years old and hopelessly bound to one man. What kind of women's liberation was that? Please, God, she prayed silently, don't let him be harmed. Not—once—more . . . He's paid enough.

She knew that Genna was right; it was the vocation. Shocks and injuries came to policemen because they solicited the dangers that others avoided; cops were going to be shot and stabbed and sliced and bludgeoned and bruised and pummeled whether God was alive or dead or paying attention or off attending to other matters. If His eye was on the sparrow, how did Packer accumulate all those scars? Where was His eye when the wall fell on Eddie Jocelyn?

The scanner . . . God, what a mistake *that* had been! Against her wishes, Packer had brought it home and showed her how it worked. The next night she'd heard his call sign—"Two Two Three in pursuit"—and for five shocking minutes she forced herself to listen as he called in. Each time he opened his mike she could hear the pounding of his engine and the screaming of the howler, and she'd heard them in her nightmares ever since.

She shuddered and pulled the sheet up across her nose, hiding herself from—what? She was becoming more fearful, newly aware of small sounds and shadows. It was as though she had been anesthetized for the first years of their marriage and was just beginning to come out of the ether and into the world of reality. She had always been able to separate herself from the anxieties of her husband's occupation, to imagine that he was just another workingman with peculiar hours, but lately she bit her nails and worried after he left for the station. Would he come home mangled from another family fight, another high-speed

[69]

wreck, another midnight rumble in the park? *Would he come home at all?*

Newspaper articles made her raise her hand to her mouth in horror: a traffic policeman clubbed brainless by a motorcycle gang, two officers ambushed in Precinct Fourteen, a police station bombed in a suburb. Once she would have shrugged those reports off; they had nothing to do with her. But now they were threats.

The shower drizzled on in the bathroom as she lay in bed and tried to analyze her new fears. The difference must be Emily, she decided. Yes, that was it. She was afraid on behalf of the baby, afraid that the child might grow up without a father or with a pathetic, mutilated father, scooting around in a wheelchair and trying to smile. She was afraid that somehow Emily would be made to pay for the shortcomings of the parents. And the baby was too sweet, too innocent to suffer. The baby didn't *deserve* to suffer. The baby hadn't selected this father who insisted on behaving like a rookie when he should be staying behind in the safety of his office and acting like a supervisor. The baby hadn't selected this father who walked around with a cold steel point impinging on his spinal cord. No, Amnee had made that selection herself, and together the two of them had brought Emily Packer Lind into the world. Maybe we shouldn't have, she told herself. But we have. We *have,* and let's stop being afraid! Let's stop worrying so much. It'll communicate to the baby, and we'll raise a fearful child. Stop acting so neurotic, Amnee. Stop it, *stop it.* . . .

Her husband galoomped out of the bathroom, pulling on clothes as he walked, talking through his undershirt. "We had some, uh, complications last night. Artie Siegl stopped this guy and chased him all the way to the freeway."

"Who?" she asked, trying to show interest.

"Just—a rapist."

She felt an annoying spasm inside. "What's 'just a rapist' mean, Packer?"

"Oh, nothing. I didn't mean anything by it." He was holding something back again; he'd been doing a lot of that lately.

"Yes, you did. You meant 'just a rapist,' no big deal. You meant it's not as though the poor man was a real criminal or anything."

"Amnee, you *know* I don't feel that way, honey. Hey, what're you so touchy about?" The hide of an armadillo! Here she was, lolling on their bed in a see-through peignoir donned especially for the occasion, and the big dumbo was wondering why she was touchy. Worse, he rubbed his hands against his cheeks, screwed up his face, and headed back into the bathroom to shave, babbling nonsense as he walked.

"I've already told you exactly how I feel, hon. Rape is, uh, it's the ultimate violation of, om, a woman's body and, uh, mind."

"You know what you sound like, Packer? A slide lecture. Where'd you learn these lines? The academy?"

The slip-slap of his shaving brush filled the silence. Then his voice came back, muffled. "Believe every word, hon. I really do."

"Sure," she said sarcastically. "You and Sergeant Molnar."

Packer moaned. At the last watch party, Turk Molnar had lectured the group on the psychological origins of rape: either the victim had asked for it in some subtle way, he said, or the rapist's mother had overstimulated the poor guy as a child. Either way, Amnee realized, it was a female's fault. She found Molnar amusing and sometimes lovable, but he should have been a short-order cook instead of a patrol sergeant handling delicate human problems. "Know what I hate?" She flung the words at the half-open door.

"Yop," Packer said. "Big Detroit cars. Captain Singletary. Cigars. Hockey fans—"

"I hate those big macho cops that go around saying women egg men on."

"Those aren't big macho cops, they're big dumb turkeys."

"You don't really believe that, Packer. If you really understood—"

"Rape? I understand it all right." His patient parental tone irritated her. "I've seen what it does," he went on. "I been there. I know what it must mean to a woman, how it must make you feel ashamed and sick and dirty and violated. . . ." He paused, as though trying to remember the rest of the text.

"Helpless," she said, halfway to herself. "Mostly helpless."

"Helpless?" said the man who understood rape.

"Words!" she spat. "Oh, Packer, you say them, but there's no way you can ever feel them."

"Why not?" he called out, sounding amused and infuriating her more.

"You're the wrong sex, that's why, and you're in the wrong job. You're a cop, not a social worker. Isn't that what you always say?" Her voice was trembling.

Packer emerged from the bathroom and took her hands gently. "No, hon, that's *not* what I always say. I—I just didn't want you to hear about it."

"Hear about what   ?"

"The, uh, incident. Last night."

"What happened?"

"The girl was, uh . . . She was—you know—"

[71]

He lowered himself on the side of the bed and draped his arm around her slender shoulders. Wisps of lather curled from the underside of his chin; he smelled like a barber shop. "Uh, eight blocks from here," he mumbled, looking at the rug. "On—on Meredith. A woman was, uh, murdered. Strangled."

Her hand touched her throat so fast it made a sound. Rape had always been her own special fear. She had never experienced the classical female fantasy about the brutal, rapacious stranger. He had never appeared in her dreams, and if he had, she would have screamed and kicked him in the crotch. Dear God, why did Packer have to tell her—

"Something else happened last night," he was going on in the same gentle tone. "When I got back to the station—"

The phone rang. God, she'd just connected it a few minutes ago. Probably they'd been after him all morning, something or other about the murder. They couldn't let the poor man alone. It wasn't bad enough he had to work through the best hours of the night; no, he also had to keep jumping out of bed to answer the telephone. The captain, especially, thought nothing of calling him at any hour of the day, as though sleep didn't matter to mere subordinates. Lately she would wait till he was snoring and then disconnect the phone. Four or five hours were all he seemed to need; he'd explained to her that the Marine Corps had taught him to sleep faster than others. She wondered if the Marines had also taught him to yawn all the time, and swill coffee around the clock, like the rest of the cops.

She listened as he spoke on the phone, smearing soap against the earpiece. "Yeah, Kimmy. . . . Sure, kid. A Schwinn, huh? Got your I.D. numbers?" He grabbed the clipboard lying on the night table. "One six nine Nora Nora Ocean. . . . No, that's just police talk for the number, Kim. . . . I'll get on it, pal. . . . Sure. . . . Sure. . . . We'll put out an APB. . . . Yop, an all points bulletin. . . . See ya, kid. . . ."

Without putting the phone down, he dialed a number and reported the stolen bike to headquarters. "Give it a little extra muscle, will ya?" he asked. "The kid's a friendly."

She waited impatiently on the edge of the bed, her flamingo-tinted toenails digging arcs in the throw rug. Packer was right; she didn't want to hear about the murder, the third watch, or the chase. All she wanted was to recapture the mood of the morning, steal the moment. Why must their brief times together be contaminated by cops and robbers and murders and rapes and . . . stolen bikes? She wanted to shout, Let's forget the Ninth Precinct. *Forget the damned job!* Let's have a few minutes to ourselves. Warm, tender moments. No, not warm—*hot!*

Let's forget last night, let's wallow in *now,* in *us,* you and me. Let's fly off on our own little tangent for a while. It's okay, Packer, it's *acceptable,* can't you see that, sweetheart?

Soft noises came from the front room of the bungalow; Emily was still cooperating. "Couldn't you have asked Kimmy to call in himself?" she asked in her poutiest voice.

"He's a neighbor, hon," he answered, crossing the room in three gimpy strides and corraling her in his big arms.

She nuzzled his slackly muscled chest with its tickly snippets of silver and black. "Isn't bike theft a little—trivial?"

"Trivial?" he barked, instantly making her regret the question. *"Trivial?* Hey, just try telling Kim Chong it's trivial. The first thing he's gonna say at Show-and-tell next week is he had his bike stolen. Hon, he may be upset for six months over that damned bike. You know what I tell the watch?"

"No, what do you tell the watch?" she mocked, slowly stroking his neck.

"I tell 'em, the bad cop goes out on a bike theft and he's mad because he's not handling some big case, and he says, Speak up, kid! I got more important things to do. But the good cop, he walks in with a smile on his face and he says, Hey, son, sorry I took so long, we're just snowed down at the station. Hey, you oughta drop in and visit us sometime. Now tell me, pal, how can I help you? See what I mean?"

The baby sneezed in the living room, and Amnee's fingers began to drift along the line of ringlets above her husband's ears. She glanced down and noticed that the pup tent was beginning to reappear in his blue-checked shorts. "Hey, what. . . ?" Before she could finish her inquiry, she was buried under 225 pounds of freshly bathed cop.

"Brazen woman," he said, covering her bared breasts with his large gentle hands. She tried to answer, but his mouth found hers, and she felt the two telltale hot spots formed on her cheeks. She could never play the outraged maiden when her skin tones gave her away. Besides, the tantalizing fragrance of witch hazel radiated from his shaven face and the clean smell of good old Ipana poured from his mouth. Everything about him was fresh and clean and—dated. Ah, but he was current where it mattered. . . .

"Does the baby know we've been meeting like this?" he whispered in her ear.

"Packer, don't screw around. Oh, I mean . . . Screw around! Oh, yes, sweetie, do it. Do it, *do it!"* He already was.

She shut her eyes and saw a salvo of rockets. "Ooh ooh *ooh!"* she couldn't help saying aloud. "Oh, it hurts." Instantly he pulled back.

"No, don't stop!" she cried. She wished she could act more ladylike, but the backs of her legs were incandescent, sparks ran up and down her stomach, she trembled in the buzz and the heat. "Oh, put it out, Packer, *put it out!*"

"Put it out?" The dummy had stopped again.

"The fire, the fire! Put it *out!*" Oh, Packer, please, please, put it out, sweetheart. That's it, *that's it.* Faster, faster. *Ooh, ooh, ooh . . .*"

The phone rang again.

"Don't, sweetheart, *don't!*" she begged. But he was rolling off the bed and limping across the room.

"Oh, hi, Cap," he said. "I dunno. . . . Musta been out of order. . . . Yeah, terrible, terrible. . . . Some nut, I guess. . . . Uh huh. . . ."

As he talked, she laid her plans. She would use the large serrated kitchen knife on him, she would turn his own gun on him, but *she needed five more minutes.* . . . Or else the rest of her day would be misery. Her stomach would twitch, she'd have flashes and tingles, she'd feel pain that would start between her legs and sting and shock all over, and she'd be uncomfortable and squirmy and depressed and irritable and run out of energy and flop on the bed and bawl. . . .

"Excuse me all to hell, Skip, you're wrong there. . . ."

Five little minutes, that was all she asked. Was that unreasonable? He'd worked her up, hadn't he? No, not really. More like the other way around, to be honest. So what? She'd get those five minutes back if she had to tear his shorts off. . . .

"Skip, I *do* understand. . . . Yeah, yeah, I *know* you got a year to go. . . . But, Captain, you can't. . . . A good man. . . . Goddamn *right* I'll be in!"

Oh, sure, he'd be in; he'd bail out the precinct one more time. But what about his poor wife, consumed in flames? She took a deep breath and tried to compose herself, but it was no use. Her toes were gone. Just before the phone rang, she had curled them tightly, and now there was no feeling down there. They were probably rolling around under the covers, along with her missing climax. . . .

"Dunno, Cap. A flat tire, I guess. . . ."

The man was actually talking about cars! Dear God, the priorities of watch commanders. His wife in bed eight feet away with her feet falling off and her face heliotrope with lust, and him prattling about a flat tire. Face reality, she told herself; you're second fiddle to a bunch of cops; might as well accept it. There was a Chinese wall, and the precinct was on one side and their little bungalow on the other, and never the twain. . . .

Mother and daughter had half of him at best.

Well, it was half of a good man, anyway. Maybe she shouldn't complain. Most of her friends had lesser fractions of lesser men.

And he loved them both, she was sure of that; loved them in spite of his preoccupation with the seedy Precinct Nine and its collection of malcontents, Lower Slobbovia they called it. She would never understand his fierce loyalty to his men, his touchiness where they were concerned, his low flash-point when the newspapers criticized them or headquarters slapped their wrists or Internal Affairs came snooping around. . . . He spent too much time with cops, too: drinking beer, shooting pool, going to their endless promotion parties and weddings and christenings and—funerals. But he loved her and Emily, he loved them, yes he did. . . .

"I'll be right down. . . ." He hung up the phone and looked at his wife as if she were a stranger off the street.

"Get—it—over—here," she said in a flat monotone.

"Something came up, hon. I won't be long."

She shrieked, *"You're off duty now!"*

"Honey, a supervisor's never—"

She leaped on his back and rode him to the rug. "Hey, *hey!*" he yelped. "What ever happened to foreplay?"

She had miscalculated. It didn't take five minutes.

12

Alone in his apartment at the Loo-Ray Arms, Patrolman Gerald Yount had spent another day without sleep, the third or fourth in a row, he wasn't sure of the number. He had tried all the tricks and techniques; he desperately wanted to sleep. He knew a good rest would clear his mind, maybe end the scenes and hallucinations, ease the strain of waiting for Darlene. But sleep wouldn't come. . . .

He'd counted to a thousand and back to zero. Breathed deeply. Stared at a spot on the wall. Relaxed his muscles one by one from the toes up. Watched TV and read the Bible till the words danced like fireflies before his face. But in his own mind he knew that nothing would put him to sleep, not the counting or the breathing or the reading or the TV: nothing would give him peace till *she* returned. . . .

He could still see her strutting around the efficiency apartment, her glistening black hair in curlers, floppy robe loosely tied, breasts bobbing in and out of view. . . .

Gone now—

But only for a time. She would be back, she *had* to come back. . . .

The next two nights he would be off duty. He grimaced at the thought. He had been moonlighting, trying to keep busy, but the manager at the pizzeria had told him they were switching to Pinkerton's instead of off-duty police officers. "Drop in anytime, Gerry, you're always welcome to all the deep-dish pizza you want at fifty percent." But it wasn't the food that he would miss—he had lost twenty of his 170 pounds in the two months since Darlene had left. What he would miss was the company. Fellow humans. Just being there with people, looking over the noisy crowd, watching for the occasional hot-blood who drank too much beer and had to be steered outside. Keeping busy. Six-fifty an hour, but he'd have worked for nothing.

Would she. . . .

He grabbed at his throat. The thought that his Darlene might never come back, that he would always be alone, made him gasp for air. He stretched out his hands to ward off a blow.

Alone . . .

He couldn't face another night alone. Couldn't or wouldn't, it didn't matter. He sat heavily on the double bed where they used to sleep. His life had turned into a broken record of couldn'ts and wouldn'ts. He couldn't be alone. He wouldn't cry. He couldn't sleep. He wouldn't take pills, and he wouldn't drink. He couldn't wipe the scenes from his mind. No, no, *don't* let the scenes start up again. . . .

He rubbed his burning eyes, whirled, and buried his face in his thin bony hands. Stop, *stop!*

But the memories began to form, perfectly in focus, magnified by imagination. He groped backward for the bed, almost fell on the tangled sheets, eased his head against the flowered blue wallpaper and let his dry lips hang open as the pictures swept across his mind.

. . . A doctor's office. A cramped room, light-tan walls, a narrow table with crinkly paper, the nose-twitching smell of alcohol. A pinpoint of fluorescent light reflects off a bottle of tongue depressors. They are in the clinic for Darlene's annual checkup. Strictly routine. She always sails through: blood pressure high–normal, heartbeat strong and steady, all tests negative.

An elderly man pulls up a chair, motions him to sit. Just the two of them; Darlene is filling out forms with the nurse. A friendly chat. Cigarettes again, eh, Doc? "Well, no, Gerry. Listen, I'd like to, uh, discuss something with you, eh, man to man, okay? I mean, we're both grown men, men of the world, we both understand—things."

"Sure, Doc, sure."

"Gerry, I'll be blunt. I've been seeing you and Darlene—how long now? Two, three years? A couple of my favorite people."

"Thanks, Doc. The feeling is—"

"Gerry, you've got to stop abusing your wife's rectum."

He sprang from the bed in his steamy apartment and rolled his head from side to side like a roped calf. His eyes locked open and he searched wildly about the room for a place where he could get away from the words. Don't say that, Doctor! Please, please . . .

Gerry, you've got to stop abusing your wife's rectum.

He sees himself trying to stay calm as the doctor fidgets with a triangular pale-pink rubber mallet. Don't let on. Don't show surprise.

"I understand, Gerry. Believe me, I understand. It's—the times. The joy of sex, and all that. Gerry, I don't knock it. But—there's a limit, son."

Don't respond. Do—not—let—on. Let him finish, then get away. Figure out what to do, and above all *don't let anybody else find out.* . . .

He sees the doctor patting him on the back, trying to ease the embarrassing moment. He feels himself wanting to deny that he ever abused his wife—like that—or ever thought of such a thing. Why, anal sodomy is a penitentiary offense, it's in the penal code along with high crimes like robbery and arson and murder. How could he commit an offense like that with the woman he loved? Something so—dirty. So— vile. . . . But instead of a denial, he hangs his head.

But we never did it, Doc! He wants to shout the words, but above all else he must hold his tongue. He must keep the darker secret: that he has been cuckolded in the cruelest way. Men killed for less. . . .

"Delicate tissues," the voice above the starched tan coat was saying. "Inflamed . . . Possibility of infection . . . Can get nasty . . ."

"Yeah, Doc," he mutters. "It was just one of those, you know—*silly* things that married people do. Just a, a, a stupid thing we fell into. . . ."

Who fell into? *Darlene and who?*

Halfway into shock, he had sat in their bedroom that same night and taken his wife's confession, his black eyes refusing to cry or even blink.

Well, the affair wasn't her idea, she began; the policeman had started phoning her a few months ago after a chance meeting in the, uh, park.

A police officer? Was it. . . ?

No, Gerry didn't know him, he was, uh, with the county; he was a, well, uh, an older man. Recently divorced. He was lonely. It was all *so* innocent. In fact, she'd hung right up when he first called.

Yes, she insisted, she *had* hung up. But when he called back the next week, she was intrigued, flattered, and finally agreed to meet him for a drink. Just one drink . . .

No, she didn't really know why. Bored, maybe. Gerry was gone so often. She cried at night, missing him. And when he was home, he was so, uh, detached and, uh, critical. Loved to tell her she was putting on weight. Didn't he. *Didn't he?* And one day she found that she had stopped missing him, she even welcomed his absences. Who knew how these things happened? Her life had become dull and meaningless. Gerry was—suffocating her. . . .

He was—*what?*

Yes, that was *exactly* the word. Suffocating!

Then Mark—let's call him Mark, she said, even though that wasn't his name—Mark started seeing her once or twice a month. . . .

Oh, heavens, *no,* they didn't have sex! What did he think she was? It was only—talk and companionship. Two lonely people . . .

"Angel, the doctor said—"

"I don't care what the goddamn doctor said!" She'd jumped up and pulled her thick black hair back from her face, blotchy with anger or—embarrassment? "Do you believe the doctor or your wife?"

"He just said—I mean, there was evidence—"

"Of what?"

He had found himself unable to answer.

"*Of what?*" she asked, pressing her cheeks flat with rigid fingers.

"Of—of—" He couldn't go on.

"You goddamn wimp!" she shouted. "You goddamn—pious wimp!" She strode back and forth across the small room. "You're panting to know the details, aren't you? And you can't even say the words yourself. Okay, Mr. Wimp! Then *I'll* say it. We—*fucked!*" She bit into her lower lip as she spat the word like a dart.

"Darlene, angel—"

"We fucked. Fucked, *fucked,* FUCKED!" She was almost screaming now. "We did it—every—way. Understand, Mr. Wimp?" Her tears began. "And he never once acted jealous, or said I was putting on weight, or I looked, I looked sloppy around the other wives, or he was, he was, he was ashamed to be seen in public with me. He, he loved me, Gerry. *Loves* me, I mean." She turned away. "He loves me. He does! *Yes he does!*"

She ran into the bathroom, and he followed, stumbling, trying to comfort her, aware only that the woman he loved was suffering.

"No, *no!*" she said, wrenching away. "It's over now, Gerry. I'll leave. That's what you always wanted. You made that plain enough."

What he always wanted?

No, he'd only wanted a loving wife, a presentable wife, sharing with him at home, helping to build his career, *their* career. Working side by side with him. For *them*. Wasn't that a reasonable role? Running the home till he could build up his seniority and climb the ladder through plainclothes and then into sergeant's stripes and maybe have a watch of his own someday? Conventional maybe, but wasn't that what they both wanted? A split-level out in Villa Manor? A little rank on his collar, to give them pride? A couple of kids to love, when they had the money? Wasn't that a good future for a policeman and his wife?

The sun whitened the stained blinds of his apartment. He closed his eyes so hard that he could feel the pull on the muscles, then jerked his head as though trying to throw off his thoughts. But he couldn't throw off the memories. . . .

She had stayed for two more days, packing, making whispered phone calls, napping on the Hide-a-bed in the living room. Then as he was leaving for the station she told him she would be gone in the morning. For good. He phoned in sick and did penance alongside her bed till dawn. He understood the game she was playing: she was making a point about his criticism and his digs, punishing him for his unchristian lack of charity. When morning came she would tell him they could try again, they would do better this time, they were always meant to be together, like those old couples whose final heart attacks come hours apart.

He had sat by the Hide-a-bed that long night in the living room, while pictures of the two illicit lovers flashed across his brain. Adultery. Fornication. Sodomy. He beat off the punishing words like bats. He couldn't allow himself to think those words. Forgiveness was divine, let him who is without sin . . . They would rebuild their marriage on the rock of his forgiveness.

It was unthinkable that she would really leave in the morning. She would wake up and they would throw their arms around each other, and he would tell her how pretty she was, how precious she was to him. He would ask if she wasn't slimming down a little? And look! He had a surprise! A split of the best champagne, purple label and all, he'd run out and bought it while she slept. They would lie in bed and sip champagne and plan their new life. No, he didn't usually drink, but this was different, this was an occasion, a rededication. They would light candles and hold hands and stroll to the Frenchman's for lunch and a brandy afterward, and she would see how he was loosening up. Maybe she'd been right all along; there was more to life than work, he could see that now, and he would take her in his arms and tell her he was sorry, and they would both be better Christians for what they'd gone through. . . .

All night he had watched her stir, listened to her breathe. Once he reached out and straightened the sheet that covered her, and once he touched her ivory ear, framed by a few damp strands of raven hair, but she pulled away and said "Don't" in a cold sleepy voice.

The movers arrived in the morning. "You can't come in here," he said to a hen-shaped man with bare heavy arms.

"This Apartment Eight-ten?"

"Hold it right there! I'm a police officer."

Darlene ran from the bedroom, wet hair hanging in dripping ropes. "Gerry, *don't!* Don't force me to go to court for an order. I'll just be taking—a few of my things."

He slumped into a rocker and watched as the round man and his sinewy partner carried out the convertible sofa she'd been sleeping on, then her vanity, a tea table, their roll-top desk. "Gerry," she said, pointing to the rocking chair, "would it be okay if—"

He waved his fingers and stood up. He was only dimly aware of what was happening. His mind had covered itself with a shield, like a frog's eyes.

"The chaise?"

He beckoned again.

By the time the movers had driven off, the apartment was almost bare, except for a few wooden chairs and their old double bed and a small chest of drawers. The men had taken the condiments, the kitchen utensils, the good silver from his mother, the juicer, the toaster. He had blinked and watched, his nails mashed into wet palms. He told himself none of this was real; it was a fake, a production, a set being struck. The performance would be over soon, it *had* to be over soon. Why didn't she admit she was only trying to teach him a lesson?

He looked up to see her carrying a blue plastic suitcase that he didn't recognize. She was wearing her plum suit and the pink plastic high-heeled shoes that thinned her heavy ankles and the floppy broad-brimmed pink hat she had splurged on for Easter. "Good-bye, Gerry," she said in flat tones. "I wish I could say I'm sorry." She brushed past him and opened the door. "But I'm not."

"Wait, Darlene, wait!" His voice cracked like a boy's. He knew he sounded panicky, unmasculine. A—wimp. How could she respect a man who pleaded? But she was leaving him, it was like losing his own body, it was impossible, *and it was happening.* . . .

He jumped up and grabbed for her arm. "Please, Darlene—"

The door slammed.

His memories of the next twenty-four hours were vague, shapeless. He knew he didn't go to bed. He remembered vomiting in the living room and again in the bedroom. He walked the floor hour after hour.

He shook his head from side to side, mouth wide open, jaw hanging loose, breathing air in deep, harsh gulps. He recited stories from his childhood. Mother Goose. Br'er Rabbit. Why? *Why?*

He remembered having a terrified feeling that his heart would tear away from his chest and fly into space dripping blood, and he remembered flattening both palms against his shirt to contain it. He sang melancholy songs, trying to make himself cry. Once he looked in the mirror, saw a strange man staring back, and cracked the glass with a single blow of his fist, somehow failing to cut himself. He buried his head in a pillow and tried not to breathe. He smashed an empty catsup bottle across his skull. And he threw up till his stomach was a fiery hole. . . .

When dawn came the next day, he was still pacing the apartment from wall to wall, bumping into doorjambs, rolling on the linoleum, repeating childhood phrases dozens of times, hundreds of times, like mantras.

He was alone.

No, he could *not* be alone.

He was *alone.* . . .

He tilted his head back and groaned like a trapped animal. He slammed a fist into the broken mirror and this time opened a bloody scrape across his knuckles. He ripped tufts of black hair from his head and flung them about. And when he had finished his lamentations and contortions, she was still gone, and he was still alone. He pressed his knuckles into his eyes. But he couldn't cry. . . .

Slowly the scene passed from his brain, like the afterimage of the sun. It was two months later now, an oppressive summer day, and nothing had changed. He turned over stiffly and looked at the face of his watch. It had stopped at 6:35; he couldn't remember when he had wound it. He was stretched on the floor, his nose pressed into the worn hooked rug. He could tell it was late morning; waves of warm air pounded against his windows like tropical surf. A pigeon began to coo on the slender balcony with the chipped tiles and the loose railing, but the song broke off in a gurgle as though the bird had come to a bad end.

He must have slept. An hour maybe? *Slept?* Was it sleep when you awoke more drained than before?

He struggled to his feet and unlocked the warped sliding doors to the balcony. A hot wash of golden light flooded the empty living room as he pulled the curtains apart and staggered outside. It was eight floors down.

13

Amnee felt her husband's weight lift from her. "No, no, Packer," she murmured. "Hold me a minute, sweetheart."

"Later, hon," he said as he rolled out of bed and hurried toward the living room. "Honest to God, I got a million things on my list."

She couldn't help smiling. He always had a million things on his list. Well, at least he'd done something on *their* list.

She heard him greeting Emily in her playpen. *"Good* morning!" he said in his bumptious way.

"Mawn, Dah." The daily gymnastics were about to begin.

"How's my sweet baby today?" He would be lifting her up by the feet now. Thought she was a midget, a circus performer. . . .

"Mawn, Dah," the child repeated in a gargled voice caused by her upside-down position.

They babbled together for a few minutes and then Packer said, "Dah gotta go now, baby, be back soon," and headed toward the bathroom. Emmy whimpered briefly, and then began flinging her blocks contentedly. She was already accustomed to her father's abrupt comings and goings. She'd better be, Amnee thought. She'll be a watch commander's daughter for a long time. Please God. . . ?

She carefully folded her chiffon peignoir, stretched out on the bed, and dozed naked in the warm morning air. She was dreaming she was a twenty-seven-pound pussycat when a faraway voice broke in. Sounded like . . . It *was* Packer, speaking from the bathroom. What was he saying? Puppies? *What?*

She sat straight up. ". . . Found the four of 'em when I got back from the killing. . . . Laying there like balls of fur. . . . We buried 'em out back. . . ."

Some deep maternal instinct made her rush into the living room and pick up the baby. In a few minutes, Packer appeared in his regular off-duty uniform of heel-worn Frye boots, years-old jeans as smooth and soft as butter, and paint-spattered fatigue shirt. Why, he was dressed as if it was just another day! No murdered pups, no innocent young woman strangled. . . . Couldn't he see the whole city was in danger? More and more lunatics and killers? How could he act so—so— *normal?*

Amnee, Amnee, she reminded herself, it's his job, for God's sake. Get a grip on yourself; you married a cop, not a chorus boy.

But after he left for the station, promising to return for a relaxed dinner before his regular night watch began, she sat on the side of the bed and rocked and hugged the baby for comfort. What a frightful way to make a living! Worse than a lawyer defending murderers, worse than a research biologist handling saucers of killer germs; worse than . . . She couldn't finish. It was just too awful. Four tiny puppies— murdered. . . . And what was Packer's comment? "Don't worry, hon, it's just some neighborhood crank." *Just some neighborhood crank!* Didn't the poor dumb thing realize that a neighborhood crank could also walk into the station with a shotgun or a bomb and splatter them against the walls? Couldn't he see that? *It had happened.*

No, he couldn't see it. He claimed she was being dramatic. Thank God he'd spared her the other cliché: that dealing with psychotics and monsters and delinquents "comes with the territory." She'd have kicked him in the shorts if he'd spewed forth that old chestnut. The job, the job, she was getting fed up with the damn job. He could— She would— The whole police department could—

Okay, Amnee, out with it, she told herself, lowering Emily to the floor. Just say it, for God's sake, and be done with it.

"GODDAMN THE GODDAMN JOB!" she cried out. The baby looked up from the rug and grinned and clapped her hands.

The primal therapy made her feel better, but only briefly. The poor dead puppies impinged on her consciousness, and when she stopped thinking about the poor dead puppies she thought about the poor dead woman. God, what a place to live! Packer always insisted that their bungalow was in the safest part of Stanton Park, but what was the difference as long as thieves and muggers flourished a few blocks away in any direction? She could barely walk the baby to the supermarket without bumping into some sinister-looking hood or—what was the word? Hoodess? Yes, the neighborhood abounded in them, too, whatever they were called. Sometimes when business was slow on the boulevard, the hookers would stand at *their* corner, Packer's and Amnee's and Emily's, a little half block from *their* bungalow, and hit on passing motorists. A lovely sight for the baby in a few years. . . .

She knew what had gone through Packer's mind when they picked out the house. He might deny it, but he was like all the other career cops; the future was what they lived for: worry-free retirement with a steady pension and a solid bank account built up through the years and maybe a security job on the side. In a way it was like serving a twenty-five-year sentence; you endured, and there was no hope of parole. In the meantime, Packer kept reminding her how pleasant their block was, how *livable.* The maple trees on both sides of the narrow street touched tips in an arch, and the thin green canopy filtered out most of the summer sun, and the mortgage payments on their tidy little home were only $197 a month, and there was hardly any traffic, and wouldn't they build a beautiful place in the country with all the money they were saving?

Well, the man wasn't entirely wrong, she admitted to herself as she steered Emily into the kitchen and set about squeezing a bag of Valencias. It made for a certain stubborn peace of mind, slugging $300 of his paycheck into the mutual fund month after month after month, planning together for the future, poring through endless copies of *House & Garden, Architectural Digest,* and every free catalogue they could inveigle out of manufacturers of storm doors, awnings, Thermopane windows, home greenhouses, bidets, saunas, whirlpools, hot baths, ornamental fencing, and the like. And while they were waiting, didn't he keep the bungalow in fine shape? Just a few weeks ago he'd finished the new shake roof and oiled it down; it was already aging to a lovely silver-gray in the summer heat. Now he was working on cedar siding to match: unpainted board and batten that would provide a neutral backdrop for the primroses, rhododendrons, geums, and zinnias that she tended with loving care in mulched beds left behind by the previous owner. That was the way Amnee wanted their life: natural and uncontaminated. At the beginning of the hot spell, Packer had trucked home a fancy heat pump, purchased through the police buying pool at just above cost, but she was less than thrilled. "Oh, sweetheart," she'd said, "I want *seasons!* Regular seasons, just like regular human beings. I don't want sixty-eight degrees all the time." But he argued that midsummer temperatures were hard on the baby, and the price was right, and they'd recover the expenditure when they resold the house anyway. The instant she relented, he dashed outside and started to dig a deep hole alongside the house to seat the pump. Today he had planned to pour the footings, but as usual the stupid station had called. . . .

After him *all* the time . . .

A regular life sentence. . . . She poked and tugged at the bedspread.

Now be honest, Amnee, she commanded herself. Do you really believe you're in jail? Isn't that kind of—stupid? Aren't you and Packer really very *very* lucky?

Okay. *Okay!* She had to admit it.

Grudgingly.

But—he was just going to have to leave his damned war stories behind at the precinct. No more horror tales about deranged murderers and juvenile monsters who crushed the heads of puppies in the night.

What a lovely morning this would have been without those awful images! Maybe she could convince him to do some discreet censoring, leave out the sordid details, concentrate more on his dealings with the men, his problems with the captain, Artie Siegl's practical jokes, Willie Bethea's colorful English: the human part of his job instead of the inhuman. There had to be some middle ground between cutting off communication and scaring her half to death.

He phoned an hour later.

"I forgot to tell you something," he said.

"Oh, Packer, sweetheart," she begged him without thinking. "No more, baby. Please."

"I forgot to tell you I love you."

"Oh, Packer. I love you, too." Sometimes, for no reason, he touched her so deeply she wanted to burst into tears.

"Gotta run now," he said. "I'm sorry, hon—"

"You've got to run," she said, almost whispering. "I understand, Packer. Really. I understand."

Oh, God, she hoped she understood. She only hoped . . . .

While the baby was napping, the phone rang again. Wasn't that just like him? she asked herself, rushing to answer. Sometimes he would call three or four times in a row, especially if he sensed she was upset. "Hello?" she said.

"Hello," a heavy voice answered.

"Yes?" she said after a few seconds of silence.

"Hello," he repeated. Was she imagining, or did he seem to be talking through a cloth? Oh, the silly man!

"Packer, stop fooling around."

"This isn't Packer. This is—me." A low grunt, more like a growl. No, this was definitely not Packer. Her green eyes turned quickly toward the baby's door.

"Who are you? What do you want?"

"I'm—Koslo." The voice was hollow and cold. "K-O-S-L-O."

"What do you *want?*" she repeated, her voice shrill.

"I'm coming for you," he whispered.

The dial tone hummed in her ear.

14

Steering his loose-jointed seat-sprung old Jeep Wagoneer toward the station, Packer tried to understand the captain's vendetta against Artie

Siegl. Chrisakes, patrol cops weren't CPAs or preachers or tie salesmen, they were peace officers, and if keeping the peace meant chasing a rabbit, well, by God, you chased him, you took the risk without hestitation. It was risky business driving city streets at pursuit speeds, no matter how many howlers or Visibars you had. It was a hell of a lot more dangerous than any stock-car race or Indy 500. But you did it. You narrowed your eyes and tightened your nuts and flattened that hammer.

To the watch commander, it was similar to placing a man under arrest: once you said the magic words, you couldn't back down, you couldn't change your mind. You *had* to take the sucker in, no bargaining, no reconsideration, not even any discussion. The dude was going to the slammer, period, and it didn't matter if he pulled a blade or a gun or a bomb, by God, he was still going. Sooner or later some fool would debate this fundamental of police science, and then you had to get down in the dirt with him, *you had to,* and you had to come out on top, *you had to.* That was the difference between this and other jobs. One difference. There were plenty of others. . . .

Patrolman Artie Siegl had behaved 100 percent righteous. *100 percent!* His car let him down, that was all. Ever since the citizens' tax revolt, Packer had been firing off gripe memos about the deterioration of the precinct's cars. Fleet maintenance was no place to shave the budget. Now one of this best men had been nearly wiped out in a chase, and whose fault was it? The pencil pushers downtown who ordered retreads to impress the mayor with their thriftiness. *Patrol officers on retreads!* He shook his sweaty head in disgust.

The captain grabbed his arm the instant he entered the station, and provided a personal escort back to the sanctum. Packer felt like a schoolboy being led by the ear. "Your shift is going down the drain," the old man sputtered. "I never saw so many screw-ups on one overnight report in my life. *Phnfff!"*

He held his tongue. Nothing would be served by challenging the man in one of his foul moods. Maybe the toilet was acting up again. A few months back, a trusty had run through the station shouting "The toilet overflew, the toilet overflew!" and the captain had almost suffered a cardiac arrest.

Now the precinct commander's voice trembled with mixed aggravation and self-pity. "You know they woke me early on account of you yay-hoos? Cracka dawn? I don't spend enough time around this sty, I got to come in and ride *your* beefs. *Phnfff!*

"My beefs?" Packer forced himself to stare out the window. A trusty was gassing up a squad car, averting his face as though the smell was

offensive. Too bad the cars didn't run on muscat. . . .

"Right! *Your* beefs!"

"Who called you in early, Skip? The chief?"

"Never mind."

Packer understood. Julius Singletary was a man who hated to admit
that he took orders. He thought of himself as a fatherly figure, stern but
just, guiding his precinct with a steady hand, delegating authority when
necessary but always maintaining tight control of *his* subordinates and
flunkies, *his* vehicles and weapons, *his* cleaning aids and fixtures. He
was a man who hated disarray, avoided surprise, distrusted improvisa-
tion, and panicked at breakdowns in his comfortable old routines.
Packer figured he must have given blood to Sergeant Jellico at one time
or another. What perfect products of the civil service system. . . .

"Why didn't you call for a dog?" the imperial potentate asked
through a castle of pudgy fingers.

"We did."

"When? Back in the station?"

"No. About three minutes after the guy did the heel and toe."

"Three minutes?"

"More like two."

"I assume you made that request over the air, I mean you didn't send
up flares, did you?"

Packer didn't rise to the bait. What was eating the old boy this
morning? The pups? No, he wasn't the sentimental kind. He'd groused
about the dogs from the first day, never contributed a dime to the
Puppy Fund, complained that his men were wasting time around the
enclosure, and who paid for all that chicken wire, anyway?

Or maybe he'd found out about Agate. Turk Molnar swore he'd seen
the henna-haired Mrs. Singletary strolling out of a motel with a young
stud, high noon, smiling and wobbling from too much booze or cooze
or something. Packer had ordered the sergeant to put a lid on his
mouth. *Tight!*

"Jellico called for the dog on the radio," Packer answered. "I heard
it myself. Couldn't've been more than a few minutes after the, uh,
collision."

"You mean 'collisions.' *Phnfff!* With an 'S.'" The captain hunched
behind his desk, his neckless head screwed to his shoulders, peering out
like a shaved owl.

"Radio came back and said it'd take a couple hours," Packer said.

"Sure they did."

"Skip, it was after midnight. The K-nine handler was in bed."

"Dog was sleeping too, eh? Rin Tin Tin hung up his Do Not Disturb

[87]

sign, right? Well, what was the logical thing to do next, Lieutenant, when you couldn't get a dog and there was a dangerous felon loose?" Without waiting for an answer, the captain snapped, *"Call in a chopper!* So why didn't you?"

"We did."

"You *did?"*

"Yop. We did."

"When?"

"Soon as Jellico heard he couldn't get a dog."

The captain's bloodless lips hung slack. Then he spun toward the wall and mumbled something about checking the 24-hour radio tape at headquarters to find out who was lying. . . .

"You do that, Skip. You'll find it's just the way I told you. You know Dick—uh, *Richard* Jellico. He goes by the book."

The precinct commander snorted. "Wish I could say the same for the rest of your watch," he said, swiveling around and adding another emphatic *"phnfff!"* from his endless supply of *"phnfffs."*

"Who you got in mind, Captain?"

"Does the name Arthur Siegl ring a bell?"

"Artie?" Now *why* was the man so hot for Siegl's ass? What had the featherweight done wrong? No denying that he'd lost a rabbit, but what cop had never lost a rabbit? It was rare but it was also inevitable: the law of averages. Losing a rabbit wasn't a capital offense. It even happened on other watches, in other precincts. The only place it never happened was on TV, for Chrisakes. But the television cops didn't have to run on retreads. Neither did any others, far as he knew. . . .

"Yale," the captain said. His phony way of pronouncing "Yeah." *"Artie.* Motormouth Siegl. The one that hears the birdies sing."

Packer's eyes turned to slits. "Gimme ten guys like Artie Siegl and I'll run this precinct so tight there won't even be a pinochle game out there, not a punchboard," he said evenly. "Artie's as good as any street cop I ever knew, and that includes me and you."

"Try that speech on Internal Affairs."

"I.A.U.'s coming?" He might have known. They were as inevitable as worms in a grave. And just as understanding.

"Any minute."

"What's the beef? A rabbit got away, our puppies got killed, or we banged up some cars?"

"Here's the beef." The old man shoved the morning paper across his desk. A boxed story on page one told how a wanton sex murderer pulled his stolen car to the curb and patiently waited to be arrested, then led the P.D. a merry chase and finally did a disappearing act while

[88]

a dozen cops sat in their wrecked vehicles working on their needle-point. Packer had to admit the writer had a way with words. In six paragraphs, he managed to make the whole third watch look like Laurel and Hardy. Too bad nobody tipped him about the pups. He'd have split his readers' sides over that. . . .

Packer slapped the newspaper on the desk. "Skipper, Artie Siegl used perfect procedure in this thing. *Perfect!* He gave Radio the license and description before he made the stop. He even ran the car for warrants. How many guys take the trouble to do that?"

"Jesus Jones, it's right in the new manual. 'Immediately transmit license number and description on all Class B traffic violations.' *Phnfff!*"

"Yop, it's right in the new manual. So what?" The 90-degree temperature wasn't aggravating enough, now he had to sit and listen to quotes from the handbook he'd helped to revise. It was 12:30 in the afternoon and he should be pouring cement for his heat pump: anything but jawing with a man with cotton eardrums. "The manual says you got to shine your badge every day, too, Cap, and you can't accept a cup of coffee, and a million other rules that not one man observes a hundred percent and I didn't and *you* didn't when you were in uniform, Skip, now let's be truthful, for Chrisakes."

"He wrecked three cars. He let a killer walk. Is that something I used to do when I was in uniform?"

"*He blew a tire, Cap!* Those lousy retreads. Siegl's one of the best wheelmen we got, you know as well as I do."

"Did you read his report?"

"Read it and screened it."

"Read it again." The captain slid the three pages across the desk.

"I know every word."

"Show me where it says he blew a tire."

"I assumed—"

"*You* assumed. *Siegl* assumed. *I* assumed. But I.A.U. isn't gonna assume, Lieutenant. The fact is your punchy hero was driving up a straight stretch of hill, no oncoming traffic, no passing traffic, no goddamn traffic at all, when he lost control of his car and aborted an important chase and caused three different wipe-outs. *Phnfff!*"

Packer grabbed the report and read aloud from the second page: "'. . . Was proceeding west about eighty-five or ninety miles an hour when the steering wheel wrenched from R.O.'s hands, causing the vehicle to spin. . . .' See, Cap? The wheel wrenched from his hands. The poor guy had a blowout."

The old man tilted back in his chair and stared through reptilian puffy eyes. "You been running a shift how long now?"

"Come on, Skip. What's the difference?"

"Two years, right?" The captain wrinkled his putty nose twice. "And in two years you never learned to weed out the phonies, did you? Nobody ever lies to Packer Lind, nobody ever improves a story, nobody ever twists things to his own advantage. Far as you're concerned, the third watch is a bunch of goddamn wood nymphs, right? Well, lemme tell ya about this broken-down prizefighter you wish you had ten of. His car is up at the motor pool, and there's no goddamn flat! His car went out of control, banged off two curbs, laid rubber almost a hundred yards, rolled up and over on its roof, and it *still* hasn't got a flat tire or anything wrong with the steering. Your boy lost it, that's all. Probably looked up and saw a flock of geese. Thought he was back in the ring, throwing a fight. Thought—"

"How do you know all this?" It was an effort for Packer to maintain his composure. The precinct commander ought to be backing his troops every inch of the way, but instead he had already tried Artie Siegl and found him guilty, and on the basis of what? A bunch of half-baked deductions and conclusions that would make the lowest-ranked municipal judge spin in his black leather chair. "Where're you getting your information?"

"Antonelli. And don't think he didn't enjoy telling me." Captain Ralph Antonelli, chief headhunter. Commanding Officer, Internal Affairs. An uncompromising shoofly whose smiling countenance created group paranoia in every precinct station in town.

"What do you want me to do, Skip?" Packer asked, trying to collect his thoughts. Regardless of what I.A.U. had found at the motor pool, he was convinced that something had gone wrong with Artie's car. Street-model patrol cars weren't meant to be driven flat-out for long stretches. He had assumed there was a tire failure, and so had Artie. If not, then some other major failure. . . .

"We got to make our move before I.A.U. makes theirs," the captain was saying, unconsciously calling attention to his paunch by rotating his hand against it, the star sapphire on his little finger catching the light from above. "You suspend Siegl, make a quick investigation on the precinct level, then give him a couple days off with a reprimand in his jacket. Time he gets back, I'll have him transferred outa here."

Packer counted to ten, ran his hands through his thick hair, looked at the floor, tugged at his good ear, inhaled deeply, and gripped his chin in a tight hold. Then he counted to ten again. Then he yelled, "When am I supposed to do all this? HUH? Oh, I know you mean today. But WHAT TIME TODAY?"

"An hour or so'd be fine, Lieutenant."

He rose to his six feet four. "Is that why you called me on my off-time, Cap? To dump on Artie Siegl for you? 'Cause it's too close to your retirement time and you're scared to death of controversy?"

The old man's chins quivered and he spouted spit. "What? *What? Phnfffff!"*

He was still sniffing as Packer continued. "Count me out! First place, Artie Siegl just got flopped here from downtown, remember? That innocent little crack he made? Artie's record can't take another rap this quick. He'd be greased for sure, and *he doesn't have it coming!"*

"Goddamn it, Lind, you don't tell *me*, I tell *you! Phnfff!"*

Packer walked toward the door. "You want an investigation?" he said over his shoulder. "Okay! You got it! By *me*, personally. But don't tell me what I'm gonna find or what action I'm gonna take. The third watch is mine, Captain, just like the precinct is yours. If I blow one, then bring *me* up on the charges."

"Depend on it. You got till tonight. Now siddown!"

"Huh?"

"C'mon, c'mon. Sit, Packer. Sit!" Suddenly the old man sounded less sure of himself, deflated. Maybe that crack about retirement had been out of line. Hey, wait a minute! Packer warned himself. If anybody's out of line around here, it's Singletary. *Don't let him up!*

"We got another, uh, problem," the captain was saying.

Packer tried to remember what else the third watch had been involved in. Oh, Christ, the dogs. The old man had just been getting his breath; now he'd start the *real* outburst. *What kind of police station are you running here at night, when a bunch of juvenile delinquents can come in and kill four puppies right under your nose and blah blah blah and Jesus Jones if that ever gets out to the papers I might as well put in for early retirement and blah blah blah and if you can't run things any better than that I'll get somebody who can and blah blah blah. . . .* Packer lifted his big hand from the door knob and turned.

"This one's strictly confidential," the captain was saying just above a whisper. "Right now it's between me and Lieutenant Barker and a couple guys at Radio. Let's keep it that way. If I.A.U. gets wind, somebody's in deep trouble. Maybe it's me, maybe it's you, maybe it's the whole precinct. Get me?"

"Uh, no," Packer said, taking a seat on a folding wooden chair.

A train approached from the south, shaking the ancient walls, and the old man's words were muffled as the big diesels pounded by the window. ". . . Saw them distinctly, two uniformed officers. Twelfth and Pomander. Midnight. Getting it on."

"Say again, Cap. *What* happened?"

He felt the blood flow into his face as the old man repeated the story and issued another order: "I want you to find those two faggots and then leave the rest to me. I'll have those degenerate bastards transferred so far they'll have to come to work by plane."

"Hold on, hold on," he heard himself saying. "What time was this? Midnight? Twelfth and where?"

"Pomander."

Packer bit his lower lip. Why the Christ had he assigned that new patrolwoman to ride with Billy Mains? He'd had some crazy idea of confronting the male-female problem directly. *Stupid!* If you wave a steak in front of a Doberman, he's gonna grab it, isn't he? That horny little Billy Mains, he'll never change. *Never!* Skinny little cracker-ass sex hound, saunters around with that loose-hipped easy stride of his, like his boots don't touch the ground, and waits for the women to slip to their knees. By the looks of things, one did. Christ, he'd thought more of Mary Rob Maki. Thought she had more pride in her uniform, more common sense. Something about the way she carried herself. Well, he wouldn't act like the captain; he'd reserve judgment, at least for the moment. And if somebody had to take a fall, he'd take it himself. You don't whip a Doberman for a handling error. . . .

"I'll sort this one out, Skip. It's gotta be some kind of misunderstanding." His words tasted like pool chalk on his tongue. Christ, he didn't even convince himself.

"Sort out that other geek, too. Your boy Siegl. Three goddamn cars wrecked and a killer on the town. *Phnfff!* Dumb yay-hoo . . ."

Packer ducked out the door. Thank God for small favors, he said to himself; the old man didn't mention the dogs. He hustled down the corridor and almost bowled over three men as he made the turn. The long lean one was Captain Antonelli of I.A.U. and the other two were his sucks.

It was another steambath day, but they looked cool.

15

Billy Mains awoke with a smile and scented his room with satisfying puffs of gas. After a long day of bad dreams, he'd finished up with a good one, his favorite; he could depend on it a few times a month, and the beauty part was that none of the dream was made up, he'd lived every exciting second, and the details were framed on his bedroom wall: the whole four pages from *Official Detective*. He could read the title from his waterbed:

THEY LEFT A TRAIL OF BLOOD

Cocksuckers left a trail of blood, all right, he said to himself, but at the end it was their own. Fucking animals! Robbing all-night gas stations and making the attendants kneel and suck them off and then—*pow!*—a bullet between the eyes. Stone executions. Six dead, one guy blinded. They'd still be leaving a trail of blood if they hadn't made the mistake of hitting an Arco station just as Patrolman William F. Mains turned the corner in his unmarked U-car. A couple of punks with acne. Sniveling, sobbing, dropped their pieces and begged for mercy. "Don't shoot, Officer. Please, please, *don't shoot!*" He'd have burned both their asses if the district car hadn't pulled up. Well, one dead homo motherfucker was better than none. Now the taxpayers had the privilege of paying the other creep's room and board for the rest of his natural life. Billy's solution made better sense. "He drew on me, sir," he testified at the inquest in his angelic manner, and the coroner's trained jurors returned "justifiable" in about eight minutes.

Too bad the police review board didn't have the same sense. Scumbags! So what if he'd been two miles outside his district limits at the time of the shooting? "Flagrant and systematic insubordination," the reprimand said. Sure, and if he'd followed orders he'd have been down at the ferry dock patrolling for pickpockets. Big fucking deal! THEY LEFT A TRAIL OF BLOOD. At least *Official Detective* appreciated a guy with balls and smarts. . . .

He pulled himself into a sitting position on the edge of his waterbed and lowered his pale, wiry legs to the parquet. A skein of mud-colored hair dangled over his forehead; he lifted it back to cover the round bald spot that was spreading across his skull like the Mongolian crud. "Losing ground," he bemoaned out loud. "Christ, I'm 36 years old and I look 40 already." A terrible fate for a man in love with guns, women, and midnight.

An oval picture of himself in army fatigues mocked him from the rock-maple dresser. It showed a gap-toothed, baby-faced recruit with freckles, curly red-brown hair, a button nose, and a shy, innocent look that he still practiced in front of his mirror and seemed to have misplaced somewhere in the 18 years since Fort Riley. Damn, he'd have to bag some rays, get rid of that jailhouse pallor. Fucking swimming pool, it hadn't been usable for the hottest three weeks of summer. Just when he needed it the most.

He touched his toes to a white synthetic throw rug three inches thick and looked wearily at the textured zebra stripes that were starting to peel from his walls and the lavender flocked Styrofoam ceiling with the four-by six-foot inset mirror that had cost a month's pay, and worth every dime if it didn't collapse on somebody's bare ass one of these nights. He tottered to his feet and looked out his sixth floor window. The municipal sewage plant was going about its business, four matched rotors that turned relentlessly night and day atop four tanks covered with a greenish-brown froth. Looks like our goddamn swimming pool, he grumbled to himself as he turned away.

Well, he'd been suckered, all right. He had a pile of bills and duns and final notices to prove it. With two ex-wives on the alimony dole, he hadn't been able to afford a mansion. But this condo, The Tahitian, had looked too good to resist. $250 maintenance, 1-bdrm. eff., singles only, no pets: a swinger's paradise. The TV commercials had shown all the chickies lolling around the pool, jugs spilling out of their maillots. There'd be parties every night, Ping-Pong and pool and volleyball and fashion shows, and six girls fanning him at poolside and shielding him from the sun with their tits.

Looked great on TV. A real bargain.

Except that the filter-chlorinator on the pool was fucked as usual, and the super was off to Europe or Paris or someplace. Mosquitoes as big as bees bred in the filthy water, and water bugs swam in the olive-colored slime. His closest neighbors turned out to be a blue-haired crone who used a walker to get to the mail slot and a middle-aged bulldagger with the body fragrance of a dump bear. There was a rumor that the frizzied pig down the hall would chew the eel for a couple of Harvey Wallbangers, but her moustache turned him off. Maybe in a few years . . .

Then he remembered, and the smile returned to his aging baby face. *My partner the policewoman . . .* Mary Rob Maki, you—are—*fucked!* It's just a matter of time. *Gotcha!* The careful way he was going about it, he couldn't miss. He'd drive her off a wall, he'd have her begging him. . . . "Please, Billy, please, can't I just—lick it?"

He flopped back on his black satinette sheets and watched as a feeble erection raised a few degrees, then subsided. He closed his eyes to concentrate on Maki, then opened them quickly. Goddamn it, the D.B.s were back, pestering him. Come to think, he'd dreamed about them all day. A Rose Bowl parade of dead bodies. An endless caravan of D.B.s passing before his eyes. White D.B.s, black ones, mulatto ones, yellow ones, green ones, orange . . . A fashion show of cadavers.

It was silly, it was nuts, it was driving him bug-fuck, all this heavy dreaming about stiffs. And the craziest thing was he kept flashing on bodies that went back ten, twelve years, remembering the stink and the bedroom windows black with new-hatched flies and the syrupy red-black blood oozing from twisted mouths hours, even days, after death. *Why couldn't he just forget?*

He knew exactly why. Because D.B. calls characterized the whole shitty boring job of patrol cop. D.B. calls showed how low he had sunk. Did plainclothes cops in undercover cars ever catch a D.B. call? Shee-it! When he was back in U-cars, they *created* D.B.s, they didn't handle them.

Every time he had to check a body, poke for the pulse and placate the hysterical relatives, spray the deodorant and call the fucking coroner, he was reminded again of what he was: a common ordinary harness bull in a common ordinary monkeysuit, and of what he had been: the hardest charging plainclothesman on the department. What if he'd been a little—undisciplined? That was a matter of opinion anyway.

There were nights when he swore that his next D.B. would be his last; he'd drive straight to headquarters and stick his badge up the dispatcher's ass. Fuck you, man! Go sniff that rotten meat yourself. You're talking to Billy Mains, you're not dealing with some thick-skulled bull cooping behind a billboard.

On the occasional days when he was the sole occupant of his waterbed, he would blink and squirm, remembering the indignity of D.B. calls, and he always came back to the fat woman in the detached coachhouse when he was a police cadet. Furnace running wild, must have been over a hundred degrees, and the queer son wiggling his hands up and down and whining over and over, "Dear dear dear *dear!* Oh, officer, we just *know* something's wrong. It's been *days* since Mummy called." The body was on the floor in the bathroom, bloated like the fat lady in a sideshow. The twin red eyes of a rat peeked from a ragged pocket it had eaten into a mountainous buttock. The bulbous arms had puffed out like overcooked hot dogs ready to burst their skin. There wasn't enough Fresh-gard in the world to wipe out the smell. His T.O. had run around spraying a whole can of the stuff, hit every corner of the three room house, even sprayed the body itself. Then they closed the door and waited outside ten minutes, the way the instructions said, and still the place reeked when they went back in. As Billy watched, his eyes watering, a bloody bubble formed in the D.B.'s mouth like a kid's balloon, and he grabbed his T.O.'s arm. "Sir, she—she's alive!" He laughed, the goddamn training officer actually laughed. Well, he was playing his role. Mr. Superior, teaching the eager rook the facts of death. In hot weather, a body always seethed and heaved and twisted, he explained, unless the maggots got a good head start and cleaned it out fast. "By the way, kid," the T.O. had added, "if you find any big maggots, scoop 'em out and put 'em in your hat. There's always somebody around the station wants 'em for bait. They pay good, kid."

He gagged at the memory. And now here he was, back on uniformed patrol, the same boring routine, the same nightly drudgery, the same debasing, demeaning, insulting D.B. calls. *Fuck!* Didn't they know that patrol cops were one breed and plainclothesmen another? "Yeah, you've had a few good collars," the deputy chief had told him, "but we can't have plainclothesmen making up their own rules. Report to Packer Lind at the Ninth. He'll work with you. And you'll work with him. Get me?"

He thought of his old T.O. again: another supervisor who was supposed to work with him. Standing over that rotting woman and laughing at his own jokes, just as though the house didn't stink like a cave full of roasted gooks. What kind of human beings could crack wise under those conditions? Patrol cops, he answered himself as he slid out of bed and padded the four steps to his bathroom. Patrol cops laugh at anything. They *better* laugh, anyway. Bend, don't break, that was a survival technique, and laughing was a good way to bend. Too bad it hadn't saved his T.O. The county found him dead a few years later. He'd driven into the hills and parked with a fifth of Jim Beam and a .41 magnum. The first round was a hesitation shot; it burned right across his fly and into the door of the car. The second caught him in the groin. He was a D.B. himself when they found him, dead of shock and loss of blood. Billy wondered if the deputies had laughed. Laugh, boys! Bend, don't break, remember? What was the T.O.'s name? Hallington? Hallaway? Halowell? Christ, it was fourteen years ago, he couldn't remember. Forgetting his T.O.'s name—wasn't that another way to laugh at a dead body?

In the irritating shower that sizzled and chilled in spurts, he thought back on his required interview with the department shrink a month ago. What a snow job! Why, *of course* I'm happy in my work, Doc. Wouldn't change jobs for the world. It's great being a cop, Doc. So *rewarding*. I just jump out of bed every day looking for a new challenge. The headfucker had smiled and scribbled a few notes and that was the end of it. No bullshit counseling, no medicine, no tranquilizers, no nothing. Some of the guys came out of the creepy little office with prescriptions up to their hairlines—Thorazine, Librium, Valium, everything but leeches. That's how Johnny McClung got started on the reds. The shrink prescribed them for sleep, but he forgot to tell Johnny to turn off the booze first, and now the poor guy was walking three feet above the ground, busting juveniles for jaywalking and pulling his shield on strangers in bars. The lieutenant didn't know the story yet, but when he found out—Billy shook his head.

A trickle of shampoo seared his eyeball, and when he stared into the shower stream to flush away the soap, the spray changed from tepid to scalding and made him yelp. Two hundred and fifty fucking bucks a month for maintenance, and what did the goddamn super maintain? He maintained his cock, that was about it. He certainly didn't maintain the fucking plumbing system. Didn't maintain the pool. Didn't maintain . . . Shit, it was simpler to remember what he *did* maintain. Yeah, that's right. *His cock.*

He grabbed a towel, swabbed out his sore eye and resumed his struggle with the shower. Sometimes life sucked. *Most* of the time. Should he have said *that* to the shrink? Should he have told—the truth? That the world was fucked, his job was the purple pits, the goddamn city was a mess? That you could accomplish a hell of a lot more with a slapjack or a wrist rocket than you could with the crummy court system? Should he have said that the world was drowning in do-gooders? Assholes, in other words? When he thought of do-gooders he remembered the Buddhist monk going up in flames in Vietnam for— what? Was there any percentage in trying to help people? If you redistributed all the money, the poor would be poor again inside of a month. You could be fucking sure it wouldn't take the crooks long to get their share. Who was the first jerk that said crime doesn't pay? "Somebody that doesn't know shit about crime," he said aloud as he lathered his washboard stomach skin with mint deodorant soap. Crime pays good, crime pays the best. Fucking hoods are driving Bentleys while kids are starving in magazine ads. What makes sense anymore?

He stepped from the shower and toweled off, still beefing to himself. He stretched and said, "Too much, too much." He rubbed a spot on his foggy mirror and stared into a dull amber eye laced with red. He breathed on the cleared space to fog it up again, forced a smile, and said in his best command voice, "Suck it in, Mains! And—fuck'em all!" His coat of arms: *Fuck 'em all!* That was the wisdom he lived by. . . .

For the rest of this day and night, he decided to entertain no more downer ideas, no more cheap-ass harness-bull philosophy. The best philosophy came from the head of your dick anyway. You never found a D.B. in a waterbed. He looked at the message on the toilet cover knitted by one of his satisfied customers: "THE PATHS OF EXCESS

LEAD TO THE GARDEN OF WISDOM. Blake." Smart bitch, the one who knitted that. Women went to a lot of trouble for him. They— did things.

Yeah, and whatever they did, it was never enough. . . .

Goddamn it, how come?

Why did he always have to raise the ante? Why wasn't he ever satisfied? He'd had partners who screwed their own wives year after year, claimed they never got tired of it, the same humping in the same way, twice a week. Himself, he would die of boredom. Where was the challenge? The biggest kick was to take some prissy broad from Mrs. Featherington's Finishing School for Girls and turn her into a fuck machine. Make her do it all. Make her *beg* for it. "Fuck me, Billy. Fuck me!" Make her put out like—

Darlene.

Well, it was a waste of time thinking about *that* whore. . . .

He could tell it was another hot day even though his air conditioner kept his room at a steady sixty-five. Usually it cycled once or twice an hour, but today the unit was dripping with sweat, working itself to death, off and on, off and on, every few minutes. Must be in the nineties outside. . . . He took another look in the steamy mirror. Christ, he was destroying himself with sleep. Look at the goddamn bags! Six hours' sleep today. Ruining my health. . . .

Jesus, what a hunk she'd been! What a hot cocksucker! Risky dangerous business, though. He knew the rules as well as anybody: chippying was acceptable, but *only* if you didn't embarrass the P.D. and *only* if you didn't mess with police wives.

Well, it wasn't his fault. She'd pushed it. He'd had all the gash he could handle at the time, but the cock-happy bitch wouldn't take no for an answer. . . .

He made a long chirping sound as he stepped into cherry-colored nylon shorts with a white-lightning stripe. She had weird tastes for a girl brought up in a small town, practically a milkmaid. Somebody was saying just the other night at the Slammer that farm broads were always the kinkiest because they'd watched it all as adolescents: bulls with slick red hard-ons, stud horses with gray lumpy dongs two feet long, sheep humping each other, males licking males, a whole fucking barnyard pornie flick going down in 3-D, commonplace, exactly the opposite of his own tight-ass upbringing with all those aunties quoting II Thessalonians.

At first he'd been glad to oblige Miss Darlene. No skin off his ass. A little off hers maybe; a couple of times he'd corn-holed her dry. But Christ, every day? It got so bad she'd leave messages at the precinct under a code name: "Phone Amelia Thudpucker soonest!" Or she'd drop notes signed "Desperate" in the condo mailbox. No pride: a typical nympho. One afternoon he'd told her he couldn't see her for a while, that he had other pigs to poke.

"Pigs?" she asked.

"Isn't that what you are?"

"Pigs?" Her eyes widened.

"You're all pigs."

She loved it. She was beyond shame. She phoned the precinct a few days later and left the name "Sally Shoat." It was a wonder her stupid husband, Gerry, didn't tumble, the way she practically advertised it. Maybe he knew all along. Or maybe the dumb prick didn't *want* to know. There were husbands like that. If they didn't see the actual infidelity on-scene, it wasn't happening.

He grabbed his electric razor and wiped the mirror dry with a towel. Christ, he could still see the blue-white scar where she bit him on the shoulder. Two months ago! Wild cunt! Always screamed when she came, out of control, embarrassed him with the neighbors. And then— *zip!*—like a curtain dropping, she was gone, back into the woodwork, nobody knew where. And Gerald Yount staggering around the precinct like a robot, barely able to talk. Brooding about—a pig! How could you figure a guy like that? Why, Christ, he ought to hunt her down and slap the piss out of her, give her something to think about the next time she walks. But some guys had no guts. *No guts* . . . Any son of a bitch laid a finger on a wife of Billy Mains, he's wind up with his cock in three different townships, like his old T.O.—Hallingford, was it? He wouldn't wait fifteen minutes! Well, maybe Yount never found out about them. Strange dude. Nobody could ever tell what he was thinking. A big brooder. Kept everything inside. Maybe he knew the whole story and was planning his move. No, not a yellow scumsucker like him. . . . Still, it wouldn't be smart to give him an opening. . . .

A clean-shaven aromatic Billy Mains walked into the compact kitchen and popped a couple of pre-fab waffles into his toaster, slathered them with margarine and raspberry syrup and a gob of Dream Whip and crunched them down in a few gulps while leafing through *Guns and Ammo.* He slurped two strong cups of instant black coffee and decided to double up on the waffles. Calories were no big deal when you stood five feet eight and weighed 150. Besides, a guy had to go for it while he could. In a few hours he'd be back in the monkeysuit, dying of boredom, hoping to Christ some fool would come out of the shadows and draw on him. And the worst thing was: nobody would. Every night was a monotonous round of burglary investigations, family fights, runaways, barroom rumbles, shoplifts, and—oh, sure, at least one D.B., with his luck. And a report to write on every fucking case. *Every fucking case!* Several times a shift he'd say, "Okay, asshole, I'll give you a pass this time," just to avoid the bullshit paper work. And *still* he was up to his ass in it. Holy fucking Christ, what a boring job. . . .

Wait, he'd forgotten again! Mary Rob Maki. *Patrolwoman* Mary Rob Maki. Yes, indeedy, let's keep it nice and formal. A line from an old Randy Newman song skittered through his head: "You give me a reason to live, you give me a reason to live. . . ."

Jeez, was there any chance the lieutenant would split them up? No, no way. Not after his perfect behavior last night. He'd be in her pants in a week, two at the most, and worth the wait. He crossed his yellow-brown eyes as he thought about the bulge in the blouse of her uniform. He had thirty-eight-C in the pool, and he was probably low. Shit, she could be a forty, a forty-two. Goddamn right! He'd known broads that looked like dainty little thirty-two's or thirty-four's and when you unsnapped them, out would come a couple of great big blobs, soft and white as overcooked frog meat. They'd been playing them down all the time, Christ only knew why. A tight-ass bitch like this Maki, all business, all shined-up professionalism, she was that kind, or he didn't know Thing One about cunt. And *still* her tits stuck out. They were so big there was no way she could conceal them! His *partner!*

The second he'd found out Packer Lind was pairing them off, the schemes had begun to whirl in his brain. I got to have that, *got to have it,* he told himself for three days and nights. And so do five dozen other cops in the precinct, a voice kept answering. What'll work? What'll pique her interest? There's a special touch that'll drop every broad's pants, one special stroke tailor-made for her and her alone. If you had the smarts, you could always dope it out. . . .

Suddenly it had come to him: *the sure-thing approach.* Obvious, once he'd thought of it.

Driving David Three with his new partner, he had slipped smoothly into the role: strong and silent, reserved, a little bored, *superior.* Exactly the opposite of all the other cops with their eyes bulging out whenever she gave them the time of day. *That* was the gimmick! Act like the perfect senior partner breaking in a rook. Detached. Aloof. She'd come in her uniform with fascination. . . .

He'd caught her glancing at him as he tooled the car through the district. Well, how could she *not* go for a Billy Mains? She must have the hots for cops, or else she'd still be teaching high school English. That's why the old switcheroo would work. She'd keep wondering:

Why doesn't this one make his move? What's the matter with me? Am I losing my sex appeal? She'd go nuts wondering why he was so different from the others.

He walked to the window of his narrow living room and slid the curtain open on its imitation-brass rings. A trapezoid of sunlight splashed against the champagne-colored rug and climbed the wall, illuminating a vivid purple seascape on black velvet. He yanked the curtains closed again and flipped the switch on the miniature motor-driven spotlight and its three rotating gels and watched the alternating colors play over the original work signed by Dominguez of Tijuana. Impressive! No wonder the broads started ripping off their clothes whenever he turned on that light. On a window ledge a red-beaked Kiwi bird dipped its beak up and down in a fishbowl: his latest conversation piece from New York. He made a note to add water. He could keep a girl's attention for fifteen minutes explaining how that thing worked, and in the meantime his hand would be creeping up her thigh. He stepped lightly around the seventeen assorted pillows, the room's only furniture, and walked back to the kitchen to consider an eye-opener. The wet bar had cost $250, his latest loan from the credit union, but it was worth at least $600, according to the Furniture Mart salesman who'd knocked it down to "police price."

He slid his hand under the bar and pulled out a nearly new bottle of 7-Crown. What the fuck, a little splash never hurt anybody. He poured the shot with steady hands. It was broad daylight, but who bothered about time on this goofy third watch? Happy Hour was whenever you were in the mood, and thinking about Mary Rob Maki had cheered his spirits.

He stepped back into the living room and flicked the TV to "Edge of Night" with his magic-control box. God, he hoped the airline stewardess hadn't been written out of the story already. She was maybe twenty-two, twenty-three, a cunning little stunt, looked like she had a couple bowls of jello under her blouse.

Ah, there she was! Holy Christ, what a pair! She was wearing a nightie today, everything under layers and layers of chiffon and lace and other shit. Why did so many ginch go out of their way to hide their best features? Like Maki . . .

He leaned forward on his mound of pillows and watched for movement beneath the gown. There! They jiggled! Oh, my aching dick, he said to himself, I can't stand it. *Can't stand it!* Look at that beast! Isn't that Emmy material? Isn't it? *Isn't it?*

At the commercial, he poured himself another shot.

16

Packer's nose crinkled and his clear blue eyes began to blink as he inhaled the stagnant air that hung in blue-gray ribbons in the police garage. The smells brought back the equipment shed where he'd worked side by side with his brothers every spring, fixing up the tired old McCormick tractor and the plows and the harrow. On the other hand, the police garage was the lair of dirty Mike Phelan, and the thought quickly curdled his nostalgia.

Packer enjoyed a brotherly rapport with his fellow officers, but he bridled at certain types. Sometimes he helped Amnee pick beetles out of their garden; that same prickly scratchiness came to mind as he knocked on the oil-stained door with its black imprint:

MOT R POOL
Micha 1 E. Ph lan, Lt., Cmdg.

"Oh, it's *you,*" the garage boss said, turning "you" into an epithet. No trace of warmth illuminated his yellowing face, and he didn't offer to shake. He sat behind a worn desk reading *The Star,* his long thin shoes propped against the wall.

"Some kinda hot, isn't it?" Packer said, trying to be civil. "I came to—"

"I know why you come," Phelan said, picking at the tips of his mustache. Packer tried not to show his revulsion. His own face was clean-shaven, but he had experimented with mustaches and porkchop sideburns, anything to conceal his multiple scars and defects, before finally deciding that it just wasn't worth the required clipping and trimming and preening. Where did an old goat like Phelan get the *ego* to maintain that silly waxed mustache? The thing tapered to a greasy point on each side and perched above his lip like a matched pair of Pekingese turds. Well, maybe when the rest of your hair consisted of a clipped gray tonsure around a bare dome, you made the best of what you had. He tried not to stare.

"The answer is no," the commander of the motor pool was saying. "N-o."

"N-o, huh? And all these years I thought that word was spelled with an 'e.' N-o-*e.*" Sarcasm was all some people understood. "What's n-o supposed to mean? N-o about what?"

Phelan ignored the question, picked up *The Star,* and replaced his feet against the grimy wall. He was wearing stained coveralls; Packer figured he was trying to look like a supervisor who worked side by side with his men, in case the inspectors dropped by. Probably had the stains sewn in. In all his visits to the motor pool, he had never seen the commanding officer lay a finger on a car or a tool. A flopped sergeant, Evert Donofrio, ran the operation while Phelan lazed in his office, surviving till pension time. Packer remembered how close the kinky son of a bitch had come to the penitentiary. Saved his own ass by turning snitch in the big corruption scandal.

Packer couldn't imagine a supervisor rolling over on his men, but he also couldn't imagine running a vice squad that practically had cash registers in every car and changemakers on every belt. Any more than he could imagine sporting a waxed mustache at fifty. Well, there was one consolation. Even if Mike Phelan played the survivor game for another thousand years, he would never make captain; the press and TV would see to that. The media all had his number. He'd never work the streets again, either.

Packer made a production out of pulling up a chair and flopping into it with studied carelessness. "I asked you a question," he said slowly.

Phelan turned a page.

"I asked you a question, Lieutenant," Packer repeated. "And I'll sit here till I get an answer."

He could almost hear the bones rattle under the coveralls as Phelan growled, "Always were nosy, weren't you?"

Packer hefted his boots to the desk and began to whistle softly.

"Take my advice, junior," Phelan said. "Forget that green-and-white. It don't exist."

"When can I inspect it?"

"Drop in the thirty-second of August. We're having open house."

"What's that supposed to mean?"

"I.A.U. put a seal on that car. Bottled in bond. Off limits. Now why don't you git?"

Packer reached across the unlittered desk with his long arm and grabbed the phone. Phelan watched, then turned back to his newspaper. Packer's fingers were shaking with annoyance as he dialed the three numbers, and shaking more when he had finished the conversation with the patrol chief's aide. The car *was* impounded, and only I.A.U. and Fleet Safety were authorized to see it, by order of the superchief himself, now closeted with the mayor. Something about a page one article in *The Star* that morning. . . .

"A coverup, eh?" Packer said to Phelan as he banged down the phone. "A fix. Right down your alley, eh, Phelan? They finally found something you can throw yourself into."

"Do tell."

"What'd you do? Replace all the tires as soon as they brought the car in?"

The sharp beak returned to the edges of the newspaper. You couldn't anger the man, any more than you could anger a beetle. Survivors survived, they didn't get emotional. Packer left.

Outside, he found Ev Donofrio, former sergeant and chief grease monkey, on a creeper under a command car. "Hey, Ev," he called down. "How they hanging, pal? How's Martha and—the kids?" There were two of them, a boy and a girl, but he'd be damned if he could remember their names; it had been two years now since he'd testified for Donofrio at a disciplinary hearing.

"Packer, you fucker!" the oil-spattered man exclaimed as he rolled out belly-up. "How ya been, man?"

"Problems," he answered, not wanting to prolong the meeting in case Mike Phelan took a notion to step outside.

"What problems, Pack?" the ex-sergeant asked, wiping his hands on his coveralls and offering a hand. "Oh, yeah, Siegl's car—" His face clouded.

"Ev, is it here?"

Donofrio turned his back to the office door, sheltered his grimy fingers with his body, and pointed straight up.

"Second floor?" Packer asked.

The sergeant nodded and pointed a finger sideways.

"In the back?"

Donofrio nodded again.

"No chance to—"

"No chance! It's in a locked stall. The lieutenant has the key."

"Any windows?"

Donofrio frowned. "Windows? What're you gonna do, Pack, break in?"

"Forget I asked, Ev."

The garageman smiled and lowered himself to his grimy creeper. "Forget you asked what?"

Packer bent over and said, "Remember me to, uh, Martha and the kids, huh, Ev? Listen, we oughta get together for dinner sometime. Lunch, maybe, huh? Something like that?"

"Hey, good idea! Gimme a call."

"For sure, buddy."

Walking back to his Jeep, he felt like a hypocrite. How many conversations like this one could he remember? "Great idea, we'll have to get together, ya ya ya," and that was always the end of it. If every cop had lunch with every cop he promised to have lunch with, there'd be a nationwide food shortage. He liked Evert Donofrio, sure, but he was closer to the men of his own watch and even closer to his wife and daughter, though Amnee didn't always seem convinced. Where would he get the time to socialize with Donofrio?

It was too hard to figure. You risked your life with these men, made confessions you'd never make to anyone else, met under the bridge with them and shared rivers of beer with them, and told war stories with awful admissions: you took them to your heart and you—loved them. Yes, that was the word, even though no cop would ever breathe it aloud. Then two years later you were saying you'd have to get together for a lunch you knew would never happen. Was that kind of fakery built into police work? Or was it just the nature of friendship? There were times when he wondered if friendship even existed, if life wasn't all a matter of self-interest. Was he going to bat for Artie Siegl because Artie was a friend, or because it was in his own interest to defend his watch?

Neither one, he thought, pumping himself up. I'm going to bat for Artie because it's goddamned unjust for everybody to be ganging up on one little cop just so they can have a patsy for the newspapers. It's a hell of a lot easier to throw Artie Siegl to the wolves than to admit that the whole patrol division runs on cut-rate equipment, because *that's* the chief's fault, and the mayor's, and pols never admit mistakes.

Plain, old-fashioned injustice . . . You could even call it corruption. No wonder he was running around dripping sweat when he should have been home with his family. . . .

He shrugged and lifted his orthopedic boot to the slickly worn jump step of the Jeep. The hell with it, he said to himself. No—more—thinking. I'm a cop, not a shrink. Men do what they *have* to do, and then they shop around for a nice label to put on it. People go nuts trying to figure these things out. Probably there's a half a dozen reasons I'm trying to help Artie. Probably it's all one big messed-up recipe: two cups of self-interest, one cup of real friendship, a couple tablespoons of annoyance at Singletary, a teaspoon of contempt for Mike Phelan, a dash of aggravation at I.A.U. and—what the hell, throw in a splash of taco sauce and a jigger of bourbon. . . .

It didn't matter, because the end result would be the same:

He was going to look at that car.

It took a while to connect with Artie by telephone. "Oh, Packer!" Rebecca Siegl answered in a pleased voice. "How nice!"

"Hi, Becky. Listen, this is a rush call. Where's the great man?"

"You won't believe it." She laughed.

"Try me."

"He's out—jogging."

"You're kidding."

She laughed again. "Doing roadwork. Said no rabbit would ever outrun, uh, *his* ass again. Whatever that means."

"Oughta be at the police surgeon's getting checked over."

Packer could hear the gasp. "Checked over? For what?"

Oh, Christ, another wife in the dark. Didn't the poor woman read the papers? Didn't she watch TV? All the news shows must have covered the story of the cop who let a killer walk. Well, it wasn't his place to give away a husband's secrets.

"Just kidding, Becky," he said.

"You've been hanging around with Artie too much."

"Yop. Anything for a laugh."

She told him to call back in an hour, at 4 P.M. He took a leisurely spin to the scene of the three-car crash and found the pavement chalked in yellow and barricades along both curbs. The road was open, but there was no way to park and look around. He glimpsed a man in green coveralls and a police cap. What were they looking for in the woods? The killer? I.A.U. couldn't possibly be that stupid. The rabbit was two states away by now. Probably planning his next caper. . . . Well, what *were* they looking for then?

He drove back to town and dialed the number in a phone booth that felt like a microwave oven. The voice answered, "Fight crime, it's your dime, Officer Siegl speaking."

"Artie? Packer." A truck rumbled by and cut off the response. No loss. Artie always wisecracked for a minute or two before letting you state your business. *Fight crime, it's your dime.* . . . That was an improvement on his old answering routine: *Just a minute, I'll see if I'm here.*

"Artie, listen, pal, I want you to call in sick a few nights."

"Sick? Me sick? I never felt better." This was followed by a faked paroxysm of coughing, retching, and gagging. "I—*cough cough*—I just—*arghhh!*—I just run—*cough cough!*—a tenth of a mile."

Packer shook his head and pulled the door tight, entombing himself in glass. The phone booth was on a main arterial, Bennington, and he wouldn't be surprised if I.A.U. had a shotgun mike trained on him from a parked truck. He cupped his moist hand over his mouth like a two-dollar snitch and said in a low voice, "Now listen, Artie. You got a

[106]

whiplash, pal, understand? You didn't realize it till you woke up this morning and couldn't move your neck."

"Hey, not a bad idea, Pack. You testify for me? Oughta be good for a couple G's insurance money. We can go hand in hand to Pago Pago."

"Artie—"

"Two guys are talking. 'Have you been to Pago Pago?' 'No, I haven't. No, I haven't.'"

Packer scrunched his heavy shoulders over the phone and raised his voice. "Artie, goddamn it, quit clowning! Listen! Call the precinct right now. And stay on leave till you hear back from me."

"Why sick? I'm in shape, Pack, I'm—"

"Artie, I don't care about your goddamn health. I mean, I do, I do. That's why I need one night, maybe two." He didn't want to fill in the details. If Artie showed up tonight, he'd have to be furloughed on the spot. Captain's orders. But if he phoned in sick . . . Singletary hadn't covered that possibility.

"I'm a problem, huh?" The little man sounded contrite. He might be silly, but he wasn't stupid.

"You and the whole precinct. We're in the shit, pal. If it's any consolation, I'm deeper'n anybody."

"It's no consolation. What'd *you* ever do wrong—besides those ax murders when you were a kid?"

"Artie, listen. When you lost control last night, did you feel anything, uh, different? I mean about the car?"

"The front end dipped and I was, like, floating, spinning. Quicker'n it takes to tell."

"The front end dipped?"

"Yeah. The left front. The way it would in a blowout."

"But there wasn't any blowout," Packer said, confused.

"That's what I.A.U. told me."

"I.A.U.?"

"Invited themselves for tea this morning, did a little interrogation. Routine. That's what they called it, anyway. Like a routine kiss from a chain saw."

Packer wiped the sweat off his forehead. He wondered how much the health clubs charged for saunas. This one was only a dime. "What'd you tell 'em, Artie?"

"Just what I told you. It felt like I blew a tire. They said unh-uh. Fleet Safety went out to the scene this morning and did a reconstruct. Said one of my front wheels popped off, but that was from the stress of skidding sideways. Said my car was mechanically perfect. I must of just lost it."

"You kidding?"

"That's what the man said, Pack. Driver error. Wrote it down in front of me. 'Left front wheel came off after control lost by driver.'"

"Pretty hasty conclusion."

"Well, you know those Fleet Safety guys. They're experts. Isn't that what they always say?"

"The wheel popped *after* you started to spin?" He still couldn't believe it.

"Right."

A rivulet of sweat dropped from his chin to his worn old boot. The propped-up phone slithered down his ear. "What made you lose it in the first place? I mean, that's not like you."

"The front end dipped, I'm telling you. Dipped sharp. And when you're doing ninety—"

"I know, I know. You tell that to I.A.U.?"

"It's the truth, Pack. What else am I gonna tell 'em?"

He pursed his lips. Poor Artie. He was such a good-natured soul, he automatically assumed everyone else was. Despite twenty-six fights, he was still a sucker for a sneak punch. He was too busy being Mr. Niceguy, jester to the world. On the way to the gallows, he'd reach out and pat the preacher's arm and tell him the one about the Reverend Brown. He could make the most outrageous remarks and fail to comprehend why people got sore, because he, Artie Siegl, had meant them only as jokes, an innocent way to pass the time. How would he ever understand what the top brass were trying to do to him now?

"Artie, do what I asked you, okay, pal? Friend to friend. Stay home a shift or two, till you hear from me."

"Hey, I can take care of my—"

"STAY HOME, GODDAMN IT!" The heat had made him over-react.

"Okay, *okay*," Artie said. "Hey, don't hang up! You hear about the dogs?" Christ Almighty, not another joke!

"The dogs," Artie repeated. "The puppies."

"Oh. Yeah. I'm the one found 'em."

"Can you imagine, Pack? I mean who . . . ? I mean whattaya suppose—"

"Somebody's trying to send us a messages."

"Kids."

"Kids send messages, too."

He was starting to say good-bye when a piece of unfinished business came to mind. "Say, Art, I forgot to ask you. What'd you stop the guy for?"

"Told you last night. A piss-ant traffic violation."

"A T.V.? What kind?"

"*Don't ask.*" God, this conversation was like two blind men playing chess. Through a screen door. Inside a furnace . . .

"Artie, the heat's getting me, pal. I'm in a sealed booth. Now tell me straight: *What was the TV?*"

"You gotta know?"

Packer inhaled deeply. "Yop," he managed to say. "I gotta know."

"It's in my report. Broken taillight. T.C. Three-Four-Eight."

"The stolen car had a broken light?"

There was a second's hesitation from the other end. "Uh, I didn't say that, Packer. I said my *report* said he had a broken light."

"But—"

"Okay, okay, I been jacking you off."

"Not like you, Artie."

"I know, Pack. It's just—" The usually strident voice sounded tired. "I been thinking about it, ya know? Lying to—*you?* Ya know? It's been—on my mind. I, uh—I stopped the guy, om uh—"

Another long hesitation.

"Yeah? C'mon, Artie. You stopped the guy—for what?"

"Driver of the Month."

Through twelve years in uniform, Packer had never falsified a report or approved a falsification of anything except the most trivial details. He explained this carefully into the wet mouthpiece. Falsification was a serious malfeasance, grounds for outright dismissal. He knew it was done on other watches, but it would never be countenanced on his—

"All right already," the ex-featherweight interrupted. "Do what you gotta do."

"I'm *gonna* do what I gotta do!" he said emphatically. "I'm gonna, uh, leave it go this time."

"Who's surprised?"

"And, uh, Artie?"

"Speaking."

"Never mind what Fleet Safety says, I wrote you up okay."

"For what? For losing a rabbit?"

"No, for some pretty fancy driving. Anybody else hit the curb at ninety, we'd be having an inspector's funeral for him."

"Hey, you're not just blowing smoke up my ass?" The poor guy had been bobbing around in the toilet bowl for so long he couldn't believe a good word would ever be said about him.

"I'm dead serious."

"Hey, that's really nice." He sounded elated, almost high.

"Well, I gotta be—"

"Wait, Pack. *Wait!* Don't hang up. Guy says, 'Hey Charlie, you coming tonight?' 'I dunno,' he says, 'But I'll be breathing hard.' Hey, wait, *wait!* You know my friend McGivern, the famous cunnilinguist? Author of *The View from Here?*"

Packer lurched from the booth. He was as drenched as if he'd just hauled himself up on a desert island. He sloshed over to the Jeep; the leatherette-covered driver's seat had been toasted by the direct rays of the sun. He swore he could hear a sizzle as he climbed in and aimed the car toward the Plymouth agency on Market.

It was 4:55 in the afternoon, and the auto mechanics' union liked its members to knock off promptly. He wanted to be there when Manuel Garibay emerged through the side door. The chief mechanic owed him a favor, owed him more than one favor, in fact, if you counted scaring the crap out of Manuel's son Chickie to get him off angel dust for good. Manuel said his missus was still paying for novenas for Packer at Our Lady of Guadalupe, and it was two years now, and Chickie straight all this time, delivering for the cleaners.

Garibay came out on time and grabbed Packer's hand with two of his own, knotted and brown as walnut. "My fren', my ol' fren'! How jew do-een, Mr. Packer? How jor wife? How jor family?"

"Fine, fine, Manuel. Yours?"

"Good, Mr. Packer. *Muy bueno.*"

"I want to ask a favor," Packer said abruptly, ushering the wiry man over to the shadow of the Jeep.

"A favor for *jew? Jew* got eet!"

"Inspect a car for me."

Manuel Garibay turned his master mechanic's eyes on the slumping old Wagoneer. "Mr. Packer, *amigo,*" he said, waving his gnarled knuckles. "I dun theenk—"

"No, not this heap. Listen, Manuel, I'm pressed for time. How about midnight?"

"*Ay Chihuahua!* Eenspect a car at meednight?" The moist brown eyes peered deep into Packer's, as though they expected to find the answer to some old Anglo riddle encoded there. "Uh, chure, chure! Anytheen jew say, Mr. Packer."

They agreed to meet a block from the police garage.

17

Her reaction to the hollow-voiced caller was to look at the phone as though it were a ticking bomb and then put it down very slowly. Dear God, she said to herself, the baby! She ran into the living room. Emily was marching in a tight circle to her Mother Goose music, her plastic pants and diapers bunched around her chubby thighs. The cheerfully resonant male voice said:

Hello, children! I want to sing a little song about three blind mice. . . .

She swept the baby into her arms. "Emmy, oh, Emmy," she said softly. "Oh, my angel . . ."

"Mommy not cwy? Not cwy, Mommy?" There it was, the infantile sixth sense. Packer called it baby-radar. She had taken pains not to cry, not to sound hysterical or even upset, but as he once said, you couldn't sneak your feelings past baby-radar any more than you could sneak the dawn past a rooster. She lifted the child over her head and looked into her pale-blue eyes, miniatures of Packer's. Tears were forming, the little rose-colored lips were shaking.

"No, Mommy's not crying, angel." She eased the baby down and hugged her close as the tiny fingernails dug into her neck. She rocked back and forth and sang along with the enthusiastic baritone voice:

. . . To get a little rabbit skin!
To wrap the baby bunting in!

When she heard Emily singing contentedly out of tune, she gave the child an extra pat on the bottom and set her down. "Emmy okay now?"

"Emmy 'tay, Mommy."

"Mommy has to make a phone call, sweet baby."

"Mommy talk Dah?"

"No, not Dah, angel." With trembling fingers, she reached into the littered playpen and gathered an armful of colored cardboard blocks and erected a small tower on the coffee table. "Now you make it higher, okay, Emmy?"

"'Tay!" the child burbled, and swept the blocks to the floor.

Amnee backed toward the phone. Then she remembered the doors. She ran into the kitchen and through the pantry and pressed her narrow body against the thin back door as though werewolves screamed outside. Packer had installed three locks, but two were open. She slid the bolts with clumsy fingers, then dashed through the bungalow to the front door. Emily's new tower was one block high. "See?" the child sang out.

The spring lock was in place, but the deadbolt was open and the chain lock hung limp. She secured the door quickly, cracking a fingernail, then leaned against the fragile wood and emptied her lungs. Thank God she had talked Packer into the extra protection. If they had to live in Precinct Nine, at least they could make their bungalow safer. Not safe, but safer. Nothing in Stanton Park was really safe. If an intruder wanted to come in, he'd find a way. A wrapped brick through a window—that was a popular daytime technique. How did a housewife guard against something like that? They should have moved to the suburbs a long time ago. The captain lived five miles from the city limits, and both the other watch commanders lived in the suburbs. But her husband wouldn't think of it. "If I can work in this precinct, hon, we can live in it," he had argued.

"But Packer, every day you read about robberies and shootings and muggings and everything else in Stanton Park. Sweetie, it's just not safe here."

"If I do my job, it'll be safe."

That was two years ago, before Emily. Were they safe now? Of course not. Last night there'd been a sex murder, and today there was—

The caller.

Smiling broadly for the baby's benefit, she hurried into the bedroom to phone the station. The windows! She'd forgotten the windows. She stumbled from room to room and checked. Three were unlocked: open invitations. There was a small crack in the pantry window. Had it been there before? Packer would have to replace the pane today. Somebody could slide a wire through there and . . .

Dear God, what was she thinking? There were neighbors close on both sides, all she had to do was scream or run out the door or—

Who in his right mind would threaten a police lieutenant's family?

Her own words echoed in her head. *Who in his right mind . . . ?* Exactly! The caller wasn't in his right mind, how could he be? And that only made it worse.

But he hadn't really threatened, had he? He'd only said . . . What *had* he said? "This is Kolso . . ." No, Koslo. He'd spelled it. K-O-S-L-O. "This is Koslo . . ." No, he said, "I'm . . ." He said, "I'm Koslo, you'll . . . I'm coming for *you.*"

She shuddered and dialed the precinct number. *I'm coming for you.*

How aggravating to be a woman. So many forms of rape. . . .

Maybe it was just a prank. But didn't he realize how he frightened her? She was alone. Helpless. No, worse than helpless. She had an infant to protect. This was no game, didn't he understand? Was that the way phone nuts operated? Working on your fears, your built-in childhood terrors and nightmares?

She could still hear the voice. The hollowness. The hesitations. The hint of a laugh . . .

Ellen Beemer had had a caller. A breather. Didn't say a word. Panicked the Beemers right out of Stanton Park and into a house they couldn't afford in Lakeside.

"Ninth Precinct, Officer Collins speaking."

She couldn't connect the name with a face, but a different watch was on now, and she knew only a few of the men. "Er, this is Amnee— Lind? The lieutenant's wife? Is he around?"

"Hi, Mrs. Lind. No, he's not here right now."

"Would you know where I could find him?"

"No, ma'am." It felt unnatural to be "ma'amed" at twenty-one, but she knew the respect was for her husband, not herself. Still, it had a reassuring effect. "Hold on a minute, will ya, Mrs. Lind?"

She heard a muffled conversation off the phone, then a familiar voice. "Amnee? It's Lieutenant Barker. Sam. Say, Packer was in with the captain a coupla hours ago, but I haven't seen him since."

"Oh, my God." A slip. She'd wanted to sound calm. It couldn't help Packer to be known as the husband of a hysteric.

"Is something wrong, Amnee?"

"No, uh, nothing," she said quickly. "Is he on the air, Sam? Oh, no, he's got the Jeep. It doesn't have a radio."

"Listen, honey, if there's something wrong, we'll send a car." God, he was *concerned*. She must have sounded awful. You couldn't fool babies and you couldn't fool watch commanders. Not when you were as upset as Amnee, anyway.

"No, no," she said, aware that her voice was quaky. "Just ask him to, uh, call if he comes in. Okay, Sam? Tell him—something happened."

"Okay, Amnee," the strong voice came back. "And remember, we can be there in a few minutes you need anything. Anything at all, okay, hon?"

"Yes, okay, Sam. Thanks, thanks a lot." She put the phone down and brushed at her eyes. God, it was touching, the way they hung together. But if they didn't protect one another and their families, who would? Policemen didn't rate anymore, they'd lost their Norman

Rockwell image. Their own ingroup was as separate from the rest of society as though they were criminals themselves. And Packer was the rallying point for Precinct Nine, she knew that. "We love that husband of yours," Artie Siegl had told her, "and there's not a one of us that's queer except the chief."

Police brotherliness. Police affection. Or was it just a siege mentality: us against the world? They said there was a line of blue uniforms a block long waiting to give blood after Packer was shot. Three bullets in his body, lucky they were .22s. Given up for dead, but the surgeons worked in teams for nine hours and brought him back.

And what was the payoff? she asked herself as she sat staring at the silent beige telephone. Another ribbon that he refused to wear, and a commendation in his jacket. *What good was any of it?* Did the telephone caller give a damn? Did it matter to Koslo who her husband was, or what he had been through?

Well, that wasn't fair, either, she told herself. You couldn't blame your husband's job for a psychopath's behavior. Some things just happened; you didn't have to deserve them. Probably he found their name in the phone book. Or dialed a number at random.

No, that couldn't be. He said he knew Packer, he went out of his way to make that statement. Didn't he? He said . . . *What* did he say? *No, I'm not Packer.* But how did he know the name in the first place? They were listed in the phone book under "S.J. Lind." Had *she* mentioned the name first? She wished she could remember. Usually her memory was strong, but the call had left her rattled.

Dear God, he *had* to come home soon. She would be a wreck till she saw that hacked-up Mount Rushmore face, till that great bulky form blotted out the light in the doorway and he took her in his arms and patted away the fright. She knew her fear was irrational, she knew it was as crazy as the telephone call in its own way. She wondered if she would have acted this way a few years ago, even a few months ago?

They didn't have enough time together, that was the problem. One problem, anyway. Love—oh, yes, they had love—more than any two human beings deserved. But so little time to share it. Six nights out of eight he would leave for the station at a quarter to seven, an hour before the change of watch, and when she complained, he would argue that he couldn't get his work done any other way. "But that's a ten-hour day!" she insisted. "You go in an hour early, you stay an hour late, that makes ten hours. Aren't cops supposed to work an eight-hour day?"

"But I'm not a cop, honey. I mean, I'm a cop, yeah, but I'm a supervisor, too. There's a whole new G.I.B. to memorize every day, there's—"

"G.I.B.?"

"General Informational Bulletin. You know, 'Kansas City Police report white male age blah blah driving stolen Ford Belchfire blah blah en route your city. . . .' There's memos from the other watches; there's crime reports and field interview reports, F.I.R.s we call 'em; there's wants and bulletins and a dozen other things to read; maybe two three memos from the old man on the condition of the toilet, stuff like that. See what I mean?"

No, she hadn't seen what he meant, but she'd learned not to debate the point. Whether she argued or not, he would be out the door at the stroke of 6:45, headed for the damned precinct. Why resist the inevitable? His old friends said he'd always put in long hours, even before the cutbacks in personnel, even before he made rank. Showed up early to work on his personal charts and notebooks: missing cars, suspected pushers, burglars active in the precinct, suspicious persons. He still kept a thick loose-leaf book full of head shots and data, called it "my family album." He collected information about Precinct Nine the way others collected Micronesian stamps. A way of life. But now that he had Amnee and the baby . . .

It didn't matter. The man would never change. Where was he right now, when she needed him desperately? He'd made sergeant in six years, lieutenant in four more; he'd make captain in another six or seven years, and if that little piece of steel didn't move over and slice into his spine, he would retire as a major or a deputy chief, unless . . .

Unless he kept acting like a rookie, she said to herself. Night after night, patrolling the back alleys of the precinct like an ordinary beat cop, looking for—what? Well, he liked working the street, that's all. And the craziest thing was, he didn't have to do it, he didn't have to endanger himself at all; he could plant himself behind his desk and serve with distinction. Sue Barker said Sam almost never used his car, and he didn't go to work an hour early, either. And everybody knew that Steinmetz, the second-watch commander, spent the day doing crosswords, while his sector sergeants handled the precinct. Lieutenants were for paper work, couldn't Packer see that?

"Damn you, sweetie, come home!" she said under her breath. She should have shown him the story she clipped last week, about the convict who walked out the gates of a penitentiary and hired a cab and went straight to the home of the policeman who arrested him and killed the entire family including a dog and two gerbils. Somewhere in Nebraska, she thought. Or Nevada . . . ?

Had Packer angered Koslo somehow? Sent him up, years ago, maybe in another precinct?

Why else would the man call and threaten her?

A barbecue smell reached her nose. She jumped up and ran into the kitchen. A drip of tuna and noodle casserole had bubbled over the side of the clay pot and lacquered itself to the cookie sheet. She lowered the heat again and lifted Emily into her highchair and began piling finger foods on her tray: string cheese and banana slices, hamburger bits and slices of cold zucchini from the day before. The casserole was beginning to look dry and unappetizing as it gave off little volcanic puffs of steam. But if she took it out, he might have to endure a lukewarm meal, and she couldn't bear that heavy a responsibility. Let it toast and burn and char—he preferred his food blazing hot anyway, even on a blazing hot day like this. He always ordered his steaks well done, insisted that they be "cremated." Well, today he'd have a cremated casserole. . . .

She dabbed at the baby's face with a dishcloth and glanced at the kitchen clock. In five minutes it would be 4 P.M. He'd promised to be home for their regular lunch at three. *Promised*. Gave his absolute word. Said "for sure."

Dear God, where was her husband? Where was her strength?

There was a light tap at the kitchen window.

She screamed and turned, both hands covering her face. The baby jerked and dumped her milk.

It was their song sparrow, the one that always delighted Emmy, made her laugh out loud. All summer long the little brown bird made love to its own reflection.

She rushed to pick up the frightened infant, lifted her from the highchair and held her close. She calmed quickly to her mother's warmth and said, "Bu'd! Bu'd!"

"Yes, sweet baby," Amnee said, pretending to share the child's delight. "It's our bird, baby."

Damn you, bird! she said to herself. The next time you scare me like that, I'll twist your fool head off.

She cradled her daughter in her arms and tried to stop shaking.

18

Gerald Yount sleepwalked about his overheated apartment searching for his lost wife. He rocked and almost toppled as consciousness hit him like a club. He braced against a wall, looked around, and blinked. She was still gone.

His heart pounded as he ran to the kitchenette and slammed his .38 service revolver on the table. A pattern of whorls in the coating of dust showed where he had spun the S&W before. When it pointed directly at him, he picked the loaded weapon up, shoved the barrel deep into his mouth, cupped the grip in his right hand, and slowly eased the hammer back with the thumb of the same hand.

Slowly . . . Slowly . . .

The hammer clicked safely into place. It wouldn't always. God's will be done. . . .

The climbing sun baked the old apartment walls as he stuffed his revolver back into its holster. His panic was growing now; he had to move fast before the ceiling began to fall, the building began to sway, the world shook and rumbled under his feet. He ran for the living-room closet and slammed the door in time to cover up the first yell. He buried his outcries in a wool jacket because he was afraid the neighbors would rush to sympathize with him, and he would rather be dead than an object of pity.

He fell to his knees and had a momentary vision of his blood boiling out of his nostrils in little pink puffs. He crawled into the bedroom and flopped on the unmade bed in his shorts. The printed patchwork bedspread was already twisted into knots by his writhings; the exposed mattress was spotted with mildew. There was a strong smell, but he was barely aware of it. To him, the apartment smelled like yesterday and the day before. He sat with his eyes half closed as scenes and nightmares reeled through his mind, shrieks and cries of pain and outrage. . . .

Darlene, when they were both sixteen. A confession. Now that he had pinned her, she had to tell. Last summer, at church camp, a boy had, had touched, had touched—her breast. Bare. A boy named Paul. No, she *didn't* like him, it had just—happened. "I didn't even know you then, Gerry. I wouldn't have dreamed . . ." The thought of another boy's hand on her naked breast had crashed over him like a wave. For weeks, he ignored his schoolbooks, picked at his food, spent hours in bed, head pressed between two pillows. He questioned her incessantly. "Was that all? *Was that all?*" She was a virgin when they married two years later, but he still felt sick to his stomach when he thought about Paul. He drove four blocks out of his way to avoid passing a place called Paul's Auto Body Shop, flinched when he was introduced to men named Paul, refused to see a Paul Newman movie, or read a book by anyone named Paul. He detested the name, detested the saint and the town, detested anything that reminded him of his wife's offense at fifteen. One night after they were married, he said to her, "Darlene, was there—anything else?" She told him he was acting crazy. . . .

Why had he tortured himself like that? And tortured her? All those years . . . Now she was gone. When she came back, he would take her in his arms and forgive her for what she did then and what she did later with—the policeman. They would be together again, Gerry and Darlene—no, Darlene and Gerry. They would finish their lives together. God's plan.

"Kid, you needa get your ashes hauled."

He jumped and looked around the bedroom. The voice had been vivid, loud. No, he was remembering again, he was back inside his head. The sergeant had said it a few nights ago. Turk Molnar. "Do ya a lotta good, kid. I don't care how bad you feel. Shit oh dear, when I got my divorce, I seen so many broads my dick like to fell off. It's—it's—therapy. You'll be shitting in the tall cotton again, good-looking kid like you. Line yourself up one of them station-house groupies, hear? Billy's got a list. Little poon'll work wonders. . . ."

No matter how he tried, he couldn't imagine himself with a station-house groupie. Lying on his sodden bed, he thought of "Uniform Olga." Poor woman, she wasn't right. A sub-moron who chased policemen, bus drivers, sailors, garbagemen, anyone in uniform. Billy Mains had arranged a mock birthday ceremony for the pitiful thing and everybody stood around snickering while she unwrapped her "present." There was an explosion of laughter as the gift fell on the parking lot. Knee pads. Gerry had turned away, ashamed for one of God's children.

Still, he felt stirrings. It had been—two months. The idea of using his own hands seemed sinful, shameful; it was something he had never done. So—weak. Sometimes he thought about available women on his old beat. *Why don't you drop back for a cool drink, Officer? I make a terrific banana daiquiri.* The divorcee on East Fremont would sit up till three in the morning reading hot paperbacks and then put in a burglary call. She didn't care who responded, as long as it wasn't one of the new patrolwomen.

Sometimes he thought about Genna Jocelyn, a police officer's widow, married for ten years to Eddie Jocelyn till he got killed at a fire. She had set herself up as unappointed social director of the precinct; Gerald guessed it was in memory of Eddie. She was a lovely, soft, maternal woman, slender like the lieutenant's wife, Amnee, but much shorter. She sent cards and cakes on their birthdays, gave watch parties and promotion parties and retirement parties, told everybody she was "the backup for the whole precinct." Billy Mains said she was the backup, all right; all you had to do was throw her a lot of bull about the lonely life of a police officer, the quiet dedication, the love of the job. "When she starts to sniffle, whip it out," he'd said with his usual delicacy.

Billy Mains . . .

Talk about pathetic creatures. . . . What could be more pathetic than a man who kept a "life list" of conquests taped to the inside of his locker, actually encouraged brother officers to read it?

Forget him. . . .

Could Billy have been—the one? The one who, who—abused Darlene? The latest Paul?

BUT THAT'S OVER NOW! ANCIENT HISTORY!

He walked slowly to the kitchen and put on a pot of water for instant coffee. *Kid, you needa get your ashes hauled.* The ugly ways cops put things! That was the trouble: it was all ugly. He couldn't imagine sex without Darlene. At twenty-four, he had never known another woman. Never wanted to, never would. Those restless stirrings—they were only for his wife.

Suppose, just suppose, that Darlene and Billy . . .

No, NO!

He remembered every word his partner had said as they drove the long nights together. Mains always circled back to the same subjects: his boredom, his nostalgia for the old days in undercover cars, his collection of—Gerry cringed at the word—cunts. "In U-cars, you get all the hot calls, see, kid?" he would say out of his crooked slash of a mouth. "Something going on all the time: shootings, stickings, busting pimps and ho's. 'Up against the wall, motherfucker!' 'Spread 'em, *spread 'em!'* And so much crease you need an extra dick. Begging for it!"

He poured the boiling water into a chipped plastic cup with a half inch of black dregs in the bottom, and sipped without remembering to add instant coffee. He carried the steaming cup into his darkened bedroom and sat in his undershorts on the bed, while the sharp voice of his former partner cut through his brain, babbling about his career in plainclothes as usual. "I was always shit-hot for action, kid, off duty or on, ya know what I mean? They use to say, 'If Mains is on duty, he'll put you under arrest. If Mains is off duty, he'll put you *to* rest.' Ain't that a bitch? I was a fucking menace with a sap, too. Palm sap, knuckle sap, slapjack, I'd break faces, knock out teeth, snap a wrist. One zap, and the cocksucker goes down."

"Where'd you learn that?" Gerry had asked, repelled and fascinated. He and Darlene had come from a village where there were two peace officers, one for nights and one for days: glorified crossing guards with soft words for everybody and wooden clubs that stayed in their ring holders.

"To use saps?" Billy Mains was saying. "I dunno where I learned it. Gift of God, I guess."

He gulped the oily hot water till his lips burned, rubbed his sweaty hand across his face and felt his heart pulsing behind each exhausted eye, and there in his reeking bedroom he saw Billy Mains, watched the busy hand with the tarnished-silver academy ring reaching up to rearrange the thinning brownish hair. "So you're all geared for action, and you gotta have it, kid. *Every night.* If there's nothing breaking, you shake a few ex-cons and slash their tires. Maybe wipe out the windows on a pimpmobile with your wrist rocket." Before he was assigned to ride with Billy Mains, Gerry had never heard of the oversized hunting slingshots that could shatter a Cadillac's windshield at a half-block range. Street justice, they called it. Untaught at the academy. Mains always said a wrist rocket was the court of last resort when a Leroy was running underage ho's and you couldn't prove it.

". . . And then I got flopped back into uniform," his old partner rattled on, as clearly as though he sat across the room. "Back into the green-and-whites with a young rook for a partner, no offense, kid. You wanna know why I hate the goddamned monkeysuit? A blind man can make you six blocks away, that's number one. You might as well put on a fucking pair of sandwich boards that say 'cop,' know what I mean? Wearing that thing, you got to laugh when you feel like crying, cry when you feel like laughing, you got to put on a fucking act all the time. 'Oh, yes, ma'am, I'm sure your husband was a fine man, I'm *so* fucking sorry he's fell over there dead, I'll order the meat wagon for you, ma'am, you poor dear.' You're laying the sympathy on with an ax when all's you feel like doing is puking your guts 'cause the old crock's uppers fell out when his heart stopped and he's crumpled up in a puddle of warm piss and it's your second D.B. of the night and you can't wait for the end of the watch and having a coupla drinks and then some nook, ya know? Wearing the blues, you play a role, you're a monkey in a cage. If you pick your nose in public or leave a fart, some snitch calls I.A.U. You're looking behind your back all the time, on your guard, defensive. And the action's gone, kid, the—action—is—*gone.* You get desperate, you start looking for it, you start creating it. Maybe you find it in the bottle. Pussy. Gambling. Some guys turn into crooks, just looking for excitement, a little challenge. Lookit me, kid. Three years working a U-car in plainclothes, busting heads, humping it out, and now I'm cruising the neighborhood looking for—what? An old lady to help across the street? A drugstore clerk to take to the night depository? That's *police* work? That's a job for a guy used to patrol Commercial Street, for Chrisakes? You know what they say about Commercial Street. You don't? Where ya been, Gerald? They say if you gave this town a high colonic you'd stick the tube up Commercial Street. And I had the fucking place so quiet you coulda conduct church service there, no offense, kid. . . ."

Billy Mains receded, still prattling. A wild man! Another of Gerry's losses, but not high on his list. He could always find a new partner. Somebody would be willing to ride with him, if Packer Lind ever let him off the desk. . . .

He looked at the door to the closet, *her* closet, the one where she had hung her dresses and slacks, proudly lined up her four pairs of heels on the floor, carefully stacked the rest of her clothes in neat piles on the shelf: shirts and blouses at the far left, then bras and panties and slips, and jeans and slacks neatly folded at the far right. He walked over and grabbed the knob and started to turn it before realizing what he was doing and pulling back. It was a cedar closet, aromatic and pungent, and the scent and the memories had disturbed him so much that he had sealed it off with masking tape. She had left a few things behind; they were safe inside her closet till she came home.

He walked back across the bedroom and pulled aside the scratched yellow-brown window shade and looked at the plug of traffic inching its way below. The bank clock showed 1:35 in the afternoon; foul gray exhaust fumes swirled off the hot pavement, mingled with the roasted air, and rose in sheets toward his balcony. An open sedan, an antique, chugged by, its two female passengers wearing string swimsuits. A streamer on the side of the car advertised a new supermarket. One of the women, a blonde with creamy breasts spilling out the sides and top of her string bra, waved giddily up at him. Sodom and Gomorrah. He let the shade fall closed. They wondered why they got raped, showing themselves off like that in public.

A woman had been strangled the night before, while he was working the desk. Probably she'd walked around in skimpy clothes: immodest, sinful, inciting weak men to lust. Maybe the sin was just in being a woman. "They all want it, don't let 'em tell you different," Billy Mains had insisted. "Girl Scouts, it might take me an hour or two. If it's the mother superior, gimme an extra night. There's a key that'll unlock 'em all." Billy had waved his middle finger and said, "AND HERE IT IS!"

Last night's killer had a key, too. A pair of strong thumbs in the throat. Gerry had read and filed the reports, tried to put them out of mind, then found himself reading them again, slower this time, before the watch ended at 4 A.M.

Sitting on the edge of his disheveled bed, he tried to imagine what kind of animal would strangle a helpless woman and scrawl a filthy insult across her belly. How could a man become depraved enough to commit a crime like that? It was beyond understanding.

After a while, he was aware that he was slumped across the foot of the bed, one leg dragging the floor, eyes closed tight. He straightened up and plucked a T-shirt from the dirty clothes on the floor. The heat pushed air across the shadowy room, lifting dust in slow ascents. He staggered back to the window; the bank clock showed 4:55 P.M. But wasn't it—

Earlier?

A few minutes ago it had been 1:35, and he had been standing at the window, thinking about—

Thinking about— What had he been thinking about?

He couldn't remember.

19

"Hi!"

She jumped at the deep male voice. He'd come up the back steps without making a sound, opened the locks, and walked in.

"Packer!" she yelped. "Don't you *ever* do that again!" She stomped her size five and a half sandal, but it made no noise on the throw rug and only enraged her more. *"Never—again!"*

Emily howled in her highchair, and Packer rushed over and consoled her, his mouth drawn down in sympathy. "It's okay, baby. Here, Emmy, have some cheese? Look, Dah eats it. Um-*mmmmmm,* that's good, baby. Good, good . . . Um-*ummmmm!* Sweet little thing . . ."

She slid the puffing casserole from the oven, talking breathlessly as she worked. "I had a caller. A breather. No, not a breather. He said— some things. Said he wasn't you, he was—Koslo. Somebody named Koslo. Said he was, he was, uh, *coming* for me. Oh, Packer, I was just—petrified."

"A U.C., huh?"

"U.C.?"

"Unidentified caller. There's a lot of that going around. The hot weather and all." He arranged his chair at the kitchen table and grabbed a fork. First things first. Apparently his appetite took priority over his family's safety.

"Packer," she said, holding her voice down for the baby's benefit, "I don't care *what's* going around, sweetie. *I* had a threatening phone call this afternoon. Me. Your wife. At home alone with—our baby. And I realized, I mean, what could we do if somebody *did* come after us?"

His chair squeaked, and she felt his arm around her shoulders, his large fingers brushing lightly at her brown hair. "Hon, relax! Nobody's coming after you. Everybody's getting calls. Next time, hang up right away. He'll get bored and dial somebody else. It's juveniles, mostly. No big deal."

"This was *no* juvenile."

"You'd be surprised. Some of these kids sing bass."

In between quick glances at the blue and white wall clock, he kept · insisting there was nothing to worry about. In between waves of nausea and trembling, she repeated that she was scared sick. Nothing like this had happened to her before. "He knew our name, sweetheart, don't you see? So it wasn't just some kid getting his, getting his—"

"Rocks off," he added politely, a noodle draped across his heavy jaw.

"He said he was coming for me. *Coming for me!*"

He didn't comment. She could have strangled him, full mouth and all.

"So I'll have to go through day after day like this, Packer. Day after *day,* don't you see?"

He slurped a half cup of coffee in one swallow and said, "Whatta you think'll happen, hon?"

"I worry—he'll try—well, he might—he might try to come in here. Like he said."

"In broad daylight?"

Why was he being so *dense?* "Anytime! In the afternoon when you're out. At night when you're working."

"Honey, the district car's never more than a few minutes away."

"Where was the district car last night?"

He rubbed his buttered lips with two slow swipes of his blue napkin and squinted at her through the fringe. "Oh, *that's* it! The sex killing. Now I understand. Honey, you shoulda mentioned that sooner."

He walked around the little drop-leaf table and knelt by her chair and took her face in his hands. "Amnee, look, that guy's *long* gone. He's probably not even in town. He knows Artie made his profile, so the last place he'll caper is here."

"Caper?" she said, jumping up. "That's what you call a sex murder? You call it a *caper?*"

He looked perplexed. He climbed slowly to his feet and wiped his hands on his jeans. "Caper's just a word, honey. It could mean a rape, a burglary, it could mean anything."

"You mean, like, the Manson case was a, a caper? The Martin Luther King assassination?" She began removing the dishes from the table, clanging them together.

"Come on, Amnee, stop getting hung up on words. Yop, the Manson case was a caper. Technically. The Crucifixion was a caper. It's just a—a word we use."

"Just a word." She dumped his saucer into the sink, chipping an edge. "Unimportant little words for unimportant little—capers. Rape. Torture. Murder. I understand. It's all in a day's work. *But this one involves your family!*"

He exhaled loudly and let his broad back slump against his chair. "You're really shook, aren't you?"

She turned sharply from his view; she'd be damned if she'd let him see her cry. If he didn't get the point—

"I've never seen you like this," he said. "Honey, it's—you're—you're overreacting. There's nothing to worry about. Must be a thousand of these weirdo calls every day."

"But not to us."

"What's so special about us? We're in the phone book. 'S.J. Lind.' Anybody can call. Mosta the time these nut cases don't even look up a number—they just dial." He ambled to the sink and looked deeply at her. "Hon, you got me worried. Not about any damn-fool U.C. About *you.* I never saw you scared like this, about—anything."

She turned on the garbage disposal and tried to compose herself. Yes, she was terrified. No, it wasn't the first time. More and more lately . . . A subliminal scene flickered across her brain: Amnee Lind is in her living room, daughter Emily in her arms, and a man is stalking them with a straightedge razor, whipping and slicing through the air, closer and closer, and *there is nothing they can do. . . .*

She bit her lip, and Packer pulled her close and stroked her honey-colored hair. She began to sob openly, unable to hold back. "I've always been k-k-kind of, kind of scared, Packer, but I didn't, I didn't want you to know, baby. I didn't want y-y-you to think less of me."

He looked surprised. "Think less of you? Because you get scared? Why, every woman—"

"When we first met, I remember thinking—marrying Packer—I, uh, I won't have to be—to be scared all the t-t-time."

He stopped stroking and stiffened. "Is *that* why you married me?" For a tough cop, he was certainly vulnerable. And wasn't everybody, in one way or another? Wasn't that the whole point?

"I married you because I loved you," she said.

"Still do?" His big head was tilted to the side. Coyness didn't become him; he looked like an off-duty clown.

"Oh, Packer, you know I do."

His face relaxed. He smiled. "Then why are you so scared?" he asked, pulling her to him again.

She spun loose and shook her head. Moron! "What's being scared have to do with loving you? Oh, Packer, you're so, so *dumb* sometimes! Can't I love you and still be worried?"

"If you love me," he said, "you know I'd never let anybody hurt you."

The childlike police logic made her seethe. It seemed intentionally— dense. Dear God, was she finding out after nearly three years of marriage that he was just another dumb cop? "Packer," she said shaking her head, "sometimes you're hopeless. How can you protect us when you're not here? Do you think you can protect us with your silly machismo when you're out chasing some drunk driver five miles away?"

"I'll have the district car check the house tonight."

"You will *not!* They'll take an ad to spread the news, your damn gossipy cops. 'Poor Packer Lind, he's got a problem at home, we have to hang around his house all the time.' The captain—he'd be thrilled to death."

His lips turned down, the way Emily's sometimes did. He looked like a tardy schoolboy. "Then what do you want me to do?" he asked.

"I don't know. I just don't know." She looked at the clock. "Maybe pay some attention to you-know-who. She's picking up the anxiety vibes. She, uh, c-r-i-e-d today when I got the call."

"Cried? How'd she know?"

"Same old thing. Baby-radar."

He hefted the child from her highchair, finger food smeared across her face, and hauled her giggling toward their wrestling ring: the living-room rug. She could hear them through the swinging door:

"What's this, sweet baby?"

"Cup. For make yo-goo."

"Yo-goo?"

"No, Dah. Yo-goo. *Yo-goo.* Make yo-goo in cup. *YO-GOO, YO-GOO!*"

"Amnee," he called out. "What's yo-goo?"

"Yogurt."

"Oh," he said, dropping his voice again. "Yogurt. Make yogurt in cup. That's nice, baby. *Big* girl. Hey, what's this?"

"Book. Goldiwocks. Fwee bay-oos. Mommy gave."

Amnee heard a loud chirp. "That's a kiss," he said. "Daddy gave."

The two of them were quiet for a few minutes, and then she heard him preparing his nightly exit. "Can Dah have his squeeze now?"

"No! No no *no!*"

"Come on, sweet baby. Dah has to go to work, honey. Just one little squeeze?"

"No! No 'queeze!"

"Okay. Okay!"

The door opened and he shuffled in ahead of the careening child. He walked to the sink and whispered in Amnee's ear, "What's eating her, hon? She won't give me a squeeze."

"She's starting her 'no' stage, that's all. Babies like to say no when they're around a year and a half, two years old. Assert their independence. So they can be people instead of toys."

Emily hugged her father's knee and began to sniffle. "What's she crying about?" he asked in a panicky voice.

"She wants a squeeze."

"But she just said no squeeze!"

"She didn't mean it, Packer. It's just her 'no' stage. I told you."

"I swear I'll never understand babies," he said, swinging the child high over his head.

"Female babies, anyway," she said under her breath.

He disappeared into the back and returned with a small handgun in his palm. "Honey," he said, "I'm sorry. I was unreasonable. If you're scared, you're scared, and there's no use pretending you're not. I'm just a little, uh, preoccupied, that's all."

"What's that thing for?" she asked, stepping back.

"For you, honey. I had it in my footlocker. It's perfect for a woman. An old Iver Johnson five-shot. You'll never need it, but it'll make you feel better."

"It makes me feel *worse!* You know how I am about guns, Packer. I'd rather have a boa constrictor in the house."

"Look, I'll just put it where you can reach it and the baby can't, okay? Then you won't have to sit around and worry about prowlers and U.C.s."

"I'd never shoot a living thing. *Never.*" She took another step backward, and her stomach did a flip-flop at the thought.

"Even to protect the baby?"

"I couldn't, sweetheart. I just—couldn't."

"Listen, hon, you don't have to shoot anybody. What you do is, a prowler comes around, you pop one cap through the roof, see what I mean? He'll run like a scalded bear."

"Suppose he doesn't run?"

He looked uncomprehending. "Amnee, for God's sake, anybody that walks into your field of fire, he's a nut case, and you got four rounds left to dump him."

"*Dump him?*" This interminable jargon. "What's that? Another police expression?"

"Yop. Dump him. Stop him, shoot him, kill him, I don't care how you say it. If it's you or him, why, sure—you dump him!"

Dear God, he was mistaking her for one of his men. He was giving her a lesson in killing!

"Packer, I can't!" she said. "I never touched a gun in my life."

"Show you everything you need to know in five minutes."

"No!"

"Not even to protect Emmy?"

"No, not even to protect—oh, Packer, what a rotten way to put it." He was being so unfair, he deserved to have a sniveling woman in front of him, wiping at her eyes with a damp handkerchief. She felt her self-control ebb away, and she let go again. "Why do you have to do this dirty job?" she asked, her voice shaking. "Do you think anybody appreciates it? Teaching your wife how to kill, for God's sake! What kind of a life do you call that?"

His big face flashed a look of shame, almost of guilt. "Honey," he said softly, "it's my—work, that's all." He sat heavily. "You take a job and you stick it out. It's part of, of being a man. I dunno—" He interrupted himself and looked apologetic as she glared at him through a wash of tears and mascara. He knew damned good and well how she hated phrases like "being a man." As though being a man was— extraordinary.

"I don't always understand it myself," he admitted quickly. "But a cop's life—it's just what I picked, honey. Maybe it was a bad choice. But I made it."

"Well, I didn't."

"You never knew me as anything else," he said gently.

"Oh, Packer." She sank into a chair and sobbed in her hands, and he crouched alongside and pulled her to him. "Oh, Packer," she said again. "What a silly argument. Oh, sweetheart." She turned her damp face toward his. "I know you're proud of your job, sweetheart. I *know* that. I'm proud, too, baby. But I'm so, I'm so—scared."

"You can't help it," he whispered, squeezing her thin shoulder and laying his head against hers.

He was right; she couldn't help it. She remembered a childhood scene. A man had kicked a woman. He had come thundering across the room like a runaway stallion and kicked her as hard as he could kick. In the side. Knocked the poor sickly woman into a wall. It was just like a cowboy western, except that Amnee was four years old at the time, and they were her parents. Maybe that was a part of her fright now. Maybe that was why she was overreacting to—what did Packer call the man? A nut case. She could never remember a time when she hadn't been afraid of violence. Even verbal violence. And now her own husband wanted to school her in the most violent instrument of all: the pistol. The cold little hunk of metal that was invented to make it easier for one human being to kill another. To watch the victim fall, a few feet away. To see the spurt of human blood. *Ugh!*

"Where's that thing?" she asked, gritting her teeth.

He pulled the gun from a pocket. It looked like a toy, a child's water pistol, but she could see the shiny brass jackets gleaming from the sides. "Where'd you get this?"

"I took it out of Billy Mains' locker. A spot inspection. It's a—a drop weapon."

That was another reason she didn't like to discuss his work: no cop on earth spoke English. "What's a drop weapon?"

"Oh, uh . . ." His worn face contorted. He looked like a man who has just been asked if he'd ever masturbated. "It's, uh, just something that you drop, om, uh, alongside, uh, somebody."

Why was he being evasive? She bored in. He fussed and fidgeted and finally proclaimed that she would never understand, no civilian would ever understand, not even the wife of a supervisor. "Try me," she insisted. "Maybe I'm not as dumb as you think."

"It's not that, honey," he said, sounding stricken again. "It's just, there's just, om, some things you can't explain if you, uh, if you haven't uh—been there."

"Where?"

"Oh, Christ." He began a long explanation, picking his words slowly and awkwardly, and ended up disturbing her more than ever. A drop weapon turned out to be a weapon carried for the sole purpose of planting it on someone. Drop weapons ranged from Boy Scout knives to .45-caliber automatics; they were the bad cop's final defense against being held accountable. *It was me or him. Look! Here's his weapon. He pulled it on me.* She'd never dreamed that such techniques existed, let alone that they were a tradition. "There's a few cops carry 'em,"

Packer admitted. "Strapped to their ankles, hidden in their shorts, tucked in the dash of their cars. They're scared, honey, just like you. That's why they do it."

"Scared?" she said. "Scared of what?"

"Of not being backed up by the public. Of maybe having to dump a guy that's threatening somebody or a guy that's holding a gun on somebody and then finding out too late that it wasn't a gun after all, it was a toothbrush, or maybe it was a finger sticking inside a pocket, and then there's six months of shooting teams and review boards and editorials about police brutality and maybe even a trial and a sentence. It's wrong, but it's happened."

"*What's* wrong?" She'd be damned if she'd back down.

"Everything. Everything about drop weapons. The fact that a few cops carry them. The fact that they have any reason to carry them. Everything. Sometimes the whole system seems wrong." He hesitated, looked down at his boots, and lowered his voice as though he didn't want his daughter to overhear. "There was a sergeant in Detroit. Guy tried to cut him, held a shiv right at his throat—"

"Shiv?"

"A knife. When he felt the blade touch his neck, he kicked the guy backward and shot him. So a crowd gathers and somebody puts out an officer-needs-help call and there's all kinds of confusion and—the knife is gone. The sergeant gets hauled before a grand jury, charged with manslaughter; the community pressure builds, and he draws one to ten. A cop, mind you, a sector sergeant. He's on his way to the joint before a black preacher drags in a kid about five years old. Turns out the kid had picked up the shiv and took it home. It was pretty. It was shiny. Does that help you understand drop weapons?"

"That's how you justify planting fake evidence on people?"

"Come on, hon, argue fair! I didn't say *I* justify it. I *don't* justify it. But that's how some of the men see it, yeah."

"And you agree with them."

"I do *not!* But—I understand."

"I wouldn't *want* to understand something like that," she said. "Did you, did you ever carry a—what do you call them? A drop weapon?"

"I never had to," Packer answered. "I was never scared." She knew he was telling the truth. "I try to understand frightened people, the things they do, but I'm not good at it. It's like me trying to tell a civilian what it's like to be a watch commander. No way. I try to explain, but I don't get across. It's not their fault. There's only one way to understand cops, honey. Be one."

She walked to the window. It was already later than his usual leaving time, but the sun was still high and hot. He was right; she didn't understand cops. But she loved one, she understood that, and what else mattered? As she turned from the window to go to his arms, a gray sedan drove by, slowed, then sped up. A lone driver, male. Maybe Koslo was checking the place out.

Dear God, they should have moved from here a long time ago. This neighborhood would never be safe, not with a thousand Packer Linds on duty at the same time. It was awful that decent people had to keep loaded guns in their own homes. The whole city was decaying from the inside out; people were breaking down, and broken-down people committed crimes, and there was nothing the police could do about it. Cops were the expendables, victims themselves. They thought they had an effect on crime, but all the cops in the world couldn't protect a police lieutenant's wife and baby from a single Koslo. If Packer didn't know it, she did.

She watched as he kissed their daughter. He pulled Amnee to him with a strong hand low on her back. "Oh, sweetheart," she said, and clung to his strength.

She stood at the window with Emily in her arms, and the two of them waved as the old Jeep pulled away, Packer flapping his hand out the open window. Then she sang and recited "Humphrey Dumpty" and bathed the baby and tucked her in, remembering to repeat "Nighty night, sleep tight" three full times as demanded. And all the time her mind was on drop weapons and U.C.s and her husband and his job.

It was sad the way the seamy little secrets dribbled out as you lived through the years together. You fell in love with a stranger, you married him, soon you thought you knew everything about him and his work, and then you found out there were certain gaps in your knowledge. She was sure that Packer wouldn't carry a drop weapon if he were the last policeman in a world full of assassins, but she also felt that he wasn't properly shocked by the practice. Hadn't he said he found the little gun in Billy Mains' locker? And Mains was still on the force, wasn't he? The baby-faced one that always studied her legs at the watch parties?

Somehow her view of her husband had shifted; somehow he had become—slightly different. Well, she would give him space. Maybe he was right: "There's only one way to understand cops." She would accept this as true, whether it was true or not. She *had* to.

No, that wasn't fair.

She *wanted* to.

He'd been gone for an hour when the phone rang and she said hello without thinking. The hollow voice said, "Good. I'm glad you're home." Her fingers fluttered in little spasms as she dumped the phone on its cradle. Then she rushed into the bathroom and vomited.

20

It was 7:30 P.M., 1930 hours in officialese, and Packer Lind squirmed in the ladder-backed wooden chair as he studied the day's pile of reports and memos. For another half hour, the office was the province of H. P. Steinmetz, the second-watch commander, so Packer sat well away from the desk, even though Steinmetz had wandered off to the recreation room, as was his frequent custom, to shoot pool and exchange information about transfers, promotions, and infidelities, or maybe to treat himself to one of the gourmet liquids from the coin machines in the kitchen.

The R-C Cola thermometer on the wall stood at eighty-one degrees, six degrees cooler than outside, and Packer knew from experience that it would drop only a degree or two before he was relieved at 4 A.M. "This weather keeps up they oughta issue us parasols," he said under his breath, then looked up quickly to make sure no one had walked in and seen his lips move. The heat's melting my brain, he told himself. They'll be dragging me away in a canvas tuxedo.

Despite the temperature, the office felt good to him. On hot nights every brick in the antique walls gave off faint reminders of the coal smoke that had hung over the neighborhood for sixty or seventy years before the diesels came in. Some of the men said the place stank like a freight yard, but he liked the smell; it took him back to the steam trains that rumbled past his grammar school and fired up his dreams.

From out around the desk area he heard some second-watch officers writing up a prisoner. "What's the legal limit on a knife blade, Tom?"

"Three and a half inches."

"We haven't got anything to measure three and a half inches with."

"*You* do."

Packer snickered. He enjoyed the "jiving around," as Willie Bethea called it; he only wished he was better at it: quick like Artie Siegl, smart-ass like Billy Mains, even sarcastic like the captain. Policemen jived and bantered to stay close without getting mushy. They joked and wisecracked and traded insults instead of putting their arms around each other. It made sense to Packer.

"Have a mint?" another voice asked. Lieutenant Steinmetz's second watch was finishing up; one by one the men were dragging into the station to write their last reports, turn in their logs, and sign out.

"No, thanks," somebody answered. "I'm fasting."

"That fasting do anything for you?"

"Makes me feel great."

"How long you been fasting?"

"About an hour."

A sturdy young cop walked by the watch commander's office, singing softly, "Gee, but it's great, to be eating your date . . ."

Packer leaned back and sniffed. With luck, there'd be enough essence of steam train embedded in the blackened bricks to last another twelve, fifteen years, at least till he retired. The old station—well, he expected it to outlive all of them. He remembered the wooden sign that a trusty had found under a pile of rotting boards in the subbasement where the holding cells used to be. NINTH PRECINT, it announced in flowery old-English lettering on a faded blue background. The crippled barber across the street said the sign had hung over the front entrance for thirty years before the misspelling was noticed. Maybe one of Willie B's ancestors had been a sign painter. Packer smiled and imagined old-time watch commanders in stovepipe helmets and walrus mustaches sitting in this same steamy office translating their beatmen's reports into English.

"Hey, Pack," Harry Steinmetz said, walking into the office ahead of a ribbon of gray cigar smoke, "what's a three-letter word for African grazer?"

"Huh?" he said.

"Naw, that ain't it. Three letters. Middle letter's a N, or maybe a Y. Hey, is a kid's first seat a potty with a Y or an I-E?" He spoke rapidly, as though there were a prize and a deadline.

"Gosh, Harry, I don't know," he said, slightly exasperated. "Why don't you call Juvenile?"

"You're a big help," Steinmetz grumbled.

Quit your griping, Packer wanted to snap back, momentarily irked. We're the busiest precinct in the city, the paper work's a week behind, and you waste your whole damned watch on crossword puzzles. But instead he said, "Gnu."

"What?" Steinmetz asked.

"Gnu. G-N-U."

"What's that?"

"African grazer."

The day lieutenant's pencil stub moved into action. "Hey, that cracks it!" He disappeared out the door, then stuck his nose back in. "Thanks, Pack. Hey, kinda keep it—you know."

"Won't tell a soul I helped," he said, looking up from a three-page memo on Chickie's, the new franchised fast-food chain. Three pages! Chickie's had advised its employes that police officers were entitled to a one-third reduction if they signed a form marked "police discount." "Such discounts are contrary to department regulation," the captain's memorandum huffed, "and Chickie's general mgr. has been so advised." Tsk, tsk, Packer said to himself, that general manager ought to go stand in the corner. Next thing you know, he'll be molesting children.

Oh, Christ, that wasn't funny, wasn't funny at all. Not the way things were at home. He thought about phoning Amnee. But if he called her too often, he would only reinforce her idea that there was something to fear, and by God, there *wasn't*. It disturbed him that she was upset; it annoyed him that a sicko was threatening his wife; it frustrated him that such things went on inside his precinct or anyplace else. *But*—you couldn't let yourself be intimidated by psychos. That was playing their game. They called to get a reaction, to hear an involuntary gasp or a frightened plea or even a shouted curse. It proved they were somebody, it showed they could be intimate with another person, it confirmed they were—human. Invariably when the dicks busted a U.C. he turned out to be a klutz, a loser. The last one he remembered was a fifteen-year-old runt with terminal acne, sitting in his room masturbating while he dialed at random, scared and excited at the same time. You couldn't let lames like that upset you.

Easy for him to say. He wasn't the one stuck at home with a baby; he was a big strong man with a .38 service revolver on his belt; he lived in a world of hot loads and palm saps and clubs and tear gas and Mace and eighteen-inch riot guns. Yeah, and drop weapons, too. Shielded like that, your perspective was distorted. It was impossible to feel Amnee's fright, he knew that, no matter how much he loved her. He just had to be gentle and understanding, maybe even fake it a little.

Besides, there was still a stack of paper work to digest before roll call. The Crime Analysis Unit report blared, "DANGEROUS PERSON—APPROACH WITH CAUTION!" John Allen Smith of Salt Lake City was back in town and believed to be capering; he'd been stopped by officers from Precinct Five and appeared to be under the influence of narcotics; he'd once shot an officer in Rock Springs, Wyoming. Okay, he'd remember that. John—Allen—Smith, W-M, 6-6, 265, pale complexion. A big mother. Sunken face looked like something hacked from mozzarella with a garden tool. No sex offenses on his sheet. Too bad—it might have been a start. "White male, six six, two sixty-five . . ." He repeated it three times till he had it memorized, then turned to the weekly poop sheet put out by the chief's secretary. "Retirement party set for Maj. Don Kesler." He would attend. Kesler had sat on the board that passed over eleven names to recommend him for lieutenant.

An item was headlined DEATH—RETIRED OFFICER. P. W. "Pete" Hansford had died of a skull fracture after a fall from his porch. Packer shook his head. Died as he lived. Spent twenty years on the P.D., half of them with Gilbey's gin on his breath. Rest in peace, Pete, and may it always be Happy Hour wherever you are.

The traffic fatality summary at the bottom showed three for August and twenty-eight for the year. Down from last year. Next thing you knew, the chief would be issuing a press release crediting the Driver of the Month campaign. Oh, Christ, poor Artie! Well, he'd get to that problem. . . .

There were ten items on the Precinct Information Bulletin, and one caught his eye:

ITEM 5:   Information on two Suspects apprehended attempting to steal Light Bars from top of Police Patrol vehicle parked at Pct. 9. Suspects had all the bolts out and were cutting the wires when they were apprehended at 1600 Hours. See Case 76-375832.

Suspect #1: GONZALEZ, Federico L., 6495 Eighth. White/male/16. 7/2/63. 5'8" 120 lbs. Brn hair. Dk. Comp. Wears glasses. Drives 71 Ply 2 door green Duster reg. to Lee Higman, 639 Ave. J. Occ.: Student.

Suspect #2: CAMPION, Wildred James., 876 Fourth W. White/male/15. 5/1/64. 5'4". 130 lbs. Brn hair. Med. Comp. Occ.: Runaway.

Someone had stapled a snip of light-green computer print-out to the item. It showed that Gonzalez had been handled three times before: "Shoplifting, susp. sent.; Assault, served two weeks Juv. Hall; Susp. of narc., no disp. shown." Campion was a cherry.

He reread the item till he had it cold. A long shot maybe, but a couple of kids who would try to vandalize a patrol car in broad daylight might just be trying to show their contempt for the P.D., and how different was that from sneaking up at midnight and clubbing the station-house mascots to death? He made a note to send somebody down to the juvenile lockup for a discussion with GONZALEZ, Federico L., and his young friend, CAMPION, Wildred James. If they weren't already sprung. God forbid the poor little fellows should have to spend more than an hour or two in custody. Might stunt their growth.

The light flickered on the telephone base and he heard the deskman say, "Just a minute. He's right here."

Amnee seldom phoned, preferring to let him choose the time, but somehow he knew she was on the line. Without waiting for the deskman to buzz him, he picked up the phone and said, "Lind."

"Packer, he, he called again!"

The line sounded hollow; somebody was listening. "Just a second, hon," he said. He flattened his hand across the mouthpiece and called out, "It's okay, Dale, I got it."

There was a click. What had the second-watch deskman heard? *Packer, he called again.* No big deal.

"What'd he say, honey?"

"He said, he said, 'Good. I'm glad you're uh—you're home.'" Her voice sounded as though it came from her stomach.

"Okay, hon, it's *okay.* Just slow down. What'd *you* say?"

"N-n-nothing. Just 'hello' when I, I picked up the, uh, phone."

"Not another word?"

"No."

"Then what happened?"

"I hung up."

"Good!" he said. "He'll give up on you and call somebody he can get a rise out of. A *live* one. You did right."

"Oh, sweetheart, I'm still shaking. Oh, Packer, how'm I ever supposed to sleep tonight?"

"Take one of my pills." He had an old bottle of Empirin No. 3's for back pain. "One won't hurt you."

"I couldn't, sweetie. I, I don't want to b-b-be wiped out." Her voice had more vibrato than an opera singer's.

"You mean you'd rather stay wide awake and listen for the boogyman? Honey, you're like a little kid." He tried to keep his tone light, but he was losing some of his patience. It was one thing to suffer from irrational fears; it was another to cultivate them, and to avoid taking a few simple steps to protect yourself. First she refused the gun, and now—this. One pill and she'd be relaxed eight or nine hours. In the new light of morning, her mysterious caller would just look silly.

"I'm sorry, Packer." Her voice broke. "I'm so, so—sorry." She stopped.

"Sorry for what?" he asked gently.

"For, for—b-b-being so scared."

He cupped his hand around the phone. "Listen, Amnee, there's nothing to be scared of. Honest! It's *okay!*" He reminded himself to keep the tension out of his tone. "I love you, honey, depend on you,

[135]

you know that. So does Emmy. And we don't want to see you tearing yourself up like this, honey. Hear?"

She sniffled.

"Now listen. I'm gonna have David One pass by every hour tonight. Wait! *Wait a minute!* Nothing official. They're not just cops, they're friends, hon. They'll be glad—"

"It's all so—unnecessary."

"We're gonna do it," he said emphatically.

Out of the corner of his eye he saw three men in civilian clothes rush past his door. Patrolman Johnny McClung was in the middle, and he could swear the other two were supporting him. Oh, Lord, what next? He heard a giggle, then footfalls dragging up the wooden stairs toward the locker room and the showers.

". . . Do whatever you say, sweetie, and don't you worry about us," Amnee was saying. "We'll be, uh, fine." Her voice was strained; she sounded eighty-one instead of twenty-one.

"You got the revolver?"

She seemed to hesitate. "Uh, it's—in the house."

"Put it under your pillow. In between the pillow and the slip."

"Under the pillow." She sounded drugged already.

He promised to phone after roll call. "No, *don't!*" she begged him. "Don't call unless you have to. I'll think it's—him."

"Okay, hon. Go to bed early. And—relax, hear?"

"I love you, sweetheart."

"I love you, honey."

That was the way they ended most of their conversations. He knew some of the men joked about it. Tough shit. Cops thought of themselves as hard cases, too tough to use words like love. But inside they were mostly infants, begging for affection and attention. That's why they brought in lost dogs and runaways. You could squeeze animals all you wanted without feeling weak or unmanly. You could squeeze them to death. . . .

Now how had he started on *that* subject . . .?

Oh, Christ, something had to be done about McClung. Quick. He headed for the staircase to the locker room, then retraced his steps. "Dale," he said to the day deskman, "do me a favor. Go tell Johnny McClung to report to me right away. I'll cover the phones for you."

"Sure thing, Lieutenant."

Dale Collins came back down looking troubled. "McClung's, uh, busy, Lieutenant," he said, averting his eyes.

"Busy? Whatta you mean, busy?"

"He's, uh, he's in the shower."

Okay, if that was the way they wanted it. He headed for the lockers. By unwritten law, the big dimly lighted room upstairs belonged to harness bulls, no supervisors or brass hats need apply. He missed the give and take with the men, getting ready for roll call: the odor of sweat and hair spray, shoe leather and after-shave, metal polish and leather cream, gun oil and the slightly burned smell of uniforms fresh from the cleaners in their clear plastic bags. He sneaked a deep sniff and walked into the shower room.

Johnny McClung was standing naked and flabby on the duckboards, a grin like a tic on his splotchy red face. "Whattaya say, bosh—boss— Lieutenant?" The words skittered up and away, and McClung grabbed for a sink and held on.

Packer tried to look enraged, but he couldn't bring it off. He settled for a serious look. How could he be sore at a typical cop with a typical ailment? Did you get mad at cops for getting shot? Alcoholism was an occupational hazard.

"Get dressed quick," he ordered. "I don't want the men to see you."

A pair of matched faces, black and white, peeked around the corner. He shoo'd them fast with a snap of his head. "Move it, John," he said. "Dry off and wait for me in the Crime Analysis room."

"Crime 'Nalyshish . . ."

"You wait there!"

In the old days a man like Johnny McClung would have been allowed to destroy himself and maybe a few others in the bargain. Packer had seen it happen. On his first tour, twelve years ago, there'd been a veteran cop named Owen Sanders who drove to work via various bars night after night. "Has to get himself up for the job," Packer's T.O. had explained.

"Get himself up for *this* job?" Packer echoed, baffled. He was a wide-eyed cadet himself, and he thought any man would exchange his house and bride for a chance to be a cop at night.

"Yeah. Some guys are like that. They get tired, they get bored. Some of 'em get scared."

"After twenty years?"

"That's the way it happens, kid. Some guys piss their pants the first time they go out; they *never* get over it. Some guys are shit hot for action and they roll outa bed one morning and they're finished."

"Why?"

"Who knows? Most cases, they didn't realize what they're getting into. All they thought of was the badge, the power, the pussy. Then they find out they gotta go up against a crazy man with an ax, or break down a door with an armed robber behind it, or maybe climb on a window ledge eight floors up. They seen it all on television, but that was *Dragnet,* that wasn't *them.*"

One night Owen Sanders had stumbled hard into Packer in the rec room, and instantly the sozzled street cop squared off to fight. The young rookie grabbed him by the arm and bent him down, and as he leaned over he caught the sour smell of used bourbon. Packer walked away feeling sad. Sanders' wife had died two years before; he was alone, surviving. A few minutes later the sadness turned to annoyance when he watched the drunken cop open his car door; the man was preparing for a long night's patrol in a sensitive salt-and-pepper area, carelessly cradling his riot gun with its load of double-0 buckshot that would stop a Kenworth truck. Still half drunk or worse, and on his way to uphold the law. "Don't worry," the T.O. had whispered. "We'll cover for him." That meant that the other cars would jump his calls. Or maybe the dispatchers would be tipped to take it easy on the guy tonight. Packer despised that kind of buddy system. How could it help Owen Sanders become anything but an old, sick drunk? Exactly what he became. Now he was in a home, messing his pants and dying of paresis, and when you asked his name, he would shake like a clothes dryer and say, "O-o-o-o-officer S-s-s-s-s-s-sanders" when he could speak at all.

For a few years, alcoholic cops had been routinely packed off to "drunk school"; the course set the city back $2,500 per man, cheaper than the $25,000 to train a new recruit. But the taxpayers' revolt had put an end to that kind of economics. Nowadays drunken cops were canned. Who gave a damn if the force lost a good man, a fellow human being who could have been salvaged? Departmental strength was still being trimmed, and attrition was welcomed in any form. At least by City Hall.

Well, attrition was fine for others, Packer said to himself, but not for Precinct Nine, thanks. John McClung had been a respected narcotics detective, then started boozing after his partner was killed in an ambush and the police grapevine blamed McClung for incompetent backup. Packer didn't know the sordid details and didn't want to know them. "He's a good cop and he's getting a bum rap," Turk Molnar had told him when McClung was transferred back into uniform. That was good enough for Packer. And the new man had stayed straight.

Until tonight.

Well, there was one step left. Put him on ice. Give him a harmless job around the precinct and look after him, pump him up, make him feel worthwhile again. Packer would handle the rehabilitation one on one. He figured Gerald Yount needed a change anyway, sitting at that desk night after night staring into the gumball machine. Let's shift Yount back to a one-man car, he said to himself, and put McClung on the desk. Not much of a risk, and it might help both men. But not tonight— Oh, my God, not tonight! That's all I need: a call from Singletary or I.A.U. and a plastered deskman answering. . . .

He grabbed an ampule from the Breathalyzer drawer and went back upstairs to the Crime Analysis room. It was tiny, like most of the rooms in the sagging station, but it could be locked from the inside. McClung slumped in a chair breathing hard, his face the color of stewed tomatoes. "Blow through this," Packer said, handing over the plastic bubble.

"Lieutenant—"

"Blow! *C'mon!* Roll call's in ten minutes and I got things to do."

McClung put the mouthpiece to his slobbering lips and exhaled weakly, eyes rolling up like a window shade. "Blow, goddamn it!" Packer said. "Quit holding back."

The reading was .15 blood alcohol. Patrolman John McClung was 150 percent drunk by state law. "Sit!" Packer ordered.

The older man ran his hands through his curly silver hair and looked at the floor. "I know," he muttered. "I got it coming."

"Got what coming?"

"Huh? I dunno. *Huh?*"

"Listen to me, John. Who saw you come in the station?"

"Saw—*me?* Collins. Om, uh, Reichert and Rollie Beemer, they kinda steered me, uh, helped me, uh, you know, they kinda insisted me up the stairs."

"Anybody else see you?"

McClung shook his head in a lazy circle. "Looks like *you* did," he said.

"Okay, Johnny, you hide here till roll call's over. Then I'll have somebody drive you home. Drink the rest of the night or sober up, that's your business. But when you report tomorrow, I'm putting you on the Breathalyzer, understand?" McClung nodded sheepishly. "Tomorrow night and *every* night, you got that? And if you ever register over point oh five, it's—"

"Lieutenant?"

"What?"

McClung started to sniffle. It seemed to Packer that he was suffering from more than just a crying jag, that his stricken face expressed some deep pain.

"I been having, having, I been having, uh, trouble—"

"Johnny, I don't have time now. Tomorrow night we can talk; you'll be working the desk. Right now I'm giving you your last warning. Point oh five or higher, okay? That means if you have a coupla beers before you come to work, you're furloughed on the spot."

When Packer reached the bottom of the stairwell, he saw a familiar figure riffling through the arrest reports. He spun and took the steps three at a time back to the Crime Analysis office. "Lock this door," he told Johnny McClung, "and don't open it for anybody but me. Let 'em break in, but don't open it!"

McClung returned a look of wet servility. He looked as though he'd been bawling. Packer wanted to say a kind word, but this wasn't the time.

The newcomer was gone when Packer returned to the watch commander's office. "Where . . .?" he started to ask the deskman. Dale Collins was already crooking his thumb toward the captain's office. Me, I don't know nothin', Packer said to himself. I'm just a poor broken-down supervisor doing his job. If the old fart wants me, he knows where to look. . . .

A bright red envelope marked "Confidential—Eyes Only" rested on top of the W.C.'s in box. He slit it open and started to read the medical examiner's protocol on

CASE OF BETTY EVANS

"This is the body of a fairly well-developed white female. . . . Multiple hyoid fractures . . ."

That was enough. The guy had crushed her windpipe. Poor girl, she never had a chance. Imagine Artie Siegl mistaking the killer for a Driver of the Month candidate. Couldn't happen again in a hundred years. A thousand. . . .

Artie Siegl . . . Oh, God, what if he showed up? With *him* in the back. . . . Packer grabbed the time chart from its clipboard on the wall. Thank Christ! Siegl was marked "S" for "sick." Somebody had accidentally done something right. He stepped behind his locker and pulled out his uniform, still sweat-damp from the night before. With an honored leader aboard, he'd better put on the monkeysuit.

"Er uh, you here, Lieutenant?"

"Hello, Mills," he said, recognizing the rookie's voice.

"I just thought I'd step in, let you take a look—"

Packer stepped around his locker and froze. The new man had been to the hairdresser's. Tightly sprung curls clung to his head like a basket of steel wool. "How d'ya like it, sir?" The dizzy twit actually seemed proud.

"That's not the question," Packer said, still trying to comprehend. He didn't think the department had an official policy toward frizzies, but Afros were banned, and what was a frizzy but a white man's Afro? He'd never seen one on a cop before. Of all the half-assed—

"I got it today," Tennyson Mills said proudly. "Place called Mr. Evelyn's."

"Mr. Evelyn's?"

"Yes, sir. A new, uh, barber. They tried to give me a discount, but I wouldn't go for it. Basic Police Manual, page eighteen, right? Whattaya think, Lieutenant?" Mills turned around like a model on the runway, arms outstretched, and Packer had to resist an urge to kick him in the nuts.

"Let's go to roll call and find out how somebody else likes it," he told the smiling recruit.

"Somebody else? Yes, sir. Who's that?"

"The captain."

21

Julius Singletary tried to conceal his disdain as the third watch lined up for roll call. Jesus Jones, what an aggregation! If these were cops, what did the criminals look like? The beer-bellied hunky sergeant bellowed, "Group—ten-HUT! Dress right—DRESS! Come on, dress it up! Smoliss, move forward. You throw the whole line off. Read*eeeeeee*—FRONT!"

The Precinct Nine commander sniffed and turned away. This watch didn't even *attempt* to look military. He forced himself to think about other matters as Packer Lind ran down the first half of the roll call, but the dimwittedness of some of the answers drew his attention back.

". . . Reichert?"

"Heerp."

"Desk tonight. Bethea?"

"Present."

"Beemer?"

"Yo!"

"You two're David One, as usual. Mills?"

"Here, *sirp!*"

"Zebra Four. Mains?"

"Yep."

"Maki?"

"Here."

"David Three for the two of you. Smoliss?"

"Huh?"

"David Five tonight. . . ."

Let's see now, the captain mused: of the answers so far, all were improper except one. The woman: Maki. Answering roll call wasn't all that complicated, was it? The book said, "Supervisor shall state the officer's name, and the officer shall answer 'Here,' unless, of course, he is absent." The most simple-minded instruction in the whole damned manual, and one out of seven of these yay-hoos got it right.

"All right, officers," the lieutenant was saying, "the captain will inspect."

Julius Singletary was in no mood to be checking navel lint and ear wax on a bunch of delinquent harness bulls—his mind was already galloping ahead to a showdown with Agate; he would get in tonight if he had to tie her down; goddamn it; he needed some relief!—but first something had to be done about the inept third watch. He was on the premises for one purpose: to stir up his sickest shift. He'd get their attention if he had to pull his snub-nose and pop a couple caps at their feet. After that, he'd have a few personal remarks to make to the most overrated watch commander in the city: the big stoop clomping behind him like a Swedish immigrant.

The captain bellied up to the line. "When's the last time you polished your badge, officer?"

Patrolman Reichert looked hurt. "Polished?" he asked.

"Yale!" the captain affirmed. "Polished! You know, rub-a-dub-dub? *Phnfff!*" Several of the others giggled. "Dummy up!" he said, glowering down the line. "That ought to be easy for you bunch of dummies. Reichert, the next time you report for duty with a badge that looks like it came from an archaeological dig, don't report for duty. Understand?"

The rookie Mills was an improvement. His shoes were black plastic, the kind that held a shine till the soles fell off. His pants were freshly pressed. There were two sharp military creases down the front of his blouse. The visor of his hat gleamed with wax, and the hat itself—the hat itself seemed to perch about three inches above his head. Odd effect. Like it was floating. Now why the hell—

"Take your cap off, son," the captain ordered. Packer Lind inhaled audibly, as did several of the patrolmen.

The hat seemed to rise spontaneously as Mills touched it, and a nest of curls sprang into sight. The rookie shook his head lightly, like a bathing beauty after a swim, and continued to stand at attention, his eyes looking left and right and up and down.

The captain took two steps back and scratched his Santa Claus nose. Then he walked behind the row and examined the hairdo from the rear. "Okay, okay," he said. "What's the joke? You doing a fruit patrol tonight? Vice asked us for help again?"

"No, sir," Mills answered. "I—" The rest was inaudible.

"Speak up! *Phnfff!*"

"Sir, I—"

"Take that goddamn thing off!"

"Sir—"

"He can't—"

"It's not—"

"Er uh—"

Several men were talking at once: Mills, Lind, Molnar, and one or two others. "AT EASE!" the captain shouted. "GODDAMN IT, SHUT UP!" He was coming to a terrible realization. The growth atop Mills' head was—not—a—rug. But what *was* it? He'd seen the kid a few days before and he'd looked perfectly normal. Now he looked like a mulatto musician.

"Okay, okay," the captain said, trying to regain his dignity. "Now you tell me: what *is* that?"

"It's—it's the latest thing, sir," Mills said in his high voice.

"The latest thing," Molnar explained.

"It's the latest thing, Cap," Packer Lind clarified the matter.

"In what?" the captain asked.

"In haircuts, sir," the rookie said. "It's a perm—uh, a permanent. A frizzy they call it. You get it done once a month, and after that there's no muss, no fuss, no bother. Just comb it out—"

"And disturb all the mice?"

Mills smiled appreciatively. Several men laughed out loud. Apparently they were under the impression that inspections were some kind of recreation period. "Give him a break, Cap," a voice called out. "He's got sickle cell anemia."

"It's strictly regulation, sir," Tennyson Mills insisted.

"Where?" the captain asked. "In Zambesia?" He didn't know if there was such a country, but if there were, its citizens were bound to wear frizzies. What was next in Precinct Nine? Rings in the nose? Codpieces? Jesus Jones, some of the old precinct commanders would have self-destructed, they saw a hairdo like this.

"Yes, sir," Mills went on in that college-educated whine of his. "It doesn't touch my collar in the back and it doesn't go below my ear lobes and it's no longer than four inches maximum."

"He's right, Cap," the lieutenant said softly. "It looks a little odd, but—"

"A little odd?" the captain squealed. *"A little odd? Phnfff!* Listen, Miller, Milton, Mills, whatever your name is, regulation is what *I* say it is, get me? And I say that goddamn fungus on your head *isn't.* I say you got twenty-four hours to get rid of it. I say you come in like that tomorrow, I'll take away your gun and issue you a spear."

"Yes, sir, Captain, sir."

"Phnfff!"

The rest of the inspection was equally inspiring. Patrolman Bethea wore his tie an inch to one side, like a hangman's noose. His partner, Beemer, had decorated his blouse with flecks of pepperoni pizza hold the onions. Patrolman Mains wore his cap at a forty-five-degree angle, and when the captain ordered him to straighten it, the hat slipped automatically back into the old position. "That's just the way it sets," Mains said, and the captain told him to report tomorrow with a new hat or a new head, one. Patrolman Smoliss wore scruffy boots that looked as though they'd been issued in the Boer War, topped by a threadbare pair of argyle socks. "Where'd you get those socks?" the captain asked.

"Dime store, Cap."

"They're not regulation, Smoliss. Black is regulation."

"Yeah, but Cap, they don't show in the car."

"DON'T YOU GET OUT OF YOUR CAR?"

"Get out of my car?" Smoliss looked confused. The captain realized he shouldn't have used such big words.

One officer passed inspection, and to his annoyance, it was the female: Mary Rob Maki, standing at crisp attention, gut sucked in, chest stuck out. He almost bumped into her twin booms as he passed. Goddamn broad was a menace to navigation. Momentarily he thought of Agate, waiting at home, and suppressed a sigh. Mrs. Julius Singletary sagged a little, to be honest maybe six or eight inches, but the stuff was still there, she just had to prop it up a bit when they went to parties. His palms tingled. Tonight, when he got home . . .

But first he had to deliver one of his patented inspirational addresses. "Efficiency's way down," he began, pacing back and forth in front of the line. "Some of you, uh, people, anything you do takes an hour. Sixty minutes minimum! *Phnfff!* Don't deny it!" Nobody did. Most of them stood like upright mummies, faces set in plaster. He glowered at the floor and went on: "You're *so* damn slow! Why, I've clocked you two hours on a simple burglary report, and if you get involved in anything on-view, it's half a shift lost. *Yale!* Half a shift! *Phnfff!"* A pungent odor wafted to his nostrils. Smoliss had struck again. No wonder the men called him Smelis and refused to ride with him. The captain walked to the other end of the row. "Now why this slowness? *Why?* I'll tell you why! *Phnfff!* The first half of the time is spent on the case. The second half is spent, uh, goofing off. You don't clear till long after you're finished, and *you* know it and *I* know it! *Phnfff!* You sit in the coffee shop for an hour writing paper and gossiping with two other cops doing the same thing. Now—this—will—stop! *Phnfff!"*

He looked up and down the line of wronged faces, each projecting the message that the captain was absolutely correct and the other officers should mend their ways. "That's all, Lieutenant!" he said, and turned smartly on his heel, scraping the toe of his tassled loafers on the worn wooden floor.

"Take your posts!" the watch commander's voice barked behind him.

Back in his office, he punched the intercom and summoned Packer Lind. "You taking care of the personnel problems?" he asked.

"What ones you mean, Skip?" the big lieutenant asked.

"Well, for one, that little dipshit Siegl."

"Oh, Artie. Yeah, I'm taking care of him."

"What about the Greeks?"

"Greeks?"

Jesus Jones, didn't the guy understand anything? You had to repeat and repeat. "Yale. The queers. Twelfth and Pomander. Squad car. *Your* watch, *your* men. What's the matter, you losing your—"

"I'm working on it, Cap. Gimme a while."

"A while? What's the problem? You only got so many men, you only got so many cars, you only—"

"It could've been any green-and-white in town, Skipper. Not just the Ninth. That's—how many? Ninety, ninety-five cars? I can't question every cop was on patrol last night."

"Why not?" It sounded as though the W.C. was trying to weasel out of the assignment. Well, he couldn't blame the poor boob. Imagine two of your men loving it up in a squad car. Sick. *Sick!* He'd lay a bet one of them was the rook. A frizzy, for God's sake. Next thing you knew, they'd be showing up in wedgies.

"I'll run it down, Skip. Just let me do it my own way. Another shift, maybe two at the most. I'll lay the whole thing in your lap, one way or the other."

"I'll be waiting." He shoved the press advisory at the lieutenant and said, "Whattaya think of this?"

Packer Lind hefted the release in his hand as though evaluating it by weight, like bologna. "What's to think about it, Cap? Headquarters puts out a release for any capital crime, right? Girl died of multiple hyoid fractures, wasn't that it? Strangulation murder. Routine case for the dicks. Or am I wrong?" He talked as though the subject disturbed him.

"You're right—you're wrong," the captain said. "Now listen close." He enjoyed the feeling of springing a surprise. Usually it was the other way around, with the lieutenant supplying the inside story to the precinct commander. "I had a call from the top," he said, lowering his voice conspiratorially.

"The top?"

"*You* know." The captain leaned forward and almost whispered. "Himself talked it over with the coroner and they decided to leave some of the facts out of the press release."

"Such as?"

"Such as this is no simple strangulation murder. The autopsy showed the girl was, uh, she was violated. She was—tortured."

"Why leave it out of the release, Skip?"

"Because we don't want the media to know the gory details. The public would shit. Old ladies'd pass out. Plus we got to hold back a few points so we can match other sex cases for M.O."

The lieutenant nodded as though he understood. It was standard procedure to withhold some intimate details of a major crime; made it easier to screen out the crazies who always lined up to confess.

"What was left out?" Lind asked, still not looking especially interested. "I started to read the protocol, but I was interrupted."

"You won't believe it," the captain said, savoring the moment.

"Skip, I'm the guy found the Schultz woman with the American flag up her ass, remember?"

"Would you believe—sulphuric acid?"

"Sulphuric—*acid?*"

The captain paused again. It wasn't always this easy to shock policemen, especially supervisors. "Sulphuric acid," he repeated. "Regular car-battery fluid, full strength."

The watch commander's blue eyes closed hard. "Cap, you're not telling me—"

"That's exactly what I'm telling you. Poured a whole goddamn bottle down her throat."

"Jesus."

"That's what the deputy medical examiner said, too. 'Jesus.' Another young wise-ass, fresh outa medical school. Unflappable, you know? But not this time. Said the tongue and throat were eaten away, lung tissue, whole upper G.I. tract turned to mush."

"The smell," Lind said, shielding his eyebrows as though from a bright light. "That must have been the smell."

"What smell?"

"When we went in. Like—like disinfectant. We thought maybe she'd just cleaned her apartment, or fumigated it."

"Didn't anybody look down her throat?"

"Not while I was there."

"No mouth-to-mouth either?"

"No. Good thing, too. With all that acid."

"How come no mouth-to-mouth?"

"The aidmen came in right behind us. They used those plastic breathers. Wrapped her up pretty fast, the way I hear." He looked at the ceiling. "Terrible thing, Skip. Terrible."

"Yale. A certified whacko woman-hater, and he's loose in our precinct and Christ knows where he'll hit next. We can thank your Artie Siegl for that. You said you were—"

"Taking care of it, yop."

"Now look. The lid's on the acid number. Tell your men to keep it that way. Homicide dicks're all over Stanton Park, chief even specialed some extra men from Robbery. If this guy's M.O. gets out, Precinct Nine is finished. First they'll lynch that goddamn Siegl and then they'll take after the rest of us. Starting with you and me. *Phnfff!*"

The lieutenant mumbled something.

"What?" the captain asked.

"I said that's my neighborhood where it happened. Stanton Park. We live about a mile from the house."

"I know where you live. You *still* don't know about the acid, understand? Don't tell your neighbors, don't tell your wife—"

"I guarantee I won't tell my wife."

"Don't tell *anybody! Phnfff!* And for God's sake, Lieutenant, next time you handle a case like this, don't send a lightweight to make the arrest. Send the best you got, send backup and more backup, the Hundred and Second Airborne if you can get 'em. Don't leave it in the hands of an Artie Siegl, for God's sake."

"Cap, I didn't leave it—"

"Shape your watch up, Lind, that's all I ask. You used to be a competent supervisor. I don't know what's got into you lately."

The W.C. looked pained. Probably hurt the poor guy's feelings. Too bad. There was more at stake than one yay-hoo's feelings. Captain Julius Singletary had to survive exactly thirty-nine more weeks to qualify for retirement at 75 percent of base pay. Then bye-bye Cul-de-sac Lane and hello Baja California. A couple of his old cronies already lived there like archdukes.

"You finished the lecture, Captain?"

"Yale. That's it—for now." He tried to smile. "Do your job, Packer! *Phnfff!* That's all I ever asked."

"That's all I ever did," the lieutenant said over his massive shoulder. He walked out the door and slammed it so hard the walls shook.

Let him go, let him go, the captain said to himself with a shrug. You can't push too hard on supervisors, not in this hot weather. You depend too much on them; they can screw you up good and proper. You have to keep the fear of God in them and still be friendly, that's the formula.

Thank Christ he didn't have to work with these yay-hoos much longer.

22

"... And when you're on a traffic stop, never stick your head inside the car window," Billy Mains was telling his partner. "That's a good way to get a free ride."

Mary Rob Maki turned in his direction and her medium-length auburn hair swirled around her face. Her big emerald eyes told him she was sucking up every word. Silly bitch. Didn't they teach 'em anything at the academy anymore? This stuff was basic.

"A free ride?" she repeated in her soft voice, eyelashes fluttering as he steered the patrol car between a truck and a taxi and headed onto Hudson Avenue.

"They can touch a button and roll up the window on your neck like— *that!* Happened to a cop I read about once. A spook—I mean a black dude closed the window on him and emptied a forty-four magnum up his nose."

"Dead?" Her mouth hung open now, revealing a hot-pink tongue about three inches long. His ass tightened on the seat.

"Raw meat!" he answered. He wished to God they were anywhere but in a prowl car.

"Shot him over a routine traffic stop?"

"The dude had a D.B. under a blanket. That's what you always got to remember. There's no such thing as a routine T.V. stop."

"T.V. stop?"

Jesus Christ, this ginch was dumber than Smoliss. "T.V. Traffic violation." He tried not to sound superior. That would come later, after he got her out of her clothes.

"Oh, I knew what *T.V.* meant," she said, tapping him playfully on the service stripes. "It's just—there's *so* much to remember."

"Well, you're coming along." He used his most approving tone. She was coming along, all right. She'd be coming along on his waterbed before noon.

They had cruised their district for several hours now, handling a series of boring, routine calls. "I just want to learn *everything* about *everything*," she'd said at the start, and he had fought to keep from laughing out loud.

"Stick with me," he'd said, arranging his face into a smile.

Their latest customer had been an aged black woman, so short she could hardly see over the dash of her Studebaker. He'd laid on the courtesy with a power shovel. "Evening, ma'am, may I see your license and registration, please?"

"Glory, glory, what I did?" The plastic cherries on the old woman's hat clicked together like snooker balls.

He glanced to the side to make sure that Maki was watching closely. "You failed to yield the right of way, ma'am, and that's a no-no."

The woman tittered nervously. Her dried-up fingers shook as she produced a wallet that was worn so slick he could see his face in it.

He held up his hands in feigned shock as though he would *never* touch anybody's wallet. "You wanna take out the license and registration for me?" He looked them over with a studious expression, then smiled into the woman's weather-beaten face. "Mizz James, you still living at Two One Three Four Meridian?"

"Y-y-yas sir."

"You wanna tell me what happened?" Christ, his partner was standing there wiggy with admiration. He was handling this piss-ant stop like a Chinese diplomat. That was the way to make time with a dedicated ginch like Maki. Overwhelm her with professionalism. Stay cool, detached. Hit on her—by not hitting on her! Genius!

"Well, I was fixin' to slide over one lane," the old woman said, looking everywhere but into his amber-goggled eyes. "I didn't see no cars coming, so I—" She pulled out a big white handkerchief and slid one tip under the side of her wire-rimmed glasses.

Maki reached in to offer a pat of comfort, but he motioned her back, winking lightly as though to convey that he had a textbook reason for his detached approach and he'd explain it later.

"Didn't see no cars coming," the woman repeated, sniffling. "So I pult on over."

"I see," he said in a judicial tone. "Well, I'm afraid you almost caused an accident there, missus."

Her voice went squeaky. "But, Officer, they wasn't no car coming—"

"No, ma'am," he interrupted firmly. "There weren't any cars in ɩ lane when you moved into it. Just a bus."

"A bus?" The old woman's face dropped and she tilted her face away. "A—*bus?*"

"Yes, ma'am," he said. "Now if I might suggest, missus, the next time you change lanes, look carefully. Make sure the lane's absolutely clear. Okay, ma'am?"

"Yas, sir," the woman said. "Does you has to gimme a ticket, Officer?"

He looked sideways at the redhead. He prided himself on knowing how to handle spades; Mary Rob Maki couldn't help but be impressed.

"Tell ya what, ma'am," he said sweetly. "Me and my partner here, we're in a pretty good mood tonight. Right, pard?"

"Eh—true," Maki said, gulping.

"So we're gonna give you a pass, ma'am. You just drive carefully now. Okay, mama?"

The birdlike face broke into a toothless smile. "Lordy mercy, Officer, Gawd bless *you!*" She started the engine and called out, "The Good Book say, 'Go and sin no more.'" She cackled loudly and revved the old clunk's engine up to about 5,000 rpm's. "Gawd bless you too, miss." Then she shot into the street without looking and bumped along the lane divider till she was out of sight.

Back in the green-and-white, Billy noticed that his partner was scribbling. "Don't log that stop," he said. "If you log too many, they expect it every night. Just leave it 'general patrol,' something like that."

"I wasn't logging," she said. "I was just—making a note."

"Making a note? What for?" He looked over and saw a small blue pad.

"I, uh, just make notes once in a while. So I'll remember. That was nice."

"Nice?"

"The way you handled that old lady."

"Thanks. Well, I oughta learnt something. Fourteen years. If a guy don't learn how to handle a T.V. in fourteen years—"

"Some never learn."

"Well, yeah," he said modestly.

He went into his motivated-career-cop act, driving in and out of traffic with one hand on the wheel and the other reaching down occasionally to adjust the radio, as though the entire metropolis would be in mortal jeopardy if David Three were to miss a call. He eased the car over toward his old waterfront district, along the bumpy railroad crossings and spurs, through a shadowed area of corrugated sheds and warehouses, past lines of empty cargo vans stacked three deep. He slowed the car to a crawl past the side fence of the old steel mill, now beginning its second century of tinting the night air scarlet, and detoured around the rolls of blued ribbon steel stacked by the private road. A mangy mutt appeared in their headlights and he resisted an urge to speed up and put a little excitement into their lives, but instead he swerved the car into a loading area where stacks of ship's piping turned green in racks and scrap-metal cubes were stacked in tall pyramids and a fleet of new Toyota pickups covered a space the size of a football field.

He was just starting to show his partner the dock where he'd shot it out with the Mafia hijackers when they caught another radio call. A dead kid, nineteen or twenty, a stone suicide. No note, but three different sleeping-pill bottles, all empty. The super had found the body after he heard the kid's gray tiger cat yowling outside.

For once, a D.B. call was painless. No muss, no stink, no bother, and the coroner's assistant hurried in with his smelly cigar and took over. "Off we go in the heat of the night," Billy said with relief as they resumed their patrol.

Mary Rob was quiet, huddled in the corner, her nyloned knees drawn up.

"Did that get to you a little?" he asked softly. Her position was giving him a hard-on.

"A little," she admitted, turning away. "He was just—a boy. Lying on his bed like that. So—dead."

Well, the ginch was certainly observant. Usually when the heart's stopped and there's a big wet circle around the crotch and the mouth's wide open and the arms and legs are as stiff as reinforced concrete— usually that's a fair indication the dude is dead. She was sharp, all right. He bit back the sarcastic remarks he felt like making and said, "You'll get used to it. Take my word. This one was a snap anyway. Empty bottles all around, victim not dead long enough to, uh, give off any, uh, aroma. You take last week, we had one—"

"That thing on his face," she said in a queasy voice.

"The birthmark?"

"Yes. Port-wine stain, I think they call it. Sad."

"Yeah," he echoed. What the fuck, if she thought it was sad, he'd go

[151]

along. Personally he had other things on his mind. A D.B. was garbage, old meat; the sooner you forgot about it, the better.

"I thought they could remove birthmarks like that," she was saying. "Cosmetic surgery? Something like—surgical tattooing?"

"Not when the stain covers half the face," he explained in his role as senior partner. "A little splotch here and there, yeah, they can hide it." He didn't have the slightest idea what he was talking about, but she'd never know. He let her brood awhile. Women were moody anyway, even when they didn't have their periods. She knew where to go if she needed comfort.

He heard the call and spun a tight doughnut. "Hey!" she yelped, reaching up and grabbing at her hat as the centrifugal force jammed her against the door.

"We just caught a Two Four One," he said crisply. "Family disturbance. See the woman Thirty Six Forty Seven Jackson. Write that down, will ya?"

Maki grabbed for the mike and acknowledged the call as he floored the gas and flipped on the siren and lights.

Goddamn, this must be black, he said to himself. There wasn't a white family within a half mile of the 3600 block of Jackson. The whole neighborhood was solid spook. On hot nights they spilled from their shotgun houses and wined it up in the streets and some of the hotter bloods would blow a little dust and go out and gang-bang one of the black sisters or stick up a liquor store. Tradition. And if you tried to make an arrest the word went out like a conference call and pretty soon you were up to your ass in dinges. Well, they'd better not fuck with Billy Mains. He tapped his pockets and felt the saps: palm and knuckle. His Mace can was charged. His ebony nightstick was cored with lead, and his .38 service revolver was loaded with 200-grain dumdums backed up by another dozen rounds in a pair of auto-loaders on his belt. Let the Nigerians revolt; they'd piss their loincloths when they saw who drove up.

The dark unpainted bungalow sat behind a sagging broken-toothed fence. Someone had decorated a spindly dead maple with lids from tin cans; empty pint bottles dangled from several branches and reflected the revolving lights from their Visibar. There was no sign of life from the house. "Over here," a small voice whispered. "Over here, polices, please."

A skinny girl of about fifteen slipped from behind a withered bush. "It's my mama," she said. "Somebody gotta help me, mister. Oh, *please!*" Her eyes rolled in their sockets like marbles. Typical scared spook, right out of a 1950s movie.

Maki stepped in front of Billy and put her arm around the trembling girl. "What is it?" she asked. "What's the matter with your, uh, your, mama."

"C'mon now, talk up, kid," he put in, backing his partner. You had to be firm from the beginning; otherwise they walked all over you. The new cop would learn.

"She sorry," the child said. "She real sorry tonight." He noticed that the girl had Rastafarian braids on her head like little black snakes. Well, your spook chicks didn't have much to do with their time. Just make the regular circuit from the welfare office to the liquor store, drop down to Grand Street to shoplift a few groceries and drugstore items, maybe visit the boy friend and do some weed and get fucked in the ass, and then back to the welfare office again. Christ knew none of them worked. What was the unemployment figure for young blacks: 40 percent, 50 percent? Closer to 100 percent, he figured, except in prison laundries.

"She gone hurt herse'f." The girl started to sob. "Oh, I be so scairt she gone hurt herse'f." She covered her mouth with a slender brown hand. "Pass on inside, y'all can hear for yourse'fs. Got to hush, though. Mama—you cain't never be sure"—she stifled another sob—"cain't never be sure what Mama gone do."

The girl led the way into a darkened living room, proportioned for pigmies. Everything was cheap and undersized, the sofa only two pillows wide with bare springs sticking out, and three small chairs without backs grouped around a drooping card table. The heat hit Billy like a fist, and he took a deep breath. "Listen," the child said.

At first he heard nothing. Then his ears picked up a baby's cry, followed by a woman's gentle voice. "Dahlin'," the voice cooed. "My sweet dahlin'." She began to sing: "La la la la, la la la la bye bye, do you want the moon to play wiv . . .?" The voice trailed off and the baby began to make gurgling sounds, giggling and laughing and then saying clearly, "Mama," mouthing it the way spooks did, so that it sounded like "Ma-oo-mah, Ma-oo-mah." Christ, it was late for a baby to be up. That was another thing about the colored: they had no sense of time. Sleep all day and play all night, it didn't matter. He remembered an old Artie Siegl punch line: "Yeah, but what's time to a pig?" Fun-*ny!* What's time to a pig?

"All right, miss, what's the problem here?" Billy said in his no-nonsense tone. He didn't want to spend the whole night in this dinge house; he'd never been able to stomach the smell of their leftovers, always kidded Willie Bethea that soul food was mule's assholes and chopped pig dicks, fricasseed till tender, basted with goat come.

"Wait," the girl said, holding a finger up to her thick purple lips. "I'm gone peep in on her now. Y'all jes'—stay back and watch. Please?"

She opened the door on a dimly lighted bedroom. A tall, pipe-thin woman with a loosely bandaged arm stood in the middle of the floor, holding a small box to her ear. Jesus Christ, it was a radio. Goddamn jigs, they were always glued to their radios.

". . . Yo' daddy's in da cotton field," the woman sang. She looked down at the radio lovingly.

"Ma-oo-mah," a baby's voice repeated. Where was the kid?

"Mama right here," the woman said in a surprisingly strong voice, holding the radio up to her cheek. "Mama gone take care of you, sweet thing." She did a little circular dance step. "Mama *always* gone be here, sweet chile. Mama *always* gone be wiv you, angel dawlin'."

The young girl approached slowly and said, "Mama?"

The woman pressed the box against her other ear and did a slow waltz around the room, bumping into the bed and the bureau. "Mama?" the child implored. When there was no response, she tugged at the woman's slip. "Please, Mama! We got company." The woman showed no sign that she'd heard.

The girl walked out of the room and shut the door. "She don't know me no mo'!" she said, burying her face in her hands. "Lawdy Lawd, my mama don't know me no mo'. What can I do?"

"You the complaining party?" Billy asked.

Mary Rob Maki whispered, "Let me!" She knelt and held the girl about the tiny waist. In a few minutes the story came tumbling out. The woman's son Arthur had died at fifteen months. The family had a tape recording that had been made on Arthur's birthday. The mother played it constantly, wouldn't give up the cheap tape recorder, spent part of her welfare money on batteries, hardly ate and hardly slept and didn't—didn't take care of herself. Tonight she had hacked at her upper arm with a bread knife. The daughter had wrapped the wound in a dish towel to stop the bleeding.

"And then you called Nine One One?" Maki said in a sweet voice.

"Yes'm."

"Good for you. That showed good judgment." She was running the show now. Well, let her handle it. If she liked to get tight with spooks, she was in the right district. She could throw away her .38 and do social work for the rest of her life. If you can stand the smell, you got it licked. Another Artie Siegl line. . . .

It took thirty-five minutes for the wagon to arrive and take the woman away, still conversing with her tape recorder, and another thirty minutes to round up an auntie to look after the sobbing young girl. Saying good-bye, Maki kissed the kid lightly on the lips. Jesus Christ! He couldn't wait to tell the guys. Kissing a spook on the lips! Policewomen! Now he was surer than ever where they belonged: on their backs or on their knees. But *not* on patrol.

The radio crackled again. "Any car vicinity David Three district. A D.B. at Six Oh Eight Gaylen Avenue."

Maki grabbed for the microphone, but Billy said, "No! Chrisakes, don't touch that damn thing."

"Why not?"

"One a night's enough. We need an upper, not a downer." He forced a laugh. Maki looked pissed. Tough shit. She'd have to learn you couldn't lap up every call in the district, you'd go off your gourd with two-bit burglaries and break-ins and barroom fights and worst of all those goddamn D.B.s with their clay faces and the howling relatives and the stink that stayed with your uniform through two or three cleanings. "Besides," he added, trying to sound businesslike, "we haven't cleared on the family disturbance yet. That's why Radio's looking for somebody to handle our D.B."

"Well, I don't see why we don't take it. It's our district. Won't the sergeant . . .?"

"Molnar? He could care."

The slow voice of Ernie Smoliss cut in over the radio. "David Five. Responding to Gaylen Avenue."

"Perfect," Billy said to his partner. "A D.B. handles a D.B. That's what I call fair. Now we can clear." He motioned toward the microphone.

"David Three," the policewoman said. "Clear on the Two Four One."

"David Three," the dispatcher replied. "Meet your lieutenant at the station."

The watch commander was tapping his big foot when they walked in. "Mains," he said, "I want to see you alone." Good, Billy thought. A special assignment.

"You could start on the paper," he suggested to his partner. She was already heading for the typewriter, a blank report rippling in her hand.

He followed the W.C. into the little office. "Siddown!" the lieutenant snapped. He didn't sound overly friendly. Well, the guy was under pressure, you had to make allowances. He clomped around the desk and began talking from a stand-up position, and Billy couldn't believe the words that came out. "I *know* what you been doing and I want it stopped right now. *Tonight!* Goddamn it, Mains, *clean up your act!*"

All he could manage was a strangled "What?" while he tried to decide what the brass had on him now. There was the kinky switchboard operator at headquarters, but nobody knew about that; sometimes they got together at her apartment, and besides it was nobody's business what the two of them did off-shift, or in what position. There was the secretary in the Safe and Loft squad, married to a sailor overseas, but that little deal was over. They hadn't screwed in a month; she was such a fucking bore. Likewise with the meter maid downtown. Came too fast—no challenge. It was like turning on a faucet. Let's see—there was . . .

Darlene Yount.

Jesus Christ, they'd found out about Darlene! Gerry Yount must of copped. Or else she came back and snitched. Maybe she made an official beef. But *why?* Oh, my ass! This—is—*bad.*

". . . Don't sit there and play dumb," Lind was saying. "You were made, and you were made *good.* A very reliable witness. Jesus, Bill, I thought you had better sense. How the Christ could you do a thing like that? You realize the spot you got me in?"

"Pack, I didn't—"

"How many beefs you think I can ride for one guy? Huh? Answer me that! You got the captain on my ass, you got half the dispatchers running around laughing at us, you got the whole watch downgraded."

"Look, Packer—"

"I mean, I always knew you'd fuck a fire hose, but *in the front seat of a prowl car? At a busy intersection? In uniform?* I think you've gone soft in the head, man. You—you're—mental!"

Billy took a deep breath and rolled his eyes. Somebody was mental, all right. The last time he'd screwed in a patrol car was twelve, thirteen years ago on the Pier 18 parking ramp, and it wasn't a screw, it was a blow job, and the broad pulled away too soon, which was exactly why he didn't mess around in cars anymore.

"Lieutenant," he said, "I don't know what you're talking about. What's that suppose to mean, 'the front seat of a prowl car'? Who? When? *Me? Never me. Never!"*

The W.C. shook his shaggy head slowly and ran the back of his hand across his forehead, beaded with sweat like a fresh-waxed car in the rain. "I can't believe it. One of my best men shining me on. Didn't you hear what I said? *Somebody made you, Mains.* A respectable business-man, on his way home from a meeting. He saw the uniforms, thought it was a couple queer cops. Twelfth and Pomander. Midnight. You were the only car within miles, for God's sake. It *had* to be you, man! You and—your partner."

Billy managed a smile, trying to show how laughable the accusation was. It was almost enjoyable to be in such a righteous position, to sit here listening to the riot act and for once to be completely in the clear. *Of all the pussy Lind could have mentioned, he brings up the one broad that I haven't even held her hand yet! How righteous can you get?*

"I'm gonna file on this," the watch commander was saying. "I didn't intend to, but if you're not gonna cooperate—"

"Cooperate?" he said. "Hey, what kinda number you doing on me? Is this somebody's idea of a joke? Huh? Listen, *nothing* like that happened. Hey, you're not even close!"

The lieutenant's blue eyes narrowed and darkened; he lowered his heavy head and raised one eyebrow. "Then what *did* happen?"

"You said Twelfth and Pine?"

"Pomander."

He tried to think back. Last night he'd stuck to his strong, silent role, hadn't said much of anything, just drove around the district showing her the ropes, letting her watch an old pro in action. "What time last night?"

Lind had a sheet of paper in front of him. "Midnight," he read.

"Who's your snitch?"

"Never mind. A businessman, that's all. Drove by, saw the two of you humping away on the front seat."

Impossible. Impossible! "Twelfth and Pine?"

"Pomander I told you."

Billy shut his eyes tightly and screwed up his face till his upper lip touched his nose. He had taken the wheel right after roll call. They had stopped for a 931 around 11:30. By midnight, they were—by God, they *had* been at Twelfth and Pomander around then. "Oh, Christ, what a relief," he said. "Twelfth and Pomander. Sure, Packer, sure. That's where I pulled over and told the broad she could drive awhile. She was so excited, Pack, ya know, barely out of the academy and all? She started to get out and walk around the car, and I told her—I just, uh, told her to scoot over my, uh, my lap instead of wasting time getting out and, uh, going around, so—"

"So?" The lieutenant looked annoyed.

"So she did."

Lind nodded his head and said, "Sure. Sure. And how long did it take her to scoot over your dick—I mean, your lap? Five minutes? Ten minutes? Maybe a half hour?"

"Packer! Jeez, you never believe a guy, do ya?" He tried to sound hurt, victimized. It could be turned to his own advantage later, when the truth came out. "Took about two seconds. Swear to God, Pack, *two or three seconds!* That must of been when the snitch was driving by. Hey, call her in! She'll tell ya."

"I'm not calling her in, you simple shit," the lieutenant said through jaws that tightened as though he were chewing wood. "I'm not a goddamn den mother. I'm running a watch, Mains. If you get your nuts in a crack on official duty, I'll back you all the way. But anybody that plays stinky pinky in a patrol car—"

"Packer, you know me better than that!"

"I know you. That's the problem."

"Aw, Jeez." He felt a noose tightening around his neck. Two harness bulls screwing in a patrol car. What was that old expression? Hanged for a sheep? He was being hanged for a jerk. Fucked without benefit of a kiss. Him, Billy Mains, of all people. And never more righteous in his life. . . .

"You're still denying it?"

"Look, Lieutenant, I hate to say this, I hate to embarrass my, uh, partner, but the only way we're gonna square this beef is bring her in. Go ahead. She'll tell ya. She's not afraid to talk up."

Lind made a chirping noise with the side of his mouth. "That's the way you want it?"

Billy nodded.

"Okay." The W.C. snapped the intercom. "Send in Officer Maki."

There was a charged moment between the two men. "Packer," Billy said, breaking the silence, "I—"

"Button up, Bill. And keep it buttoned when she comes in."

"Yes, Lieutenant?" the red-haired policewoman said as she glided into the room.

"Where were you, uh, last night, uh, around midnight?" Lind said, looking wildly about the room. "I mean, ar uh, with respect to, I mean in the vicinity of, om uh, Twelfth and Pine."

"Pomander," Billy corrected.

"Om, uh, yeah. Twelfth and Pomander." A line of sweat tracked from Lind's tousled hairline all the way to his chin. Let the fucker squirm, Billy said to himself. Let him sweat himself the way he's sweating me. And all about—nothing. A bum rap. Somebody would hear plenty about this.

"May I check the log, sir?" Maki asked. Look at her, Billy thought: smiling, innocent, just like me. And naïve. Poor bitch don't know the fix is in, somebody's greased it for us pretty good.

"No," Packer said. "Go ahead and use your memory. Now, uh, think back. Twelfth and Pomander. Midnight."

Maki tucked a frond of dark red hair behind her ear and frowned.

"Let me see now. Twelfth and—Oh, isn't that where we changed seats?"

Billy started to respond, but the W.C. said, "Dummy up, Bill! You changed sides, huh? And just exactly, uh, how did you change sides?"

"I slid across," she said.

"Slid across the seat?"

"Well, no, sir, I didn't exactly slide. I had to sort of, oh, eh, lift up and over my partner." She paused; her green eyes narrowed, and her mouth fell open. "Lieutenant, you don't mean . . .? You're not suggesting . . .?" She turned and looked at Billy, and he shrugged and lifted his shoulders.

Packer Lind held up one hand and then rubbed his eyes. "What time did you say you changed?" he asked in a low voice.

"Lieutenant, if it really matters, sir, I can show you on the log," Maki said, looking puzzled.

"Go ahead."

She came back in with her finger on an entry. *Ptn. Maki driving. 0002 Hours.* "I remember writing it," she said hesitantly. "I was, sort of— proud."

The watch commander hid his big face in his big hands. He spun around in his chair and faced the wall. Then Billy heard a distinct burp. No, it was a half-swallowed cough. When Lind turned toward them again, he was dead-pan.

"Both of you," he said, "pay attention. Do I ask too much of you? Of any of my men—my officers? Tell me that. No, don't answer! Now I'm asking one thing, one little thing. Okay? *One little thing?*" His voice had changed from stern to annoyed to pleading.

"Yes, sir," Maki said eagerly.

"The next time you switch seats?"

"Yeah?" Billy said.

"Get out and walk around!"

"Sure," Billy said. "Why not? If it'll make you happy." He looked over at Mary Rob. She was making notes again.

23

For a while after they left, Packer stared at his dull-green wall and thought of the joke about the sign at the nudist camp: ANYONE PLAYING LEAP FROG MUST COMPLETE THE JUMP. God, it must be a bitch of a job to be Billy Mains! Sixteen hours a day chasing tail, and then getting in trouble the one time you're innocent.

He thought about calling home: Amnee could use a giggle. But it was after eleven, she might be in bed, and anyway she had asked him not to call tonight, the ring of the telephone would just make her nervous.

Now hold on there, Packer told himself. Just wait—one—damn—minute. Suppose she needs some encouragement? Suppose she's still rattled about this afternoon? I'll just—

He dialed the first four numbers, then picked up his portable radio instead. "Two Two Three to David One."

"David One," Willie Bethea's resonant voice came in.

"What's your location?"

"Southbound on Washington, approaching, eh, Amethyst."

A block from his house. They must have just rolled past. He'd asked them to check hourly; that meant they'd drive by every twenty or thirty minutes, if he knew Rollie Beemer and Willie B. "Received," he said, and added, "Thanks." The other cars would think he was going soft in his old age, thanking a team on the air.

A long time ago he had learned not to sit around brooding about problems. "Just list 'em up and knock 'em off," his old gunny sergeant used to say. His big feet up on his desk, Packer listed 'em up:

Problem No. 1: Amnee's caller. A case of female hysteria, not that he blamed her. That problem would dry up and blow away, as long as she refused to respond to the nut.

Problem No. 2: Billy Mains and the redhead. Another big nothing. Packer prided himself on reading faces, and he knew Mary Rob Maki had told the truth. There'd been no "fruit cops" getting it on at Twelfth and Wherever it Was; some nosy motorist had jumped to a wrong conclusion; there was a lot of that these days, especially where cops were concerned.

Problem No. 3: A crazy killer loose in the precinct. Well, this one might turn out to be a continuing problem and then again it might evaporate. The dude might be long gone. But if he *wasn't*—Packer rubbed his boxy chin ruefully and twisted his reconstructed nose to the side—if the psycho hit again, every cop in Precinct Nine might as well throw his badge in the drink like the policeman's eternal hero, Dirty Harry Callahan. The whole city knew that a Precinct Nine patrol cop had had the guy square in his sights. . . .

Which brought up:

Problem No. 4: The case of Artie Siegl.

Packer looked at the clock: 11:50 P.M. In ten minutes he was supposed to meet Manuel Garibay, the master mechanic. He grabbed his radio and hurried out, then doubled back and fumbled in his bottom drawer next to a bottle of Canadian Club he kept to console cops who had drawn blood. Ah, there it was! A small hard-leather case that looked like a cosmetics kit. He hadn't used his lock-picking outfit since his short stint with Safe and Loft, seven or eight years back. He ran his thumbs across the pads of his thick fingers. Gnarled and calloused: as sensitive as an elephant's toenail. Too much hole-digging and yard work; he'd have to tell Amnee to let up on him. Christ, he could barely pick his nose, let alone a police lock. . . .

Behind a cigarette's glow, Manuel Garibay was waiting in his car a block from the police garage. Packer eased his Fury into the shadows and called, "Ready, Manuel?"

The little Mexican flipped the butt away and climbed out of his Trans-Am Pontiac with the chrome air filters. Typical mechanic's wheels, Packer noticed. Could have bought a lot of frijoles with the money that went into that package of power. "Anytheen jew say, Mr. Packer," Manuel answered.

"Climb in my trunk, pal."

"Een—jor trunk?"

"Right." Packer stood to one side and stretched out his palm, like a butler ushering an honored guest.

"Mr. Packer," the mechanic said, his dark eyes trained on the stars, "no can do eet. Have close—closetro—how jew say eet? Closetro—"

"Claustrophobia?"

"Closetrophobia! *Si!* No can be in close place. I get—frighteen."

"Manuel, you're with *me*, buddy. It'll only be for a few minutes."

"No can do eet." He folded his short arms across his chest and shifted his gaze from the stars to his feet.

"Manuel—"

"I know, I *know*. I tol' jew I do anytheen jew say." He sounded annoyed at himself but adamant.

"Then, please, Manuel, *por favor,* get in. It's—important, Manuel. Trust me once."

The Mexican peered inside the open trunk. "What's dot?"

"My evidence kit, police equipment, blank reports, junk. That's a portable generator over there. Get in, Manuel. There's still plenty of room."

"A few meenutes?"

"Five or ten, probably less."

"Jew promeese?"

"My word on it."

The mechanic started to climb inside, then looked back anxiously. Packer said, "A few minutes, that's a promise."

When the little man was curled on the trunk floor, Packer carefully closed the lid. He gunned his unmarked car down the narrow side street and up the ramp to the second floor of the police garage and tucked it into an open stall. He snapped on the blue-white light bar over the work bench and grabbed a box of tools, intentionally making a lot of racket. He had just lifted the Fury's hood when a voice said, "Hey! What's— Oh, it's you, Lieutenant."

"Whattaya say, Frosty? How they hangin'?" Packer stuck out his hand and greeted Sergeant Forrest M. Allen, busy shining his flashlight around the walls, a smile pasted on his sly face. Pay attention, Packer warned himself. Frosty Allen was another survivor, a man in his early fifties with long rodent's teeth and a simpering attitude whenever he spotted the metal bars of rank. Underneath, he was frightened and jumpy and worried like most survivors that any day he would get his ass in a crack and lose out on his pension. The commander of the motor pool, Lieutenant Mike Phelan, attracted these weak sisters like roaches and worked their fears for all he could get, including, Packer suspected, the odd kickback here and there.

Allen gave him a soft handshake and said, "Car trouble, Lieutenant?"

"Frosty, I'll tell ya," he said, abandoning his friendly smile for a faked look of aggravation. "There's a ping in that son-of-a-bitchin' engine and it's been there a month and nobody seems to know how to take it out. Tonight I'm driving around the precinct and all of a sudden I realize the worst noise pollution in town is the knock in my own goddamn engine." He rapped the hood with his heavy hand and said, "So here I am. Where's the timing light? I'm gonna fix this mother if it takes me clear into the first watch."

"Hey, friend, we got experts can do that for you," Allen said, studying Packer's face like an algebra book. "Just bring it in tomorrow."

"I already brought it in, Frosty. Four times now."

"I don't remember no—"

"Always on day watch. Donofrio looked at it. Phelan worked on it himself."

"The lieutenant worked on it?" Allen's expression showed how often the commander of the motor pool dirtied his hands on an engine.

"Yeah. If you can call it work." Packer laughed. "Said it was the distributor, he'd have it fixed in an hour. I picked the car up and drove away and—PING! Hey, Frosty, where's the timing light and the plug wrench and the other stuff?"

"Jeez, Packer, the manual says . . ."

What did it take to get rid of the guy? Usually he prostrated himself before anyone above the rank of sergeant. Maybe there'd been a crackdown, another economy memo from headquarters. A few cops had a habit of sneaking their personal cars into the garage at three o'clock in the morning and performing everything but complete overhauls. Packer had heard rumbles.

The motor-pool sergeant walked alongside the unmarked police car from front to back, stopping to lean over the trunk. Jesus Christ, had he caught on? Had Manuel coughed or something?

"Okay, Lieutenant, seein's it's you," he said, turning sharply. "Let's see, the timing light's over here. I'll unlock the cabinet, that's where the gappers are. We'll tune this thing so fine you can balance a wineglass on the block."

Now the old crock wanted to help! Any second Manuel Garibay would start pounding on the trunk and screaming: Packer had had experience with claustrophobes before, and when they blew, they blew sky-high. "No, no, Frosty," he said. "Let me do it myself. It's a—a challenge, ya know?"

"You really wanta get in the grease?" The old sergeant's smile didn't extend above his lips, but he didn't dare make an issue. Survivors never did. That was how they became survivors.

"Yeah, yeah," Packer said impatiently. "Come on, Frosty, get outa here." He raised his voice to cheer Manuel. "Lemme go to work."

"Okay," the sergeant said, backing off obsequiously, "but if anybody shows, you drove up here on your own and you're working on your own. Deal?"

"Deal."

When the footsteps receded down the concrete staircase, Packer opened the trunk lid and said, "Okay?"

Manuel Garibay spurted out like a jumping bean, staring back at the open trunk as though it had attacked him. "Stay in there a few more minutes," Packer insisted. "I'll leave it unlatched, make you feel better." The mechanic flopped back into the trunk like a sleepwalker, wet brown eyes open wide, thick black hair in rat tails slicked with sweat.

Artie Siegl's wrecked green-and-white lay on a flat-bed trailer behind a double door of heavy cyclone fencing. A new brass Schlage lock secured the hasp. It *would* be a Schlage! Goddamn things were tough. Back in Safe and Loft they used to say it was easier to get into a Sunday-school teacher.

He tried three rakes before he found one that fitted the keyway. He held the rake with one hand and inserted the tension bar with the other, feeling like a garbageman doing surgery, and slid the rake back and forth trying to line up on the pins. Nothing clicked. All new locks were hard to pick, but this one was impossible. Maybe he wasn't pressing hard enough on the tension bar. He bore down, and the pick bent like babbitt metal. Balls! Now both the picks were jammed in the keyway.

Footsteps sounded from the concrete staircase. He scuttled into the lee of his Fury, moving like a raccoon on feet and fingertips. When he reached the opened hood, he raised his head.

"How we coming?" Frosty Allen called from the top of the steps.

"Oh, it's—coming," he answered, slowly rubbing his fingers on the throttle cable to pick up some grease.

"Just wondered. I didn't hear no motor noise."

Christ, the guy was snoopy. Packer imagined him sitting down there analyzing the sounds through the ceiling. Well, it was his own goddamn fault. Nobody can tune a silent engine: he should have remembered that. "Oh," he said, groping about for an explanation that would make sense, "I was looking for—the wrenches. Where the hell . . .?"

"Watch out," Allen said, laughing dryly. "They'll bite ya."

A full set of color-coded wrenches was suspended on a wall rack in front of the car. "Jeez, Frosty, I looked everyplace but straight ahead," he said apologetically. "Thanks."

He jumped inside the car and turned the key. The engine purred. Well, he could explain that away. "It only pings under stress," he would say. But the sergeant was looking around the back of the patrol car again. Christ, he'd noticed the trunk wasn't closed all the way! No, he was attaching the long rubber hose that vented exhaust fumes out the roof. Another stupid oversight. Manuel's wife was already saying one set of novenas.

"Lemme know, you need anything else," Allen said with mock cordiality, strolling toward the stairs and peeking over his sloped shoulder. Thank Christ for leather heels, Packer said to himself. They weren't regulation, but neither was anything else in this gloomy garage. If he hadn't heard those loud footfalls, Sergeant Forrest Allen would have caught him picking the lock, and then what? A midnight shoot-out in the police garage? Hell, no, but there'd have been a ton of trouble. Explanations, reports, maybe a review board; depended on how far the brass wanted to take their goddamn secrecy. What was Artie Siegl's car doing under lock and key anyway? What was there to hide from the man's own watch commander? Why the Christ had they made him a supervisor if they intended to conceal things from him?

Oh, Jesus. Manuel!

Packer yanked up the lid of the trunk. The little mechanic looked ashen. He took a deep breath and raised his arms slowly. "Cramp-ed," he said. "Arms are cramp-ed." He made "cramped" a two-syllable word. He looked scar-ed, too, but he didn't complain.

"Just a few more seconds," Packer said, returning to the jammed lock. He tugged at the twisted tension bar with a heavy pair of pliers and ripped it free. The rake fell out and rattled on the floor. If he'd bent any pins in the Schlage, it would take a hack saw to beat the lock.

The tension bar was beyond repair, but there was a thinner one in his kit. This time he inserted the rake tenderly, the sweat streaming off his forehead, and when he heard a click he bit his tongue and yanked. The lock held.

Maybe this was a new, advanced type of Schlage. He had heard of expensive magnetic locks that were unpickable except with sets of magnetized cobalt picks that cost hundreds of dollars. The city would never authorize a lock that expensive. Not these days. Not with patrol cops running on retreads—

A hand touched his shoulder and he jumped and whirled.

"Manuel!" he said. "Chrisakes—"

The little Mexican nudged him aside gently and grabbed each pick by thumb and index finger and tilted his head about five degrees and popped the lock open in less than a minute.

"How . . .?"

"I juice to work in New Jork," Manuel explained.

Packer gulped and opened the heavy screened door. "That's the car," he said, his heart still bumping his rib cage. "The left front end failed at speed. I need to know why."

"Hwhy?" Manuel said, rubbing his fingers. "Mr. Packer, jew kiddeen me? I can tell you hwhy from here. Front hwheel come off."

"*Sshhhh!* Keep it down, Manny. Listen, I know the wheel came off. But that was *after* he lost control. Something went wrong before that."

"Hwheel came off . . .?"

"In a spin-out. After the driver already lost control."

"*Comprendo.*" He shook his head knowingly. "Now jew wan' know hwhat hoppen—"

"What made him lose it in the first place, right! Now listen. Be as quick as you can. I'll be working on my car."

"Uh-kay." The Mexican sounded hesitant. Maybe watch commanders didn't smuggle mechanics into police garages at midnight in Guadalajara. Then he shrugged and turned toward the wrecked green-and-white.

For ten minutes Packer leaned over his own humming engine. He lifted the oil filter and the air filter and blocked the choke till the car almost quit breathing, then worked the throttle rod in and out to vary the sound. He killed the engine and fired it up again, then began shorting the plug leads to the block one by one to change the engine rhythms that he suspected were being monitored at the foot of the stairs. He had just tightened the number two plug when Manuel asked for a flashlight.

Packer handed over his six-cell Kellite and the mechanic padded back toward the stall. A few minutes later he beckoned Packer to join him. The Mexican was focusing the beam tight on the bare left-front wheel drum. The five threaded lug bolts stood out sharply in the light. "Feel," he said.

Packer grabbed a bolt and quickly pulled his fingers back. The threads were rough and irregular, like a file.

"See?" Manuel said. "Next one ees same. And deese one too. T'ree bolts. Stree-ped."

"Stree-ped?"

"Stree-ped? Stree-ped. *Como se dice?*"

"Stripped?" Packer said. "Sure they're stripped. They were stripped when the wheel went. The lug nuts ripped right across the threads, tore 'em up. So what?"

The mechanic pointed to the two remaining bolts. "*Mira!* Touch!" Packer felt them. They were unblemished, smooth. "Hwhy deese two not streep-ed?" Manuel asked, lowering his voice like a Mexican revolutionary. "Ees seemple. Was no lug nuts on deese two in first place. Hwheel was mounted weeth t'ree—"

"With three nuts instead of five?" Packer asked, slightly confused.

"*Correcto.*"

"So—"

"Dee hwheel fly off. *Ay Chihuahua!* Hwhat kind of mechaneecs jew got, send jew out to chase *criminales* weeth two nuts meesing?"

Packer touched the bolts again. No tight steel grip had ever torn across these threads. "But they said the wheel popped off because the car slid sideways," he insisted to Manuel.

"Someone ees ly-een."

"Ly-een?"

"Makeen up story. *Ly-een.* Jew can see weeth jor own eyes hwhat makes hwheel fly off. Ees driver alive?"

"He's home sleeping."

"*Madre de Dios.* Ees a miracle." Manuel Garibay crossed himself.

Packer's mind raced ahead. Did lug nuts ever loosen and fall off accidentally? He'd never heard of one coming loose, let alone a pair on the same wheel. . . .

"Okay, Manny, climb back in the trunk and let's get outa here," he said. "You'll be home in a few minutes."

The mechanic wrung his leathery hands. *"Una mas* miracle," he said.

Packer eased the trunk lid down till it clicked. He was settling into the driver's seat when the howler sounded in the distance. A chase. The noise grew louder, switched from howl to hi-lo to siren and back to a screaming howl. Must be passing right under the window, Packer said to himself. He started to pocket his lock kit and suddenly realized the chase car had entered the building. He ducked instinctively as the intruding car shot up the ramp and skidded ninety degrees to a stop directly behind him, blue lights spinning, dark silhouettes springing through the doors, howler still howling. All he could think of was poor, trusting Manuel Garibay, huddled in the sealed trunk like a murder victim, hearing that deafening racket a few feet from his ears.

"Shut that goddamn thing off!" Packer shouted, jumping from his car with the kit still in his hand. The howler died with a final chirp, and he looked into the faces of Lieutenant Mike Phelan, head of the motor pool, and Captain Ralph Antonelli of I.A.U.

"Hold it right there!" Phelan barked.

"Check his hands," Antonelli said. "He's got something in his hands." The tall, skinny captain, a few inches taller than Packer, sounded pleasant as usual; he was known as "the smiling assassin." A few years ago, he had led the department's fight against entrenched corruption. Smiling all the time.

Mike Phelan reached for Packer's hand, but something made him hesitate. "Whatever he's got there, it's evidence," Antonelli said calmly. "Get it."

"Come and get it, Mike," Packer said. "It's my glasses case. Come on, take it off me. We'll see how far it'll go up your ass."

A click of scurrying heels announced the arrival of Sergeant Forrest Allen, breathing hard. "Anything I can do?"

"No, you done your job," Phelan said, backing away as though Packer were a charged wire. All their voices bounced off the walls of the big garage area and came back from the purple-black shadows muddy and muffled.

"What's going on here, Lieutenant?" the I.A.U. boss asked pleasantly.

Packer thought about Manuel's discovery, and Artie Siegl. Removing two lug nuts from a chase car wasn't much different from planting a bomb. It was attempted murder. There was no time left to stand around jawing.

"Captain," he said, "I got very important business. Police business. Back your car out of my way, will you, please?" The Visibar lights were still projecting a light-show on the walls and faces.

Antonelli took a half step forward. "You haven't answered my question, Lieutenant. What—"

Packer opened the door of his car. "I don't know what you junior G-men are up to," he said, sliding inside, "but whatever it is, your plan just went tits-up."

"What's that supposed to mean?" the I.A.U. boss asked, smiling thinly.

"Somebody's stupid campaign to get Artie Siegl—it's dead now. We just found out"—he quickly corrected himself—"*I* just found out what made him lose control."

"What?" Phelan asked, his face a mask.

"I think you know the answer as well as I do. The left-front wheel—it popped off before the spin, not after. It—"

"Fleet Safety said—"

"Fleet Safety's wrong. A driver like Artie Siegl doesn't lose control unless there's a goddamn good reason. Now what do you suppose made that wheel come off?" He leaned out his car window to see if all three were paying attention. Antonelli was smiling; Phelan stood alongside, his face changing to a bored sneer, and Frosty Allen stood behind his boss, surviving. "It popped because the car was sent out with two lug nuts missing on the left-front wheel. Siegl was running on three instead of five. And I can prove it."

Antonelli's smile faded for an instant, then returned as Mike Phelan said, "That's bullshit, Cap. He's just covering up for one of his men. He's famous for that."

Packer weighed the possibilities. He could lead the three of them back into the other stall and patiently show them the stripped and the unstripped threads, but would it be safe to tip his hand? He couldn't assimilate the idea of one police officer trying to injure or kill another, but stranger things had happened. Who was involved in the sabotage? All three of them? *None* of them? Anything was possible. He couldn't take the chance of letting them know what he had: an expert witness in the trunk of his car, plus his own testimony on what he had seen with his eyes and felt with his hands. Something was filthy stinking *rotten*. . . .

"Stripped threads, anything like that," Lieutenant Mike Phelan was insisting to Antonelli, "that was after he already lost control. Happens all the time in spins. Them wheels aren't designed to go sideways at ninety miles an hour."

"Yeah, we all know your story," the angry Packer said, deliberately keeping his voice down. "But you're a liar, Mike. We all know that, too."

He started his engine and began to inch back toward the command car. "Now the next question," he called out his window, "is why you motor-pool assholes didn't find this out for yourselves. No, wait! I think I got it. It's always simpler to put the blame on some poor flatfoot, right? Some dumb jerk that's already in the shit? I mean, that's easier than a lot of bad publicity, right? I mean, this is a helluva scandal, sending a chase car out with only three lug nuts. That wheel's gotta pop sooner or later, doesn't it? How'd you ever make a mistake like that, Phelan? A guy like you with twenty years."

"I—"

"Get outa my way!" Packer shouted. Somebody had tried to kill one of his men, and maybe the somebody was one of these three. "MOVE IT!" he shouted.

He raced his engine. No one budged. The smile had leached off Antonelli's face, Phelan looked sulky, and Frosty Allen's busy eyes darted back and forth from one of his superiors to the other.

"Ay Chihuahua!"

The voice was muffled, but to Packer it sounded like a P.A. announcement. "What?" Antonelli said, looking around.

"I said, *'Ay Chihuahua,'"* Packer hollered. "That means move your ass."

"Lieutenant Lind," Antonelli said, "it's my duty to tell you—"

"It's my duty to tell you to go fuck yourself!" Packer called out. "Now for the last time, are you moving your car or am I?"

"In due time," Antonelli said, edging closer. "Now if you'll just—"

Packer shoved the gear selector into "R," backed the Fury against the command car's bumper, and stepped on the gas. Stay down, Manuel, stay down, he kept repeating to himself.

The other car resisted; they'd left it in gear. Was the hand brake on? The damned thing would never budge if the brake was set. He drove forward a few feet, then reversed at full power. The command car gave, then bucked backward in a balky arc till it clanged against a concrete pylon. "'Bye-'bye," Packer said, ramming his gear selector into "D" and aiming for the down-ramp. "Hey, Frosty," he called back, "I got rid of the ping." Then he was gliding down the ribbed concrete and out on the street.

A block away he braked to a stop behind Manuel's white Pontiac. A sharp pain caught him in the backbone. Was it just strain? Or was that damned steel splinter moving again? He didn't have time to worry about it.

He opened the trunk. The mechanic lay on his side in the fetal position, his palms pressed together in front of his glistening Indian-brown face, mumbling something about *"espiritu santu."*

"It's okay, Manuel, okay," Packer said as though talking to his baby at home. "Come on, compadre, let me help you."

He reached in and gathered up the little man and deposited him on the curb. "You okay now, Manuel? Huh?" The mechanic stumbled away in the wrong direction. Packer grabbed him by the thin shoulders and steered him to the Trans-Am.

"Okay, pal, that's our show for tonight," Packer said. "I owe you one." Any second now the other three might come by and spot them. Or maybe an APB had already gone out for the outlaw watch commander who rammed a command car and made his getaway in the night. He doubted it. The I.A.U. was like the C.I.A.—discreet and devious. Antonelli and his headhunters worked in shadows: disciplinary interviews behind closed doors, strong hints about voluntary retirement: the velvet hammer.

Packer opened the door of the Trans-Am and arranged Manuel Garibay on the driver's seat. The little man reached out and hugged the wheel as though it were a life preserver. "You gonna be okay, pal?" Packer asked.

Manuel sat up straighter and began to talk at a frantic pace. "Wait," Packer said. *"Wait!* I don't speak Mexican."

"Ees uh-kay now," the mechanic babbled. *"Muy bueno.* I go home now, get some slip."

"Some what?"

"A good night's slip."

Packer thanked him again and returned to his car. No one was in sight on the narrow side street. He had to get back to Precinct Nine and begin an investigation of his own. *Fast.* Come to think, there wasn't time to drive back to the station. Any second one of his patrol cars might start another chase, or take a corner too fast, and a wheel would come off. Somebody could be killed this time. He sped two blocks to a phone booth and dialed the station.

"Ninth Precinct, Officer Reichert speaking." With Gerald Yount off duty and Johnny McClung exiled for the night, Packer had assigned the desk to McClung's partner.

"Rike, this is Packer. Listen, I want you to put out a Six Nine One for all cars in the precinct."

"When, Lieutenant?"

"Right now."

"Did you say Six Nine One? 'Phone your station'?"

"Yep. And fast."

"Uh, right, Lieutenant. What do you want me to tell 'em when they phone in?"

"Tell 'em get out and count their lug nuts."

"Uh—"

"You heard right. I want every car in the precinct to take off their hub caps and check their lug nuts. Make sure they got five on each wheel. Make sure they're all tightened down. Got that?"

There was a pause. "Lieutenant," the quizzical voice came back, "you want a Six Nine One to all cars, and when they call in you want me to tell 'em to, to get out and uh, count their, their—lug nuts?"

"And make sure they're tight. Get an acknowledgment from every car. No exceptions. Anybody's cooping or hiding, chase 'em down with another car and see they get the message."

"Can I ask you one thing, Lieutenant? Why don't we just put this out over the air? 'All cars, uh, check your lug nuts'?"

"Because the wrong ears might be listening."

He hung up and trudged back to his car, and as he drove around the corner something reminded him of Amnee and Emmy. The U.C. . . . Could there be any connection between the sabotaged car and the phone calls to the house? Ridiculous. He was acting silly, letting his wife's jitters bother him. Christ, when police supervisors started getting casabas in their throats every time a nut case made a threat, the whole P.D. might as well close shop and turn the town over to the social workers.

Still . . .

He waited till he heard Reichert put out the 691. Then he grabbed his own mike and said, "Two Two Three to David One." Bethea and Beemer would assure him that everything was peaceful on Orchard Street.

"Two Two Three to David One," he repeated after a long pause.

"Two Two Three," the dispatcher's voice broke in. "Lieutenant, David One's processing a traffic victim at St. Mary's."

A traffic victim . . . The call must have come in while he was holding his debate with the three idiots in the garage, his radio drowned out in stupid chatter. "For how long?" he asked, trying to conceal the tension in his voice.

There was a hesitation. "Since zero zero thirty," the dispatcher answered.

"Received." Since 12:30 A.M. An hour ago. . . .

He spun the wheel hard and veered into a darkened gas station, squealing to a stop in front of another pay phone. He dropped his last dime on the floor, reached into his pocket and snaked out a quarter, misdialed and redialed and waited for Amnee's sweet voice.

Four rings. Six. Eight . . .

Answer, Amnee, for Chrisakes. Answer, honey, please, *please*. . . .

Ten rings . . . Fifteen . . . She must be sleeping with the pillow over her head. No, she never does that. She likes to be able to hear the baby. And anyway, she was upset tonight; she always sleeps lightly when she's upset. *Why doesn't she answer?*

He threw the phone onto the hook, jumped into his Fury, and sped up the hill toward Stanton Park.

24

Turk Molnar crouched alongside the pool table trying to dope out his next shot, sighting with puffy gray eyes over the serrated pattern of scars burned into the rail by cigars and cigarettes momentarily forgotten during long runs and debates over whether one foot had remained on the floor. There was a time when the sergeant had been the hottest cue in the station, but his game was slipping; he had just missed a dead bank on the six, despite a full minute of careful planning.

"Must be a fucking full moon," a gravelly voice called out, ruining his concentration and his next shot. Don Reichert, temporarily assigned to the desk, walked in, griping as usual. "Every fool in town's calling me up and the lieutenant's flipped his gears," the resident grouch continued. "A couple more calls like that last one, you can stuff the desk job. I never wanted it in the first place. I—"

"Gripe, gripe, gripe," the sergeant said. How the hell had he missed that pigeon? They said older men couldn't see the edges of the balls. Well, sure, *older* men. But he was only fifty-five.

He looked into Reichert's sheep-dog face, and a popular expression popped into his head: a squeaky wheel makes the most noise. Something like that. "Now I'm gonna tell ya where the bear shit in the buckwheat," he said, trying to sound authoritative. "All you do is sit on your ass for eight hours and complain. You bitch when you're outside and you bitch when you're inside. Maybe you'd like a transfer to bikes?"

The deskman had disappeared into the kitchenette; he emerged blowing into a steaming cup of greasy chicken soup from the coin machine that had been generously marked down to a dime by a distributor who hated traffic tickets. "Yah, yah," the deskman said. "Great idea. Can I change tonight? I mean like *right now?*"

Sergeant Richard Not Dick Jellico glared up from the plastic table in the corner where four Davis quiz books were spread before him. Molnar shook his head disdainfully. He had tried to entice his junior colleague into a friendly game of eight-ball for five dollars but the scholar-sergeant wouldn't budge. Eager asshole spent every spare minute studying for promotion. Rank-crazy, absolutely rank-crazy. Guys like that were never satisfied. By the time he made chief, he'd want to make commissioner, and by the time he made commissioner, he'd want to try for Peter and Paul and all the saints. Claimed he had a system: you memorize 100 questions and answers, then move on to the next 100, and keep going till you had 400 Q&A's down pat. Then you were ready. Molnar had enough trouble with Thelma's shopping list.

Medicine-ball paunch pressed against the rail, the senior sergeant lined up the three on a combination with the fifteen, but a train rumbled past and the red ball hung on the lip and wouldn't drop. "Suck my cock!" he said.

"*Hey!*" Jellico called out.

"Oh, excuse me, Richard," Molnar said. "I know I shouldn't be using that expression while you're trying to quit." It was the latest stroke in their nightly battle of goads. Jellico could memorize like a son of a bitch, but he was pathetic on the comeback. By the time he figured out an answer, Molnar always had another zinger ready.

Reichert spoke up from one of the old stained leather armchairs that dated to the days when every merchant in town gave only their best samples to the men in blue, and a little extra in cash. "Fucking ridiculous job if I ever seen one," he complained. "Sitting there—"

"Hey," Molnar said, "you know how you can always tell a deskman?" He leaned over Jellico's shoulder and pretended to read from the quiz books. "Answer: he's the one picking his ass."

"Funny," Reichert said. "Highly humorous. I'm out there on the phone a half an hour straight, and my sergeant's in here making jokes."

"Listen, my boy, on this job you got to hang loose. Either that or go soft-headed, one. What's that you said about the lieutenant? Where's he at, anyway?"

"He's on the air," Jellico piped up from the corner. "I just heard him a while ago." He nodded toward his portable radio, parked on the desk in front of him. When Richard Not Dick took a dump, his portable radio watched him wipe.

"Called in and had me put out a Six Nine One to every car in the precinct," Reichert grumbled, licking the bottom edge of his chicken-soaked mustache.

"Yeah, I heard that," Jellico said. "That was an old-fashioned coop check, Reichert. Not a bad idea. Make sure everybody's awake. We used to pull surprises like that in the One-eight. Make everybody get out of the car and find a phone and call in."

"Is that written down in them Davis outlines?" Molnar asked, chalking his cue with squeaky enthusiasm. If there was anything griped his ass, it was honor students.

"He wasn't making any coop check," Reichert said. He ambled over to the magazine rack with its tattered copies of *Sheriff & Police Reporter, The American Rifleman, FBI Law Enforcement Bulletin, Law and Order, Nude America,* and other police publications. "This was— you wouldn't believe it."

"Give us a try," Molnar said patiently. "We're both sergeants. We seen life."

"Every car that phoned in, I hadda tell 'em count their lug nuts."

"Count . . .?"

"Yeah! Take off all four hub caps and count the nuts. And he says, 'Right now!'"

Jellico assumed a superior smile. "And you don't recognize that as a coop check, Reichert? It's a way to wake up your people good. He's no dummy, the lieutenant."

"No, *he's* not," Molnar cracked. "So what happened, Rike? Anybody in David sector got missing nuts?"

"Nope. Unless you count the goofball citizen that phoned in a few minutes ago. Sounds like he's talking out his bellybutton, his voice is so faint. Says please send somebody over to—I forget the address—send somebody over and bury the Morty."

"The Morty?" Molnar asked, standing on tiptoes for one of his famous massés. Might as well try a trick shot, he said to himself. I can't make the ducks.

"Yeah. 'Bury the Morty before it starts to stink,' he says. Then he hangs up. That's when I decided."

"Decided what?" the sergeant asked, shoving the cue briskly downward and slashing the felt.

"To have some soup. Clear my head."

"'Bury the Morty'?" Richard Not Dick was repeating. "You sure he didn't say 'Mortay'?"

"Mor-*tay?*"

"Yeah. Mortay. M-O-R-T-E. Means dead in—Latin, I think."

[174]

"It don't mean nothing in Hungarian, I'll guarantee you," Molnar said, backing away from the table as though from a tarantula. The captain would shit a brick. The last poor sucker to rip the felt was now working as a coroner's aide. "Don't it have that word in your outlines there?" he asked, thinking fast. Jellico was at one end of the long room and Reichert at the other; neither had seen the rip—yet. He had to create a diversion. If nobody noticed the damage for a while, the captain might not find out who was responsible.

"Hey," he said, noisily racking his cue, "maybe somebody's trying to tell us something."

"No way, Sarge," Reichert said, crumpling his empty cup. "The guy sounded drunk or spaced out or something. Just another weirdball, I been getting 'em all night."

"Morty means dead, huh, Richard?" Molnar asked. "Hey, suppose the guy found hisself a D.B., and he's trying to call the police, see, but he's a, he's a—he's a seaman off a ship! And he can't speak English good—"

"Oh, sure," Jellico said, snickering. "A seaman off a Latin ship."

"Just got in from Latvia," Reichert added.

"I'm serious," Molnar said. He escorted the deskman toward the door as Jellico's nose steered back to the printed page like a hound on deer scent. "You write that address down?"

At the front desk, Reichert mumbled and breathed hard and groped in the waste basket before coming up with a slip of pink paper bearing the inscription "4701 Nx Wy 3."

"That Latin, too?" the sergeant asked.

"Forty-seven Oh One Noxham Way, Apartment Three. Course that could be a bad address. I could hardly hear the guy."

"Didn't you put him onto Nine One One?"

"No. He hung up too fast."

"Well, maybe we better roll on this one. We got anybody?"

"Whole precinct's up to their ass now. The bars are closing."

Molnar grabbed a portable radio from the rack above the desk, thumbed the switch, and said, "Two Lincoln."

"Two Lincoln," Radio answered.

"Checking a possible D.B. Forty-seven Oh One Noxham Way. Over."

"You want backup?" Backup? Maybe Reichert was right about the full moon.

"I think I can handle it," the sergeant said.

"*Ree*-ceived." Some wise-ass up there. Backup for a D.B.! What a farce.

He had an eerie feeling as he drove into the warm night. There was something familiar about that address. Hadn't he once . . .? No, that was in the 4400 block. Guy went crazy, held a blade at his baby's neck for three hours till Willie Bethea took him down. But 4701—was that the cheap condo went up a few years ago? Corner of Poplar? Didn't what's-her-name . . .?

Sure, *sure!* Genna Jocelyn lived there. Eddie's widow. Maybe he'd stop and pay a social call. Poor lady, she never seemed to get tired of cops, practically held open house for monkeysuits. Jeez, suppose this was somebody's idea of a practical joke? Phone the desk, give the Jocelyn address; then some cop goes out and wakes her up. What asshole would pull a silly stunt like that? Let's see, he answered himself: Siegl, Smoliss, Wry, Beemer, Johnny McClung. . . .

Goddamn, he couldn't remember a precinct as snake-bit as this one. Dogs getting their heads stomped, weird phone calls, cops snapping at one another. What they all needed was a little less work and a little more breeze. Anything but this steady eighty-five, ninety degrees night and day. . . .

Well, it wouldn't hurt to pass by her place, anyway. Just sneak a peek. Put a little distance between himself and that ripped table. . . .

The low-profile garden apartments lay half in shadow, a few recessed green lights illuminating the flowers, as if God's own paint hadn't been good enough for the job. A threatened feeling persisted in his large stomach. You couldn't be a cop for thirty years and not learn a few simple rules of survival. One was: Never go snooping at three in the morning unless you got damned good reason and a very high visibility. Least of all the night after a big hairy killing. There were unstable types that would pop a cap through a window at a prowler, even if the prowler wore stripes on his arms and a badge as big as an omelet.

The outdoor entrance to Apartment Three dripped with ferns. Goddamn, I'm Nanook of the Jungle, he said to himself as he spread the greenery. The whole world's up to its ass in ferns; damned things get in your hair in restaurants, you can't drink a beer at a bar without a fern leaf falling in, next thing we'll have ferns in the crapper. Maybe he could uproot one tonight, just a small specimen, and put it on the pool table. Right over his failed massé. . . .

The Jocelyn apartment showed a lot of light behind the blinds, but no one answered his scratch. He knocked, then stage-whispered, "Sergeant Molnar!" Oh, Jesus, he shouldn't have said that. If this *wasn't* her place . . .

Well, it *was.* There was a little brass nameplate: Edwin Jocelyn. Christ, she still used his name two years later. Protection, probably.

Molnar had been here for a promotion party one night. The good woman laid out about six kinds of appetizers, including smoky salmon and cold artichoke butts, and when he left at midnight, the party was still going strong. Well, there was no party in there tonight. He laid his ear against the door. Dead quiet. Then why so much light? *Morte,* eh? He felt a chill in the hot air.

He tiptoed back to his green-and-white and radioed David Seven to meet him. Five minutes later two men climbed out of their car wearing annoyed expressions. Molnar had heard they were tight with the widow; maybe they knew something.

"Any reason for her lights to be on this late?" he asked.

"Search me," Patrolman Endicott Wry said.

"Well, listen, we got a call a while ago, possible D.B. Apartment Three. A little bird tells me you two guys might know how to get in."

"Sure, Turk," Sam Demaris said. "You walk up, you knock, she opens the door, and you walk in."

"That call," Wry said. "Somebody's jacking you off, Sarge."

"Yeah, I already thought of that. So what? I been jacked off before. But what if it's the real thing? *Huh?*" He nudged the little cop in the side.

"You got a point," Wry said.

The low-slung Demaris led the way along the winding glazed-brick walkway back to Apartment Three. When nobody answered his loud knock, he forced the door with a single well-placed kick. "Wait!" Molnar said, and entered first.

Eddie Jocelyn's widow lay naked, face-up, on a thin foam pallet. Her small brown eyes were open and dry, her slender wrists handcuffed behind her neck. A path of red bubbles began at her lips and ended on the floor in a maroon stain. Something was scrawled on her belly in poor block printing; at first glance it looked to the sergeant like

COCSUCKER

"Don't touch a thing!" he warned, leaning over the body. The milky white throat was crushed and stained black and yellow and blue. Somebody had strangled the poor woman, and then strangled her again and again. Usually you just saw a couple of faint purple spots, like on the Evans woman the night before.

Shit oh dear, we're in for it now, he said to himself as he unholstered his radio and called in the 010. Well, he wouldn't have to worry about the pool table. It would be a long time before the captain had a chance to notice.

25

All the way home in his blue Buick Riviera, he had fantasized about the approaching night. He pictured Agate in their square onyx-type bathtub, her soft skin absorbing exotic scents and vapors. He would follow with a cool shower and a dab of cologne at the edges of his hairpiece and then he'd mix rum Cokes, her favorite bedtime drink, a jigger for himself, a jigger and a half for her, and they'd lie in bed and listen to their Mantovani tape and talk about life, she went for romantic crap like that, and then he'd slip downstairs and mix another blast, two jiggers for her this time, and he'd drop his arm across her ivory shoulders and lightly feel her long nipples the way you test a blackberry to see if it's ripe, and then he'd move in with the other hand, just gently rub along her bush. . . .

Jesus Jones, he was getting a hard-on! Suppose he had an accident here on the freeway? Suppose somebody else had an accident and he had to jump out and take charge? Forget it! He wouldn't interrupt his trip home for an on-view multiple ax murder in the bus passing him on the right. He wouldn't stop if he saw the mayor's wife getting gang-licked by a troop of naked chimpanzees on the median strip. . . .

Agate wasn't in the tub. She was slumped in the recliner wearing her half-glasses and reading *Seventeen*. "Oh, it's you," she said, and turned a page.

He smiled and strode across the room and kissed her on the forehead and instantly regretted it. He shouldn't have moved so fast; she'd be on her guard the rest of the night. She always claimed he only kissed her when he wanted something. Well, he wanted something, all right. *Everything*. How about his second trip around the world? One every decade. Was that asking too much of a wife?

He made the required small talk for a half hour, while she responded in murmurs and grunts. He ran the bath himself, but she didn't get the hint, so he plopped his softening body in the steaming water and scrubbed off, taking special pains with the areas of social significance. After a touch of Brut and a gargle of Cēpacol, he popped a floral-flavored Cloret in his mouth and jumped under the sheet to wait.

And wait.

At 10:45 he suppressed his mingled lust and aggravation and called out nonchalantly, "Ag, you gonna be much longer? 'Cause if you are, I'll just turn out the light and go to sleep now, hon."

The irritated voice came back like a pushcart peddler selling fish that weren't moving. "Can't I ever get a minute to myself? I'm busy all day long. Just go to sleep! I'll be up—when I'm ready."

When I'm ready. ... Did that mean something? Was she intentionally teasing him? She used to do it that way, fend him off and fend him off and then give him the jump of his life. "Okay, baby," he said, trying not to show his eagerness. "See you, uh, later." Another hint. By now a blind deaf-mute bull dyke would have caught on.

Well, at least she was home, she was on the premises. Lately, she'd turned into a one-woman welcome wagon, running around the neighborhood day and night, "doing social work among the rich," as he kidded her one night when she came home all worn out from calling on a new couple from Indianapolis who had moved in down the block or around the corner, she didn't seem sure which. When she wasn't doing what she called "vizting," she was attending something known as "coffees" or running off to kitchenware parties or bridge socials or going downtown to fashion-show luncheons at the Blandstone. But she didn't seem to spend much money, thank God for that; the budget was intact and the bank account growing. Not like last year, he reminded himself as he mindlessly hefted his sparsely haired balls, when her hobby had been redoing various rooms in monochromes: royal blue had been followed by celadon which had been followed by burnt umber which had been followed by a $6,000 withdrawal at the bank. Then she contracted a severe case of furniture rearrangement syndrome culminating in the removal of his favorite lounger to the hallway "where it won't fight the colors." He had shoved it back into the living room where she had it reupholstered in a guacamole color that reminded him of the waste products of certain trusties through the years. Now the house was apparently set, fixed, satisfactorily arranged to last out their final year till resale and retirement and the dream move to Mexico. And now she was almost never home.

I'll never understand women, he said to himself, yawning widely. Christ, I don't understand *anything* anymore. Getting dumber as I go along.

He talked to himself under her faintly scented pillows. Jesus Jones, my mind's on screwing all the time. *All the time!* Was I always like this? Hell, no! Sex just used to be—something nice that happened. Two, three times a week. No big deal. Good for her, good for me, lots of laughing and giggling, and every so often she'd lean back on the pillow and stare at me like she was trying to bore a hole through my eyes and say, "Oh, Jules, I love you *so* much, Jules." And I'd get embarrassed and say quickly, "Uh, me too." I didn't used to have a burning need to, to, to—*come* all the time. Why, there were nights we'd lie side by side and talk for a couple hours, just *talk,* maybe reach out and hold hands, touch each other, kiss good night, and then start to talk all over again: about Rosarito, about cops, about life and the way we met and how good it always was. We'd make each other laugh, make each other sing, and you can never—

"Why Don't We Do This More Often?" Hell of a song. Jo Stafford. Yeah, Ag, why don't we? *Why don't we, honey?* Is it because my face sags like a bassett hound's and my eyelids have turned to crepe paper? Is it because I'm—getting old? Jesus Jones, is it possible that you don't, you don't—love me? Oh, Christ, Agate, say you love me one more time, baby. Say it. *Say it!*

He flung one of her pillows across the bed and clamped his jaws tight. Talking to somebody who wasn't even there! A police captain! And talking—mush. God, was he going sentimental? Never had *that* problem before. Where had he read lately that women reacted better to sentimentality, delicacy; women needed love-talk, flowers, presents, crap like that? The article said women hated to just jump in bed and screw. Said something about one red rose in a crystal vase could make a woman hotter than half an hour of dick.

Was that how it was? Okay! He'd give her all the extras; he'd *drown* her in extras. They were making six-carat diamond fakes now that even the jewelers couldn't spot; he'd shop for one on his lunch hour. Police price ought to bring it down to three, four hundred bucks. Ag was worth it. Oh, God, you never knew the value of something till it was gone. . . .

He woke with a sharp snap of his head. The bath water was running! He looked at his luminous dial: 11:50. Well, how long could she stay in the water? He napped again and woke to the sound of the hair dryer. 1:15 A.M. The buzzing went off and he sat up, one ear cocked toward the bathroom. Then the hair-drying resumed, and kept up till he fell asleep again.

. . . Huh? What was that smell?

She was doing her goddamn nails!

This time he climbed out of bed and padded past her to the toilet, gently dusting her naked shoulder with his hand as he passed. "You still awake?" she said.

Still hanging in there, he wanted to answer, but instead he said, "I fell asleep for a while."

"Hmmmm."

He pulled the frosted door closed and directed his stream of urine against the curved porcelain of the toilet bowl instead of splattering it into the water—"the most disgusting sound," she'd complained before he changed his technique. He pulled the Air-wick out an extra inch, returned to bed, and began to count. Anything to relieve the pressure in his groin. Soon the numbers became jumbled and a vision of the well-packed sergeant in Juvenile floated before his eyes. They were having dinner at her apartment, and the dessert course was each other. "Hey, stop!" he called out, and woke himself up. He reached across the bed and felt for Agate. She wasn't there. For an instant he felt guilty about the dream. Then a faraway sound droned in his ears. She was vacuuming the living-room rug. He looked at his watch: 1:45. What was that smell? Brut. He hated that stink, it'd be a long time before he put it on for *her* again. Fucking woman! She'd beg for it the next time. He didn't need— Some goddamn— What did she . . .? *Didn't she know*— Wouldn't—

Now she's got me wide awake, and for what? he asked himself. Too late to think about it now. I'll wait till morning. I'll get up before she does, bring her a steaming cup of coffee, lots of rich powdered cream the way she likes it; I'll slip down alongside her for a while and just rub her back. . . . Lower and lower . . . And little by little . . .

The captain was strolling nude across their *lanai* at Rosarito Beach, his erection throbbing, when he heard the ringing. *What . . .?* A naked Agate stood in the cool Mexican moonlight like an alabaster statue with pubic hairs, waiting for him to get up speed and rush at her. God, he had to hurry, his equipment might slump to the floor, the roof might—

Something clanged again, miles away. He groped wildly in the soft glow of the night light. She was asleep on his left, her mouth agape like a beached porpoise, her snores rattling the headboard. She was wearing the black silk sleep mask that looked like a leftover from a bank job. A latex stopple peeked from her ear. The phone jangled. . . .

To his right. Yes, that was it. Over there where it—always was.

He grabbed and missed, grabbed again and put the phone to his ear backward, turned it around and said, "Singletary. Are you there?"

"Captain? *Cap?*"

"Singletary!" he repeated, trying to sound as though he'd been wide awake, waiting for a call.

"Cap, this is Reichert. On the desk? There's been another, uh, case. You asked to be called?"

Now he was wide awake. "Another killing? Same M.O.?"

"Just about," the deskman answered. "Strangulation, that's for sure. This time he wrote 'copsucker' across her stomach."

"*Cocksucker?*"

At the word, Agate moaned and rolled on her side, one pendulous breast slipping from her nightgown and sliding out on the sheet like a jellyfish..Before his eyes, the nipple shriveled up and went from flat to erect. What was she dreaming about? Or *who?* He stiffened and reached for her with his free hand, but she turned on her stomach, immune to his appeal asleep as awake.

"No, sir," Reichert was repeating in his ear. *"Cop*sucker. *Cop,* Cap, not, uh, cock, Cap. You be down, Cap?"

"Yale," he said. "I'll be down in—an hour." He looked at his shrinking member and lowered his voice: "Sooner, I guess."

"What, Cap?"

"Never mind."

26

He felt like an overprotective jerk, barging in on Amnee demanding to know if she was all right. "Of course I'm all right," she said, flopping back on the bed. Her green eyes had lost some luster; he was sure she hadn't slept. "Why, Packer? Shouldn't I be?"

"Sure, *sure* you should," he said, a little too eagerly. "It's quiet in the precinct tonight. Quiet as it ever gets, every car's about two calls behind. A lot of chippy stuff. Nothing worth worrying about."

"Sweetie, for heaven's sake, why are you telling *me* all this at three o'clock in the morning?"

He realized what a blunder he had committed, belying his own words by rushing home to check on her. "It's just—it's just, uh, you were so nervous about that caller. I just thought I'd, uh, check."

She drew him down and kissed him. "Oh, Packer, sweetie, I'm so sorry."

He hugged her close. She smelled like toothpaste; she must have just gone to bed. "Sorry about what?"

"About getting you all upset and worried." She gave him an extra squeeze, her arms barely reaching around his chest. "I try not to interfere, baby, can you believe that? Can you?"

"Interfere in what?" He sat on the side of the bed and looked at her nakedness out of the side of his eyes, still slightly embarrassed at the sight of her creamy young skin after three years of marriage. On warm nights like this, she glowed like an Olympic athlete. Sleek and spare and—functional. Too bad he was on duty right now. . . .

"I try to be just steady?" she said, as though talking were difficult. "You know, old dependable? Take care of baby, stay out of your hair when you're working. But—oh, sweetheart, I was *so* scared."

"I know, I know." He held her again, and they rocked together. When he let go, she pressed close against his shirt front.

"I thought about those calls for the longest time, Packer. You know that feeling you get when you, when you're repeating something from earlier life? Like—you've been there before?"

"Sure. That's called— It's called— There's a name for it."

"I know."

"*Déjà* view," he said, snapping his fingers.

"I have that—déjà thing—about those calls. The voice. I mean it doesn't sound familiar. Not exactly. I mean it doesn't sound like anybody I know. And yet—there's something—familiar."

"You said he muffles his voice?"

"Sounds like it, uh-huh. Like he's talking through a scarf or something."

Packer got up and walked to the window and tried the locks. "Everybody wears a scarf in this freezing weather," he said, trying to lighten up the conversation. He hadn't rushed home to make her hysterical again.

"Well, handkerchief, then, or maybe part of his hand. Or a hat, something like that. I really think—" She stopped and pursed her lips and pulled the bed sheet over her breasts modestly.

"Think what?" he said, sitting down and rubbing her feet through the white layers. "Do you . . .?" He cut himself off as he suddenly realized that the general sloppiness of Lower Slobbovia had now reached the watch commander's level. In his anxiety about Amnee and the baby, he had jumped out of his unmarked Fury and left his radio in the console. They could call a disciplinary board on him for that; a W.C. was *never* supposed to be out of contact without first assigning another supervisor to take over and clearing with the dispatcher. Now his portable radio was in its slot waiting for somebody to grab it. The riot gun was there, too, but it was locked in its blue-steel rack. Well, it would serve him right if the radio was gone when he went back out. What the hell, it would only set him back $900.

"Honey, I think I know that voice," Amnee was saying. "Oh, Packer, I realize I'm acting stupid again. But don't you see? It makes him that much scarier, sweetie. He's *not* some loony—what do you call it? U.C.? He's somebody I—know. Or have known, or—oh, baby, it's so confusing. Oh, sweetheart, this job. It's—dear God, *why us?*" She was babbling now, the way she'd babbled earlier. It was a bad sign. "I mean, other families— Oh, forget it." She turned abruptly toward the wall.

"Forget what?"

"I'm sorry, sweetheart. It's something that comes into my head, but it's so—unfair. So—selfish."

"Well, let's hear it," he said, trying to catch her eyes.

"No, no, I'm going to sleep now." She lowered her head on the pillow, and her honey-brown hair framed her troubled face. For an instant, she looked like a very tired and very pretty washerwoman.

"Amnee, you are *not* going to sleep now!" he insisted. "You just wake the hell up and tell me what's on your mind, you hear? That's our deal, honey, remember? No secrets? Everything on the table?"

"Your job," she said, talking toward the wall as though she couldn't stand to confront him. "Your—job." Her voice was tight, strained, as though one part of her was forcing it out against the resistance of another part. "Do you think anybody appreciates it? The things you do? The chances you take?"

He took her small hand and stroked it gently. "Those calls bothered you more than I thought," he said softly. "I'm glad I had David One check the house tonight."

"You *what?*" She sat up abruptly, and he saw tears in her eyes.

"I had the district car cruise by every hour. Make sure you were okay. That's why I came home now. Willie and Beemer didn't get a chance to check for a while, and then you didn't answer the phone—"

"I was afraid to answer," she said, crying openly. "I thought it was him. Emily woke up and I was so scared I went in and got the gun and put it—" She slid the five-shot revolver from under the other pillow. "If you asked the car to check," she went on shakily, "then *you* must have been worried too, Packer. But you, you, you kept telling me it was—nothing."

"That's what it is, hon. Nothing."

"No," she said. "Not—nothing. I know you, Packer. You'd never assign a car for nothing. Not even for your own family. Something's going on, Packer. Something's—"

"Honey," he said, trying to sound exasperated and therefore sincere and truthful, "there's *nothing* going on." He wouldn't mention the missing lug nuts, and he wouldn't remind her about the dead pups. She was already suspicious, and her distress was communicating itself to Emily in the next room. He could hear the child making little cries in her sleep. Next would come a full-fledged nightmare, and Amnee would have to get out of bed and comfort her, and another half hour of refreshing sleep would be lost forever. It was a constant problem: with him working from eight at night till four in the morning, it was impossible to regulate the household's rest. It must feel nice, he said to himself, to go to bed with your family and wake up with your family.

Well, he wouldn't complain. The 10 percent night differential went in their savings account, and besides, a good cop worked the hours he was assigned. The job came—

He had started to say to himself that the job came first. But that wasn't true. His family came first. But the family's happiness and security depended on the job, wasn't that right? He could quit the department and get something else in the daytime, security work or maybe a carpenter's job in the construction business, but he'd never be happy off the force. Never again. And wouldn't his discontent rub off on his wife and baby, wouldn't it sour their lives together?

"I never said a word before," Amnee was muttering, more to herself than to him. "I pretended you just went to work and came home, like other men. But now—your job's pushing into our house, Packer. It's intruding on me and my baby—our baby. And we're not invulnerable like you, honey. Can't you see—"

"*What's* pushing into our house?"

She shook out her lank brown hair and punished her tired eyes with sharp little knuckles. "Somebody's threatening us because of you, Packer, can't you see that? Because of something you've done. Yes, you *do* see it, don't you? You *do* believe me, don't you? Why else would you send a car around and then run home like this? You never did it before. Packer, *what's going on?*"

He got up and smoothed his shirt. "Honey, there's a few things happening, there always is, but none of 'em have a blessed thing to do with you or Emmy or the house. Honest to God. Look, you go back to sleep and I'll go back to work and we'll talk about it later, okay?"

"You're putting me off."

"Honey, I didn't lock my car. My radio's out there, my riot gun, my evidence case. I don't think I even shut the door."

"But you really weren't worried about us?" she said sarcastically. "Oh, no! That's why you ran home and scared me half to death banging on the door."

"Hon, I just stopped by to, uh, to *check,* that's all, just to look in on you before the watch change. But I got a million things to do now. Can't we talk . . .?"

"Oh, sure, we'll talk later. We'll have breakfast together. How's that?" She sounded as though an intimate breakfast was the last thing she wanted. "Or were you going to stop at the bar first? A beer or two with the boys?"

"Honey—"

"I mean you're only with them eight hours a night, six days out of every eight, except when you go hunting and fishing with them on your

[185]

days off, and when you meet at the bar, and when you have your watch parties and your promotion parties and retirement parties, but that's not so bad, that's only two or three times a month. Go ahead and enjoy yourself with *the boys,* Packer. It's part of the job, isn't it?"

He stood silently and tried to figure out what was going through her head. Jesus, the way she bit down on "the boys," you'd think she was accusing him of being a queer. Well, you never knew about women, you never knew. You thought they were contented, then all the grievances came out in a single outburst—the slights and insults and imagined injustices. Or were they real? "Honey," he said, "why didn't you speak up before?"

"Because I wasn't scared before!" she said, sobbing loudly. "Because your job was always—separate. Now a man's calling me on the phone. Now a man's—watching me."

"Watching you?"

"I know it. I can—feel it."

He knelt alongside the bed and draped his arm across her waist. No one was watching her, he was certain of that. Beemer and Bethea would have noticed in David One. But there was a paranoia that affected stressed policemen, and maybe it affected stressed wives, too. Maybe he'd been asking too much of this child-woman all along, and it had taken these three years for her to break. "Honey, what do you want me to do? Quit?"

"Oh, I don't know, Packer." The tears detoured around her small nose and trickled to her chin, and she shook her head helplessly. "I just don't know. Maybe, maybe you could stop and think about—" She peered at him through eyes that looked like slick wet jades in the pale yellow light from the bedlamp.

"Think about what?"

"About, about why you wanted the job in the first place. Why you wanted to go through life, uh, arresting people and, uh, meddling in their lives, and—"

"I didn't take the job to meddle in anybody's life, Amnee. Chrisakes! I took it because—I don't know."

She dried her eyes with a large handkerchief that was already soaked. He guessed she'd been crying before he came home. "Yes," she said, "and now your wife and daughter can't walk to the market without being afraid. Can't answer the phone without wondering if some psychopath—"

"Honey, that's temporary, and it could happen to anybody. *Anybody!* Ministers' wives get U.C.'s. Girl Scoutmasters. I told you, hon, the guy just dialed a number at random. Nothing personal. He'll quit. Wait and see. Things change. Things quiet down."

"Till another creep comes along."

"There won't *be* another creep, Amnee." He stood up to go. "We'll talk later, honey. I gotta go now. You're safe, you been safe all the time. We just built something up, you and me, that's all."

She offered a pair of unparted lips and he put his arms around her as they kissed. "You'll see," he said, squeezing her too hard and causing her to grunt in pain.

"I guess we will," she said.

"What're you getting up for?"

"To double-check the locks behind you."

"Honey, don't worry—"

"It never helps to tell a worried person not to worry."

Well, she was right about that. It was seldom that you could chase fear with words; that worked only on small children. The best approach was to get right to the source of the worry, solve the problem if it was real and air it out if it was unreal. But—a goddamn U.C.! Who the hell ever caught one? The phone company had expensive new gadgets that they leased to the P.D. for a ton of money, and they hardly ever worked. And who did they catch when they *did* work? Lames and losers, losers and lames. But he had already given her the full explanation, and still she was panicky. Maybe she had a need to be scared, maybe there was some deep psychological problem bothering her. She was eligible for help from the department shrink, lots of wives went, almost as many wives as husbands. But this was no time to broach *that* subject. . . .

Backing out of his driveway, he turned up his radio and heard a voice that sounded like Sergeant Turk Molnar saying, "Over."

The dispatcher came back, "Two Lincoln, that's received." Two Lincoln *was* Molnar. "Verify Oh One Oh at Four Seven Oh One Noxham Way. Was that Apartment Three you said?"

"Affirmative."

Homicide. Packer hit the siren and the lights just as the rear wheels of his Fury backed onto the street. Oh, God, Amnee would jump out of her skin. He'd explain the noise later; he'd *have* to explain later, he certainly couldn't stop now. They'd better get somebody down at Forty-seventh and Noxham to direct traffic, the whole goddamn city would be headed for that intersection within minutes. The captain! Jesus, Singletary would roll for sure on this one.

"Two Two Three to Two Lincoln," he said into his microphone, steering the speeding car left-handed.

"Two Lincoln," Molnar responded.

How should he phrase it? He needed the information fast, but he didn't want to share it with all the crime freaks sitting by their scanners with saliva dripping from their mouths. "Uh, Turk, how's the, er, uh, M.O. look?"

There was a pause at the other end. He realized that Turk Molnar was trying to compose a discreet answer. "Ditto," the sergeant finally replied.

"Ree-ceived," Packer said. There was no point in rushing to the scene of the crime; Molnar would preserve the evidence. He nosed his car onto Meredith Street and sped toward the station. He passed last night's murder house and noted that the place was dark. One consolation jumped into his mind: Noxham Way was on the far side of David sector, at least two miles away. That meant the killings were no longer localized to Stanton Park. Now they could be shared by the whole city. Wouldn't the press and TV love that?

He rushed into the station to find a red-faced Don Reichert pacing the floor. "Jesus Christ, Packer, I'm riding this desk and there's a hot killing right on my beat—"

"Sit," he said. "I need you bad."

"But Packer—"

"SIT! Call Artie Siegl and tell him get his ass down here right away."

"It's ha' past three in the morn—"

"Normal working time for Artie. He won't mind."

"He's sick, Lieutenant."

"He just got better."

"But—"

"GET HIM DOWN HERE! Then put the word out: we're staying after school. Emergency meeting in the big room."

"The first watch'll be standing roll call."

"Oh, eh, right. Make it in the rec room."

He dashed for his office. As he ducked to enter, he noticed the grumpy deskman still standing, facing him. "What're you waiting for, Rike?" he asked. "A review board? Start dialing!"

"Oh. Uh. Sure."

Packer fell into his chair just as the first button lit up on the phone console. A few minutes later Molnar chugged in breathing hard. "The dicks got it," he said, making the other chair squeak for mercy. "Don't envy 'em this time. Couple young guys was catching tonight. Their assholes really puckered they seen that body."

"Run it by me quick as you can," Packer said, looking at his watch.

"Nothing fancy about it, Lieutenant. It was Genna Jocelyn. She—"

"Genna—*Jocelyn?* Eddie's—?" He felt as though someone had clubbed him from behind.

"Eddie's widow, yeah. She was strangled. Bad. Crazy. She was nekked, handcuffed behind her back. 'Copsucker' printed on her belly."

"Huh?" He was still half shocked.

"He wrote 'copsucker' on her, Packer. With some kind of black stuff, not like ink, more like—powder."

"Powder?"

"Yeah. Kind of rubbed in. Made a pretty rough job, but you could read it, all right. 'Copsucker.' Capital letters right above her bellybutton."

"Anybody checking the registration numbers on the cuffs?"

"Yeah. The dicks. If they can get into the clerk's office."

Packer usually enjoyed the ritual of changing watch: the mock insults back and forth between the two shifts, the incoming men lined up to buff their shoes on the brushing machine and the outgoing lazily pulling off their monkeysuits in front of their lockers, rendezvous plans being made for the Slammer and other drinking places, and the younger men snapping to attention and making cracks like "Carry on, Constable" as though they were the first policemen in history to use the phrase in jest. But tonight the change of shift was accomplished with the enthusiasm of an inspector's funeral. This is a sick precinct, Packer said to himself, and somehow we got to make it well. Amnee was right, in her usual intuitive way. Something terrible *was* going on.

At 4:15 A.M., after the last district car had changed crews and sped away, he faced the third-watch personnel in the rec room. "Okay, sit down, make yourself comfortable," he said. Out of the corner of his eye he saw a foreshortened form enter in a modified Groucho shuffle and heard a familiar voice say, "Okay, men, who's got the dice?"

"Sit, Artie," Packer said, relieved to see the ex-featherweight. He counted sixteen patrolmen—oops, patrolpersons—and two sergeants. Missing were Johnny McClung, home sleeping off a drunk or maybe continuing a drunk for all anybody knew, and the other deskman, Gerald Yount, on a badly needed night off. Both could be briefed later.

"I'm telling you this in front," he said, "because I know that police officers have a terrific news network and you're gonna find out the details anyway and besides I need your help. *Everybody's* help." He deliberately swept the room to make eye contact. Parts of two or three uniforms were visible back in the kitchenette: a sleeve, a shoe and pant leg, the peak of a cap sticking out from the doorway.

"Hey, you guys, come on in!" Packer ordered.

"Not enough room," somebody spoke up.

"Why, sure they is!" Turk Molnar called out. "Sit up on the pool table."

When the group was packed in tightly, Packer said in a confidential tone, "I don't have to tell any of you we've had two killings in twenty-four hours. *Bad* killings. The man is a nut case, he strangles, he pours acid into his victim's mouths. We got a witness says he stutters or stammers, whatever you want to call it. The first time out he wore a blue knee-length nylon stocking over his head. We don't know what he wore this time. Last and hardest to take, he doesn't like us. He wrote 'copsucker,' excuse me, miss"—he nodded toward the back of the room, where Mary Rob Maki was writing in a blue spiral notebook—"he wrote 'copsucker' across Genna's—across tonight's victim." He paused and looked down. "It's possible he's a police officer himself."

"What makes you say that, Lieutenant?" Sergeant Richard Not Dick Jellico asked, looking insulted at the mere suggestion.

"He used regulation cuffs tonight."

"Whose number?" Willie Bethea asked quickly.

"They're working on that."

The troops nudged one another and exchanged asides. Most of them were saying they would stick around for a while, needed or not. "Will you tell us soon's you hear?" Tennyson Mills asked.

"The *second* I hear," Packer answered. "Now listen. This was a Stanton Park matter last night, but now it's the whole precinct. So button up. We don't want a scare. Understand?"

The faces nodded.

"When word gets out that some fool is strangling and defacing women, the public'll flip. And that won't make our job any easier."

"Who'd kill Genna Jocelyn?" somebody mused aloud. "Why'd—"

"Was she raped?" Mary Rob Maki called out.

"You were there, Turk," Packer said, turning to Molnar. "How'd it look to you?"

"Couldn't tell. She was nekked, poor thing, but all the damage seemed to be around her neck. I think it was a straight homicide, me. Strangulation, but no penetration."

"We'll know for sure when the coroner gets finished," Packer said.

"Yeah," Molnar said. "Whenever that is."

The watch commander cleared his throat and tried to figure out how to put his next point. Maki was still standing in the back, next to Billy Mains. He wondered if she knew anything about Eddie Jocelyn's widow. "Om uh, a lotta you guys were friends with Genna—Mrs.

Jocelyn. If you know something about her personal life that might help, tell me or your sergeant, and we'll tip the dicks. Anything at all. And we'll keep it confidential."

"She was a good woman," Sam Demaris said. He sounded forlorn. "She was—friendly."

"She was never outa line," Ernie Smoliss said. "She—"

Packer interrupted. "I didn't mean to cast any aspersions on her. She was—she liked police officers. Some good people do. She was always straight with me. And anyway, nobody deserves to go—the way she went."

"Nobody," Demaris echoed, lifting his glasses and brushing a hairy hand across his eyes.

"Okay," Packer said loudly to end the mourning period, "there's a couple other things been going on. I don't know if they tie in with these homicides, but let's run 'em by."

"The dogs?" Jellico suggested. Faces fell.

"Yop," Packer said. "The dogs. I wish I had something new on that. But I got an idea. Those juveniles that tried to rip off one of our light bars yesterday—they might know something."

"What juveniles?" Billy Mains blurted out. Immediately a foolish grin passed over his face, as though he knew he shouldn't have asked.

Packer didn't try to hide his annoyance. "Mains, it wouldn't hurt you to read the arrest reports once in a while."

"I missed that one."

"Read 'em all! Every watch! Anybody else forget their reading tonight?"

A couple of hands were raised shyly. "Well, catch up!" he said gruffly. "This is no time for, uh, goofing off."

"What's your idea on the juveniles, Lieutenant?" Jellico asked.

"My idea's anybody that tampers with a patrol car outside a police station in broad daylight, he's sure not trying to make the P.D. look smart," he answered. "Same goes for stomping our pets in the middle of the night."

"Yeah, and how about killing a friend of the precinct and writing a dirty word on her body and cuffing her with regulation cuffs?" Molnar added. "That don't make us look none too good either."

"Wait till you hear this," Packer said, lowering his voice so that the officers in the back of the room had to crane their heads. He told the story of the missing lug nuts, leaving out the role played by Manuel Garibay.

There was a hush in the room, broken finally by Artie Siegl's excited voice: "I *knew* something come off that car before I spun."

"Lemme get this straight, Lieutenant," Endicott Wry said. "Somebody tampered with the car *before* Artie went on patrol?"

"Looks that way," Packer said. "Now listen. We're pooling what we know. That's why we're here. Keep it all working: eyes, ears, and nose. And memory, too. There's some inconsequential little thing, something one of us knows and maybe put out of his mind already, that could help us."

"Did any y'all see somebody messing around the cars last night?" Molnar asked.

No one spoke up.

"Anybody see anything suspicious around the dogs?" Packer asked.

"I fed 'em right after we relieved the second watch," Ernie Smoliss said. "They were romping and milling around and licking my hand. Same as usual."

"Anybody notice *anything* unusual last night?"

"We were on post, Lieutenant," Rollie Beemer said.

"No cars came in before one A.M.?" Packer asked. "That's when I found 'em dead."

"We did," Endicott Wry said. "David Seven. We typed up a report on a shoplift, couple other little calls. Around midnight."

"What was going on inside when you came in?"

"Nothing," Sam Demaris put in. "Stone quiet. Your office was empty, the sergeants were on the street, that's it."

"Who was here?"

"The deskman."

"What was he doing?" Packer asked.

"Staring."

"Staring?"

"I remember that, too," Wry said. "He was just sitting there looking straight ahead. I ask him, I says, 'Hey, Gerry, what's happening?' But he just kept on staring."

"We all know Yount has personal problems," Packer said evenly. "Now look," he said, changing the subject, "forget your days off for a while. You got a vacation scheduled, cancel it. I can't give you that as an order, and headquarters hasn't authorized O.T., but any of you work late, you know I'll make it good one way or the other."

Heads shook up and down emphatically, and somebody said, "We're not worried."

"We're gonna work on this as a precinct," Packer went on. "Not as a bunch of individual men." Oh, Christ, he said to himself, what a time for sexist terminology; I need *everybody*. "And women, too," he added, a little overemphatically. "Of men *and* women." Good. Maki was nodding in the back; she didn't look offended by the slight. "And we're gonna nail this son of a bitch excuse my French if it takes us seven days a week for the rest of the year. Are we together on that?"

There was a buzz of approval. Packer understood, and felt his face flush. For once, the third watch was motivated.

"Check with your sergeant for specific assignments," he said. "Is there anybody here that can't be brought in any hour, day or night?"

Silence.

"Good. Great. Let's go to work." At the door, he called back, "We'll show 'em one thing if we never show 'em anything else." He paused for effect. "This isn't Lower Goddamn Slobbovia."

27

"I don't have to tell you we got to stop this strangler quick," the captain said as the third cup of sour coffee burned through his system.

"That's right, Cap," the night-watch commander acknowledged in short tones that said all too bluntly he had better things to do. "You don't have to tell me." Packer Lind was turning into a disrespectful bastard, but why should he be different from the rest of those stupid yay-hoos on his shift? Siegl. Billy Mains. Mills and what's his name, Smoliss, all the rest of the goddamn idiots. Long on noise, short on performance. You could recruit a better crew from the morning soup line at the Salvation Army.

The captain did two squared-off laps around his dazzlingly neat desk in his pouter-pigeon steps, trying to cut a figure of authority. He had no choice but to push his problems with Agate aside and concentrate on the bloody business at hand. When he had left home at 4 A.M., her Halloween mask had been in place and her breathing was deep. He'd bet the damned woman still didn't know he was gone. Home or away, he didn't exist. Imagine! Vacuuming the rug at two in the frigging morning! She was turning him into a husband who couldn't make his own wife. There was nothing more pathetic. The thought sent pangs through his scrotum, and the doctor's words came back: "Use it or lose—"

"Who called you in this time, Skip?" the watch commander was asking, conspicuously declining to sit.

"Reichert. I left word to be called." He slumped into his padded chair and pushed up his violet-tinted glasses in case the sun arrived ahead of schedule. "Listen, Lind, tell me something," he said. He had never felt more old or tired or more at the mercy of fools and assassins. "What d'you make of this thing?"

The big man shook his head. Typical Swede. Never reached a conclusion in less than a week. The quick one was Jellico, but most of his answers came from the manual, and God help him if a little imagination was called for. And the other sergeant, Molnar, was a survivor, nothing more; you might use him for backup, but he hadn't spent five minutes as a detective. There was one supervisor with a dick's experience and a dick's smarts: Packer Lind. And there he sat, mute.

The captain cleared his throat and said, "The guy must've been interrupted last night." It was his one and only theory on the killings. "Didn't get his rocks off, don'tcha figure? Had to caper again tonight? Something—like that?"

"What, Cap?" The watch commander was switching from one foot to the other, as though he wanted to leave. Let him wait. They needed a plan. By God, Julius Singletary was still running this precinct, no matter what anybody might think.

"The killer!" he said, mouthing the words emphatically as though he were talking to a retard. "Hitting two nights in a row like that. Must've been interrupted when he snuffed that—what was her name?"

"Betty Evans. Yeah, he coulda been interrupted. Woman downstairs heard a scream, opened her door. The guy ran out, passed her on the stairs."

"That's *it*, then! She blew his act. He got the name but not the game. Either that or we got ourselves a regular nightly sex killer. I never heard of one of those before, did you? Even your man Mains needs a night off once in a while."

The lieutenant didn't respond to the dig. He seemed far away. "Cap," he said, "I keep—wondering something." He clomped over to the window that was wide open on another hot dawn. "I wonder—no, it's too wild."

"Be wild. We got to start somewhere."

"What's the chance this second killing's a copycat?"

Now that *was* stupid. Lind didn't usually go off half-cocked. "How could it?" the captain said. "Nobody knew the guy writes filthy names on his victims. There wasn't a line in the papers, on TV, anyplace. We held it back. *Phnfff!*"

"We held it back, but a lotta cops knew."

"What's the percentage in copycatting a sex killing?"

"What's the percentage in any of this stuff, Skip?" the lieutenant said. His big frame went black against the glow of a passing car; he looked like an oversized rapid-fire silhouette. "The guy's got a hard-on for Precinct Nine, anybody can see that. So he jiggers our cars, he kills our pups, and then he wipes out one of our widows by using another killer's M.O."

"Why?"

"Who knows why with a nut case?" Lind said impatiently. "We don't know his mind, Cap. He probably doesn't know it himself. Maybe he figures the first killer'll get the blame. Maybe he figures he'll walk in another guy's footprints, throw us off the track, make us look silly again."

The captain swallowed a yawn and looked at his watch: 5:15 A.M. "This isn't Fu Manchu, Lieutenant. We need something solid, not a bunch of opium dreams."

"What about the cuffs? Is that solid enough for you?"

"We'll see." Suddenly he had his second idea. "Here," he said, shoving a memo pad across the lacquered desk. "Write down the names of everybody has it in for us. Start with police officers."

"Cops?"

"Yale! Cops! Isn't that what you're thinking? That it could be—one of my men? Go ahead! Write the names down one by one. *Phnfff!*"

"Zimmerman," Lind said, scribbling.

"That yay-hoo's in Alaska, pipeline security, last I knew. Perfect job for him."

"He said he'd be back, Cap. You were pretty, uh, forceful when you, uh, terminated him."

"Okay. We'll check out Herbie Zimmerman. Who else you got?"

"Torrance. Dunlap . . ."

"Review board nailed those two, not us." Torrance and Dunlap. A couple of gross incompetents. Got themselves into a fire fight with a scared kid shooting a pellet gun, for God's sake, and shot him in the legs with riot weapons. The civil suit was still in the courts. "Who else?"

"What about—"

The phone made him jump. Jesus Jones, he had to get some sleep before long. He wondered if any precinct commander had ever been caught cooping. "Singletary," he said, sighing deeply.

"Sir, this is Sergeant Ames at headquarters. Sorry we took so long, but you know how it is."

"How is it?" Christ, he was getting punchier by the second.

"Well, Personnel and Records was closed for the night, Cap, and we had to send for a key."

"Huh?" God, his brain was sluggish. "A key for what?"

[195]

"To get into P and R and look up the handcuff registration, sir. They belong to, er uh, one of your, uh, your men, Cap. Third watch. John Jerome McClung."

"Yale? What else?" The captain tried to sound as though this was precisely the news he'd been expecting. He barely remembered McClung. Was he the flopped dick that drank?

"Nothing else, sir."

"Detectives want to talk to him?"

"They're on their way to pick him up."

"*What?* You should have called me before you called the dicks. Matter of courtesy. One of my men. *Phnfff!*"

"Sorry, sir. We're a little disorganized right now. This was—"

He slammed the phone down. "They're McClung's cuffs," he told the watch commander. "How the hell can that be? Didn't he work tonight?"

Lind looked surprised. "No, I, om, gave him the night off."

"Drunk?" He could read the answer from Packer's face. "Oh, my God."

"The dicks want him?"

"On their way."

The big lieutenant leaned forward. "Listen, Skip," he said, "call 'em off. Let me pick up McClung myself. There's liable to be trouble if a couple of dicks jump him cold at six in the morning."

The captain started to say that the matter was out of his hands, but he had second thoughts. Let Lind go out and pump some hot coffee into the guy, sober him before bringing him in. The precinct wouldn't look so bad that way.

"Hold on," he said, dialing headquarters.

"Be right back," Lind said, rolling out the door in that peculiar sea gait of his.

After two tries, the captain reached a deskman in the detective bureau. Yes, sir, he would ask the chief of detectives right away, sir. No, sir, he didn't think the major would authorize the Ninth to pick up McClung; Detectives Clevidence and Dillard were already en route.

"Then hurry up and call, goddamn it!" he said.

To his surprise, the aide came back on the phone within a minute and said politely, "Chief says thanks, we can use your help. Who you sending, sir?"

"My third-watch commander. Packer Lind."

"Chief says he'd like to see McClung here within an hour. Fair enough, Captain?"

"Yale. Fair enough."

As he was hanging up the phone, Lind rushed back in. "Skip!" he said, snorting with excitement. "I just checked McClung's locker. His stick was there, a couple uniforms, some personal stuff. But—no cuffs."

"How'd you get in?"

"It was open. He musta forgot to lock. He was kind of, uh, confused when he went home."

"Seal that locker right now, it's evidence. And—"

"I already did."

"Go to his house and take him downtown. Use plenty backup. Chief of detectives wants him bad."

"On my way, Skip." The watch commander was halfway out the door. Gimpy or not, the big man could move.

"And remember his rights!" the captain called out. "Don't screw it up. *Phnfff!* Here!" He reached into his drawer and found the familiar yellow card and held it out. "Make him sign this waiver first thing."

"Cap, he's a police officer. He knows his rights."

"Make him sign!"

"You don't really think—"

"I'm just a patrol cop like you, Lind. The dicks get paid to do the thinking, not us. Go grab the guy. Tell him it's for—public intoxication. Tell him— *ANYTHING!* I want a clean arrest! Deliver his ass to the dicks within an hour. I promised."

"He lives near here. Manor Heights."

"Good. Get moving! *Phnfff!*"

The early sun was washing out the shadows in the corners of the office, and the green walls began to glow with reflected color. Another scorcher. The captain hoped his career would survive it. Rosarito Beach, Rosarito Beach, he chanted over and over. His own little incantation for times of stress. Rosarito Beach, Rosarito Beach . . . It seemed a million miles away, and who would be with him when he got there?

28

It bothered him to call Amnee and tell her he would be home much later than usual, but he had to do it. To his relief she answered the phone on the second ring, and her voice sounded relaxed. Putting on an act, maybe? He doubted it. It was almost 6 A.M., daytime. Hysteria faded with light. He had noticed the phenomenon before, not only with his wife. Little old ladies who slept behind Fox locks and burglar alarms would carry their beaded purses through the heart of the ghettos as long as the sun warmed their backs. Sometimes they paid the price with cold cash and broken heads.

After the short call home he hurried into the rec room to look for backup. Almost the whole third watch was hanging around after-shift. Some were shooting pool—sloppily, he noted; there was a long gash in the felt. They had other things on their minds. Wait till they heard about Johnny McClung. Nobody in the Ninth was close to McClung except his partner, but the poor drunken guy was one of them, another Lower Slobbovian, and now he was in trouble up to his tin. Packer wondered if a man with fifteen years in the detective bureau could possibly murder a woman and leave registered handcuffs on her body. Well, it made as much sense as Artie's jiggered car or the dead puppies or the Betty Evans killing with bare thumbs and battery acid. It made as much sense as a police officer coming to work drunk. Alcoholics did crazy things, they were true psychos, at least while they were drinking. Johnny McClung qualified.

"Turk," Packer said, leaning over the chubby sergeant, "wanna go for a ride?"

"Who is it?" Molnar said, fingering his flowing Magyar mustache.

Packer whispered, "McClung."

"Shit oh dear."

"Come on. You're his sergeant."

The two supervisors hurried toward the door. Packer remembered his promise just in time. "Hey, listen, everybody," he said loudly. "Thanks for staying. You showed me something, all of you." He lowered his voice. "The cuffs were signed out to Johnny McClung. That's not for repetition, I don't have to tell you."

"You gonna—arrest John?" Don Reichert asked, his long face drawn even longer. Packer couldn't blame the man for being upset; McClung was a likable partner, when he was sober.

"He'll be questioned, Rike, that's all I know. We're going out there now. Who wants to back us up?"

"Back you up?" a voice asked incredulously.

"Orders," Packer explained.

They all stepped forward, including the woman.

"Hey, we're not picking up Martin Bormann!" Packer said, forcing a smile. "Willie? Rollie? You two follow us out. Park across the street and a little bit past the house, okay?"

"Lieutenant?" The stricken Reichert was shouldering his way to the front of the group. "Let me do—something."

"Cover the rear door, Rike. Take whoever you want."

"He'll be a pussy, Lieutenant," the sad-faced man said in his rumbly voice. "I guarantee you. Johnny'd never hurt nobody. Except maybe—Johnny."

The three teams walked outside, Reichert bringing up the rear with Artie Siegl, subdued for a change. Packer said, "Don't use the radio unless you have no choice. He might have a scanner."

"He does," Reichert said. "But his wife keeps pulling the plug." Packer thought of Amnee, and the universality of police experience. He'd have to disconnect their own scanner, sell it for whatever he could get through the police bulletin. Amnee needed no reminder of her husband's occupation. What police wife did? Maybe home scanners were strictly for police freaks, groupies, the poor souls whose thrill was to overhear the turmoils of others.

Manor Heights, where McClung lived, was a cheapjohn real estate development of the late forties: bungalows row on row, stucco chipping, paint blistering and peeling, roofs covered with gap-toothed green asphalt shingles bleached by the weather. Off by themselves stood a few carefully preserved old homes that made the others look even seedier by contrast.

Packer had never visited the McClungs, never been invited, even though Johnny was always friendly and polite. As the Fury slid to a stop a few houses down the block from No. 5216, he saw why the McClungs didn't entertain: they didn't even keep up what little they had. Heavy drinkers seldom did. There wasn't time, and there wasn't energy; they were happy to get through an eight-hour shift and rush to the bottle, if they hadn't been nipping all day on the job.

The two supervisors gave the backup cars time to take their posts, then stepped out into the soupy morning air. "Let's leave our caps," Packer suggested. "The less we look like cops, the better it'll be for John with the neighbors."

"Good idea," Molnar said. He flipped his sweat-stained hat back inside and slammed the car door shut.

Half of the McClungs' parched front lawn had been trimmed; the rusty mower remained on the grass, marking the point where pride had run out. Ahead of it, the weeds were nearly a foot tall. An old Mercury Monarch, gray over blue, sagged on cinder blocks in the driveway; someone had smashed the windshield. The walkway to the house was made of dusty brick, but half of the bricks were loose and the other half gone, revealing the chalky dirt below. Around the tilting wooden porch, wild thistles choked the few ornamental plants, and the two evergreens were brown and scraggly. A wide hedge divided the house from its nearest neighbors; it was carefully clipped on the far half and running wild on the near. Packer turned to Molnar, and Molnar looked down.

Somebody opened the door a crack, then eased it closed. Packer tapped the bell and waited, inhaling the resin smell from the dying trees. The heat made them sweat like the station's walls. He reached down and touched a drooping pansy in a pot; the faded flower was the color of a tattoo on a corpse.

He rang again. "There's a lady home," Molnar whispered. "I seen her."

Packer drummed with his fingernails and said, "Johnny! Open up!"

"Who izzhut?" a slurred female voice asked.

"Johnny McClung live here?" Packer called out. A matched pair of drunks; that's all they needed.

"Who wants ta know?" The words were heavy and indistinct. Maybe she'd been asleep. He'd give her the benefit of the doubt, for the moment. This police family needed every consideration.

"It's me," he said. "Packer Lind. Johnny's, uh, friend."

"His *what?*" The woman peeped out a side curtain, and he saw her face clearly. She looked like a tired old prizefighter in a wig.

"I'm his, uh, watch commander. Down at the station."

"Not home." She'd never make it as an actress.

"Ma'am, we'd just like to talk to John for a minute." He *had* to be home. The bars were closed, all except a few after-hours joints like the Slammer. "We're, uh, friends of his."

There was a commotion inside and then the woman's muted voice: "It's your funeral."

The door creaked open and Johnny McClung swayed in front of them in a stained orange jumpsuit, unzipped down to belly hairs that shone in the pale morning light like a day-old city snowfall. "Lieutenant!" he said, smiling broadly and standing at a slight angle toward the street, as though preparing for the inevitable fall. "Sarge! Hey, you guys come on in! Lemme pour ya a li'l, a *little* libration." He made them welcome with a broad flourish, and Packer realized the man was probably drunker than when he had registered .15 on the breath machine.

"You the guys was boozing with him?" the woman said accusingly. Packer couldn't help staring. Every trace of color had been drained from her skin. Her gray hair hung lank and raggedy, as though she trimmed it in the dark; her face was furrowed and pale; her eyes reflected no light. She was bent and thin; he estimated she was somewhere between thirty and sixty. "You the guys?" she demanded, poking him with a stiff finger. "Huh? *Huh?*"

"We're not the guys, missus," he answered gently, closing the door behind them so the neighbors couldn't witness the sad extravaganza. "We're here to collect John."

"Collect John?" she said, cackling derisively. "Well, go ahead and collect the damn bum. Who's stoppin' ya? What'd he do this time? Drunk on duty? What else is new?" As she spat the words, Packer noticed that half her face seemed frozen; the sound came from the left corner of her mouth only, and when she blinked, her right eye hung wide open. Was it a hangover of her own? Some weird disease? He didn't know what to make of Mrs. John McClung, standing there glowering, a spot of saliva sticking to the right corner of her mouth.

"Hey, come on, come on, party up!" McClung tugged at his supervisors' sleeves as he spoke in a high, excited voice. "Siddown, siddown! Hey, Ginger, you pour, huh? Okay, toots?"

The woman made a spitting noise and walked from the room.

"Excuse her, boys, excuse her," McClung said, still smiling. "She's a little, uh, peculiar on the stubject, the study, the *subject* of, uh, alco, alcol, alcolhol." He took in air and smiled with the conviviality of the practiced drunk. "Hey, glad you stopped by!" He emitted a powerful belch. "Glad you came to the party." He dropped his voice to a conspiratorial tone. "How's things down the station? Can't run a precinct without J. McClung, Two Two Nine Three Six, uh, Eight. Am I right, Sarge? Right, Lieutenant?" He reached up and shook Packer by the shoulder.

"Yop, that's what I wanted to tell you, Johnny," Packer said quickly, glad for the opening. "Couple things came up, we needed your advice. Wondered if you'd maybe give us a hand." He felt a wave of pity. Johnny McClung should have matured into a distinguished-looking middle-aged man; he was the dark type of Irishman whose charcoal-black hair turns to silver instead of gray and whose blue eyes brighten with the years. But the face that wobbled in Packer's eyesight was bloated, splotchy with sunburst veins, the nose turning into a rosy lump and the eyes as dead as the woman's. The liver can absorb only so much sour mash, he said to himself. Then—*blooey.* It produces a Johnny McClung. But why? That was the pity of it all. *Why?* He had known so many McClungs in his twelve years in uniform.

"Hey, let's get going then," the teetering man said. "Just gimme a minute first. Okay?"

"Sure," Packer said, throwing Turk a quick look. "Where you going? We'll help you."

"Hey, thanks!" McClung flashed an off-white cap-toothed smile that gave a hint of how he must have looked as a young man, then floated down a narrow hallway with a picture of the Madonna on one wall and the graduating class of St. Margaret's parochial school on the other. Packer stayed close on his left, ducking his head, and Molnar just behind. The woman lingered in a doorway, listening, but she backed out of sight when they turned into a bathroom.

"You can have that stewbum," she called out. "He's yours! Get the rotten bum out of my sight."

"Just take it easy, Mrs. Mac," the sergeant said. "We'll only be a minute."

"Take him!" she screeched. "Take him away!"

McClung ran the cold water and stuck his head in the sink. Then he raised his dripping flushed face and reached into the medicine cabinet and gulped a big red capsule before either of his escorts realized what was happening. "Uh, what was that, John?" Packer asked.

"My—just my, my—medicine," he said. "Yeah, my medicine."

Molnar palmed the container and passed it to the watch commander behind the drunken man's back. It was Seconal, thirty milligrams a pop, a dose heavy enough to put a sober man to sleep in twenty or thirty minutes, and a drunk in less. "Why'd you take that?" Packer said, annoyed at the sneaky move. "That's a—sleeping pill. That's bad stuff, John."

"I need 'em, Lieutenant," McClung said, slipping to his knees in front of the toilet. "I'm so—sick." He began to sob.

"Suck your pills!" The woman's voice came through the walls like a knife through a cardboard box. "Suck your pills and bawl! Goddamn bum! Bum! *Bum! Goddamn bum!* BUM! STEWBUM!" Packer couldn't tell if she was crying behind her shouts.

"Okay, Mrs. Mac, we'll be getting out of your hair now," Molnar said as they lifted the man like a marionette and steered him toward the door, his feet barely moving along the worn plastic tiles. A litany poured from the house as they walked him down the front steps. "Bum! Bum! Goddamn *bum!* Goddamn shitting bum! Goddamn bum! Bum bum bum bum . . . *Goddamn shitting fucky bum* . . ." Poor woman, Packer thought. Poor, sad woman. Doesn't even know how to curse. Just blurting out any ugly sounds that come to mind. The words are unfamiliar to her, you can tell by the way she uses them. Looks like she spent half her life in church, kneeling and lighting candles. By the looks of her and the looks of him, it'll be a close race to see which one lights the last candle. . . .

Molnar drove, Packer alongside, McClung in back. "Sorry, I'm sorry," the drunk mumbled as Packer pushed the automatic door lock.

"About what, John?" Packer asked. He tilted to hear the man's weak voice.

"Can't shut her up," he was saying. "Never *can* shut her up. A fine up—up—*upstanding* woman like that, too. Tried everything. Can't shut her up." He put his trembling hands over his tufted pink ears as though she were inside the car screeching. Half-turning on his seat, Packer made a discreet study of the hands. There was no trace of any dark substance. But there'd been plenty of time to wash, drunk or sober.

"Where ya been hanging these days, Johnny?" Packer asked, as though making idle conversation.

"Hanging?" The jerking head snapped up as though someone had tightened a string, then fell back to the chest. "Oh, just—here 'n' there," he said suspiciously. "Why?"

Packer asked, "Where's here and there?" then leaned across the seat and whispered, "Slow it down, Turk!"

"I thought the captain said—"

"*Slower, Turk!*" Packer whispered, then said in a loud voice, "Johnny and me, we're just having a little talk. Right, John?"

"Li'l talk," McClung said, friendly again. "Old times, stuff like 'at." Packer wondered when the Seconal would take hold, and what the reaction would be. Kids who popped reds stayed up for days, but the drug was meant for sleep. He had to keep the man blabbering.

"Say, John, you been to the Slammer lately?"

"Shlammer? Not that goddamn joint. Never catch me drinking in there. Not since I was, uh, transferred. I go—I go—" He batted his eyes wildly.

Packer said quickly, "One of the guys was saying, he was saying he had a drink with you at the—the— Oh, I forget the place."

"Huh? Musta been the Green Onion. No, Samarini's. I was there tonight. Hey, wait a minute, that's—unaccurate. It was last week. I had a few couple little drinks at Samalini's. Isn't that okay?"

"When?"

"Dunno. Last night. Tonight. Uh, yesternight."

"Been drinking two days straight?"

McClung smiled and nodded, as though proud of his achievement. Packer tried to remember the watch schedule. "Turk," he asked under his breath, "was he off when Betty Evans got it?"

"Yeah."

Packer groaned inside. "Been on a toot, huh, Johnny?" Could this pathetic drunk have—

"Toot. Toot-a-toot-toot!" McClung began to sing in a thin tenor voice. "Me and Rosie O'Grady, all over town. We licked the lights fantastic. . . ."

Packer interrupted. "Where'd you drink, Johnny? Come on, pal, you can tell *me*. It's Packer, pal." He hated himself for the same old hypocrisy, the false friendship. Pretending that they were asshole buddies from way back, when in fact they knew each other only as flopped dick and watch commander. And all the time, Packer thought, I'm helping one of my own men dig his grave. And the worst part is I don't have a choice. Not a *hint* of a choice. If this man killed— Goddamn it, I'm doing my job as a supervisor, as a cop. Maybe it's time for a switch. Maybe Amnee's right, as usual. Maybe—

"Where'd I drunk—eh, *drink?*" McClung asked.

"Yeah. Where you been hanging the last couple nights?"

"Tol' you already. Samino's." Another syllable amputated from Samaralino's bar and grill. "Blue Onion. No, the Purple Onion." The color was wrong both tries. "Washbury's." He must have meant the Washington Avenue Bar, or maybe Richberry's. "The Pirate's Cone. *Cove.*" He got one name right at last. "Then me and some, uh, acquaints, uh, some companions, we dropped over to the park, had a couple bottles of wine, sherry, stuff like 'at. Had a few on a, on—a bus. Pissed on the driver. *No!* Pissed *off* the driver, that's right, uh, Packer did you say?" He laughed hollowly, and coughed into his shaking hand. His lungs rattled like toy castanets. The pill was taking hold.

"Johnny, do you know Genna Jocelyn?"

"Jozlin? Whuzzat? Whuzza Jozlin?" He turned his wobbling head at the mention of the name, and now his red nose was pressed to the window as they approached the big granite City Hall.

"Genna Jocelyn, John," Packer said. "Genna. Eddie's widow."

"Oh, *that* Genna Johnson!" He jerked upright again. "Genna. Yeah. I know her. Nice lady. Genna's her, her last name, you said? *Huh?*" His eyes rolled upward like a window blind, and crossed and uncrossed as they came back down. "Never knew her, Lieutenant. Never been, uh, popperly innerduced, I guess you'd call it."

"You seen her lately?"

"Who?" He slumped deeply into the seat, knees splayed wide. "Oh, you mean *Genna*. Seen her at the Onion. No, the Samaro's. I mean Samino's. She was drinking with us. Wasn't I?"

"Don't ask me, Johnny."

"Hey! That's right! Joyce Genna Johnson. Jo*han*son. She bought, she borrowed, she ob—ob—*obtained* a bottle wime. *Good* wime. 'At's right! Wouldn't kid you guys. Terrific broad, Joyce. Gen'rous with her time, gen'rous with her, her, her money. Very nice person, know what I mean?"

"We know what you mean, Johnny," Packer said. He turned toward Molnar. Their eyes locked; Packer nodded, and they swung into the entrance marked "Official Business Only." It was 7:10 A.M. They eased past a car with four polished gold stars on its bumper. The chief was in.

29

Once again Gerald Yount had lost track of time. He knew only that the sun was shining straight into his eyes and therefore it was morning. He stumbled along the busy street toward the Loo-Ray Arms; his legs were stiff, as though he had overextended himself running or walking. He had stomped across the night, he was sure of that. Hour after hour. The counselor at church had said walking would help him sleep. Still too soon to tell. But his legs were wobbly, and the sun was searing his eyes. Must be coming to his turn soon. What was the next street . . . ?

Locust.

Three more blocks. Or was it farther? Was he three blocks from home or three miles? He wasn't sure.

He slumped against a cement bench, sluggishly waved a bus off as it veered to the curb to pick him up, then staggered to his feet and turned in a full circle and plodded on into the sun.

He had to sleep today. Had to fight off—the scenes. When had he slept last? He had a dim memory of dozing during the night. Wasn't it in a park? He remembered a band shell, a line of chipped Greek columns in whitewashed plaster, a mossy stone bench like the one at the bus stop. The moon had shone through the openings, and then it seemed as though he'd blinked his eyes, and when he opened them the moon had moved two columns down the row. Had he slept two columns worth? How long was that?

The residue of nightmares littered his brain. When had he dreamed them? Maybe this night? Years ago?

His mother handed back his report card, her face in rigid lines. "Why the B, Gerald?" she asked. Her yellow eyes shot sparks like a Catherine wheel.

Pictures . . .

He was being sent away again. The train towered over him in the station, engine pounding low and powerful, scaring him speechless. His mother smelled of lilac as she gripped his mittened hand. When she let go for the last time to hand his bag to a beaming black man with a gold badge on his flat black cap and long horse teeth and skinny black shoes, he broke loose and locked his arms around a steel pillar. His mother's boy friend hurried over to wrench at him with sandpaper hands and breathe dirty words in his face.

Why had he dreamed those dreams? He wasn't even sure they came from real life. His childhood was lost to him. *Real life:* where did it begin and end? He would understand nothing till she came back.

Two boys cradling skateboards made a wide detour around him. He stopped and stared, and they vanished in the dancing air above the sidewalk. He had a flash memory of black kids swarming a police car and asking silly questions about his guns.

Would those same children be afraid of him now?

He rubbed his eyes and made them tear, and the tears burned and slickened down his face.

Could he have been running from somebody all night? Was that why he was so exhausted?

The long train began to slide from the station, but he clung to the pole. "Let loose, ya little prick ya!" Breath like dung . . .

He tripped and almost fell across a curb at Fletcher Street. Two more blocks . . .

He was aboard now, nose flat against the cold glass, searching the receding crowd till all the faces became a single face: his mother's. He remembered not to cry.

He had to—keep moving. Had to—get to the apartment. Maybe she'd be there.

What was her name? They all had the same name.

Darlene.

30

Packer found the station strangely quiet when he returned from the Central Lockup at 8 A.M. The first watch was on the street, the lieutenant and the two sector sergeants were gone from their desks, and the captain's door was closed. Proably talking to the dicks or the chief's office, he assumed. Poor Skip. He'll be on the phone all day, wearing himself out going "Singletary!" and *"Phnfff!"*

In the rec room, remnants of the third watch huddled together, four hours after their shift ended. Probably want to see if they can be helpful, Packer figured. Well, they can. "Artie?" he called out. "Can you come in a minute?"

He carefully shut his door behind the little cop. "Artie," he said, "think hard. That guy you stopped the other night—any chance he was John McClung?"

Siegl made the face of someone sipping a health drink. "Jeez, Pack, I never, uh, really saw the, om, dude. I only got, uh, three or four feet when he—"

"What'd he look like from the back?"

"Well, uh, I was looking for his hands, Packer. You know how I operate on a T.V. First I get a good make on the hands, see that they're empty. Then I look the guy over. I mean, shit, you don't expect to be stopping Jack the Ripper, do you?"

"Artie, you're a goddamn good cop, we all know that. There must've been something you noticed besides his hands."

"Yeah. Well. The guy was white. He was wearing something on his head—a watch cap, maybe. Dark. I got the impression his hair was blond."

"Or maybe—silvery gray—like McClung's?"

Artie fidgeted in his chair. He seemed to shrink down into the flyweight division. Packer knew the feeling. Righteous or not, nobody liked close questioning. But nobody liked sex killings, either. "I wish I could help ya, Pack. But the guy—he rabbited *so* fast."

"Okay, Artie, let's come at it from a different direction. Can you say positively it *wasn't* Johnny?"

Siegl was staring at the floor in front of him. His bland unreadable gaze shifted to the cracked picture of His Honor the Mayor, and then made a meticulous study of the backs of the three lockers used by the watch commanders. Finally he mumbled, "No. But I'm just—guessing."

"Ask Reichert to come in, will ya, Art?" This was no time for cat-and-mouse games.

"I'm sorry, Packer."

"Don't be sorry, Artie. You know where you can get me, you remember anything."

"Uh—yeah." He turned for the door, then compressed his lips and spread his hands. "What can I tell ya, Packer? Christ, the guy coulda been a Martian, ya wanna know the truth. It happened so—*fast!* When I say the hair was blond or gray, that's just a quick impression. I could never swear in court to it." He sounded thoroughly apologetic. Good.

Maybe he'd go home and dredge up some memories. Sometimes small details came back to witnesses. Sometimes small details solved big cases.

"Send Rike in, will ya?"

Packer felt vaguely traitorous, grilling his own men; he knew the instincts he was bucking. Johnny McClung might be stone guilty, but nobody in the precinct wanted to prosecute a brother officer, guilty or not. Artie had bobbed and weaved; Reichert would play slow and dumb. He was a truculent man anyway, disenchanted with the system, and he was McClung's partner, a relationship closer than marriage in many ways.

"You wanted me, Lieutenant?" His eyes slanted downward, creating the look of a bereaved bloodhound. He had never seemed more sullen or unfriendly.

"Yeah, Rike. Johnny was drunk, we took him downtown. I guess you know why."

Reichert nodded about a quarter of an inch. "Will they . . .?"

"Last I heard, the dicks were gonna hold him till he sobered up, then ask him a few questions. You know, the cuffs? I asked him a few myself."

"Uh-huh."

"Said he'd been on a two-day toot. Said he'd had a drink with Genna. The feeling I got, he barely knew his name."

"Um-hmm."

"Has he been drinking in the car?" Packer stabbed the question quickly, hoping it would catch Reichert off balance. But the man just sat there blinking his cowlike brown eyes.

"Rike, listen," Packer said, leaning forward. "I swear I'll never use this against Johnny, you, or anybody else. Swear to *God!* Has he been drinking on duty?"

The blank face turned away. "Don't ask me that."

"Listen to me, goddamn it! Your partner's in jail. There's a couple homicides hanging over him, Murder One all the way. The death penalty's back now, man, and the public's always gunning for cops. Now gimme an answer! I can't help Johnny if I don't know the truth. The D.A.'s office—they'll be trying to burn him."

Reichert looked up slowly. "And you're not?" he said accusingly.

The defensiveness of the patrol cop; there it was again. You could go to the mat for them time after time, cover up their mistakes, lie to their wives, overstate their efficiency reports, guzzle hooch with them, and risk your goddamn ass for them, but the claws always came out if you got snoopy.

"I won't lie to you, Rike," he said evenly. "If I find John's guilty, I'll be the first to testify. But right now I'm on his side and I'll stay there till I'm proved wrong. If that means I'm prejudiced—then I'm prejudiced. The D.A.'s gonna be prejudiced, too. He'll go balls-out for a conviction; he's got to get the mayor off his ass, the media, the public. The way things are, Johnny's gotta take the fall. His alibi stinks, he admits he was drinking with Genna, and they found his calling card on her body. He's too fucked up to help himself, and nobody else can help him if they don't know the truth. You follow me? Now I don't care if he was shit-faced drunk on duty every night of the week, that's ancient history now, but I *got* to have some place to start. Now spill it, for Chrisakes! *Has he been drinking in the car?*"

Reichert looked up, then back to his patrol boots. "All the time, Lieutenant," he said in a low gargle that Packer had to strain to hear. "All the time."

The news was almost a total surprise. McClung had fooled him, at least till last night. For over two months he had seemed straight, an efficient, sober cop. "How the hell come I never noticed it?" he asked, feeling foolish.

"I read some place if a guy drinks constantly he never gets a hangover and he always looks sober as long as he don't go wild and overdo it. I mean at least till he falls on his face. That's the way Johnny drank. Many a night he'd come to work and I wouldn't even recognize he was juiced till he'd say something a little—out of kilter, you know? But I can't remember a single watch when he didn't suck maybe a pint of vodka, like a steady flow—drip, drip, drip. Like somebody getting one of them whattaya call it? Intravenious feedings. Course, on his days off, he may of drank more."

"He went on binges, it looks like. At least his last two off-days. What about the goofballs?"

"Goofballs?" Reichert's look of surprise seemed genuine. "He had pills for a heart condition, that's all I know. Took a couple every night."

"Just a couple?"

"Goddamn it, I'm not his mother!" Reichert stopped and swallowed hard. "I'm sorry, Packer. I didn't mean—"

"The pills, Rike."

"I didn't see 'em close up." He kneaded his hands and sat on the front inch of his chair and spoke to the floor. "He coulda been popping pills when I wasn't looking, that's what I meant. I wasn't studying him every second. He was always sticking gum in his face, anyway."

"I know. Juicy Fruit." Packer made a mental note to keep a closer watch on all chewers of aromatic gums and candies—he was still chagrined at failing to spot a habitual boozer on his shift. What the hell good was a watch commander who didn't know his own personnel? "Did he talk about—women?"

"About *what?*"

"Women."

"Lieutenant, God is my judge, I don't think John had an outside interest in the world except Glenmore vodka. Even his wife. You meet her?"

"Yop."

"Then you know the problem. You talk to her?"

"Um-hmmm. Briefly. What's the matter with her face?"

"That's some kinda—condition. Bell's Palsy, I think they call it. Half the face goes dead. Nerves. John figured it was his fault. It started after—that other thing."

"*What* other thing?" Packer was aware of sounding slow-witted, but he couldn't help it. Maybe he *was* dumb; he'd have a bitch of a time proving otherwise, the way things were going on his watch.

"You know," Reichert mumbled. "When he was on the dicks. His partner getting, uh, shot and all."

"I heard some gossip," Packer said. "The usual crap: he didn't back up his partner, he didn't—"

"Well, he *didn't* back up his partner. But—it coulda happened to any of us."

"I never heard the inside." And don't tell me, he almost blurted out. Cops had the most intense love-hate relationships with one another. Cops would hack a watch-mate's reputation to bits and then crawl through broken glass to back him up. Like young brothers in a big family. Packer had read all kinds of studies on the subject; they were full of words like "ambivalence" and "dichotomy" and "rescue complex" and "sibling rivalry," and they made about as much sense as Ernie Smoliss discussing the binomial theorem.

But now he was desperate to know everything about Johnny McClung, gossip included. Gossip could motivate, gossip could enrage, gossip could destroy a man. He tilted against the wall in his unsteady chair and locked his hands behind his head in the open body-language that said, You can trust me.

"He'd just bought one of those safety holsters," Johnny McClung's partner began in a voice suitable for the last rites. "You know, the kind where you hafta shove the weapon forward before you can draw? He'd been moonlighting a few rock concerts at night, crowd security, picking up change, and he was afraid some punk might get high and try to disarm him." Reichert stopped talking and looked around, got up from his chair and rattled the door knob, then continued in a near whisper. "The second time he wore the safety holster, he wasn't used to it yet, get me? Some jerk-off car thief drew on his partner from behind, and John couldn't unholster in time. Forgot he had the safety thing, kept yanking at his piece till the guy fired. One of those things that happen, Lieutenant, but you can see how it looked to the other dicks."

Yes, Packer could see how it looked. Above all else, partners protected each other. When the mutual coverage broke down, nobody wanted to hear excuses. *You didn't back up your partner.* The ultimate sin.

"That's when he was flopped, Lieutenant. I been riding with him since."

"When did he start the heavy drinking?"

"Right away. I'm sorry. I shoulda said something." He closed his eyes and looked away. "But I—I—I just—"

"You just followed the unwritten law," Packer said. "I never could squeal on a partner either, if it's any consolation. I rode with Maloney for a while. Remember Maloney? Vice? Shake down his own children for a buck. I suspected, but I never said a word. Probably shoulda." Fran Maloney was in the joint on the hind end of a two-to-ten for extortion and assault. "Sometimes we get all mixed up, Rike. Some of our traditions—well, maybe they don't work too good anymore. I mean, we wind up doing our people more harm than good. Maybe that's the way it was with you and Johnny. Sometimes a guy doesn't know *what* to do."

He walked around the desk and laid his big hand on the beat cop's shoulder. "Listen, Rike, I appreciate it, what you told me. You did the right thing." His hand came away wet. With the door shut, they might as well be casting ingots in the little room. It was a few minutes after 9 A.M.; Juvenile Division would be open now; and he had an urgent call to make. "Not one word leaves this room, I promised you that before, and I meant it."

"You won't tell the dicks?"

"They got their investigation, I got mine."

"Thanks, Lieutenant. Listen, if there's anything, *anything*—"

"I'll let you know, Rike."

Walking out the door, the cop shook his head and muttered, "Christ, this is awful."

"Awful," Packer echoed, sealing him out gently.

When Juvenile answered, he asked for whoever was handling the case of the Visibar thieves. *"The what?"* the female voice asked.

"Two kids tried to pry a light bar off one of our cars yesterday afternoon. Precinct Nine."

"Oh. Sure. Hold on, please."

After a few loud clicks and buzzes and muffled remarks, an abrupt young voice answered, "Donato!"

"Officer Donato, this is—"

"*Detective* Donato," the brash voice interrupted.

"This is Packer Lind, Ninth Precinct."

The voice went from smart-ass to respectful. "Oh, yeah, Lieutenant. I heard about you." And back to smart-ass. "Plenty going down, eh, Loot?" Typical young charger, Packer said to himself. The sensitivity of a Marine corporal. Where did they recruit these guys? The stockade?

"Listen, Donato, I need your help on something. Confidential for now, understand?"

"Shoot."

"Those two punks. Gonzales and, uh—"

"Campion."

"You still holding them?"

"You kidding? They blew out of here yesterday. Parental recognizance. We had 'em two hours. Longer'n usual."

"What's their story?"

"Don't ask. Pure cowshit, top to bottom. And not a goddamn thing we can do, either. Lift a finger to one of those punks and you're greased to the review board. They're the first generation in history that eat but don't shit, ya know what I mean? I mean, they sprout angel's wings before they're six years old, ya know what I mean? Why—"

"What was their story?" Packer interrupted. Every time you talked to a Juvenile officer you heard the same speech. They should tape-record it on a loop.

"You really wanna hear their fairy story?"

Packer sighed loudly. "I really wanna hear it."

"Okay, *okay!* Way I hear, you guys at Nine can use a laugh. Well, they met this weirdball in the park, see. Stoned out of his gourd, all googly-eyed and shaky, see, and the guy says, 'How'd you boys like to make a half a yard for twenty minutes' work?'"

"Fifty bucks?"

"Fifty dollars, five-oh," Donato said patiently, as though talking to an old man or a child. A little of this guy went a long way. "That's their story, anyway. So they tell the creep, 'Sure, what the fuck.' They're just a couple fresh punks, petty thieves, shoplifters. Roadrunners, ya know what I mean?"

Packer said he knew what he meant.

"Never saw a half a yard between 'em, so they ask this character what do they hafta do for the bread. Can you dig it so far, Loot? I mean, these kids must of been sniffing glue three days to come up with a story like this." There was a long pause while the Juvenile detective talked to someone behind his hand.

"I'd like to hear it just the same," Packer said. "And Donato—I'm in, uh, kind of a hurry." The phone felt like a soapdish against his ear.

"Gotcha, gotcha. Anyway, the creep says, 'You guys know the Ninth Precinct building on Lawndale?' He says all they gotta do is pry a light bar off one of the parked green-and-whites and throw it way back in the brambles. They says bullshit, and he says, 'No, I mean it. Here!' And he hands 'em five bucks each and tells 'em to come back for the rest after the caper. So—that's it. Poor little kids. Putty in the hands of the big bad dude. We get that shit *all* the time, Lieutenant. None of these juveniles ever broke a law in their life. I mean how can they get in trouble when they spend all their time selling papers and helping their moms? It's always some Big Bad Wolf forced 'em into it."

"Did they describe the guy?"

"Yeah, wait a minute, I got it right here. . . . Hey, they made up a pretty good description. Five foot ten, black hair, dark eyes, skinny as hell, acted like he'd been snorting coke or something. It's all goose shit, Loot, so what's the diff?"

"What makes you so sure?"

"Because we hear stories like that six times a day in Juvenile. Six*teen* times a day."

"You question the boys yourself?"

"Me and Detective Mathisen. Francine. My partner."

"Weren't the kids afraid they'd get caught? Stripping a police car right outside the station?"

"Listen to this for imagination. They said the guy told 'em the job was a pussy if they went exactly at four o'clock. Told 'em some of the cars rolled at quarter to four, so they'd already be gone, and the rest would still be standing roll call inside the station at four sharp."

Packer's attention picked up sharply. "That's one part of the story wasn't goose shit," he said.

"Huh?"

"That's the way we been staggering patrols this summer. Keeps at least half our cars on the street at all times."

"Yeah?" Donato sounded surprised.

"Yop. How d'ya figure those kids knew to make up something like that?"

[213]

"Search me, Lieutenant. Anything else I can do for ya? Francine, uh, Detective Mathisen just come on."

"No, I guess that's it. Oh, uh, did you get the weird guy's name?" A dumb question, but you never knew.

"Lemme check." A loud hum came over the phone; Packer thought the connection had gone bad, but then he realized it was Detective Donato humming off-key as he leafed through the file. "I think, *hmmmmmmmmmmmm*, they might of, *hmmmmmmmmmmmmm*, they might of gave us, *hmmmmmmmmmmmmm*, the creep's name. That's another way you can tell the little turds were lying. Spilled everything about this guy except the size of his jock, ya know? Too many details. Dead giveaway, ya know what I mean?"

Packer didn't disagree. Liars usually gave themselves away by telling too much, seldom by telling too little. "What name did they say?" he asked. "You remember it?"

"I'm looking, I'm looking! Uh, Crosby, Crossen, something like that."

Packer swallowed hard. "Keep looking!" he ordered.

The light sound of rustling onionskin came over the phone. "Yeah, here it is!"

Packer held his breath.

"Koslo."

31

Amnee was watching the noon news when she heard his Wagoneer in the gravel driveway. She wondered if he'd spent the morning at headquarters. The newscaster had said there'd been a series of high-level meetings. The police department didn't worry about his sleep, and neither did he. He actually seemed pleased on the days the captain woke him up and called him in! Maybe it made him feel important, made him feel like—somebody. Everyone needed to be needed. But didn't he know how much he was needed around here? Maybe it was her own fault. Maybe she wasn't communicating. Well, she'd do better. He'd see. She'd make him feel like the most needed husband in town. Because he *was*.

She started to get up to greet him but dropped back on the sofa when one of the mayor's pin-striped aides appeared on the black and white TV screen and announced that the citizens had nothing to fear, but if anyone had any information . . . She stood up again and sat down again when she recognized the police chief's face. He was being interviewed in the corridor outside his office and he was hinting smugly that there was a major break in the case, he wished he could say more, but perhaps later . . . In the meantime, he said, looking straight into the camera, the nation's finest P.D. was on the job, *ahem* and *harrumph.* . . . Pompous ass! He wasn't handling a damned thing. Men like her husband were doing the scut work.

"Hi, hon."

"Oh, Packer, sweetheart, thank God you're home. You must be exhausted, poor baby."

"Did he call again?" His broad face was furrowed, and as he spoke he surveyed the kitchen as though he expected someone else. It figured he'd be keyed up. The precinct must have been a madhouse. She could imagine Singletary stumbling around screaming contradictory orders. Well, she'd make her husband lie down and rest if she had to lock the bedroom door and bulldog him like a rodeo calf.

"Did *who* call?" she asked.

"Uh, *anybody,*" he said, brushing past her in the bedroom. He carried a metal container a little larger than a cigar box.

"No," she said. "Why?"

"Oh, uh, nothing." He hurried into the front room to the delighted squeals of Emily Packer Lind. "Just wondered," he called back. He picked the baby up and kissed her and lifted her like a barbell till the wisps of blond hair touched the ceiling. "Down!" Emmy yelped. "Dah, put—*down!*" But she was giggling all the while.

He lowered the baby to the floor and hugged Amnee at last. Then he lifted the baby again. "Packer!" Amnee said, pleased by the attention. "You must have missed us."

"You'll never know," he said, and launched into a long story about a murder and a couple of teen-age boys and a damaged light bar and a man named—Koslo.

"Dear God," she said, sinking onto the sofa. "I knew he was more than a crank, Packer. I could just—tell. Oh, poor Genna!"

"The guy hates cops, he's out to hurt the precinct any way he can. He did one of the sex killings, maybe both. Yeah, I know it sounds remote. But I got—a feeling. Genna had—she had 'copsucker' scrawled across her stomach in mascara. The Evans girl had 'slut.' I didn't tell you because we're holding it back."

She covered her mouth with both hands. "Oh, Packer!" she said, her eyes straining wide. "Oh, sweetie!"

"Hon, we've got a nut case on our hands, might as well face reality. No telling what's next or who. There's a six-state bulletin out for escapees from mental hospitals, escapees from prisons. We're checking anybody that was released lately and might have a grudge. A screen like that could take two months. Meantime, he walks. A homicidal maniac that hates cops. Who else would pay fifty bucks to have a coupla kids deface a prowl car? For *what?* He's the one killed the pups, hon, or hired somebody to do it, I'd bet my bars on it. I could show you two dozen winos that'd stomp a dog to death for a pint of Petri white. And give you change."

She felt cold all over, boneless. The hollow, defenseless feeling of yesterday had diminished overnight; now it was back, and worse. He was home to protect them, but he wouldn't always be home. When danger stalked a city, normal people could lock their windows and their doors and stay inside, but cops—cops went out and *looked* for the danger, solicited it, begged it to make an appearance. God, what a way to live!

"Sweetheart," she said, surprised when her voice came out hoarse, "I'm, uh, taking Emmy to m-m-mother's for a while. Till this—blows over."

"No, hon!" he said quickly. The baby sniffled, feeling the tension, and Amnee knelt and picked her up. "That's not the way," he was saying. "If the guy's trying to get me by hurting you, a drive to the country isn't gonna stop him. And anyway, all he's done is call. If he comes here, we'll be ready for him."

"Ready for him?" She was biting back panic; it pushed into her throat like an indigestible meal. Emmy trembled in her arms, and Amnee held her close. "You'd use us as—bait? Your own wife and baby?"

"Honey, you're upset," he said, closing the two of them in his huge embrace. "Look, I figured it all out. First I need to check the locks, windows, stuff like that."

"Check the . . .?"

"Make sure the house is tight. So the, uh, guy can't get, uh, inside. Barker's sending the district car over. When I go on watch tonight, Bethea and Beemer'll be parked down the street in an unmarked car, securing the front, and another team'll be next door at the Adamsons', covering the back. Anybody that slips through that perimeter, he's either a ghost or—" He cut himself off and stood up, as though he realized he'd made a poor choice of words.

Dear God . . . She felt faint and let go of the baby.

"Top of that," he said quickly, "somebody'll be checking around the house all the time. The shrubs, the driveway. You two couldn't be safer." She felt like telling him to stop pretending. His smile, meant to be reassuring, didn't include his eyes. He was just as jumpy as she was about the crazy man.

"The phone company's installing a tap and a tracer," he went on. "They'll give you a call."

"They're coming *here?*"

"I guess." He held up the silvery metal box. "Then there's—this." He thrust it toward her.

She shrank into the corner of the sofa. The box was police hardware, first cousin to the guns she detested. Her husband had to use tools like that in his work, but she didn't, any more than a carpenter's wife had to carry a saw.

"It's a Varda alarm," he said, opening the lid and uncovering dials and meters. "You'll never need it, but I brought it home to make you more, uh, comfortable. Less, uh, scared. With this thing, you touch a sensor and you got help at the door practically instantly. Here, I'll show ya." He pulled their single easy chair from the wall and slid the box behind it. A long thin wire ran from the box itself to a metal disc the size of a dime. He inserted the disc under Emmy's sock monkey on the empty bookshelf reserved for dolls. "There's your silent burglar alarm."

"My *what?*" She felt apprehensive with the thing in the house. It confirmed that she had something to fear. A *lot* to fear. Besides, it might—go off. Then what?

"If you see anything suspicious, all you do is pick up the sock monkey. Simple as that. The sensor tells the box to start transmitting the alarm."

"To the car parked outside?"

"To every radio in the precinct!" he said. "You'll have a half a dozen cars in minutes. In *seconds!*"

"But why do we need that?" She felt the tears brimming her eyes, and her voice was squeaky and small. "You said, you said, you *promised* me, Packer. Nobody can get in the house."

"That's right, they can't. But this way you're even protected from—from termites."

She tried a gallows laugh, but it wouldn't pass her tightened throat. She wanted to be reasonable; her brain told her to be reasonable, all her experience and all her knowledge told her to be reasonable. But it was like telling a bird to be reasonable about a snake. Reason didn't matter anymore. Reason was—unreasonable.

"Where do I speak?" she asked, leaning over the back of the chair and staring at the metal box.

"You don't," he said. "There's a tape and a transmitter inside. It's already programed. You lift the sock monkey off the sensor, and Varda starts calling in cars."

She carefully kept her back to him so he couldn't read her face. The poor man had enough problems without having to cope with an unstable wife. "What'll it say?" she croaked.

"I forget the exact words. 'Housebreak in progress, private residence, Seventy-one Eighty Orchard.' Something like that. It repeats the same thing three times a minute. Here." He handed her a small instruction manual. She turned a page at random and read a boxed message in red print: "Officers and supervisors must realize that when they respond to the Varda alarm the subject will most likely be at the scene and possibility of a hazardous confrontation is extremely high."

Dear Father in Heaven . . .

"Packer," she said, turning to face him, her cheeks punched inward by the knuckles of both hands, "I want to take Emmy to my mother's. We'll be—safer there."

"No, honey, you won't!" he insisted. He brushed her hands aside and cupped her chin in his palm. He looked deep into her moist eyes and squeezed his hard body onto the chair with her. The baby let out a joyful squeal and waddled across the living-room floor, speeding up and beginning to lose control as she approached the center of her universe. Packer grabbed her by the plastic pants and lifted her, giggling, to his knee. Then he pulled Amnee's head against his shoulder and spoke very softly. "Honey, listen. You're scared and nobody could blame you. You don't deserve what's happening and Emmy doesn't deserve it and I don't deserve it, for that matter. *But we're in it now.* The whole precinct's in it. This guy's lost control. He's hitting at us every way he can. You'll be safer here than anyplace else. You'll have a whole damn precinct looking after you, and you'll have— me. Can't you see that, hon? I can't get leave to go to Oak Forest with you—not with this guy running around, uh, strangling people. You're safest right—"

"Here," she said automatically, hardly hearing the words.

"You're gonna be *okay!*" he said, nuzzling her light-brown hair with his jaw. "Don't you realize that, honey?"

"I—realize it." But she didn't. She felt lifeless, like a robot. This— was—not happening! She wished she could harden herself into a statue. A statue couldn't be raped, a statue couldn't be mutilated. If she had to go through this, she could do it only as a robot, a zombie. Otherwise she would bend and snap the instant Packer left the house. She would run screaming with the baby in her arms to the first passing motorist, and beg for protection. She knew her strengths and weaknesses. She had opted to be a cop's wife, not a cop.

The three of them walked in single file to the bedroom, and Packer shut the windows. He disappeared into the back and returned with his Monkey Ward tool kit. He hammered large nails along the tops and bottoms of the windows. As he worked, she rocked lightly on the bed, her thin arms clasped tightly across her chest while the baby toddled around in her daddy's wake.

He said, "They're holding Johnny McClung."

She was aware that he had spoken, even heard the words, but they hadn't registered. "What?"

"I said they're—we're holding Johnny McClung. His cuffs were on Genna's body. He doesn't remember much of anything the last two days, but he says they had a drink together. Reichert says the guy's been drunk since Day One. Shows how well I know my men." He gave a sonorous yawn. It was early afternoon, but on his biological clock it was long after midnight. "There," he said, speaking with three nails in his teeth while he hammered in another. "Nobody'll ever get froo dis window. Not widdout a brick."

"There's no shortage of bricks," she heard herself saying under her breath.

"Anyway," he went on, stepping away from the sealed window, "they're questioning him. Probably got three teams of dicks stomping on him in track shoes. Poor guy, he takes goofballs, too."

"Could he have been—the one?" She couldn't bring herself to use a stronger word.

"I have my doubts, but—" He yawned again, reached for Emmy and grabbed her around the waist till his fingertips touched. "Give Dah a kiss. Um-*ummmmm*. Sweet baby."

"Mommy, too," the child pouted.

He kissed Amnee and hugged her till she was limp in his arms. "Stay cool," he said. "Who'd try to hurt a police lieutenant's family?"

Koslo? she wondered, but said nothing.

After a while, she heard him banging on the back door. "What now?" she called out.

"Tightening the hinges. Checking the locks. The place'll be a fort. Oh, listen, hon—if you have to go out after I leave, call the precinct. They'll send a car."

She slumped into a chair again, and the baby grabbed onto her jeans. "Oh, Emmy," she said, trying to keep the anxiety from her voice. "Oh, Emmy . . ."

"Mommy sing 'Humphrey Dumpty?'" the little voice asked. Amnee hummed a few lines and then turned her head away. *A police escort to go to the market. . . .*

This was not happening to anybody she knew.

It was happening to two strangers named Amnee and Emily. They would have her prayers.

The phone rang an hour after Packer left. She had halfway expected it. She picked the phone up and listened numbly.

No sound. Not even breathing. There was a light buzz on the line, as though a tape recorder were spinning somewhere. Had the phone company installed its tap? "Hello?" she said, inhaling a great spasm of breath and producing a sepulchral sound.

"Hello," the hollow voice answered. "Is it—you?"

Her jaws were locked.

"Why don't you talk?" the voice said louder.

She sat erect and forced the tan telephone tightly against her ear, afraid he would hear her intakes of breath. This was the way baby chicks acted when weasels approached.

"Talk!" he said, sounding frightened. "Talk to me! *Talk to me, for God's sake!*"

Her arm tensed all the way to the elbow. The cords in her neck shrank tight.

"Talk to me, bitch!" he said. "I'll *make* you talk to me! You just wait. *You hear me, whore?*" He was crying. "You'll talk, goddamn you! You'll talk your fucking mouth off, you slut. You'll—"

She knew she should keep him on the line, but it was out of the question. She ceased to feel, to think, to plan. She tried to slip outside of her own body: she would be an imitation person, on a stage: unreal, vague, distant. Her hand relaxed its death grip and she eased the phone on its cradle. Then she picked it up again and dialed the precinct.

32

Julius Singletary squinted into the mottled mirror in his office bathroom and raised the edge of his violet-tinted glasses like a man lifting weights. He touched the bag under one eye with lump-fingered delicacy and turned away in disgust. If this keeps up, he said to himself, I'll need a transfusion. No wonder my eyes are red. Between Agate and the nut that's tearing up the precinct, I'm getting about as much sleep as a marathon dancer. Retirement can't arrive a second too soon. *If* I make it to retirement. . . . This goddamn case could blow the whole precinct out of the water, mess up everybody's future. A review board at my age: wouldn't that look great on my jacket?

His office phone had started ringing at sunup. The first caller was the chief of patrol, Major Perkins, "just checking." Then the deputy mayor, demanding a complete fill-in on the murder with names, dates, and serial numbers. Then the chief, snapping about Lower Slobbovia and threatening to transfer the whole precinct, starting with the captain. Then the mayor called, all bluff and bluster, typical goddamn thirty-one-year-old former used car salesman who rode the Peter Principle all the way. And then the polite voice of Captain Ralph Antonelli, saying, "Jules?" The polite voice meant he wanted something; it also meant don't turn your back.

"What is it now, Antonelli?" he said, feeling irresponsible and aggrieved. "You got me cold for jaywalking downtown, am I right? You got actual films shot from an unmarked van, huh? There's three witnesses right? A nun from the Maryknolls, an off-duty judge—"

"Jules, your man McClung—"

"Oh, I get it. You're ready to file on him. Two counts of murder, one count of failing to signal a lane change. That it, Ralph?" He knew how irrational he must sound, but for the first time in a half-dozen painful calls he was talking to someone who didn't outrank him, and he needed a break.

"Jules, we got him dirty."

"Whattaya mean, dirty? You got his handcuffs on the victim and you can prove he was, uh, drinking. *Phnfff!* You got any more than that?"

"He admits he might've had a drink with her. He admits he could've been over her place. Then he gets a little cute, says he lost his memory, he wishes he could help us but it's a blank. Tell you the truth, we're not communicating anymore. I wondered—"

"Whattaya need?" If John McClung had to take a fall, a certain precinct commander might as well share the credit.

"We need a confession. Not only so we can file the charges, but—" Antonelli lowered his voice. "The mayor's office needs something to give the papers and TV."

"Where do I come in?"

"McClung's crapped out. Keeps mumbling 'Packer, Packer.' Evidently trusts your man Lind. I figure, bring in Lind and clean up the whole thing in time for the evening news."

"What time you want him?"

"Quick."

"You got 'im."

No sweat off my balls, the captain said to himself as he hung up the phone. Given a choice, he'd rather not have one of his men turn up as a homicidal maniac, but nobody could blame the precinct for a mental case. Anybody could flip his lid. Look at that guy in Texas, blew away thirteen people from a bell tower, and when the doctors did the P.M. they found a blood clot pressing on his brain. Nobody's fault, not even the killer's. The stink from this case would blow over the same way. Nine months to go. . . . Besides, McClung would never do a day of hard time. He'd be in and out of one hospital after another. Probably what he needed anyway. Brain dissolved by alcohol. No wonder he went buggy. Stomping women and raping dogs. No, the other way around. God it was hot. And God he was bushed. . . . .

He opened his eyes with a jerk and looked around his office. He was still alone. A lucky break. All he needed was one motormouth cop to spot him nodding on the job.

He jabbed at a button on his intercom, missed, then carefully leaned forward and pressed. "Barker?" he said.

"Captain?"

"Get Packer Lind down here right away."

"He's home, Skip."

"Right away!"

"Yes, sir."

For thirty minutes the captain sipped strong coffee and tended his phones before the third-watch commander stumbled in, all elbows and feet, breathing from his kneecaps. "What is it, Skip?" he said. "Whatcha—*phew!*—got? I came in—*pheow!*—on the siren."

"Go downtown and get a confession outa McClung," the captain said. "He won't put out for anybody else. Claims he doesn't remember. Same old crapola you hear from every killer. *Phnfff!*"

"I dunno, Skipper," Lind said, looking wary. "That's the same story he told me when I picked him up." It was almost impossible to get this bohunk Swede to admit that anybody on his watch would pass gas in public, let alone go on a one-man lunacy rampage.

"Packer, do this little job for me. Talk to the guy, nail it down so the whole mess'll be over before it sinks into the public what happened. Do it for the precinct, Packer. We been taking a lot of bum raps lately."

"Yop, we have. There's—"

"The dicks're probably scared McClung'll get some shyster and clam—"

"—Artie Siegl, for—"

"—Up, but this way we can go in and get him while he's still hung over. A guy'll—"

"—Instance."

"—Talk his brains out when he's hung, I've seen it a million times. Huh? What about Siegl?"

Lind looked annoyed. "You said we been taking a lot of bum raps lately. I said, Yeah, Artie Siegl. Somebody almost bum-rapped Artie right off the force. And you're the somebody. Now you're asking me to roll over on one of my own men?"

The captain blinked his sore eyes. Who the hell did Lind think he was talking to, some junior assistant at the typing pool? "Now listen,

Lieutenant," he said in what he hoped were menacing tones, "I'm not asking you to do a goddamn thing. I'm *telling* you. There's a man in Central Lockup that it looks like he killed two women in two nights and God knows what all else, flattened a bunch of poor little pups, tried to wipe out one of my men in a jiggered patrol car. Now go down there and get the confession! You hear me?"

Packer Lind sat in the small wooden chair and looked up through his eyelashes at his superior officer. If the captain was any judge of facial expressions, the look was pure contempt mixed in with the smallest touch of pity. He could handle the contempt, but the pity made him boil. Goddamn it, he said to himself, I—do—not—need—anybody's— PITY! "Get out of here, Lind!" he said, summoning up his last reserves of command presence. "I gave you an order!"

The watch commander didn't budge. "You're a study, Cap, you know it?" he said finally. "You want that pension so bad you'd mug a cripple to get it, wouldn't you? What's your limit? I mean, would you put your own kids in jail? Your wife?"

"Now just a goddamn minute—"

"And don't shake your finger at me!" The lieutenant stood up and strode toward the door. "Get somebody else to do your hatchet jobs. Do it yourself for a change! I'm no goddamn errand boy."

"Who the hell d'you think you're talking to?" the captain said. He jumped to his feet for emphasis, but teetered and almost lost his balance in the heat of the exchange and the morning. The W.C. stopped at the door and answered in a strangely subdued voice. "I know exactly who I'm talking to, Cap. A *ghost*. I'm talking to the cop that went in single-o on the Chinatown killers, the cop that practically put down the nineteen-seventy lockup riot by himself, the cop we used to call—what was it, Skip? It's been so long I can hardly remember."

The captain tried to show another flash of anger, but he couldn't produce it. Something had trickled away when he wasn't paying attention to his life. Something that just happened to—older guys. Juices drained, emotions cooled, the backbone softened. The passage of time, that's all. Nothing you could do.

"Oh, yeah, I remember now," Lind was saying. " 'Old Brassballs.' 'Brassballs Singletary.' Did you know everybody called you that? *Years ago?*"

The captain groped behind him for his chair, slumped down without giving up eye contact. Jesus, this goddamn hot spell would never end, they'd still be sitting in puddles of body grease at Christmas. "Packer," he said in a tired voice, "shut the door and—and let's talk like old friends instead of—yay-hoos."

The W.C. hesitated, then lifted his hand from the knob. "C'mon, Cap," he said in a tired voice, "quit jackin' me off. I got a million things to do."

Was the captain imagining, or had the big, beefy face softened? Maybe he was feeling ashamed, snarling at a superior like that. Maybe this was the time to wax his ass, hint about disciplinary action, threaten to flop him clear back to—no, he was already here; there was no other precinct to flop him to.

"Talk to Johnny McClung," the captain said hoarsely, his voice worn out by the long morning of chatter.

"I—"

"Now wait a minute! I'm not telling you to get his confession, am I? I'm only saying, talk to him. Get the truth. That's all I ask. Shoot the breeze with him, have a stenographer write it down, and get him to sign. Is that unfair, Packer?"

"What if the truth is that he didn't do it? What if he was just plain drunk for two days? What if he's just a poor guy with family problems, hanging on for his pension, just like—"

"Then write that down," he interrupted quickly, "and get him to sign."

"No matter what he says?"

"No matter what."

Lind creased and uncreased his old Marine fatigue cap, rubbed the brim with the palm of his hand, held it up to the fluorescent lights. He looked at the captain, then again at the wreckage of his hat. "No conditions? No deal? No—fixes?"

The captain shook his shoulders and jowls as though he'd just been hit by a cold thundershower. A close subordinate was actually asking him, Julius Singletary, Ninth Precinct commander, to promise no deals, no *fixes*. Years ago he'd have punched anybody out for a question like that. Back when he was—Brassballs. But now he was just defeated. And hot. And—anxious. He had one inducement to offer Agate: retirement. Balmy breezes, a sea-view condo on the beach at Rosarito, a new kind of life together. The final payoff for twenty-five years as a cop. . . .

Besides, goddamn it, McClung was guilty as dog shit. Practically admitted it already. Lind was an honest man, he'd get the truth. He'd never cover up a crime. "No prior conditions," the captain said emphatically. "No deals. No—" He wouldn't dignify the word "fix" by repeating it.

"I'll see what I can do."

The captain sighed and studied the off-yellow acoustic tiles in the ceiling as the door closed behind the big watch commander. His eyes fell shut in their fatty sockets and refused to open for eight or ten seconds. Or was it longer? Jesus Jones, he was tired. Last night he'd had maybe two hours of flawed rest before the deskman woke him at 3 A.M. Christ, that used to be enough sleep for a week. But he'd weighed 175 then. Hard and lean. All over. Agate couldn't get enough of him then. . . .

If I could just crap out, he told himself. I used to snap back after fifteen-minute naps. Maybe still can. But where? It'd be all over town if I got caught snoozing in one of the armchairs in the rec room. Somebody'd shoot a Polaroid picture for evidence. Half the precinct was flopped detectives anyway. Mad at the world, out to pin something on somebody. *Anybody*. Especially a precinct commander. . . .

Besides, he couldn't sleep away from home. Never could. Maybe . . . It was just a short run. . . . No, that was ridiculous. The phones and the radio had him pinned down, there'd be no rest for him till this case was cleared. . . .

But Cul-de-Sac Lane was only ten minutes away, and he could stay on the air the whole time. If anybody wanted him, they only had to pick up the radio and say the magic words: "Charlie Two." There were dozens of excuses he could use to hit the street. "Barker," he said abruptly into the intercom, "I'm gonna take a little run up to the Jocelyn place. See what I can see."

"Excuse it, Skip?" The first-watch commander sounded surprised. The captain knew why. It had been a long time since he'd worked the street, for *any* reason. That's what sergeants and lieutenants were for.

"I said I'll be on the street for a while. Hold my calls."

"Oh, uh, yeah. Sure, uh, *okay*, Skip."

Barker can't believe it, the captain said to himself. Well, I'll be home in ten minutes, hang my police radio around Agate's neck, and tell her to wake me if she hears my call. If I get thirty minutes sleep out of it, I'll be a new man.

"Om, uh, Skip?"

"What?"

"You be on the air?"

"Certainly I'll be on the air!" he snarled. "But when I'm working a homicide, I don't want a lot of chippy calls."

"Okay, Cap. We'll screen 'em for ya."

The radio-operated garage door at his home opened smoothly for a change and he slid the Buick Riviera inside and quickly pressed the "close" button. It wouldn't be smart to leave the car where the public could see it. When you were serving your last year, you had to watch things like that.

The house was hot. He listened for the whir of the air conditioner and heard nothing. "Agate?" he called softly.

There was no answer.

"Agate!" he hollered. Jesus Jones, where was the roving ambassador of neighborliness now? All he needed was one lousy hour of her time. Was that too much for a husband to ask? "Agate, *where are you?*"

He rushed from room to room. The breakfast dishes had been done, and the house was immaculate. One good thing about her, she was neat and she was clean. She'd been the one who recommended Pine-Sol to him after a short visit to the station. Before that the trusties had cleaned up with yellow soap powder provided by the city, and it left rings and residues and smelled like fresh semen. There was a faint aroma of pine in the house; Agate always finished her kitchen work by squirting a few drops of Pine-Sol in the sink, to scent the air.

Now what?

If she wasn't home, he didn't dare sleep. Maybe he could just lie back for a while, monitor the portable radio out of one ear. Where had she gone? Probably shopping. Or another one of those damned coffees. Seemed like every week a new family moved in, and the girls were always getting together for greeting ceremonies. Or meeting in the afternoons to play gin and canasta. Or going to movies downtown, "just to break the routine," as Agate explained once.

He slipped out of his tight, lumpy Florsheim boots, wiggled his toes, and stretched his suffering frame onto their bed. Ah, comfort! His eyelids were dried flaps. Police calls crackled out of his radio, balanced alongside him on the table, but most of the business was routine. If the dicks were fanned out all over Precinct Nine looking for this sex murderer, they sure were keeping quiet about it. Usually the radio traffic was heavy when a big manhunt was on. There were constant warrant checks on cars and houses that needed searching, descriptions and names and M.O.s to be run through the computer, and progress reports by all the extra troops. Ralph Antonelli must be confident he had his man. Poor McClung. Nineteen years a cop, just a year away from his fifth hash mark. Two counts of Murder One. Jesus Jones . . .

He decided to stop thinking, just close his eyes and tune one part of his brain to the radio. Mind over matter; he could do it. Goddamn, the room was bright! Agate had always refused to buy plain old-fashioned window shades, the only kind that really kept out the sun. "We never sleep here in the daytime," she argued, "and those things are so unstylish." Instead they had chiffon drapes full of little flounces and bows, great dust-catchers, and on bright days you could get a tan on their bed. Just like Rosarito Beach . . .

"Charlie Two!"

He heard his number as in a dream, grabbed the radio, and answered, "Charlie Two," trying to work up an instant imitation of a harassed precinct commander.

"Location, sir?"

"Om, uh—Sixteenth and Lorimer." Oh, how stupid! Sixteenth and Lorimer was three miles out of his precinct. What the hell would he say he was doing there? The address had just popped into his head. He and Agate used to eat mushu pork at a little Mandarin restaurant on the corner. Back in the days when she—

"Received," the dispatcher said calmly.

Now who the hell wanted his location? And why? He waited for further developments, but the radio was busy on other matters. Were they checking on him? Or was it just routine? No, nothing was routine anymore.

Goddamn it, he was home in his own bed, he was wiped out, and by God he intended to have a little rest. Every beat cop was entitled to a lunch hour, wasn't he? Well, so were captains. If he wanted to nap instead of eat, the choice was his. He closed his eyes, but the incandescence of the room reddened his lids.

He lowered his Support-Hosed feet to the rug. Let's see, he said to himself groggily, maybe I can stretch a blanket across that big casement window. . . . No, too conspicuous. Wait! Agate's eyeshade! She swore by the thing.

Now where did she hide it? He rooted around in her bureau drawers, then padded into the bathroom, radio in hand. The logical place was the drawer below the vanity, where she stored her intimate articles. He opened the drawer, didn't spot the eyeshade, but found himself breaking into a half-smile despite his fatigue. *Just look!* It still had the flowers baked on it. The Japanese enameled box that held her diaphragm. She'd been using that same cute box since they were first together. All those years . . . Sentimental value, he guessed. Women hated to part with things. He leaned down to the drawer and sniffed. She always kept a layer of Johnson's baby powder in the bottom of the box. After they were finished for the night, she would rinse the rubber ring carefully, pat it dry with Kleenex, and then place it on its own white bed of powder and sprinkle another layer on top so it would be clean and fresh the next time. God, how he loved that smell! The power of association . . .

He momentarily forgot what he was looking for as he stared at the pale-blue flowers baked into the glossy black finish. He felt almost faint as the light scent wafted to his nose. How could anybody resist taking a peek at such a treasured object?

Gently, he lifted the lid.

The box was empty.

33

Packer felt inhuman whenever he had to lock somebody in one of the holding cells at headquarters. They were little more than closets, six feet long by four wide and barely high enough to stand in, the only exposure a small window on the hall side. The admitting log showed that Johnny McClung had been in his cell for seven hours when Packer arrived, and his tiny window was covered with cardboard and masking tape. Packer figured the jail sergeant must be afraid the news media would see who was inside the cell and start asking pushy questions. Then the edge would be taken off the mayor's announcement that the crimes in Precinct Nine had been "cleared by arrest."

"Hey, John! How they hanging, pal?"

McClung batted his eyes at the wedge of light admitted by the open door, started to rise when he saw his visitor, then slipped back on the thin bed. "'Tenant, *Lieu*tenant, I asked to see you. Did they, did they—tell ya?" His voice was weak, and his matted hair was parted in about six places. The cell smelled like a refinery.

"Can we use an interrogation room?" Packer asked the young jailer.

"No, sir, Lieutenant. I'm sorry. Orders."

The jailer told Packer to knock three times on the heavy wooden door when he was ready to leave, then stepped outside and turned the key. Packer felt a chill and inhaled deeply. If life was cops and robbers, as somebody had once said, he was glad he had chosen cops. He wouldn't last long on this side of the locks. Or was he just tired? He hadn't been to bed in a long time.

McClung looked pathetic as he rocked on the edge of the slab that hung from the wall on two chains. It didn't take a great leap of the imagination to picture him as a waterfront alky in a few years. In a sense, he was already one, except that somehow he had managed to cling to a steady job. Through the kindness of others. And the stupidity. My own included, Packer accused himself. "How you feeling?" he asked, dropping into a sitting position against the wall.

"Terrible, Lieutenant. Awful. Never flet, flelt, *felt* worse. Wish they'd get me—somebody to, uh, somebody to—help me. A hospital. I need, need help." As he spoke, he shuddered, hiccuped, gasped for air. It was early afternoon; he'd now gone eight or nine hours without vodka, probably his longest stretch since the night his partner was killed. They said alcohol was as tough to kick cold-turkey as heroin.

"I'll talk to somebody for you," Packer said. "See what we can do. You shouldn't have to sweat it without help." He looked around for a bug, found no logical hiding place. The walls were sheer and smooth: polished maple. Maybe they hid it in the toilet bowl, he said to himself. Must be fun transcribing the tapes later. . . .

McClung spread his arms to shoulder height as his head fell forward on his chest. There was resignation in the motion, abject surrender. Packer was touched. If this man was an alcoholic, it was at least partially because he was a cop. And if he turned out to be a killer—would that have something to do with his job, too? Another unanswerable question.

He shooed the killer idea from his mind. He wanted to interview his brother officer without prejudice, without thinking of the consequences and the ramifications of a confession. Somewhere in his mind he could see a flickering miniature movie picture of Lieutenant Sverre "Packer" Lind seated on a witness stand, monkeysuit neatly pressed, face scrubbed pink, testifying on oath that John J. McClung, a patrolman under his supervision, had confessed to the crime of murder in the first degree on this date and had done so willingly and without promise of reward or threat of bodily harm. Packer would tell the whole truth and nothing but, and then he would turn in his badge. The entire scenario flashed across his mind as he was saying, "Johnny, what really happened last night?"

Again, the uncontrollable hands fluttered into the air, palms flat and wiggling as though no words could cover the subject. "John, listen," Packer said. "I'm here as your friend. Okay?" Yes, it was false. But it was also true.

McClung nodded, and a swatch of greasy silver hair flopped across his dull blue eyes and stayed there.

"You told me a few things when I picked you up this morning, Johnny. Let's start there."

The man shook his head and stared across the cubicle with unfocused eyes. "Don't remember, remember anything, Packer. I mean Lieutenant. Was it you, uh, did you pick me, uh, pick me—up?"

"Yop. Me and your sergeant. And you told us something about you'd been on a two-day rip and you'd had a drink with Genna Jocelyn or you went up to her place or something. Remember any of that?"

"Genna *who?*"

"Jocelyn. Eddie Jocelyn's widow."

"The thin, uh, thin little lady that, uh, the thin little woman gives the watch parties?"

"Yop."

"And they said I was, I was at *her* place?" He sounded puzzled and confused, almost inarticulate. Packer felt like a torturer. Better him than another.

"I thought *you* said it this morning, John. Something about she bought a bottle of wine? In a bar? Samaralino's? The Red Onion? That ring a bell?"

McClung flopped heavily on the cot and trembled from head to toe. Paresis, maybe. It started like this. "No," he said. *"Unh-uhh.* Don't remember, remember, anything like, like that. Oh, yeah"—he wheezed like an asthmatic in spasm—"I remember being in Sam, Sam, Samaralino's, the Onion, six, eight other places, ten. Plenty witnesses. Dozens. Drinking two three days, 'Tenant, 'Tenant, *Lieu*tenant. I, I don't deny it, uh, deny it. But that person—who'd you say her name was?"

"Genna Jocelyn. Lives on Noxham."

McClung locked his arms under his knees and rocked on his back, as though to keep from shaking. "I dunno," he said with effort. "Dunno, Lieutenant. I jes' dunno, dunno, Uh, jes' dunno. . . ." His faint voice faded completely as he slumped over on his side.

Packer slapped the door three times with the flat of his hand. The jailer must have been standing right outside; he entered in seconds, a young cop, maybe twenty-two, twenty-three years old, fresh from the academy, serving his apprenticeship in the lockup. Packer had once been detailed here for a month, still had bad dreams about the experience, never could fathom the value of the training. "What's Officer McClung had to eat and drink?" he asked.

"Nothing, Lieutenant," the jailer said, his eyes homing on Packer's wide shoulders in the Marine fatigue jacket. "He tried breakfast, but he threw up the first bite. I gave him some milk, but he spilled it."

"Any coffee in the sergeant's pot?"

"Yes, sir. I think so."

"Bring me a big mug. *Big!* Load it with cream and sugar. Anybody complains, tell 'em it's for me."

"Yes, sir, Lieutenant. Sergeant gave me orders, anything you want."

"Nice of him." Anything I want, he repeated to himself. Long as I drag a confession out of here. They'll set up a table of appetizers and

Don Perignon or whatever the hell that stuff is called. . . .

Thirty minutes later Johnny McClung was sitting on the pull-down bed, muttering answers in a weak voice, but adding little information of value. The two days were a blur. He remembered some bars, mostly because he always drank at the same places, but he clung to his story that he barely knew Genna Jocelyn, had been to her garden apartment only once, at a small party for a couple of retiring cops a month ago, and had never seen the woman before or since, "in fact I wouldn't recognize the lady if you was to bring her in here right now, Lieutenant." It struck Packer as a strangely naïve, or cunning, statement. Was he saying he didn't know Genna was dead?

"Johnny, didn't you hear what happened to Genna Jocelyn?"

"Didn't I, uh, what?" He looked up with faint curiosity in his eyes. "Well, I know something must of. Everybody keeps asking me about the lady. Christ, I got enough to do to keep up with Ginger. Runs me ragged. Calls me—bum. Every chance. Bum bum bum bum . . ." The man did a lazy impression of his wife. Packer remembered her standing at the door, shouting obscenities.

"John, didn't anybody tell you why you're in custody?"

"Public drunk. 'Partmental investigation. Something like that." He took another swig of coffee and choked, spraying the sticky fluid across the cell. "Way I feel," he said after a paroxysm of coughing, "it don't matter—why I'm in here. Feel like I'm gonna—die—anyway." He began rotating his head and scrunching up his eyelids and mouth and nose. "Headache," he said. "Somebody's beating me to death from the inside out." He giggled off-center, then wiped spit from his mouth.

"From the inside, eh, Lieutenant?" Packer wanted to quit beating on this old dead plow horse, but he had to hang in, as much for McClung's own sake as any other reason. Maybe he could find out what was behind the boozing, anyway. But hadn't Don Reichert already told him? McClung was responsible for his partner's death. Or was that just departmental gossip?

"Johnny, tell me something straight. What happened to—your partner?"

"Is that it?" He teetered to his feet and tipped over the coffee mug. "I knew that was it. Goddamn it, I knew all the time." He started to blubber. "You know what happened. Everybody knows. He was shot because I, I, I couldn't get my gun out. He had a wife and, and—four kids." The tears smeared his face. "Four kids, Lieutenant. Rachel Pierpoint, she's ten. The twins, Donald Pierpoint and William Pierpoint, four years of age. And the baby, the baby's—he was six months at the time." He slid sideways against the wall.

"What's the baby's name?" Packer asked gently.

"Jackie," McClung answered, looking up through swollen eyes. "Jackie." He covered his ears as though to keep from hearing his own words. "John McClung Pierpoint. Six months old. No, he's nine months now."

Packer grabbed him by the arm and straightened him up on the cot. He sent for a fresh mug of coffee and watched as the sick cop held it with weak fingers. And finally the story came out in a torrent, as Packer had known it would. "They set me up with a shrink a few weeks after— after, uh, Larry's funeral. God, I was ashamed, Packer. *So* ashamed. Still am. Nobody in my family ever been to a shrink before. The priest was always our shrink. I wanted to talk about the shooting; it was fresh on my mind, ya know? But every time I'd start, the doc'd say, 'Well, John, you must of had a very unhappy childhood.' 'Hey,' I says, 'don't say that about my mom and dad. Hey,' I says, 'I had a good childhood, the *best*.' He says, 'No, John, you must of had an unhappy one, but you didn't realize it at the time.' I says, 'Doc, all my trouble started with this shooting.' He says, 'John, it started when you were in diapers.' I got outa there quick. Started drinking pretty heavy. That's when my captain flopped me to the Ninth. I went back to the shrink one more time, because the guy at Personnel, he told me I could lose the whole pension, and the shrink, he starts on the same old crap, and I says, 'Goddamn it, I don't want to talk about my toilet training, I want to talk about *now,* about the department, about the shooting and all the goddamn rumors and shit.'"

"What rumors and shit, Johnny?" Packer said softly.

"Oh, *you* know. McClung didn't back his partner. Didn't know his equipment. It was true, that was the trouble. It was true." He put his head in his hands and the thin bed shook with his sobs. Packer squirmed and waited anxiously; he could almost feel the man's pain. If Don Reichert's version was correct, McClung had watched while his partner was blown away. "It was a new safety holster," the trembling man continued, sitting on the edge of the bed and looking at Packer through pleading eyes as though asking for absolution. "I fumbled with my piece for a few seconds. That's all it took. My fault, Lieutenant. A hundred percent my mistake." He lowered his head between his knees and made loud retching noises, but nothing came out; ratty strands of silvery hair brushed the dirty floor of the cell. "A bookkeeper makes a mistake, he fixes it with an eraser," he went on in a strangled voice. "A ballplayer hits a home run. But a cop"— the next few words were inaudible—"and his partner's—dead. His best friend's—gone." He ran his hands straight back through his hair and started to cry again. "I killed Larry Pierpoint, Lieutenant. I never denied it. I can't atone. The priest says I can, but I can't. There's no atonement for something like this. That's the way the men feel, and I don't blame 'em. The other day I got a snub from an old friend. A guy I use to walk the waterfront with, drink with, go to ball games with. He—"

"Billy Mains?"

"Yeah. How'd ya know? Billy. Helluva cop, and I use to match him bust for bust, you realize that, Packer? He had Pier One to Thirty, and I had the rest. Matched him *bust for bust.* You look it up. The year he had the fifty felony collars? I had forty-eight solos and split thirteen more. Including two homicides and an on-view stick-up. Nowadays he sees me at the station, he turns away. The other night I walk up to him, I hold out my arms like I'm asking for mercy, I whispers, 'Bill, Bill, what can I do about it *now?*' He says, 'You should of backed up your partner,' and walks away. Well—he's right. And he'll always be right."

"You're hard on yourself, John."

"It's a hard line of work, Packer. Who oughta know that better'n you?" His thin voice had nearly faded away from strain.

"What about—at home?" Packer asked, trying to change the subject.

"Nothing, nothing," McClung said, lying down and addressing the ceiling a few feet above his head. "Nothing—special."

"John, I saw you at home this morning, remember? Talked to your wife. She's got—"

"Bell's palsy, yeah. That's my fault, Lieutenant. This shooting thing, all the aggravation, it made her nervous. Some of the wives, they stopped talking to her. The old friends didn't drop in anymore, ya know?"

"Was she pretty normal before the, om, incident?"

McClung shook his head. "I wouldn't want to complain, Lieutenant. She's a good and decent woman. She just—can't help herself, I guess."

"From doing what?"

"See, the boys are grown. Franny's in the Navy. Johnny Junior, we don't know where the hell he is. Oakland, Tampa, someplace." His voice was nearly gone; Packer kneeled alongside the cot to hear. "Then she stopped having her period, ya know? The change of life? Hit her hard. And then—my partner, uh, my partner dies and everybody yells it's—it's my fault. She just started sitting around thinking about things. Thinking, thinking. You know, days at a time? Thinking?"

Packer couldn't shake the feeling that someone was monitoring the conversation; a couple of times he thought he had heard the giveaway click of the relays on a voice-actuated recorder. They would play back the tape and then call him in and ask him why he hadn't used his knuckles. Too bad. If they didn't like his methods, let them send in a rubber-hose team. Not that poor John McClung needed one. He'd already been rubber-hosed by life. "Then you started drinking again, huh, John?" he asked.

"Drinking, yeah. And—pills."

"Pills?"

"Seconal. Valium. Shrink started me. I found out you can pop a couple extra with booze and get a total wipe-out. Total."

"Is that what you were on the last couple days?"

"Don't remember, Lieutenant. I mean, yeah, I think so. Must of been." He brushed a shaky liver-spotted hand across bloodshot eyes, like a man genuinely searching his memory. Or was he just the world's finest hungover actor? "I mean, how would I know for sure? Last I remember, I went off-shift and hit the bars. Then I bat my eyes and I'm in this cell. That's it. Everything in between's blank. Wipe-out."

"Just what you needed, eh, Johnny?"

"Huh? Oh—yeah." His voice sounded like pebbles rattling in a can.

Packer saw the whole vicious circle, or was it a vicious sphere? Too many whirling orbits; too many collision courses; the drinking, aggravated by the gossip and contempt that showered down on him; his wife's middle-age depression, aggravated by her husband's drinking; her verbal assaults, which in turn aggravated his drinking, which in turn aggravated her depression, which in turn . . . Aw, Christ, too much, too much! And on top of the other pressures, the memory of Larry Pierpoint. He drank to relieve his guilt; she screamed "bum bum bum" for the same reason. It was all too complex for an ordinary police supervisor.

But Packer was also convinced that Johnny McClung was no strangler. If the brass had sent him here for the sole purpose of extracting a confession, he had flubbed an easy assignment. Good. In the state John McClung was in, he would have confessed to the Lindbergh kidnaping. And thought he was telling the truth. . . .

Packer went straight from the lockup to I.A.U., two floors up. Captain Ralph Antonelli was hunched over his desk, reading a stack of papers with a fierce look of concentration that changed immediately into his camouflage smile when Packer blew in past an astonished deskman. There was no time for chitchat. "You've got one of my officers in a holding cell," Packer said. "He's not guilty of a goddamn thing except alcoholism, and I got good reason to believe you know it. I want him taken to the hospital right now."

Antonelli leaned back in his chair and pushed his rimless glasses up his sloping forehead to his thin hairline. "He's being held for departmental investigation," he said calmly, still smiling.

"He needs medication!" Packer raged, banging his hard fist on the desk. "He needs treatment. He needs help, not harassment."

"He needs a lawyer, too," Antonelli said, the smile flickering out like a drowned match. "We'll be filing charges."

"You won't be filing a goddamn thing," Packer said, stabbing his finger at the scrawny captain. "You're running a bluff, Antonelli. You thought you could get me to come down here and score for you, squeeze a confession out of a sick man. And I might have, too, except for one little thing. There's no confession to squeeze. The guy's righteous, Captain. He's as guilty of those murders as you and me."

"But—"

"Oh, sure, he lost track of a couple days. And he met Genna Jocelyn once. And those were his cuffs, no doubt about it. Now, you want me to tell you why that all adds up to a big pile of cowshit?"

"Not particularly."

"Well, listen anyway! Or do you want me to tell the grand jury? Maybe we can bring back the bad old days. I can see the headline now: COP CHARGES UNLAWFUL JAILING. CAPTAIN INDICTED ON BRUTALITY CHARGE. POLICEMAN HELD IN DUNGEON et cetera, et cetera."

"I'm listening." There was no evidence of a smile now.

Packer talked nonstop. He pointed out that the killer stuttered; the woman at Betty Evans' apartment had heard him distinctly. John McClung had no trace of a stutter, even when he drank.

He pointed out that McClung had been on a well-documented binge and that no falling-down drunk could have handled an automobile with the skill of the wheelman who eluded Artie Siegl; "the car woulda been piled up six times before they hit the sector limits."

He pointed out that he himself had checked McClung's locker that night and that the padlock was open; any of several dozen men could have grabbed his handcuffs and slipped them in a pocket in seconds. Including trusties.

He pointed out that John McClung was a sick man with a sick wife; he was a listless, demoralized wreckage who showed only the faintest interest in the opposite sex, a tired, defeated cop waiting for his pension like so many others. Would that type of man have the raging motivation to strangle two women and scrawl filthy names across their skin, and stomp the life out of four puppies, and sabotage a couple of police cars, and scare people half to death on the telephone for good measure? *Would a John McClung even have the energy?*

"He's not charged with any of that," Antonelli said, his narrow eyes watching Packer closely.

"What's he charged with?"

"Public intoxication. Conduct unbecoming an officer."

Packer chortled. "Conduct unbecoming? When he wasn't even in uniform? Cap, you guys gotta cut the self-abuse! Your brains are going soft! Why, Jesus Christ, if you start charging cops with conduct unbecoming for what they do on their days off, you're gonna have the whole top brass in jail! You'll have to grab the chief!"

Antonelli nodded. "Is that about it, Lind?"

No, Packer said, that *wasn't* about it. He warned the I.A.U. boss that holding Johnny McClung had to backfire in the long run. They should be looking for a bona-fide psychopathic cop hater, not a falling-down drunk. Some crazy genius was trying to make Precinct Nine look ridiculous, and he was doing a hell of a job. All the emphasis on a drunk like Johnny McClung just served to take the pressure off the real killer. Somewhere the sick son of a bitch must be laughing himself silly at the department's stupidity.

The I.A.U. commander spun in his chair and faced the wall. When he spun back, he was smiling again. "Okay, you made your point," he said. "He's yours."

"What—"

"You on duty or off?"

"Off. Till tonight." What did the I.A.U. boss have up his sleeve?

"Take him away. Personal recognizance. That means you're responsible for anything he does. *Anything.* Including another binge. I'll have both your tins if he does. We'll hold a departmental charge open just in case."

"In case what?"

"In case you don't have the good sense to keep a couple of men sitting on him twenty-four hours a day till we break this case. If he screws up again, he'll be back in jail as fast as I can send the wagon. And this time we'll file. Does that, uh, strike you as fair?"

"It strikes me as expedient. I guess you'd rather have me watching Johnny McClung than making a case against you."

"Some might see it that way." When Packer was halfway out the door, the thin man called, "Oh, and Packer?"

"Yop?" He turned to see a wider smile than ever.

"Have a nice day!"

Packer drove a slobbering Johnny McClung home in the bouncy Jeep Wagoneer and helped steady him to the door. Ginger McClung, her eyes deep sockets, her body concealed in a faded orange wrap, backed away when they went inside, and made no move to help. "Bum" was her only comment. With half her mouth.

34

Sergeant Turk Molnar smiled with pride. "Acting watch commander." Well, who else? Richard Not Dick Jellico might know the books and manuals, but when it came to street time, Molnar had him four to one. And forty to one on street sense. The sausage-bellied sergeant gave his shoes an extra buff as he tried to lean over the shine stand in the locker room. *Acting watch commander. Um-hmmmm!* Nice sound! Then his face fell and he crossed himself in four short strokes as he remembered how he got the job. Let's hope we nail the killer tonight, he said to himself. I don't give a flying fuck if I'm only acting straw boss fifteen minutes, long as we catch that cocksucker. . . .

"All right, people, fall in!" he bellowed at roll call.

"Where's the lieutenant?" Artie Siegl asked, sniffing the air with his flattened nose as though he could smell out the answer to his question.

"With the homicide dicks. He's special-detailed till further notice."

"Who's running the watch?" Rollie Beemer asked.

"Myself. Why?"

Willie Bethea said, "Whoo-*ee!*" and rolled his eyes. Makes him look like a plantation nigger, Molnar said to himself, but I better not mention it.

"Hey, listen," Artie Siegl piped up. "Nowhere does it say that a cop's life has to be easy. Nowhere does it say there's not gonna be bad days. But this—!"

"ALL RIGHT!" the sergeant shouted. "Quit jackin' around and pay attention." He called the roll. Demaris and Wry were off; Gerald Yount wouldn't return till tomorrow night. Johnny McClung was under some half-ass kind of house arrest, with a couple of cops from every shift detailed to hold his hands. "Rike, you take the desk again."

"Aw, Turk—"

"I said take the desk!" Then in a lowered voice he added, "You done a terrific job last night." That was the way your modern supervisors operated: soft compliments instead of loud yelps. You can catch more flies with flypaper than you can with vinegar, he recited to himself. "Okay, now, listen up!" He had heard a TV watch commander use that expression. "We had an Oh-Five-Oh last night at Bob's Electronic on Shadeland. Car stereos are hot right now, so keep your eyes open.

Smelis—uh, *Smoliss*—there was three different complaints last night about kids dragging on West Nineteenth. Don't give 'em no more friendly tater-tates. Write 'em!"

"He can't write," a voice muttered.

The sergeant ignored the remark. "Now as far as the big case goes"—an instant hush fell over the gray-shirted line—"we need everybody's eyes and ears, we need everybody's help, we need everybody's, uh, prayers. Any you big-time operators got eyes for my job, this is your shot. Bring that killer-pervert-scumbag in and I guarantee you'll be the next chief. Assistant chief, anyway. Plainclothes dick for sure. Okay?"

"Anything special planned?" Tennyson Mills asked.

"*Everything* special. David One"—he nodded toward Bethea and Beemer, standing side by side like a salt-and-pepper set—"David One's detailed to the lieutenant's house tonight. For the rest of y'all's information, his wife's been getting threats, and it looks like it might be the dude we're looking for. Willie, Rollie, you already been briefed, right? Okay. The rest of you, it goes like this: There's three different cars patrolling that district tonight: Willie and Rollie are David One and there's two units specialled in from undercover cars: David Eleven and David One-eleven. Got that? Somebody'll be watching the lieutenant's house every second. Now all y'all make a note of this: there's a Varda inside. If it goes off, shag, uh, move your, uh, backside. Could be a false alarm—the lieutenant says the wife's a little jumpy, a baby and all to take care of. But fly anyway! Lights and sireen all the way. We only got one lieutenant." He lowered his voice. "And he's only got one family."

There was a murmur of assent. Good, he said to himself, I got 'em in the back of my hands. Maybe there's a little command presence left in the old boy yet. "Coupla announcements," he said firmly. He held a blue memo about three inches from his eyes; he'd be damned if he'd pull on his glasses in front of the troops. "From the chief of patrol. Quote. We are presently averaging forty-one percent department-wide on notifying Radio of the arrival time on calls. Precinct Nine's average is only thirty-five percent. Please be reminded that you are required repeat *required* to notify Radio whenever you arrive at the scene of any dispatch. Unquote. Clear? A word to the wise is efficient."

"Balls," somebody said.

"Moving along," he continued, barely ahead of an outbreak of anarchy, "this one's from the burglary unit. Subject: alarm system. Quote. An alarm system has been installed at God the Father

[238]

Pentecostal Tabernacle of Christ on Scribner Street. The alarm rings in the patrol captain's office at Haggar's Security Agency. Also, there are guard dogs inside the church at night. Be advised. Unquote."

Somebody snickered. "It's not funny," the sergeant said. "You could go in after a prowler and lose a hand."

"I'll bear that in mind, Sarge," Billy Mains said, smirking sideways at his big-titted partner, "next time I take care of my spiritual needs."

"You do that," he said sourly. "Way I hear, your spiritual needs all the help it can get. All right, now, everybody dissemble yourself around the big table. We're gonna check ammo."

A groan went up. "Special orders," he added. "Don't waste no time and energy fussin' at me. I'm just one of the hired help around here, I'm just another—watch commander, uh, *acting*. Empty them revolvers on the table and spill your belts. Come on, Billy! You got another pouch. Don't tell me, I'm looking at it, man! No it's *not* empty. There. Lay it all out. . . . Artie, change that stuff for fresh stuff, and then shoot up that stuff you been carrying. . . . Smoliss, how long you been carrying this stuff?"

"Oh, maybe four, maybe five—"

"Years?"

"Months."

"What were you gonna fire it out of? A musket? Ball and cap? Look, the powder's leaking down the sides."

"I didn't notice, Sarge."

"Get over there and exchange it for fresh. Billy, what's these cuts across the front?" As if they both didn't know. . . . That crazy Mains, he had about as much respect for authority as a sow in heat. Somebody should stomp him good. But—who?

"They must of got scratched up in my piece," Mains answered with his famous baby-face innocence.

"Here, take this new stuff. Shoot up your old stuff this week."

"Aw, Jesus—"

"*This week*, get me? And the next time I catch you with dum-dums, you can explain it to the captain. . . . Okay, hand 'em over, Beemer. Oh, my ass! Look at these bullets. Oh, Jesus . . . Get ridda this crud!"

"Come on, Sarge, they're okay. They just *look* dirty."

"*Look dirty?* Man, you could grow potatoes in there!" He ran his little finger around the jacket. "See that grease? It'll hang up in the cylinder for sure."

"Anything you say, Sarge."

"Way you guys act, you'd think you had to buy this new stuff yourselfs. Just replace the old caps and quit fussin', okay? Well, well, what have we here? Now that's what I call good ammo. You been polishing these?"

"I was at the range yesterday afternoon," Mary Rob Maki answered. "They're all new rounds." Broads! They tried so goddamned hard! But he still wouldn't trust one for backup.

When the old ammunition had been replaced by gleaming new bullets, he said, "Okay, okay, what're you all standing around for? Let's hit the street. Eyes, ears, and mouth open, and windows *down.* Get me? DOWN! We got a bad dude lose in the precinct. Let's us pinch him ourself before somebody else gets the credit. And remember, when you write up your reports, it's Molnar, acting watch commander. M-O-L-N-A-R."

". . . One way to spell it," Artie Siegl said, and ducked out the door in his jaunty featherweight's stride. Featherweight brain, too, the sergeant said to himself.

On the way to his office, he passed the Breathalyzer room. A dozen or so dicks were meeting inside with Packer and the captain. Extra cars were double-parked outside, and uniformed officers from other precincts milled around looking confused, all of them working out of a mobile command bus parked in the back.

Go get the scumsucker, the sergeant said under his breath. I'll hold down the station, give you a clear field. Imagine: a regular nightly sex killer. A bad-ass like that could ruin Lower Slobbovia's reputation.

35

Drained and pale, Amnee sat with her legs folded up on the brown corduroy couch, staring mindlessly at a still-life with apples she had painted from numbers on a whim, a work that Packer had admired so much he hung it over the mantel. Her graceful arms hugged her chest tightly, shielding her from any storms that might descend on the overheated living room, and her thin shoulders were hunched up close to her ears. The summer sun had just flickered and died with a final spasm of heat and light. Emily had been stirring restlessly in her bed for an hour; her chirps and calls had finally dwindled away. The old black and white TV was on, but the sound was off. As she turned to watch distractedly, a master of ceremonies jumped up and down and shook the hands and elbows of a contestant who broke away ecstatically and embraced a portable washer. My God, she said to herself, doesn't anybody ever win with dignity on these shows? Do they always have to behave as though they'd just won a death-row reprieve or an entire South Sea island?

She uncoiled and jumped at a sound. Motor noise, slowing down. Every blind in the house was pulled tightly shut; she ran and looked through a slit at another police car, sliding past slowly, its driver peering in. Thank you, thank you, *thank you,* she said under her breath. Please—keep coming. Till Packer gets home. Till tonight is—tomorrow.

She tiptoed into the bedroom. The tape recorder was in place, completely automatic like that other thing—what had he called it?—the Varda. If anybody phoned, the recorder would turn itself on, even before she answered. The technicians had spent an hour wiring the device. One of them had said something about a voiceprint. She wasn't sure, she'd barely been listening.

She peeped behind Emily's screen. In her crib, the child was stretched full length on her stomach, head turned to one side, thin blond hair splayed atop the *Children's Playmate Magazine* that she couldn't read but enjoyed tearing into tiny shreds as a presleep ritual. Packer had insisted on the subscription. Next he'd be buying her *The New Yorker.* Tonight *Playmate* was unripped; the poor baby must have been too hot and tired in the sealed cauldron of a room. Amnee held her own head very still and stared hard at her daughter's back. *There!* The light seersucker pajamas moved up and down in regular puffs. How many times, how many *thousands* of times had she and Packer checked behind this screen to make sure their daughter was alive and breathing? Were other parents so overprotective? She guessed not. But they had read something about Sudden Infant Death Syndrome, and never again would they take her existence for granted. She was approaching two, and soon the SIDS worry would be over. But new ones would start. Traffic, disease, kidnapers . . .

Kidnapers? Amnee, settle down, she told herself. Dear God, what possible reason was there to fear kidnapers, of all things? Hadn't Packer said over and over "Nobody in his right mind'll come near here tonight"? The neighborhood was crawling with policemen and prowl cars, the house was wired up like a space station, and what he insisted on calling "the old equalizer" lay fully loaded on an upper shelf of the bookcase.

Well, it could stay there. There was nothing that would induce her to fire that gun, least of all in the direction of another human being. *Nothing!*

But what if someone tried to hurt the baby. . . ?

The rooms were slowly darkening. She realized she would soon have to turn on the lights, but she would hold off till the last possible instant. Inside the house looking out, she had the advantage on prowlers. But as soon as she lit the place up, the situation would be reversed. She needed to see without being seen, hear without being heard. She made a decision: no lights in the house tonight. No sleep either. She wouldn't even lie down till Packer got home at 4:30 in the morning. *If* Packer got home. . . .

She tiptoed back into the living room, clicked off the TV, and repositioned herself on the couch, worn down by the hot, sticky house. Maybe he was right about the heat pump, out back in its ugly crate, the hole half-dug alongside the house. If only she could open a couple of windows, but—God, no! She still wore her apron; the dishes were stacked dirty in the kitchen. She wished she knew how to meditate, to withdraw into herself. There were people who could fold into the lotus position and float into space repeating a meaningless syllable or two. Then who would protect Emily? *But who would protect her anyway?* She told herself she had to overcome her feeling about the weapon. She was walking toward the bookcase when she heard the footfall on the porch.

She stopped dead. Her heart jumped into her throat and she gagged and pressed her palm hard against her breastbone. She was two or three steps from the gun and somebody was trying to get in. Which way should she turn—toward the baby or toward the gun?

Oh, Amnee, *Amnee!* she admonished herself disgustedly. It's the men from the precinct. Packer had said they'd do an occasional foot patrol; they'd check around the house, make sure nobody had slipped behind the bushes or hidden in the shadows.

She stepped toward the front door as the knob turned against the lock. Then someone knocked lightly.

She tried to see around the edge of the shade that covered the front window, but she couldn't make out anybody at the door. "Yes?" she called out, but the word stuck in the dryness in her throat. "Yes?" she repeated in a strangled grunt.

"Police officer," a polite voice answered. "Can you open up, please?"

Her heart thumped and her breathing accelerated. She couldn't make a decision. She pulled the curtain back a fraction of an inch and looked through the slit. In the dark greenish-black shadows from overhanging leaves she glimpsed portions of a man: a trouser leg, the back of a shirt. Was it light gray with green trim? She couldn't tell. The man knocked louder, in a different rhythm—insistent, official. "Police officer!" he said firmly. "You okay, Mrs. Lind?"

The porch light! Why hadn't she remembered? She flicked the switch alongside the door and peeped outside again. A policeman in full uniform came into view. Thank God, thank God! She swallowed hard and shut her eyes with relief. There were dozens of cops patrolling Stanton Park tonight; she was relieved they'd had sense enough to send someone she recognized.

She undid the three locks hurriedly. "Come in," she said. "God, I'm glad you're here!" In the yellow glow from the insect-repellent light on the porch, she glanced at his nameplate. Then she screamed.

36

To Packer's patrol-cop way of thinking, the strategy session had peaked after the first thirty seconds and gone downhill ever since. Almost an hour had passed, and still the planners and schemers chattered away like a convocation of crows. His own instincts told him to shag-ass, quit wasting time in this decompression chamber watching the sweat darken everybody's shirt.

He wondered about Amnee, wished he could duck outside and give her a reassuring call. God knew she was probably safer than any other woman in Stanton Park tonight, with the Varda in place and a loaded revolver at her fingertips and a half-dozen cops within shouting distance. But even with the whole neighborhood buttoned up tight, it couldn't be any picnic sitting inside an airless bungalow on a steaming summer night waiting for a psycho to make his move. What woman wouldn't be disturbed? He hadn't married Amnee for her bravado any more than she had married him for his beauty. She was a frightened child now, barely out of her teens, and she deserved his support.

And here he sat. On the slick wooden bench that had held how many thousands of drunk drivers. Listening.

". . . This Koslo could go way back, Packer." Detective Sergeant Danny Galvin had the floor. He was a missing-persons specialist, an old friend of Packer and his first wife. He was one of a dozen dicks in the room, most of them from Homicide, a few from other units. "He's a guy you sent up maybe when you were in plainclothes, maybe even before that. He gets out of the joint or comes back from another state and assigns himself a phony name and he's gonna get your ass."

Packer didn't comment on Galvin's theory any more than he had commented on the others. To him they were equally pointless: pipe dreams, visions, maybe true, maybe untrue; what was the difference? The trouble with a lot of detectives was they deluded themselves into the same ideas about crime as the average citizen. They read the same books and watched the same TV shows and movies until they actually believed that crap, they actually believed that crimes could be solved by insights and plans and deductions. *Eureka, I've got it! The culprit has to be . . . Nobody leave this room. . . .* Deep down, they knew better, but it made the job more exciting to play Sherlock Holmes, even though Sherlock Holmes never handled a 291 Barricaded Man with Gun or a 241 Family Disturbance in his life. Instead of hitting the bricks and going door to door and putting heavy heat on their snitches and interrogating every goddamn transient they could find, they wasted time at bureaucratic back-scratchings like this one, "planning" how to solve the crime, with everybody trying to score points toward his next promotion. Packer knew the difference between uniformed cops and dicks, having been both, and to him it was largely political. A detective was a harness bull with a line of bullshit, a quick talker who knew how to pass tests and impress a promotion board. That didn't make detectives any smarter than patrolmen like Artie Siegl or Willie Bethea. But it *did* make them windier. It made them like to palaver. Endlessly. Especially with each other. While Koslo went free. . . .

Ah well, Packer said to himself, I'm just tired and grouchy. Two days without sleep. And none in sight. Not while that psycho's calling up my wife and endangering my home. . . .

". . . We been checking that idea all day," Tony D'Amato was saying. He was a detective who came out of Vice to become the department's computer expert. "We checked every asshole Packer ever sent up, ever booked, investigated, every asshole any of his partners ever laid a glove on, and so far we got—your sister's."

"One day's not enough, Tony," Danny Galvin said. "That's a two-week job I ever heard of one."

"Not with the computer it isn't," D'Amato insisted, defending his gadget. "We worked all the way down to his misdemeanor arrests, but I cut it off right there. I mean, this asshole isn't gonna turn out to be somebody Packer arrested for jaywalking."

"I never arrested anybody for jaywalking," Packer said, keeping the record straight. "If I did, I'd've arrested myself."

"You ever thump a guy without writing him up?" Sergeant Jack Garrison put in. He was a wizened old skeleton of a detective who dated back to the days when techniques were simpler. "You ever bend some dude's back and keep it quiet?"

"Never," Packer said lying a little. "Only when it was necessary."

"Spent most of your time helping paraplegics, right, pal?" Detective Lieutenant Dickie Hyland said.

"That's me," Packer said, studying Hyland's robust face. No malice there. Just a plain, tough-talking dick, one of the best. "Believe me, if I'd given somebody cause—I wouldn't hold back," Packer added. "That's *my* wife and kid this Koslo's wolfing at."

"We know it, pal," Hyland said brusquely. "That's why we're here. Keep that in mind." Packer looked around. He hadn't seen the late rosters, but he knew that half the men in the room were off duty. Headquarters had asked for volunteers, and they'd arrived in a horde, begging for a crack at the case. Eventually they'd get compensatory time, or maybe they wouldn't, because compensatory-time vouchers had a way of getting mislaid. Maybe some of them were just self-servers: trying to improve their jackets or horn in on a big bust. So what? They were here, that was what counted. They could have been drinking at the Slammer or home with their own wives and children. Packer reminded himself to be grateful. His eternal questioning of people's motives, his own included, was getting him down. What the hell was the difference why they were here if they did the job?

He tried to concentrate as the voices droned on, and his gaze rested on the light-green walls of the windowless Breathalyzer room. Over and over he read the same signs: "You have the right to refuse to submit to a sobriety breath test. If you do refuse, your driving privilege will be revoked or denied. . . ." next to the full text of the Miranda warning in large black type, next to the notice over the door: "Quiet please we are recording," next to the stenciled phrases each suspect would be asked to read three times in front of the videotape camera:

METHODIST ELECTRICITY

AROUND THE RUGGED ROCK
THE RAGGED RASCAL RAN

SLIPPERY STICK

". . . Don't think there's any connection at all," the intense voice was saying when a nudge in the ribs made Packer open his eyes. As near as he could figure, the bright-eyed young plainclothesman was suggesting that the crimes might have been unconnected, random coincidence—the two murders, the killing of the dogs, the Visibar heist, the missing lug nuts, the U.C. who called himself Koslo. This was a big city, the eager young dick continued; plenty of things went down at once, and it was mathematically possible that the crimes were accidents of chance, in which case they could all save time by treating them individually. Packer tried to keep a straight face. The kid probably took a minor in math, thought the whold world ran on his theories of means, probability, and chance. Well, it didn't. What they were dealing with here was a nut case, and the only certainty was that there were no certainties. Some infinitesimally small current of electricity would leap from one cell to another in Koslo's brain, and another woman would die. And when would the police department find out? *After* it happened. That's why they belonged on the street and not in this office. It wasn't like him to be fatalistic about crime and criminals, but now, as Amnee had insisted, his own family was involved. That tended to make a man pessimistic. Or jumpy. Or both.

"What about it, Cap?" Lieutenant Dickie Hyland was saying to Julius Singletary, sitting in a corner studying his shoes. "Any ideas?"

The precinct commander raised his head. He seemed dazed. To Packer, it looked as though he'd been crying, but that was impossible. Old sea dogs like the captain didn't bawl; they made *others* bawl. He was showing his lack of sleep, that was all. He'd been routed out of bed at two or three in the morning. He was pushing fifty years old; he lived an executive's life, kept banker's hours, lunched with his cronies, and went home every day at five sharp. This case was disrupting his routine, and his beaten face showed it.

"Any ideas, sir?" Hyland repeated.

"Uh, not, uh, nothing—special," the captain muttered.

"Didn't hear ya, Cap," Hyland said.

Singletary shook his head slowly, his reddish-brown hairpiece askew, as though dignity no longer mattered. Packer knew that give-up feeling—what cop didn't?—but he was surprised to see it etched so clearly on his precinct commander's face. The standard-model, snarling, spitting Julius Singletary would have taken firm command, rattled out theories of his own, raved about "my" men and "my" precinct and "my" district, and issued a string of orders, some of them reasonable. "Well, how d'ya want to handle it?" Hyland insisted. "Half and half? Patrol division works outside and detective division inside? Something like that, Cap? Whatever you say. It's your precinct."

"Okay with me," the captain mumbled. He sounded like a man with personal problems on his mind. Well, who knew? Who knew?

"We already doubled up where we could," Packer put in, trying to draw attention from his superior. "We got fifteen men in Stanton Park alone. My place is covered like a rug."

"Where'd all the troops come from?" Danny Galvin asked.

"Every precinct," Packer answered. "Mostly downtown."

"Great night to stick up a movie," somebody said in the back.

"The chief's got cadets walking the streets, but they're stretched thin," Dickie Hyland said. "I wish we didn't need so many bodies around Packer's neighborhood, but there's been two or three calls to his house and the name matches up."

"Koslo," Tony D'Amato said.

"Yeah, Koslo," Packer repeated. "I'm sorry he ever picked my wife to call."

"Don't be sorry," Dickie Hyland said, scratching his ass. "Your house is the only lead we got. If this cocksucker's as crazy as he sounds, he'll show up if he has to walk through an honor guard with drawn swords."

"Not so loud," Packer said, half seriously. "I don't want Amnee to hear."

"You tell your child bride not to worry," old Jack Garrison said, his Adam's apple bouncing in his gaunt throat. "You tell her that Koslo's good as caught. We'll—"

Suddenly Don Reichert burst into the room from the front-desk area shouting "Varda! Varda!" Packer was first through the door. The message poured from his radio as he gunned the Fury out of the parking lot ahead of the stream of accelerating cars. "SILENT ALARM NUMBER ONE. HOUSEBREAK IN PROGRESS AT PRIVATE RESIDENCE, SEVEN ONE EIGHT OH ORCHARD. SILENT ALARM NUMBER ONE." Then an eighteen-second pause and the recorded voice again: "SILENT ALARM NUMBER ONE. HOUSEBREAK IN PROGRESS . . ."

"Please, God," he prayed aloud, "let it be a mistake." There were cops behind every bush; nobody could have come within fifty yards of his house without being grabbed. He would *never* have exposed his wife and baby to real danger. Amnee had accidentally tripped the Varda sensor, that was it. Or maybe Emmy grabbed the sock monkey. No, she was asleep by now. Well then, Amnee did it. Dusting, maybe. She was always dusting when she got nervous. Right about now she'd be apologizing to the district car, she'd be telling Beemer and Bethea it was all new to her, she didn't understand silent alarms, she'd be more careful the next time. . . .

Then he heard the resonant voice of Willie B on the radio, the same voice that had responded two nights ago on the first sex killing. Good old Mr. Cool, calmly giving out his call sign first: "David One." Willie would set things straight, clear up the confusion. "Verify barricaded suspect with hostages." *Verify?* Had he said "verify"? "Seven One Eight Oh Orchard Street. Request a supervisor."

[247]

Packer juggled his mike as he one-armed the unmarked car around the corner at Calhoun. Something inside him was frozen: he was functioning by memory, by instinct. "Two Two Three responding," he heard himself say. "Any unit in vicinity, seal the back."

"We covering front, back, and side, Lieutenant," Willie B answered crisply.

"Shots fired?" Packer asked.

"Negative."

He sighed. No shots yet. There was—a chance. Then he remembered the strangler's M.O. and kicked the pedal to the mat. He was turning seventy down Meredith Street when the strange outcry came over the police radio. It sounded like a half-suppressed moan of pain or rage, more animal than human. When the cry ended, a woman's voice could be heard faintly. "Don't!" she was saying. "Please!" It had to be Amnee.

37

Billy Mains was too aggravated to play his cool-cop role another second. "God*damn!*" he said to his partner. "Will you just listen to that?"

"Trying to," Mary Rob Maki said, her glinting red mane cocked toward the scratchy sounds of the police radio.

"Tell ya one goddamn thing," he griped as he steered the car toward South Park. "This is a dumb operation. *Dumb!* Any time you got all those cops involved in a hostage situation and Billy Mains driving a green-and-white two miles from the action, that's dumb!"

"Somebody's got to cover the other districts," the patrolwoman said in that phony syrupy voice she must have used as a teacher. "Why not us?"

He managed to suppress a scornful look only out of respect for her bra size. *Why not us?* Didn't the dumb cunt know the first thing about him yet? His record, his reputation? Radio was talking about a SWAT call-up, and here was a one-man SWAT unit being wasted on routine patrol. Why, he'd been a one-man SWAT unit before anybody ever used the term. Special weapons, shit! His *hands* were special weapons. Well, they must be holding him back on account of the broad. They didn't dare involve her on a hot call, no matter who her partner was, he consoled himself. It was the broad.

"I got half a mind to drive up there anyway," he grumbled, more to himself than to his partner. "Who they gonna send inside? Gerry Yount? Smoliss? Tennyson Mills in his frizzy, for Chrisakes?" But he ground his jaws and drove on. At his last review board a captain had taken him aside and warned that another act of insubordination would tear it for good. A big bluff, probably; still, he couldn't be sure. Better lie in the weeds awhile. . . .

But soon his boot began fluttering on the gas pedal as he thought about turning around. Wouldn't the broad cream her drawers seeing him in action? Banging down a door with the butt of his riot gun and swaggering inside behind a couple bursts of double-0 shot? "Come out of there with your hands up, motherfucker! Yeah, *you!* Put the kid down or I'll blow you away, cocksucker!" Then a single perfect pistol shot, square between the eyes. *Pow!* The force of the hot load slams the guy to the floor and the legendary Billy Mains catches the baby in midair before it gets hurt.

Talk about making an impression! Oh, Jesus! She'd—

For once, Mary Rob heard their call sign first. Deep in his fantasy, he only picked up the tag end: ". . . Barton Place. See the man."

When she grabbed the clipboard, he realized they'd just had a call.

"What's that address again?" he asked.

"Twenty-three hundred Barton."

He whipped the car into a tight U-turn and headed south as his partner picked up the mike and acknowledged. He knew 2300 Barton. How well he knew it! The ten-story Loo-Ray Arms was tired and unstylish, but several cops lived there, and one of them was the deskman. Oh, my ass, he said to himself, I don't like this. What the fuck are we going *there* for?

"Lemme see, honey," he said, nodding toward the clipboard. He perused it as though checking his junior partner's work for flaws. "Poss. D.B.," she had inscribed in her neat printing.

He bit down on his breath mint and crunched it to pieces. A possible dead body at Gerald Yount's old apartment building. He did not—like—this—one—bit. He hated D.B. calls anyway, and he didn't look forward to going back to the same damn building where he'd met Darlene Yount—how many afternoons? Five, maybe six, before she suddenly took off for her old home town and didn't even say good-bye. Not that he gave a fuck. Saying good-bye to sluts wasn't a social requirement. He still lived by the famous four F's of his high school years. A certain redhead would find that out sooner or later.

But this call . . . "See the man." And there he was, a short, stumpy old goat standing under the tattered peppermint-striped awning that led from the apartment entrance to the street. The guy had "super" written all over him: khaki pants, a chino work shirt open at the neck, smooth-leather shoes he probably bought by mail, a key ring with a thousand keys, and a bowling ball tucked under his belt buckle. Why the fuck didn't they call these guys what they were: janitors? "That must be the complainant," his partner said. Christ, what if the old dude recognized him and said something? He took another look and relaxed. Each time that he'd met Darlene when Gerry was in class, he'd used the back staircase, never the elevator, and he hadn't encountered this super or anybody else. He usually ran in luck that way.

". . . Feel kinda silly about this," the man was saying through the open window to Maki, "but it don't hurt to be sure."

As she scribbled in her notebook, Billy leaned across her clean-smelling body and said, "Sure about what?"

"There's a tenant up on eight, I hear him raving all the time, banging into things, talking loud, but there's nobody in there except him. Never. I watch. Maybe you know him. He's, uh, a cop—a policeman."

Billy's pulse began to hammer. A policeman on eight. Had to be Yount. He stayed dead-pan as they stepped from the car and followed the old man inside. "He was acting up again this afternoon, and then all of a sudden—quiet. I waited awhile and looked in. Door was unlocked. Eight-ten. Apartment eight-ten." Yeah, Billy said to himself. Eight-fucking-ten. You don't have to tell me, pop. The bedroom's in the back, overlooks Preston Street. There's an old double bed with a flowered spread. ". . . I walk inside and the front room's bare, just a few broken chairs and some other stuff all littered around like a cyclone come through. So I figure maybe he's gone south on us for the rent, but then I realize he's a police officer, he'd never do a thing like that. Yount, his name is. Maybe you know him."

"Gerald Yount?" Maki said, turning toward Billy. "Isn't he—our deskman?"

"The deskman, uh, yeah," he mumbled. "Used to be, uh, my, partner."

"Your partner?" the super said as they walked to the rear of the narrow lobby. "Did he always act weird like this?"

"Like what?" he asked stiffly. He wanted to double back to the green-and-white and fly away, find an excuse to dump this call, but there was nobody to dump it on. Something had happened to Gerald Yount, and it was their call, and no way out.

"Oh, coming and going all hours, ranting and hullabalooing like I told you. Always—"

"Wait a minute," Billy said as the super pushed the elevator button. "Who made the complaint about a D.B., uh, a dead body?"

"Oh," the super said, looking chagrined. "Well, that was me, Officer. I went inside the apartment, see, just looking around, not meaning to be nosy or anything. I mean you live your life and I'll live mine, understand? But this guy's been acting, uh, strange for weeks now, and I thought—well, I thought maybe he, he done himself some harm, the way the place all of a sudden fell quiet."

The ancient elevator whined and clacked upward. "You found a body?" Maki asked.

"I walk into the bedroom," the super said, telling the story at his own speed. "I figure I'm gonna find him stretched out or something, but all I can see is this big bed with the covers and sheets all matted together. Looked like they haven't been laundered since his wife left."

"His wife left?" Maki asked. The dizzy broad. Didn't she ever listen around the station? Anybody that didn't know the Gerry Yount soap opera had to be deaf or dumb or both. In this case, probably both.

"Yeah. They split up six, seven weeks ago. I'm not suppose to know, but you can't help hear things."

Jesus H. Christ, Billy said to himself, Yount must of sucked the pistol. Or stepped into the airshaft or off the balcony. What if there's a big investigation? They could bring Darlene back, question her, put on some heat. . . .

Never happen, never happen, he assured himself. He wished he could be sure. No, it *couldn't* happen. That wasn't the way the P.D. operated. When cops killed themselves, whether it was New York or L.A. or Peoria or anyfuckingwhere, the lid came down tight. Half the time, the story didn't even make the papers. Cops and reporters worked together; you could always make a deal, spare embarrassment for the family. *And* the P.D.

Besides, what was there to investigate? The fact that Darlene Yount had been a nympho? A kinky bitch that liked her vice versa? Couldn't happen. God, he hoped not.

". . . Then I noticed this, uh, odor," the super was saying apologetically as the elevator doors parted on a hallway that smelled like corned beef. "Look, I'm no expert, but I seen human dead before. World War Two, we found a Frenchman, in the bottom of a bombed house. Two weeks gone. He was—"

"You said you smelled something in the apartment," Billy said impatiently. Who gave a fuck about a dead foreigner when the whole world was collapsing?

"Oh, yeah. Well, I noticed this, uh, aroma. Nothing that would knock you over, y'understand? But it was *there*. And I mean the bed was all messed up and sweaty, but what I smelt wasn't simple B.O., ya

[251]

know? It was—different. Like that dead Frog. So I went down and dialed Nine One One."

They had reached the familiar metal door of 810, and the super reached around and hefted the heavy chain of keys from his belt. "I'm feeling kinda silly about this," he said, the keys rattling in his hand. "I mean, bringing you, eh, officers here. I mean, a dead mouse, it smells exactly the same as a dead human. Probably all it is. Under the bed or something. We don't have a lot of mice, but once in a while one gets in a trash can and carried up."

"Don't feel bad," Maki said. "It's our job."

Billy stepped inside the darkened apartment and called out in a quavery voice, "Uh—*Gerry?*" Christ, he'd have to watch himself. He'd almost said, "Darlene?"

The front room was exactly as the super had described it—a mess. Splintered chairs. Ripped papers. Broken glass. The shades were drawn, but the place still sizzled with trapped heat.

The old man snapped on the bare overhead light; it illuminated a circular imprint on the ceiling where some kind of shade had been flush-mounted. Billy remembered an upside-down Tiffany type of thing: red and white plastic. "In there," the super said, pointing toward the back.

"That the bedroom?" Billy asked, trying to sound unknowing. He turned and peeked at Maki; she looked even paler than usual in the harsh light, and her hand brushed lightly against the back of his shirt as the two of them walked through the abbreviated hallway that led past the bathroom to the rear. Bits of glass crunched underfoot.

"Right in here," the super said, snapping on another switch.

The bedroom smelled like an open tomb. "Jesus," Billy said. "Break a window, do something." God, how he wished he was up in Stanton Park, shooting it out with a barricaded suspect. Anyplace but this rank apartment. Anything but another D.B. It wasn't fair to bring him back here like this. *Find 'em, feel 'em, fuck 'em, and forget 'em.* You shouldn't have to return to their bedrooms and go through—this.

"Please, stand back and don't touch," Mary Rob was saying to the super. Preserving evidence already. These female cops were slaves to procedure.

"Whattaya think?" the old man asked.

She fell to her hands and knees and checked under the bed. "Anything?" Billy asked, pinching his nostrils.

"A lot of cigarette butts," she answered. "Stubbed out on the floor. The wood looks like burnt toast under here."

"What else?"

"A paperback. A hankie. *Ugh!* Filthy!"

He stepped to the closet door and noticed that the edges had been sealed with masking tape. "What's this?" he said.

"A closet," the super said.

"Yeah, but why's it sealed?" He had a premonition.

"Don't ask me," the old man said, moving back a step or two. "I'm not the one done it. I told ya: the guy's funny. He's—not right. Why'd a man tape his own closet?" As he spoke, he stared at the sealed door, and his eyes grew wide and round and filmy.

"Maybe we better call the coroner right now," Billy said, tasting his lunch in his throat. He had never been afraid of another human being, but this particular D.B. call was one too many. He shied from the closet; he knew the smell that would pour into his nose and into the weave of his uniform and permeate the hairs on his head, and he could not stand one more D.B. *Not one more D.B.!* He was a cop, not a mortician, and this dead body was too goddamn close to home.

"Better check inside that closet, don'tcha think?" the super said. "In case it's a mouse? A cat? Something maybe crawled in by mistake?"

Billy took a deep breath. Goddamn, he *had* to check the closet, and there was no way he could fob the job off on the coroner; they would think he'd cracked up, calling the meat wagon over a smell. Citizens mislaid bolognas and months later screamed murder. People made mistakes.

His hands were shaking. He couldn't let the others see how disturbed he was; he had given away too much already. He slipped his locker key under one line of tape and stripped it to the floor, and the smell of protein rot eddied from the crack. He wiggled his head and tried to take short breaths and yanked off the rest of the tape.

"Stand back," he said, as though there might be a bomb inside, as though he was bravely trying to protect the others. A bomb, he said to himself. I should be so lucky. . . . He turned the knob and looked in.

The closet was large, paneled in cedar. A beam of light bobbed around: Maki's Kellite; he had forgotten his own. The bouncing rays splashed over a plum-colored women's slacksuit arranged neatly on a wooden hanger, then on a pink nylon blouse hanging next to a lacy black padded bra that had been stretched around a wire hanger as though it still supported a woman's breasts. On the ledge above, a wide-brimmed hat in light red looked as new as the spring sales.

"Now lower," he ordered, breathing through his mouth, and his partner played the flash down the back wall till it touched the floor. The bright elliptical puddle of light fell on an almost new pair of pinkish high-heeled shoes parked side by side. Then the beam moved haltingly to outline the shiny edges of a large clear-plastic grocery bag, heavy-gauge, tied off at the top. Inside was what looked like the head of a large doll.

Billy leaned over. An open-mouthed Darlene Yount leered up at him.

His eyes rolled back in his head; he coughed and swallowed the sour taste that gushed into his mouth. The light wiggled and wobbled like a home slide show, and he reached around and grabbed the black cylinder from his partner's hand.

Next to the head, he found a naked torso lying upside down in a dry-cleaning bag, and another bag bearing a swollen pair of legs, crossed at the knees. He wiped a sleeve across his nose, blinked his yellow-brown eyes, and dropped to his haunches. Through the clouding twist-tied bags he saw that the skin had begun to split and fall away in sheets, exposing translucent yellow fat. Across the heavy thighs a thick green layer of mold clung like spilled gelatine. The ass . . . He shuddered and covered his mouth with his hand. *Oh, my God, there's something up her ass. . . .*

He forced himself to push the flashlight closer. He swallowed spit and bile as nausea squeezed his stomach like claws.

The bottle had once held champagne; he recognized the familiar dimpled base. But the base was all he could see, jutting from her distended rectum like a green lens. The rest of the bottle was inside her body.

Jesus, he thought Oh, Jesus, Jesus, Jesus. Did she die that way? *Did she die that way?* He scrambled to his feet and rushed toward the bathroom.

38

The captain loosened the irritating seat belt in the elephantine command vehicle and wished to God his yay-hoo driver would step on it. "This the fastest we can do?" he called out.

"She's not made for speed, sir," the driver said. He was a leathery midget of a man who had found a niche for himself after twenty years on a beat in South Park. Looked like a jockey, the captain observed; he huddled over the steering wheel as if he were piloting flesh instead of metal. How the hell had shrimps like that gotten themselves hired back in the fifties? Must've been a shortage of humans. . . . .

They stooged along at thirty miles an hour; at this rate it would take five or ten minutes to get there. No real hurry anyway. Seldom was in these hostage situations. The area was saturated with cars; men on foot covered Packer Lind's house from vantage points in the vacated homes all around. The perimeters had been set up early, fast, almost without radio communication, although the captain had heard his watch commander barking out a few orders. A SWAT unit was due. And Captain Julius Singletary was en route in a fat green and white command vehicle that looked like a retired school bus from the Jones Junior High in Toledo, except that its sides were reinforced with slab steel and its windows were made of inch-and-a-half plastic and its various drawers and compartments held enough weaponry and equipment to handle a brigade of assassins, provided the assassins weren't holed up in a private residence with an innocent woman and baby.

The captain gripped a milk-white overhead strap as the command bus swayed around a corner on its soft shock absorbers and almost sideswiped a new Jag. He couldn't keep his mind off the missing item in his bathroom. What kind of cop am I? he asked himself, and answered with a disgusted shake of his head. My watch commander's wife and child are at the mercy of some nut, my precinct's shot to hell, and all I can think of is—my wife. Who's she with? *Why?* All those years. Kept her high on a pedestal. Yay-hoo! *Stupid* yay-hoo! Stupid, *stupid,* STUPID . . .

For a few seconds he entertained the idea that he had misinterpreted the evidence. No. Impossible. Open and shut. What could she say? She was having her diaphragm cleaned and pressed? Sent it out for alterations? No, she was—with somebody, that was all. Probably been going on for weeks. *Months.* Explained everything. Vacuuming at 2 A.M. Headaches. Eight-day monthlies. The whole goddamn thing. . . .

"Please don't come close to the house. I'll have to kill anybody that does." Huh? *What?* The radio. The captain leaned toward his speaker. Christ, the guy had sounded nonchalant, meek. Well, didn't most psychos? Hard to reach them. You couldn't jolly them out of their rage because they weren't in a rage—they were just plain *off.* And *off* was the hardest to handle.

But what was that racket that came over the speaker earlier? The outcry like a wounded animal. Where did that come from? Were there two men in Lind's house? And where the hell did they get hold of a police radio? Maybe Lind had left one behind. Or maybe—maybe a cop was in there. That was all he needed: a crazy cop with hostages.

"Charlie Two to Two Two Three," the captain said into the microphone.

"Two Two Three," Packer Lind's voice acknowledged. He sounded surprisingly calm. "Professional" was the word. The captain wasn't surprised.

"I'm a few minutes away in the bus. What's the situation?"

"No change, Charlie Two. We've set the traffic perimeter. You heard the message? Uh, the *messages?*"

"Affirmative."

"I'm ready to open contact."

"Negative on that," the captain answered quickly. Better to wait till they'd worked out an approach together. Of course Amnee Lind could be getting murdered in the meantime; the baby could be screaming for breath under the psycho's thumbs. That was the chance they had to take. Hostage-takers always had that advantage: the first hostile move. And no amount of force could deny them. "Stand by, Two Two Three," he said. "We'll set up at Orchard and Meredith."

"We evacuated the Safeway parking lot. That's a little closer." Christ, the guy was always one step ahead. Well, he had the most at stake.

"Received." If he remembered correctly, they would have a view of the house from the supermarket parking lot. The side of the house, anyway. "That's approved," he added.

The bus moped along, its wailer giving a false impression of speed. The tires hissed against the tacky asphalt, heightening the illusion. They were a mile or so from the scene. "Kill the noise," the captain told the driver. You never knew what might set a loonie off: a glimpse of a police uniform, a snotty remark on the radio, maybe just the arrival of another car with its arrogant siren. Take things easy; that was the first rule. De-tune the tension. Stay calm and relaxed; put on an act if you had to. Handle the suspect the same way you'd handle a rogue bear with slobber dripping off his fangs. Respectfully. Gently. Time was your main weapon. The captain knew all the clichés; but he also knew that at the end it would come down to execution. And if the suspect was a cop himself, he'd know the procedures, he'd know how the game was played. He'd be onto their tricks. The situation would become . . . impossible.

All that sniffing around, the captain muttered under his breath. Making a fool out of myself, splashing on that pansy-ass cologne and pretending to sleep. . . . *Hours.* While she was setting her hair and doing her nails for—him. Or *them.* Afternoons, that was her playtime. No wonder she wasn't interested at night. *Hooray, hooray, matinee.* . . . All those months pretending she was the neighborhood welcome wagon, and one dumb yay-hoo falling for it. Jesus Jones . . .

The radio was quiet for a few seconds. Everybody must be waiting for him to set up his C.P. Waiting for—the honcho. Well, he was still a cop, wasn't he? A precinct commander? A respected leader?

Maybe.

Christ, they must suspect something around the station. Those nosy cops. They *had* to know something. All that time sitting in his office mooning about Baja California. Playing everything safe. Figuring up the retirement pay till he ran out of scratch pads. Doodling pictures of saguaro cactus and sailfish. . . .

He'd take the bitch to Rosarito Beach, all right. He'd turn her over to one of those spic pimps he'd heard about: the S-M specialists with the whips and the snakes. . . .

No, he wouldn't.

Because it was his own fault. . . .

The hell it was! What was wrong with the action he gave her? Still brought her off, didn't he? *Didn't he?* No, maybe he didn't. Women were born actresses. Georgeanne used to say she came every time, but then she told the marriage counselor that he bored her in bed. *Bored her!* Goddamn broads. *What did it take?* AN ELECTRIC COCK?

"You say sumpin, Cap?" the driver said.

"Did I *what?*"

"Thought you said something, sir."

"Well, I didn't. *Phnfff!* Just mind your—mind the road." Jesus Jones, had he talked out loud? Was he that far gone?

He wouldn't confront her. He wouldn't do or say a thing at all. He patted his expanding middle and tried to shape his face into a smile. There were better ways to get even. There were women who went for solid men. Men of rank and standing. *Superior* men. The captain swallowed hard. Two can play at one game. He turned away from the driver and dipped his head quickly to wipe each eye on his shirt. She'd get hers. Oh, God, why did she have to do it? Agate . . . Oh, Agate . . . *Why* . . . ?

Two blocks from the address the scene began to resemble a battle zone. At each intersection a green-and-white stood diagonal watch in the center, engine idling, roof lights spinning, helmeted occupants cradling riot guns and leaning into their radios. "Charlie Two at the location," the captain said.

"Charlie Two arrived with the command vehicle," Radio echoed.

Well, he was a respected part of something, anyway. He was the head of a unit that did useful work. Indispensable. What the hell more could he ask? To be acknowledged, recognized; wasn't that the idea?

The way the dispatcher just acknowledged him? The way all those eager faces looked up and *respected* him as he drove past in the command bus?

The midget driver backed the ponderous vehicle into place with two deft swings, and Packer Lind shoved through the door. His eyes were rubbed raw; his thick head of gray-black curly hair overflowed onto his forehead in limp coils, and his usually immaculate uniform was open at the collar and shapeless from sweat. Behind the watch commander, the captain recognized a few others from the precinct. "How's it look?" he asked.

"Bad," the lieutenant answered. His big open face was empty of color. The captain turned away. Emotion was exactly what they didn't need. They had to reach deep inside themselves, Lind and all of them, and draw out cold precision, cold technique. Discipline! They needed to behave as though two chess pieces were threatened inside that house, not two relatives. "You ordered me not to open contact," Lind was saying. He sounded as though he wanted to argue.

"That's right, Lieutenant," he answered. "Now fill me in, from the top."

"Cap, I'd like to try and approach from—"

"I said fill me in!"

"Willie?" the lieutenant said, his head jerking around." Speak up. Fast."

"We was parked a half a block away, watching the house." Willie Bethea said, pushing himself to the front of the group. "The dude popped out of the bushes and walked up to the door."

"You get a make?" the captain asked.

"No. Seem like he come outa nowhere. He, like, materialized. One second the porch is empty, the next second he's banging on the door, ya know? He had a monkeysuit on, so maybe we didn't react fast enough. By the time we realized he wasn't, uh, authorized, she'd let him in." Bethea paused and bit his heavy blue-black lip. "I'm sorry."

Being sorry wastes my time, the captain said to himself. "You say the suspect had a police—"

"—Uniform. Yes, sir, Cap'n. A regulation green-and-gray."

"The guy's a cop, Skip," Lind put in. "Got to be. He has one of our portable RCA's, and he knows to use it."

"Houses all been evacuated?"

"Half a block in every direction," Sergeant Turk Molnar answered.

"What was that first transmission?" the captain wondered aloud. "Sounded—garbled."

"Dunno," Lind said. "I heard Amnee, uh, my wife in the background. I'm sure of that. Skipper, let me talk to the guy. I'll work out an exchange. I'll deal with him, Captain. Let me try anyway. Then if I blow it, nobody—"

"Packer, you know the hostage procedure as well as anybody. You're personally involved. That rules you out."

"Cap," the big man pleaded, "let me make just one contact. *One!* Skip, it's my—"

"I *know* it's your wife and baby in there, goddamn it! You think I'm fucking stupid? Now back off! *Phnfff!* We don't even know what he wants yet."

"He's irrational, Skip," the lieutenant insisted. "He doesn't know what he wants himself. We got to open contact—"

"Sit!" the captain ordered. He turned to the bus driver. "Gimme my radio!" The jockey yanked the microphone from the console and passed it across at the end of a long spiraled coil.

"This is Captain Singletary, Precinct Nine," he began slowly. "I'm calling the party inside the house with Mrs. Lind. Can you hear me, sir? Please acknowledge."

The men crowded around. To the captain, they seemed to breathe in unison, as though they had rehearsed. A hand snaked out and turned the radio volume up to "10," but nothing came from F-2 except background noise.

"Charlie Two to Radio," the captain said.

"Charlie Two." The dispatcher sounded bored, as though he was handling a routine warrant check.

"I want all Precinct Nine traffic off this frequency. The, uh, party has already contacted us on F-two. Let's reserve it for him." A subtle way to butter the psycho up, the captain figured. A special channel just for him. . . . That was another rule: inflate the subject's ego, make him feel important. Recognition was what they craved. Pathetic sickos . . .!

"*Ree*-ceived," the dispatcher acknowledged. "All Precinct Nine units, switch to F-seven. Repeat, Precinct Nine communicate on F-seven till further notice."

Once again the captain addressed the little black microphone in a steady voice, trying to sound neither patronizing nor threatening. "Sir? The, uh, gentleman in the house? This is Captain Singletary again. I want you to know we're here to help in any way we can. *Any way we can.* Could you tell us, sir: how can we help you?"

Static poured from the radio speaker. Static and nothing else.

Where was Agate right now? Was she . . .? No, she couldn't be. Oh, yes she *was*. . . .!

Green-and-whites and unmarked cars had been pulling in and

making screaming stops around the parking-lot command post. Men in dark-green jumpsuits lined up outside the door of the bus. A blond hulk with the build of a pro wrestler and silver bars on the collar of his jumpsuit elbowed his way inside and said, "Okay, Cap, thanks a lot. We got it."

He recognized Elmer Frosch, the head of the SWAT unit. "You got what?" he said as more men in jumpsuits squeezed aboard the crowded vehicle and elbowed their way toward the lockers full of automatic rifles and machine pistols and tear-gas grenades and other riot gear.

"Didn't you request us, Cap?"

"I certainly did not," he said. "I'm—"

"Headquarters verified the call-up," Frosch said, taking little side steps toward the back of the bus. "That's the procedure."

"I know the procedure!" the captain snapped. "Move your men outside and stand by, Lieutenant. Thanks for coming. When I need help, I'll let you know."

"But Captain—"

"Stand aside!"

Frosch paused and looked around at his men. Another goddamn charger, the captain observed to himself: 99 percent balls and 1 percent brains. How'd a guy like that make rank? "Lieutenant," he said, "I'm busy now. If you'd just—"

"Captain, we been specialed in—"

Packer Lind slid behind the SWAT lieutenant and provided a gentle nudge with his forearm. "Do what the skipper ordered," the watch commander said, his voice trembling. "You're in the Ninth now."

Frosch reacted to Lind's nudge with a mild shove of his own, and Lind reacted by failing to budge. "Clear—*out!*" Lind said. The SWAT lieutenant took a short step forward and stared level with Packer's eyes.

"KNOCK IT OFF!" the captain shouted, surprising himself with his command presence. "Frosch, I gave you an order. NOW MOVE!"

The SWAT leader returned a long look, then walked slowly down the middle exit of the bus. When he hit the pavement, his men crowded around and began buzzing and chattering.

Now there was police work to do. The captain tried to form a mental picture of the scene inside Lind's bungalow, but it eluded him. Who was there, and why? "This is Captain Singletary again," he said in a low-key voice. "Could you tell us what you need, sir? We're here to help, you can count on that. You won't be hurt, you understand, sir? Can you hear me? Who's in there with you?"

"I can hear you," a faint voice answered. It was deeper than average, and it sounded contemptuous and tentative at the same time, like someone not used to command, someone who aspired to be a bully but was slightly unsure of his ground. Okay, the captain said to himself, there's a way to deal with a guy like that. Kiss his ass. Kiss it repeatedly and unashamedly till he loses that insane need to feel superior. Stroke the mad dog's fur and gentle him down and then—snap his spine fast and clean.

When the channel fell silent, he said, "May we have your name, sir?"

"No," the man answered. "Wait. Yes. I'm—Koslo."

Someone tapped the captain on the shoulder. He turned and Packer Lind whispered, "That's the U.C."

"What U.C.?"

"The one's been calling Amnee," the lieutenant explained in a tight voice. "Skip, he's completely psycho. We got to—"

The captain shook his palm in front of the watch commander's face and depressed the transmitting button again. "Glad to know you, Mr. Koslo," he said with mock cordiality. "Listen, my name's Jules. Can I ask you one favor, Mr. Koslo? Let's all just take it easy, buddy, okay? Please. We'll get along just fine, okay? We won't do anything radical out here. You have my word on that. *Nothing radical.* Okay, Mr. Koslo?"

"Keep your distance," the voice answered. "You make one move this way and everyone in this house is dead." The voice had turned so flat and emotionless that it sounded like a recording device.

"You have my word, friend," he repeated, trying to sound like an old drinking buddy. The Dutch-uncle approach. Establish a rapport with the suspect, force him to relate to you as a person, not as cold metallic vibrations coming out of a piece of plastic. It wasn't much of a plan, but it was all they had at the moment.

Agate's red mouth opened to a slick wet erection. . . .

The captain blinked and held his eyes tightly shut, then shrugged the scene away with a sharp shake of his head, like a man sniffing ammonia. No time for that now. . . . There'd be plenty of time later. *Years* . . .

In the command vehicle, the only sound was light static from the radio speaker. Nobody wanted to miss a transmission. In the subdued glow from dull-green lights in the back, a few shadowy figures wriggled into jumpsuits and jackets of SBA, soft body armor, the densely woven synthetic that turned away bullets. The captain squinted and confirmed that the men were from the Ninth. *His* men. Good. Those chargers from SWAT should wait for something more in their line: an escaped cage of Bengal tigers, maybe, or an invasion of Sikh warriors. This situation called for a scalpel, not a meat ax.

He cupped the radio in his hand. It wasn't wise to lean on a hostage-taker, but it was worse to lose contact. "Mr. Koslo, remember, sir, if you need anything we're right here to help. You, uh, okay for food?" Of course they were okay for food; they were inside a well-stocked house. But the question would serve its purpose. *We care about you, Mr. Koslo. We'll even give you food that you don't need. . . .*

The man spoke again after a full minute. "Bring Darlene to the porch!" It was an order, and this time the captain sensed no underlying lack of confidence. He realized that he couldn't afford a single mistake, that the suspect, crazy or not, had regained command of his emotions. That's what often happened with these crazies. They started scared and nervous, pissing their pants, feeling out the situation and getting accustomed to their new power and finally settling in like bank executives, bossing people around and making outrageous demands and threats. It didn't matter, as long as you kept things *cool.*

"You want us to, uh, bring, uh, *Darlene* to the porch?" the captain repeated. Who the hell was Darlene?

"Affirmative," the man in the house answered. "Right now."

"Darlene?" the captain asked again, stalling.

"You heard it. Darlene." The voice sounded far away. He was talking more softly, or his battery was weakening. "You took her away from him. Now bring her back. Do you read me—Jules?"

"Uh, yeah, we got that, friend. Yes, sir buddy, we got it. Om, uh, could you give me her last name?"

"You know her last name," the voice said, a little higher in pitch now. "Bring her to the porch. *Fast!*"

"Listen," the captain said, "stand by for a minute, will ya, Mr. Koslo. We're, uh, having some radio problems. You're fading on us. Let's see if we got your message right. Bring Darlene to the porch?"

"Affirmative."

"Okay, okay, that's received. We got your message and we're gonna work with you, Mr. Koslo. You bet." He tried to think of a stall. Reasonable people didn't take hostages; you were always dealing with a short fuse, and you had to gain time, make unkeepable promises, agree with the disagreeable, the impossible, *anything.* But—

S-t-r-e-t-c-h . . .

When the man fell silent, the captain said skittishly, "We'll need some time, Mr. Koslo," then realized he had forgotten to punch the button on the radio. He pushed tightly and repeated, "We'll need some time, Mr. Koslo," fighting to control his own voice. All this explosive situation needed was one jumpy person talking to another, and Packer's wife and baby were gone.

"How much time?" the voice asked suspiciously.

"Quick!" the captain said to the group surrounding him. "Who's Darlene?"

"The only Darlene I know is Gerry Yount's wife," Packer Lind whispered. "*Was* his wife, I mean. They been separated."

The captain pushed the button. "We're not sure of Mrs. Yount's location," he said. He held his breath. Darlene wasn't a common name, and he hoped to God they were talking about the same person. Christ, it was tricky dealing with these mental cases! Any second he expected to hear gunshots; then it would be too late for SWAT or the Ninth or anybody else. And the failure would be his own. Well, that was the way it was supposed to be. The precinct was his own, wasn't it? Goddamn right!

"You know where she is," the man said evenly. His voice was as hollow and cold as though he were speaking from a mausoleum. "You put her there."

Thank Christ, they were talking about the same Darlene. The captain resumed breathing. He tried to visualize the man standing in Packer's living room, eyes wide and staring, holding Amnee Lind at the point of a gun, and the baby. . . . The captain couldn't think about the baby. "Now bring her to the porch," the voice was saying. "Acknowledge, please." His signal was fading fast.

"Uh, stand by a second, Mr. Koslo. I got your message. Just give me a second." He turned to Lind. "Where's the woman now?"

"Darlene? Left town, last I heard." The W.C. gulped and looked anxiously at the radio, as though he wanted to grab it.

"Molnar!" the captain snapped. "Call Yount. See what you can find out. Right away! Ask—"

The static stopped pouring from the speaker and a thin familiar voice said, "I'm cocking my revolver now. Do you hear?" There was a metallic click.

"Uh, we hear, Mr. Koslo," the captain said, somehow managing to sound calm while his heart pounded inside his clammy shirt. "It'll take a few minutes to, uh, get Darlene here, Mr. Koslo. Wait a minute. *Wait a minute!* I just got word. She's—she's—on her way! *She's on her way, Mr. Koslo!*"

The captain wondered if the sound of gunfire would carry from inside the Lind bungalow to this command bus parked fifty or sixty yards down the street. Oh, God, he hoped not.

. . . Maybe some of the men knew about Agate. . . . Laughing at him . . . Figure of ridicule . . .

"How long do you estimate?" the weak voice asked.

"She's, uh, caught in the midtown traffic," the captain said, improvising wildly. "It'll be, uh, let's see"—might as well try for the moon—"maybe an hour."

"It's ten after ten," the faint voice said. "At eleven I'll shoot the lady."

"Received," the captain said anxiously, then deliberately repeated in a calmer voice, "That's received, Mr. Koslo. Got your message. We're trying, buddy. If there's any way . . . We'll be"—better not promise—"we'll be working for you."

He relaxed the tension in his cheeks and throat. He had bought some time. A little. This was the way negotiations were supposed to go. Increasingly intimate. First names as soon as comfortable. And words like "buddy" and "pal" and "friend" when you could slip them in naturally. He would work on that in the next exchange. At least they had—what?—fifty minutes. Not much, but it was better than instant massacre. The man sounded capable of anything. No hint of emotion, of feeling. A killing machine. . . .

The captain peered out the window. A half-dozen SWAT members were reflected in blue and red from a brightly lighted beer display in the supermarket's windows.

. . . Jesus Jones, Agate could be rolling around in a motel bed right now. . . .

"Cap!" Turk Molnar cried out from the telephone in the midsection of the bus. "Billy Mains, he, he answered the phone at Yount's! They just found a D.B. looks like Gerry's wife. Nobody knows where Gerry is."

The captain looked out the bulletproof window toward a corner of Packer's bungalow barely aglow in the blue-white streetlight. "They do now," he said under his breath.

39

Still in her dish-washing apron, Amnee braced her bare ankles against the legs of the wooden chair and tried not to pass out. Her cheek hummed like a tuning fork where he had clubbed her. She reached up, trying to check her face for blood, but in her disorientation she forgot that her hands had been threaded backward through the slats of the chair and cuffed behind her. She groaned as the metal pinched at her bones.

"Be still," he said from the other side of the living room. "I told you to be still."

His voice was as cold and flat as it had been from the beginning. If he hadn't hit her at first, smashed her face with his truncheon after she ran from the doorway and tripped the alarm, she would be just as frightened. Of all the men on her husband's watch, he had always seemed the wimpiest, the least likely to succeed as a cop, but tonight he was terrifying. Black hair poked from his head in ragged tufts, as though he had hacked at it with a knife. His dark-brown eyes looked like an oil sump in which the pupils swam like bugs. He lurched about the room like a sleepwalker, the gun wobbling in his hand, aiming— everywhere.

She remembered that Packer had told her something about him a few months back. Something—disturbing? What was it? Her addled mind refused to release the information.

A pulse throbbed in her throat, fast, then slow, then fast again. Once she had read that an irregular pulse was a symptom of shock. How did you treat shock? By breathing deeply? Her heart had started pounding when she first saw his nameplate; now it wouldn't regulate itself. Dear God, dear God, she said to herself, I've got to slow down, I've got to clear my head, make myself coherent, at least to myself. She gulped for air, couldn't get it down, tried several shallow breaths, but the lack of oxygen in the warm room panicked her, and she started to black out.

Then she remembered what Packer had told her about—whatever this man's name was. His wife had left. Yes, *yes*. His wife had left, and he would sit at the desk at night and stare. Or did she have the right man? It was always perplexing; there were sixteen or eighteen on the watch, and not all of them went to the gatherings where she could meet them. She hadn't seen this one more than a few times. God, what *was* his real name?

Now she watched wide-eyed as he crawled on his hands and knees to the front window and peered out. He turned and said something into his portable radio, but not loud enough for her to catch the words.

Yount.

That was it. George? Jerome? *Gerald.* Gerry Yount. Married to a large woman. Doreen?

She couldn't associate the behavior of this menacing man in her living room with the meek patrolman she had known as Gerry Yount, husband of—yes, *Darlene.* A woman of medium height but thirty or forty pounds overweight, dark lacquered hair that looked as though it would shatter if you touched it, a Slavic face striking in profile but a shade too broad from the front, and a lovely complexion. She showed up at one of the wives' parties and talked all evening about the sex appeal of cops versus athletes. No one had missed her when she failed to make the next meeting, or any others.

But why was he wearing a nameplate that said "Koslo"? And why was he so—changed? The herky-jerky movements, completely unlike the docile Gerry Yount she had met. The voice—the voice was Koslo's, not Yount's voice as she remembered it, not even close. She had often talked to the third-watch deskman on the phone; his voice had been soft and his manner had been mild and withdrawn, like a man afraid of making a mistake, of being corrected by his superiors. And now he was—Koslo. Could she have been so mistaken? Could there be two men so alike and so different?

At the moment he was giving orders. "Be quiet," he said, not to her, not to anyone she could see. "Be quiet and listen. I'm going to kill you now, understand? It's your time now."

But he wasn't talking to her.

The baby!

No, he wasn't talking to Emily either. He was talking to—the far wall. His eyes were focused on a single spot on the beech paneling, an imperfection in the wood; he was directing his words at a knot in the pattern. "You're dead," he said, then laughed—a deep, rolling laugh like a villain in a scary movie. "You're dead anyway. Climb into your coffin. Go ahead. You're *dead*. Dead, dead, *dead* . . ." The voice droned on as he strolled about the room, marching past her without pausing or looking down, as though he had forgotten she was lashed to a chair by her own arms. Each time he reeled by, eyes riveted on the paneling, almost stumbling, she looked down so he wouldn't catch her staring.

Oh, God. Why was this happening? What had she done?

No, it wasn't anything *she'd* done; it was something her husband had done. But what? Packer was the mildest of watch commanders. Too easy, that's what they said about him. Artie Siegl told her the men thought of him as a pussycat; they took advantage of him, went over their sergeants' heads to get his permission for days off and compensatory time they didn't have coming, and Packer always gave in. Or did he refuse to give in once, and now somebody was getting even?

The man stood above her chair, studying a furry white rabbit on the bookshelf. The little five-shot Iver Johnson lay inches away, underneath a moth-eaten teddy bear she had played with as a child. Would his eye catch the glint of blue-gray metal? He seemed fascinated by the white bunny, reached out and grabbed it from the shelf, and as she watched pinched its neck.

Dear God, this maniac mustn't find the baby. . . .

But he'd made no effort to search the house. Emmy was asleep in the back, behind her Chinese screen. Or was she sitting up in bed, getting ready to talk to her dolls, the way she sometimes did? Amnee wanted to call out, "Mommy'll take care of you! Daddy's coming home!" Oh, God, how she wished she could say that! For an instant she realized how much of her strength, their strength as a family, flowed from Packer, and now he was—gone. *Gone.* The world was reduced to her and Emmy and Yount. No, he was Koslo now. He had drifted to the other end of the room, giving more phantom orders in his hollow voice. It was her and Koslo, and she was helpless. She couldn't protect her own infant. Oh, sleep, Emmy! Sleep, baby! Not a peep, sweetheart. Emmy Packer Lind, for God's sake, *not a peep!*

She'll be eighteen months old tomorrow, Amnee realized. She has hair so blond it's almost white, and blue eyes the color of her daddy's; she has trouble with R's and can't pronounce L's; she distrusts men but she's friendly with women and cats and she loves her bubble bath and Paddington doll and sunsuits and salt-water sandals and small animals but not big ones and this awful, sick, insane man is going to find her and kill her. She's never had a haircut or an ice-cream cone; she's never gone to a party or a dancing class or a movie. She's—incomplete. How can such an incomplete life be threatened? She screamed inside: *it's not fair!* No, *no!* It's—unnatural.

If she could only reach him. If she could just get him talking, then maybe Packer could intervene. He was out there. Somewhere. Guarding them. He wouldn't let anything happen. Not to his Amnee, his Emmy. . . .

But what could Packer do? Yount—Koslo—had already threatened to shoot if he heard the slightest sound of entry. How could anybody save them from the outside?

No, no, that's not the question, she told herself. It's "How can *I* save us?" It's up to *me.* God in Heaven, where do I start, shackled to a chair and my baby asleep in the next room? *Give—me—strength.. . .*

"Please," she said. "Please—Mr. Koslo?"

He didn't stir from the couch where he was slumped.

"Mr. Koslo," she said louder.

He studied the floor, then his gun, turning it over and over in his small hands. His eyes were blank and unblinking, the deep sockets gaping so wide that they looked like holes in the dim light. "Please," she repeated. "Sir. *Mr. Koslo!*" She would get him talking, keep him occupied, draw attention from the next room. And then—then what?

"The poor man," he began mumbling. "The poor man . . ."

"What poor man?" she asked. Oh, God, would he respond? It would be a sign. It would be—something.

"The poor man," he repeated. He raised his head and looked in her direction through uncertain eyes. The skin around his forehead and eyebrows was a painful pink, as though recently burned. "You're that lieutenant's wife?" he said in a slightly questioning tone.

"Y-y-yes," she answered, anxious to please him. "Yes." Her lips trembled. She was so mixed up that she wasn't entirely sure whether she had spoken or just thought the words.

She saw him blink slowly, then again, squeezing hard with his eyelids. His forehead crinkled into ridges of flesh. Somehow he managed to look less human as Koslo than he had as Yount. Or were they two different men? His butchered hair poked sharply upward, like a weapon; his thin body seemed more muscular under his disheveled green and gray uniform, and his voice was pitched at least an octave lower than she had remembered. She didn't understand. Why this masquerade? Why was it so—thorough? He was really Yount. Wasn't he? He *had* to be. But who was he trying to fool? She *must* figure it out; she mustn't give up.

"She left him," he announced, turning the barrel of the pistol away and then shakily back in her direction. "Oh yes she did!" he said abruptly. "You can't deny it. *She—left—him.*" His voice had risen in pitch, and she cringed in fear as it picked up volume. "She won't come back unless he forces her. That's what I keep telling him. She won't come back, no, no, *never.* Not unless he forces her! That's it! She won't come back unless he makes her! Unless we—"

Suddenly he ran to the window and looked out a crack. "Unless we kill cops," he said slowly.

Again she watched the hollow eyes and the flushed upper face. "Unless we kill—pigs. Pig wives. Pig girl friends. Pig kids. Pig pets . . . Enough of them . . . She'll come back then. She'll come back to save them. She, she—loves pigs. If we just kill . . ."

She tried to shut out the words. She pursed her lips and looked at the dark ceiling. She wished she could seal off her ears, but the cuffs held her hands, and she was beginning to lose feeling in her arms. Think about something, she told herself. Concentrate on another subject! This—isn't—happening. It's—a dream. A phrase from an article about the Kennedys entered her mind: "There is no suffering like the loneliness of a parent who outlives his own children." Why did she have to dwell on that? What if they went at the same time: mother and daughter? Would it be so hurtful then? Wouldn't there be a certain—symmetry to it?

But that would leave Packer. Her mother had warned her, "He's already sixteen years older than you, and women live longer than men. You'll be a widow a long time, Amnee."

Wrong again, Mother.

Packer would be the only victim. Amnee wouldn't suffer long; he'd have to kill her fast, with cops waiting to rush in. Maybe the baby wouldn't suffer at all. Oh, she hoped not. Please God . . . Let that little light go out quickly. While she sleeps, Lord? Would that be—acceptable?

Packer would be left to suffer. Another wife gone, his only child . . .

Oh, Packer, sweetie, I'm so *so* sorry. I didn't mean to open the door, angel. But I was nervous, Packer, I was—afraid. And he wore a uniform, and I knew his face. . . .

"Please," she pleaded. "Please . . . Gerry."

He looked across the room at her through eyes that tracked oddly, out of phase with each other.

"Aren't you—Gerry?"

"Koslo," he said, his head slowly turning. His gun hand slumped, and his eyes rolled back in his head till she could see only the muddy whites.

"Please," she said, surprised at her boldness. "Mr. Koslo. These handcuffs. They're cutting me. Won't you loosen them? Won't you, please?"

The gun drooped more in his hand, as though it was too heavy a burden. Restrained or not, she would be just as much his prisoner shackled or free; she weighed one-hundred pounds and had a horror of violence and he was a full-grown man with a gun. But it would be a start. It would be a sign of—compromise. A step. If she could do nothing else, she could throw herself across her baby, protect the child to the end. She would do it. He would have to shoot Emily through her own body. Then she remembered: this man was a strangler. How long would it take him to squeeze the life from an infant?

He holstered his gun and stumbled across the room and knelt alongside her chair. He pulled off his key ring and selected a small silver key, and as he tried to slip it into the handcuffs, he whispered hoarsely, "I'm sorry, miss. It's—him. He does these things. He's—bad."

The nameplate KOSLO waltzed and wiggled in front of her eyes like a billboard seen across a stretch of desert. It had been lettered in stark black ink on a piece of cardboard attached to a safety pin. Why had he gone to such trouble? She realized it was useless to wonder why. It was useless and dangerous, she told herself as she braced to see what he would do. There was no why. He was demented, insane; something had twisted his mind beyond reason, beyond logic or order or intelligence. *There was no why.* He was crazy. *That* was the why. She was alone in a room with a lunatic locked in another personality and holding a loaded pistol on her. She would be dead long before anybody figured out why.

The human being she had once known as Yount the deskman raised himself to his feet and picked his way back across the living room like a blind man without a cane. She pulled at her hands to lift them into her lap and rub the circulation back. She was yanking hard before she realized she was still in the cuffs. He had started to free her, then stopped. Why? Had he forgotten what he was doing, leaning around her body? Why had he stopped?

There was no why. There would never be.

"Tell 'em twenty-five minutes," he was whispering. "That's when I open fire. Twenty-four minutes and—fifty seconds. Unless they bring her here. To the porch. Twenty-four minutes and thirty-five seconds, I start the killing. Tell 'em. *Tell 'em.*"

Amnee jerked her head in frustration and blew a strand of hair from her eye. She heard a low groan and saw that his head had flopped on his shoulder and his eyes had fallen shut. From the back of the house, there was a matching outcry. The baby was stirring in her sleep.

The man stood up, weaving from side to side. Then, frowning crookedly, he headed on wobbly feet toward the sound.

40

Packer reached the phone in two long steps. There could be no mistakes now. *No mistakes!* "Gimme that," he said abruptly. A frown creased Turk Molnar's fleshy face. Why did the old fart have to be so goddamn dumb and slow? Packer took the phone from his hand. I'll explain later, he told himself. He knew what was bothering the sergeant: the new rule that any officer who was personally involved was disqualified from hostage situations. Well, screw the new manual. It covered generalities; this case was a specific. And it was beginning to look as though there was a specific cop involved: Gerry Yount.

"Mains?" he said as he shoved the warm phone against his ear. "Yeah?"

"What's the situation? How old's the body?"

"Om uh, coupla months." Mains sounded tightly coiled.

"Homicide for sure?"

"Champagne bottle, uh, uh, up her ass. Probably um, um, bled out." Mains sounded like a hysterical old woman. It was out of character.

Packer tried to keep his own voice dead level: "What shape's the body in?"

"It's, it's, oh Christ—she's—they'll need, they'll need, uh, paper towels to get her, om, uh, out of here. Listen, uh, Packer, can I, um, call you from another, uh, another phone? We're still inside."

"Better stay put. We don't know—"

"Goddamn it, I already puked. Whattaya want from me?"

"Stay put! You hear me, Bill?" What was the matter with the guy? Stuttering and stammering like a green rook. He certainly wasn't a cherry on D.B.s. *"Listen to me!* Where's her clothes? In the apartment?"

Mains made a noise like a man dying, but Packer realized he was just clearing his throat. "One, er, uh, outfit. Hanging in the closet. With the b-b-body."

"Anything else?"

"P-pants, shoes, everything."

Packer reacted without thinking. "Get those clothes over here right away."

"Packer, the coroner—"

"Fuck the coroner! Knock him down if you have to. We got to have those clothes, Bill. We got to have 'em now."

"At the C.P.?" Mains sounded close to the edge. How could you figure? Billy Mains upset? The old charger? "They, they, they *stink,* Packer! Oh, Christ, I couldn't, uh, I couldn't stand to be in the s-s-same car with 'em."

"I gave you an order, Mains," he said, trying to force authority across the phone line. If only he'd been dealing with Artie or Willie or some cop who hadn't built a career on ignoring procedures. Mains should have been canned a long time ago. Whose fault was it? Every supervisor's. *Every one.* When you made the first compromise with a guy like Mains, he owned you. "Bring—those—clothes—*here!"* He spat the words out. "Put 'em in your trunk and crank that siren and—*fly!"*

"But—"

"Right now!"

Mains was still whining and balking when Packer hung up. It was like training a cat.

Now that he had bent himself out of shape issuing the order, Packer wondered why he'd asked for the outfit. Well, the reincarnation of Darlene Yount had to start somewhere. Maybe they could wave a white flag and hold the pantsuit in front of the bungalow and claim that Darlene was on her way, she was just changing or something. Was that really Gerry in there? But the voices were totally different, and Packer couldn't picture the timid Yount ("Right, Lieutenant") as a killer.

Maybe they were both inside, he thought: Yount and Koslo, working together. That would make more sense. How had they hooked up? Could Yount have seen Koslo enter and followed him in? *Why?* Yount was running, had to be. His wife's body was thoroughly dead, dead for months, Mains had said. If the deskman hadn't killed her, why had he concealed her death?

He had to be the killer.

But how did you get from there to the two sex murders? It was flat impossible for Yount to have strangled Betty Evans; he'd been on the desk the night of the murder. Every *second*. Packer had sat inside his own little cauldron of an office, doing paper work. *Es-ca-ped.* The only time he'd left the station was when he rolled on the 010, and by then the victim was dead. It had taken hours to lie in wait for Betty Evans, strangle her, pour acid down her throat, write "slut" across her belly, get into that wild chase with Artie Siegl and then slip away. *Hours.* Gerry Yount had been sitting a few yards from Packer the whole time.

But if not Yount, then who? *Who was in there now with Amnee and Emmy?*

Yount or Koslo, it didn't matter, he reminded himself as he lowered his head and made his way to the front of the bus. We've got to get the guy out of there whoever he is, to save—my family. No! To save—*the subjects.* The civilian hostages. The—*victims.* He had to think of them that way, depersonalize them by a great act of will, or he would be reduced to uselessness. That's where the new manual made sense.

Please, God, save me from my helplessness, save me from my fear. For the first time in my life, I'm scared to death. I'm shaking. Please, God, don't let me fuck up. . . .

His head scraped the underside of a grenade launcher that hung from the ceiling in a chain-web sling. The command vehicle was a weapon of war: as bulletproof as a tank, bristling with fire power, lockers crammed with riot weapons and machine guns and machine pistols and sniper's rifles and tear gas and Mace, closets in the back stacked with bulletproof vests, lead-lined aprons that hung below the knees, bulletproof helmets with bulletproof visors, jumpsuits lined with SBA, SWAT coveralls, gasproof coveralls, gas masks, asbestos outfits that would withstand six-hundred degrees. . . .

And nothing to help his wife and baby. Not a goddamn thing. . . .

He lowered his head and squeezed his face into a blank mask. Singletary would run him right off the bus if he showed any emotion. The old man was fully in charge. It had been a long time.

"Cap," he said, "what's happening now?"

"I positioned SWAT. We may hafta rush the house."

Packer gulped. Not those trigger-happy SWAT troopers! "Cap, you won't—"

"Of course I won't! Not unless we hear shots. Not unless—we have to."

"You'll wait . . .?"

"We won't endanger the—anybody."

"Thanks, Cap. Thanks a lot." He touched the precinct commander on the arm, but the captain turned away.

"And he hasn't said anything new?" Packer insisted.

"I won't lie to you. Nothing."

He leaned across the command desk and squinted at the only corner of his bungalow that was visible in the streetlight. All he could distinguish was the line that separated the new cedar board and batten from the old white planked siding. He'd have to finish the job; also finish pouring the footings for the heat pump, so they could use it to cool the house in this heat wave. Especially with all the doors and windows sealed. God, it must be hot in there. A goddamn oven . . .

Amnee . . . And Emmy . . .

He caught a glimpse of movement at the Orchard Street entrance to the parking lot. The captain had lied: something else *was* new. An ambulance had been called in. He looked again. No, *two* ambulances. They parked side by side, roof lights off, drivers waiting with itchy hands on the steering wheels. In his mind's eye he could see Emmy being lifted gently aboard. Did they have tiny stretchers for tiny patients? *Packer, knock it off! Keep your mind on—work.*

The quavery voice of Turk Molnar broke in. "How much time left, Cap?"

"Uh, twenty, twenty-one minutes," Singletary answered, glancing up from the plastic street map that swung out from the wall on thin wires.

"Isn't he saying anything at all?" Packer asked. He knew he sounded nervous. He wanted to be quiet, let the captain concentrate, but he couldn't hold back. How could they just sit here and do nothing? The guy inside might not be bluffing.

"I told you. He dummied up."

No, Captain, no, *no!* Packer wanted to shout. That's the *one* thing you can't let happen. Their only hope was communication. "Skip, did you try—"

"I tried raising him. Three, four times. No answer. I'm giving it a rest now. Don't want to piss him off."

"What's he doing, I wonder?" Packer asked half aloud.

"Doing?" the precinct commander said. He shook his head and looked back over his shoulder with a grim expression. "He's running out the clock."

41

When nothing had been heard from inside the house for five or six minutes, the captain spun his selector dial to F-7 and whispered into the microphone, "Charlie Two to David One."

"David One," Willie Bethea's steady voice came back.

"Whattaya see?"

"Can't see nothing from here," the deep voice returned. Bethea and Beemer were in the house next to Packer's, watching the south wall and the rear exposure.

"No sounds?"

"Negative."

"No—shots? Loud noises?"

"Dead quiet, Charlie Two. Every shade's pulled, the lights are out, there's no signs of, uh, life."

"Received. Stay on post. Who's got the north exposure?"

"Zebra Five. Mills."

"Charlie Two to Zebra Five."

"Zebra Five," the rookie's voice came in alertly. "I can see the whole north wall and most of the back, sir. Everything's quiet."

"Received. Charlie Two to whoever's across Orchard."

"David Five," Ernie Smoliss responded. "I'm inside Seventy-one seventy-seven. Residence of, uh, Mrs. Steve, uh, Walker. She's a widow, sir; resides here alone. I'm by the front window. It's—" Jesus Jones, couldn't the dummy keep it short?—"it's pretty bright, sir, with the streetlight. I got the whole front porch. Thought I seen somebody peek out a while ago, but no sign of the perpetrator. I can see the door good. It hasn't moved. Guarantee you that, Cap."

"Received," the captain said curtly. "Shorten up the next time. All you men, I don't want to know what you don't see. Tell me what you *do* see. *Phnfff!"*

Where was Agate right now? What would he see if he could see his own wife?

He turned as Molnar handed him a phone on a long extension cord. "It's the chief," the sergeant mouthed.

"What chief?"

Molnar looked aghast and clamped his hand over the phone. *"The* chief," he said in a stage whisper.

The captain grabbed the phone. "Chief? Listen, I'm under a lot of time pressure here. What . . .?"

"You can't talk?" the mellow, saccharine voice poured over the line. Goddamn politician! He'd perfected that piss-elegant style for interviews and public appearances; now he used it all the time. Even on old friends. He used it when he was awarding medals and when he was cutting nuts. The captain could guess which of the two was coming up.

"Chief—"

"I just got a red-line call from the SWAT lieutenant, Jules. He says you won't relinquish."

"That's right."

Was she lying stripped in some sleazy motel?

"Listen to me, Jules," the chief went on calmly, as though he were discussing the next senior officers banquet. "We've trained our SWAT teams to handle hostage situations. Do you read me, Jules?" Then the voice hardened. "Pull off those stumblebums and give it to Frosch." Then back to the golden voice. "Are we on the same wavelength, Jules?"

"Al, this is a *precinct* matter."

"A precinct matter?" The chief spoke slowly as though addressing a retard. "You call a hostage situation a precinct matter?"

"Look, the guy's jumpy. Flash one riot gun in front of him and we got a dead woman and a dead kid on our hands." He hated himself for talking so plainly in front of Packer, but the chief didn't comprehend subtlety.

"Don't you think Frosch knows that? He's trained—"

"I'm not relinquishing to SWAT, Al," the captain said. "I'm going with my own. We got—an interest."

. . . Sprawled on a disheveled bed with a little edging of semen around her mouth.

"Then I'll have to order SWAT in, Jules."

Enough time had been wasted. There were less than twenty minutes to go and he had to think and plan—and act. "Don't order a goddamned thing, you phony prick!" he blurted into the telephone. "If you special anybody else in here they'll have to fight ten of my men first. *And we got the bus!*"

The chief's answer was barely audible. "This is on tape, Jules."

The captain almost cracked the phone in half as he banged it down on its cradle. *"This is on tape." What do I give a shit? My wife's gone; my bars might as well be gone, too.*

There was a stir at the door. He swiveled in his chair and saw Billy Mains and a policewoman climbing aboard. The skinny cop was waving his arms and telling anyone who would listen, "That's him! That's Gerry in there! I know him! It's Gerry faking his voice. Hey, Cap, I drove with that guy six months, remember? He's not kidding me. I can influence him, he'll listen to me, Cap! Let me try to talk the sucker out."

The policewoman Maki followed her partner through the entrance door, holding a pile of clothes at arm's length. The two of them stank like goats. Old dead goats. No, old dead humans. It had been years since the captain had covered a D.B. call, but he remembered the smell. Any cop would. Then he also remembered: the two of them had just found Darlene Yount's body.

"That's *him* in there!" Mains chirped, jutting his aging baby face into the cone of light from the pull-down lamp. "You can make book on it."

Turk Molnar spoke up. "How can it be Yount? He was on the desk the night of Betty Evans. He can't be the acid killer."

"Maybe that first killing—inspired him," the captain said, thinking out loud. "Something about the M.O. fired him up. Wouldn't be the first time. Maybe it was that word on her stomach. 'Slut,' right?"

"'Slut,'" Packer Lind said quickly. "I don't believe it, Cap, but that second killing coulda been a copycat."

"Yeah," the captain said. "You already said that once." He slapped his hand on the table and said, "It's Yount in there. We'll proceed on that basis."

"Absolutely," Billy Mains echoed. "Listen, Cap, I can handle him. Believe me—we're tight, real tight. He's a—pussy, Cap. Look, somebody's gotta make a move. Let me go, Cap. I know the guy like a brother. Christ, we—"

The captain held up his hand for silence and spun the selector knob to F-2. "This is the captain," he said into the mike. "Calling Mr. Koslo. This is Jules, Mr. Koslo. Come in, please."

Silence. Or was that an answer way in the distance, too faint to be understood?

"Mr. Koslo," he said again. "We're still right here, friend. Listen, is there something we can do for you right now? What do you need, sir? We'll do anything within reason, I promise you that. Okay, Mr. Koslo? Darlene's on her way; I just heard from her. Respond, please. *Give me an answer, please, sir.*"

Once again the captain thought he heard a weak reply. Uncertain, he turned questioningly to the figures huddled around him in the dim light and saw the heads shaking slowly.

"Cap, gimme a chance!" Billy Mains pleaded. He was so excited, he looked ready to piss his pants. "I know—"

Turk Molnar threaded the long phone line to the command desk. "It's the shrink," he whispered. Oh, Christ, the captain told himself, the whole goddamn department's sticking its nose in. When did I ever need this much help? Then he remembered: the dispatcher was under standing orders to alert the shrink in hostage situations. Sometimes a quick psychological evaluation could help. The captain motioned to Packer Lind to pick up the other line in case the doc needed any information about Yount. "Doc?" he said, and didn't wait for an acknowledgment. "We got a young officer, calls himself Koslo, real name Yount, he's holding a lieutenant's wife and baby in their home, orders us to produce his ex-wife or he'll kill everybody. Oh, yeah, and we just found his ex-wife dead. Murdered." He paused to get his breath.

"You say the man claims he's Koslo but you know him as—"

"Yount. That's it exactly, Doc."

"Any doubt he's really Yount?"

"None," Packer put in.

"Tell me quick, Jules. This, uh, Yount had any big emotional problems lately? A demotion? Personal problems? A new beat, something like that?" The shrink's words tumbled out; the captain had to concentrate to catch them. "Jules, hold on! Isn't he the one whose wife walked out? You sent him in for consultation and— Yes, I remember! He resisted like hell. I figured give him a little space, reschedule him later."

"Right, Doc," the captain said, "but how did he turn into Koslo all of a sudden?"

There was a slight pause, then another avalanche of words. ". . . Multiple personality . . . Old story . . . Extreme stress . . . Mind snapped, simplest way to put it. . . . Another identity took over."

"Maybe. Maybe not."

The captain looked at the clock. Fifteen minutes left. "What's your advice, Doc? Tell me quick. We got a time problem."

"Do what he says. Anything! If he wants to be, uh—Koslo did you say? Then treat him as Koslo. That's who he is right now anyway."

"Can't we snap him out of it?"

"Out of what?"

"Out of being Koslo. Back to being Yount. Yount was a quiet guy. Koslo's a crazy."

"Sometimes a strong shock'll bring them out. A long sleep. A change—"

"But—"

"Best leave him alone. Stall! Keep stalling! When he's ready for reality, he'll come back. Too bad you can't watch for the symptoms."

"What symptoms?"

"Usually they get a dizzy spell, a fainting spell; maybe they'll be overwhelmed by a mood swing, slide into a deep depression. May even lose consciousness, blank right out. When they wake up, they're back to normal. Whatever normal is. Listen, Jules, I'm in the car now, be there in another ten or fifteen. Treat him gently—buy some time."

"Right." The captain shook his head and avoided Packer Lind's intense stare. So that's what it added up to: treat him gently and buy some time. Exactly what they'd been doing. All the rest had been the usual psychological jargon: mood swings, reality, depression, shock. . . . Who needed that bullshit? Koslo, Yount, whoever he was—he still had Packer's wife and kid, multiple personality or not. Maybe he didn't do that first killing, the Evans girl, but he sure as hell killed Eddie Jocelyn's widow; he practically announced it was a cop, the inscription on the stomach and the handcuffs and all. And now he was cranking up to kill again. . . . Another police family. . . . It wasn't the clearest homicide pattern he'd ever seen, but it was sure as hell a pattern.

There were thirteen minutes left. The captain decided to follow an old rule of thumb: "Do something, even if it's wrong." He turned to Billy Mains and spoke emphatically. "Try to raise him on the radio. Slow and easy, get me? *Slow and easy.* Calm yourself first. Take some deep breaths. That's it. Keep it nice and light and conversational. Okay? Ready? A few more breaths. Okay, now. Here." He passed the mike across.

Mains punched the button and held the black instrument tight against his lips, and the captain reached out and nudged it an inch or two away. This was no time to be popping P's. "Yount?" the patrolman said in a raspy voice. "Can you read me?"

The captain leaned forward and whispered, "Call him Koslo. *Koslo!*"

"Koslo?" Mains went on, slower this time. "This is Billy Mains.

Hey, buddy, this is Bill. Your old pardner? Come in, pal. Gimme a roger. Okay, uh, Koslo?"

Not too bad a performance for an excitable type, the captain said to himself. But there'd still been too much tension in his voice. It wasn't easy, a situation like this. You had to sound like you were just an old friend discussing the weather or your latest fishing trip. Two lives hung in the balance, but the other guy didn't care about life and you had to act as though you didn't care about it either. It was like making friends with a rabid dog.

"There's somebody answering," Packer Lind said. "But it's faint."

"I think he's responding," Molnar put in. "But his battery must be gone. He can hear but he can't respond, Cap, that's my impression."

Jesus Jones, the captain said to himself, no wonder the guy's been quiet for so long. Oh, my God, maybe he thinks we're pulling his chain. Ignoring him. Taking him cheaply. If the manual made anything clear, it was never discredit a hostage-taker, never talk disrespectfully to him; break your ass to make him feel like a goddamn maharajah, the emperor of the world. . . .

Well, they couldn't run the risk of losing contact. The captain grabbed the mike and spoke carefully. "Mr. Koslo, sir, this is Jules. Sir, we think maybe your radio's not putting out. We can't hear you, friend, and we think you're trying to tell us something. Mr. Koslo, please, listen closely, so there's no misunderstanding. Okay, sir? Okay, buddy? Now listen: *nobody's gonna move in on you, do you understand that?* Okay, what I'm gonna do, I'm gonna go around to the neighbor's house just to the south of you. The big bungalow with the dormers? I've got a portable loudspeaker. A bullhorn? I'll talk to you from there, across the driveway. Okay? Remember, nobody's moving in, Mr. Koslo. Let me emphasize that, friend. We're just trying to keep our lines open. Okay, pal? Okay? Can you give me an acknowledgment on that, buddy? I'd appreciate it."

This time there was dead air and static.

"Okay," the captain said to the men around him. "I'm going. There's no other way. *Phnfff!* We got to stay in contact or it's over."

"Wait!" Lind said. "How about trying the phone first?"

"Dial it," the captain said. Christ, he mustn't be as cool as he thought he was. Forgetting to try the phone! The obvious thing. . . .

When the lieutenant had finished dialing his own number, the captain took the phone away from him. He didn't want Lind talking directly to anybody in that house. Too risky. . . .

The phone buzzed against his ear. Again. Again and again. . . .

When he realized no one would answer, he asked Lind to re-dial. This time he let the phone ring a dozen times. Koslo, Yount, he must have ripped it out. More time lost. "No use," the captain said, "I'll have to go."

Eleven minutes left. . . .

"Cap, the guy's crazy," the watch commander said from his bent position. He was the only one in the command post who had to lean to avoid the ceiling. "He'll shoot, Skip. We know that. Let me go. It's my house. It's my—"

"It's my precinct," the captain said. "Now listen. I'm taking Mains with me. He knows Yount well; maybe he can help. You take over here. Yeah, I know you shouldn't be involved. The hell with the manual. Just remember: nothing radical." He reached up and slapped Lind on his broad back. "We can handle it."

No, Agate wouldn't be in a motel now. That wasn't her style. She'd be at home in the bathroom, buffing her nails for—him. . . .

"Cap," Turk Molnar said nervously, "go the back way. Approach the house from the other side, where he can't see you."

"Thanks for the advice, Sergeant," the captain said as he grabbed a bullhorn offered by a patrolman. "Did you think I was gonna tromp right across the kill zone?" Molnar grinned sheepishly as the captain turned to Mains. "Let's go."

The anxious little cop stepped on the captain's heel as they climbed out of the bus. A few leftover SWAT troopers gave way as the two men from Precinct Nine walked toward a green-and-white. The captain heard a few muffled cracks. He knew they wouldn't be the last.

Used to call him "Old Brassballs," did they? What would they call him now? *Who gave a fuck what they called him?* Some whacko yay-hoo cocksucker was threatening a defenseless woman and child; there was a job to do, and by God he was gonna do it.

His way.

Rosarito was a silly dream anyway.

42

When the man disappeared toward the bedroom, Amnee wrenched so hard at the handcuffs behind her back that she could feel the metal slice into her flesh. She tugged upward till the pain in her thin wrists made her lose her breath; it felt as though the harsh edges had cut to bone. She knew he could hear the cuffs clanging against the rungs of the chair back, but she couldn't stop. She had to break free. He was stalking her baby.

In the dark hallway something moved, and then he emerged carrying Emmy by the back of her plastic pants while her legs and head dangled. She made a noise, part whimper, part question, and Amnee called out, "It's okay, baby. Mommy's here, sweetheart. Everything's so . . . nice." Familiar words in a lilting tone, almost sung. A ritual between mother and daughter. *The world is safe, Emmy.*

In the dim glow of streetlight that leaked around the edges of the blinds, the baby looked more confused than frightened. Amnee realized that a dream must have awakened her; now she probably thought her daddy was carrying her into the living room for more of their roughhousing.

The man lowered her to the floor and straddled the tiny body with its vulnerable bare legs and chest. Amnee looked at his heavy black boots and thought about the dead puppies.

"Come to mama!" she called out, her breath catching in her throat. "Come, honey. *Come, Emmy!"*

The baby clutched the uniform pants and softly said, "Dah." Then she said, "Dah?" and began to sniffle.

"Shut up," he said.

"Let me hold her," Amnee begged. "Please. I promise—I'll keep her quiet. She's only—eighteen months." Cramped against the wooden chair, she was afraid she would pass out any minute. She bit her lip till she tasted salty blood; someone had to protect the baby. . . .

The man walked a wavery line to the front window and looked out the crack between the curtain and the window frame. Faint tints of blue and red splashed alternately against the shade; she guessed a patrol car must be parked nearby. She had heard him talking to someone on his radio. To Packer? He must be out there. Somewhere. What did this crazy man want? What could her husband possibly give him?

Her gaze fell on a milky-blue bowl of wilted daisies that drooped almost to the dully shining surface of an end table. That evil, rotten, disgusting man wilted my daisies, she said to herself in blind fury. Damn him! Damn damn god*damn* . . . No, it wasn't him, it was the heat. Funny, the heat didn't bother her. But she knew it was hot: stifling outside and even worse in here with the windows shut and locked. The baby must be feeling it, but she wasn't feeling it herself. She wondered where her senses had gone. Her hands were dead lumps; flashes of pain shot up to her shoulders, but a numbness was settling in there, too. She wondered if the numbness would reach her brain. *It couldn't.* She had to hold on.

Clumsily, the baby sat up, but made no effort to crawl or stand. When she sniffled again, the man turned and aimed his gun at her and said, "Boom!" A bent smile flicked around his slobbered lips, but it didn't reach his death's-head eyes.

Emily's gaze went up the gray-white pants with the green stripe and across the gray-white shirt with the green patches and stopped at the face. She began to babble excitedly. Amnee understood one word, "Man!" Now the baby knew this wasn't her father. And she let out a shriek.

"Make her be still," he insisted, looking frightened by the noise.

"She won't, she won't, I can't!" Amnee said, fighting her own hysteria. "Can't you see? She's—afraid."

"Mama!" the baby cried. "Mama mama mama *mama* . . ."

He stepped toward Amnee, the planes of his face altering spasmodically in the shadows. "She won't hurt you!" she called out, realizing how ridiculous the words must sound. "If you'll just let me—"

But he was already kneeling behind her chair, the key ring jingling in his hand. "There," he said. "There." Slowly she slid her left hand onto her lap, the cuffs still dangling from her right wrist. She saw that she was abraded but not cut; the skin was raw and oozy at the wrist bone. She rubbed her hands between her knees, trying to restore the feeling. There were prickles and shocks of pain, but she rubbed harder. Without thinking, she lurched toward the baby, but he shoved her back down, almost tipping the heavy wooden chair. "Don't you move an inch unless I tell you," he said.

"Y-yes," she said. "But—the baby—"

"Here," he said, lifting the infant one-handed and dropping her on Amnee's lap. "Keep it quiet."

Emily screamed again and dug her fingernails like tacks into Amnee's neck. "It's okay, baby," she murmured. "It's okay, it's *okay*." She rocked back and forth on the straight-backed chair and whispered the old, soothing words. As the baby slowly stopped shuddering, Amnee realized that somehow the two of them had gained ground. Maybe they had only postponed the inevitable, but they were still alive, unharmed, unviolated. There was hope. A minute ago there'd been none. As she rubbed gentle circles against the baby's back, she noticed that the wild pounding in her own heart had slowed, her breathing was easier, and she was acutely aware of everything that was happening. She was scared, but she was no longer stupefied. The improvement encouraged and puzzled her. The most horrifying possibility was now taking place; an insane man held their lives in his uncontrollable hands and there was no one to help, and yet she wasn't falling apart, she wasn't collapsing, she was taking the only action that could be taken under the circumstances: calming her baby. Next she had to calm a full-grown lunatic. Emmy's life depended on it. If he lost control . . .

For the first time, she wished she had the gun. The—option.

She glanced over her shoulder at the bookcase, shrouded in shadows. The little revolver was on the third shelf, under the teddy bear. He mustn't catch her peeking. She was still repelled by the thought of firing a pistol, but at least she could entertain the idea. If he lifted one finger to harm her child . . .

She didn't understand the change that was coming over her and she couldn't try. It was taking her last reserves of mental energy to stay calm, stable, to prepare for whatever she would have to do, for whatever was—unavoidable.

Did that include taking the life of another human being? Or maybe shooting him blind? Or paralyzed for life?

She didn't know. If it came to something so final, so irreversible, he had made the choice, not her; he had made the choice when he emerged from the back room with a helpless human being in his hands as though he were carrying a satchel. With that action, he had ceased to be human himself.

Amnee, Amnee, she told herself, patting the sobbing form in her arms, you're into self-delusion. You're trying to—what was that expression Packer used?—to jack yourself up. You'd *never* shoot a gun, you'd *never* take aim at another person.

I wouldn't?

No, you wouldn't.

Not even if . . .?

Oh, God, *God,* put that little gun in my hands!

The man had sat down heavily on the sofa, one wavering hand pointing his weapon in their direction, the other holding the portable radio to his ear. He seemed to be talking, but she couldn't distinguish words. When the baby quieted at last, still gulping, Amnee realized that the poor crazy man was reciting a mantra. "Me me me me me me me," he chanted. But it couldn't be a mantra, because he suddenly stood up and clawed at his pallid, clean-shaven face and said, "That's how they think, that's how they live. Me me me me me me . . . *Me me me me me me me me me . . .*" The baby jerked in her arms as he threw his head back and yelled, "ME ME ME ME ME ME . . .!"

Then he spun and almost fell, took a step backward, and clawed the air behind him for the couch. He looked dead on his feet. She wondered how many days he'd been awake. If he would just doze long enough for her to sneak the few steps to the bookcase. . . .

She couldn't take the chance—yet. Not even if he closed his eyes. It was too risky. The baby . . . He would kill; he had made that plain. He would fire and fire till they were both dead. She knew what was in those tooled-leather pouches on his belt. At least a dozen ugly silver cartridges in each. How many slugs did it take to end a year and a half of life? Or how many fingers, deftly applied? She bit the old panic back, refused to indulge in it. She swallowed hard and sucked air and swore not to yield again to her own weakness. She might die, she might have to watch her baby die, but neither of them would die of fright or cowardice. She squeezed the child tightly and whispered in her ear:

> Go to sleep,
> Go to sleep,
> Go to sleep
> Little Baby. . . .

The man's head was slumped almost to his knees. "How can they do it?" she heard him say. "Animals. *Animals!* It's me, me, me, me, all the time. Me me me me me me . . ."

Then his voice became almost matter-of-fact. "He should kill himself. That's it! No, he can't! How can he? *Are you baptized?*"

For an instant she thought he was questioning her, but when he stared into the darkest corner of the room for his answer, she realized he was having a conversation with someone else. Or no one. There was nothing in that corner but an old Canadian spinning wheel Packer had picked up at the Trash 'n' Treasure. "ARE YOU BAPTIZED?" he yelled into the blackness. "No? . . . Oh, my, that's what I was afraid of. Maybe she'll—come back. Sure, she'll be back. They, they promised." He raised his wrist till it was a few inches from his inflamed eyes. "Six minutes," he said. "They have six minutes. Said she was downtown, caught in traffic." What in the name of God was this psychopath talking about?

He sprang to his feet and cried, "No! *No!* There's no traffic this time of night. They're lying to me!" He put his head in his hands and started to shake. "They lied to me all along. Jules—Jules lied." He sounded devastated by the deception. "She's out there," he said, his voice quaking. "She's there right now. With one of—them." He sounded like a lost child, forlorn, terrified of being abandoned. Her mind flashed back to a movie scene. "We were walking in a crowd," a young woman says, "and you let go my hand." *Dr. Zhivago:* she had seen it when she was nine, cried at the poignant words. *You let go my hand. . . .* Every little girl's fear, and maybe every little boy's. Yount, Koslo, whatever he called himself—he had spoken in the same lost tone. He was an abandoned child now, he was frightened and forsaken, and for an instant he made her forget his gun and his vicious threats and his trembling hands and what he must have done to other women on other nights.

This was the moment. He was still. She had to take the risk. "Gerry?" she said.

He stared at the floor; his lips moved soundlessly in the semidarkness.

"Mr.—Koslo," she said louder.

He peered across the room as though he were seeing her for the first time.

"Can we—talk?" she asked, as tentatively as though she were approaching a lost child in a park. "We'll listen, Mr. Koslo. We're—your friends."

He looked glassy-eyed at her, his lower lip wobbling, his head bobbing toward his chest as though he could no longer support its weight. All at once he began to cry, tiny sobs at first, then great moaning outcries, his thin body twitching and twisting. He fell back on the sofa and lifted his knees from the floor and hugged them with both arms and then held the pistol flat against his chest as his body shook violently. He cried for three or four minutes, and even after the sobs had turned to deep strangled suckings of air, his body continued to jerk like the puppet of a spastic puppeteer. At last he dragged a uniform sleeve across his streaked face, sniffed a few times, and raised the barrel of the gun so that it pointed shakily at them. "I'm sorry," he said gently. "I'm—he's sorry."

"About what?" Amnee asked, pulling back reflexively and holding the baby tighter.

"He's sorry. He's really sorry." His body shook again, and he coughed and cleared his throat.

Stay calm, she told herself. For God's sake, stay calm! She rotated slowly in her chair so that Emmy was half sheltered by her body. At the first shot she would fall, even if it missed. She would fall and hold the baby beneath her, and maybe he would go away, or maybe Packer would break the door down before there was time to finish them off. Or maybe Koslo, no, Yount—maybe he would run. Maybe, maybe . . . Their lives hung by a string of maybe's.

He looked across at them with empty eyes. "Gotta do it—for him," he mumbled, his tight lips barely moving. "Gotta—get her back. Darlene. Mrs., uh, uhm, Yount. She won't come back, unless—unless he—unless I—"

His gun hand shook, and he brought his other hand up to steady it.

"Unless you what?" Amnee asked, bending her shoulder across the exposed face of her child.

"Unless there's, uhm, blood," he said. "Unless there's a body to, to replace, to replace, uhm, uh, her—body."

He wasn't making sense. He had passed out of the stage where anyone could understand him. He was off in a science-fiction setting of his own creation, where new bodies replaced old ones and there had to be—blood. What could she say to bring him back?

"Mr. Yount—"

They both heard it at the same time: a thumping sound from the back of the house, as though someone had thrown something heavy against the outside wall along the driveway. "What?" he said, jumping up, his eyes widening. "Don't move!"

His gun clicked. Dear God, she said to herself, did he pull the trigger? Did it misfire? Will it be— *now?*

No, no, he had *cocked* the pistol. She remembered now. You pulled something back and the metal went—*click.*

He crossed the room in a couple of strides and yanked the baby from her arms. With Emily dangling again from his one-handed grasp, he strode toward the rear of the bungalow.

Now Amnee's life was meaningless. All that mattered were the screams of her only child.

In a second she was out of the chair and scrabbling with her uncuffed hand under the teddy bear. *There!* She cradled the gun in her right hand, fumbled with it till her index finger was firm against the trigger, and turned toward the sounds. You feel nothing, she instructed herself. *Nothing.* You are calm, you are composed.

The baby's screams filled the house in waves, eliminated the rest of the world, blotted out rules, laws, morality, gentleness, decency. . . . Oh, God, I can't let her be hurt. . . . *Not one finger* . . .

A shot rang out. Loud. Close.

She hurried toward the hallway that separated the living room from the rear of the bungalow. Her hand was outstretched; she would gun him down the instant he came into sight.

She heard heavy footsteps approaching from the back room, and another wail from the baby. They were coming back. Emmy was still— living. Then she heard another shot. Too late. It was too late now.

She dropped the chunk of steel into the deep front pocket of her apron and ran back to the same chair, the loose handcuffs jingling like cheap jewelry. She would wait till she couldn't miss.

The baby screamed again, louder. They were coming through the hallway. She *was* alive! *Emily was alive!* But was she—in pain?

My own flesh and blood is calling for me, Amnee told herself slowly, but I won't hear the sound. It won't affect me. I *refuse* to hear her; I blot out my baby's cries. There is something I must do with utter, calm serenity.

Now I can kill.

43

Scheme after scheme had tumbled through Billy Mains' busy brain like clothes in a dryer, till he was hardly able to sort them out. For one of the few times in his life, he felt vulnerable, besieged. Not by people, but by events. That Yount . . . *Jerk-off cocksucker!* Who'd he think he was kidding with this Koslo shit? Then he remembered the D.B. Oh, Christ, Darlene's body. Darlene's . . . head. But hadn't he seen worse? What about the old artist in the Heights that sucked both barrels of a ten-gauge and distributed his brains all over the ceiling of his darkroom, and a bloody hunk fell on Billy as he opened the door? *Fell on my head! A fucking piece of brain!* Wasn't that worse than the scene in Yount's closet? No, it wasn't. He hadn't known the artist. He hadn't been—intimate—with the other D.B.s of his career.

"Let us off down the block," the captain was telling the driver of the green-and-white. "We'll approach through the front yards."

Big deal, Billy said to himself. Big—fucking—deal. Imagine slinking through front yards to approach Gerry Yount. Or any other yellow-bellied hostage-taker. The brass hats pussyfooted too much in these cases. The guy was a coward from go. Would a real man hide behind an innocent woman and child?

Now what was the smartest way to handle a weak sister like Yount? Did you genuflect and ask His Holiness what you could do to help? Fuck, no! That was just encouraging the asshole, feeding his ego. What you did, you used your command authority loud and clear. *Loud and clear!* You got up in his face, you made it plain you wouldn't bend an inch. Of course you had to have big balls to operate like that, but whoever said Bill Mains didn't have big balls?

"Far enough," the captain said in a hushed voice, as though the mighty Gerry Yount could hear him halfway down the block. "Take it easy. Don't squeal your brakes."

As they slipped from the car, the captain beckoned Billy into a crouch. Christ, how had he gotten teamed up with this old crock? Everybody said he'd been a charger in his day, but that was folklore. When was his day? The fifties? Beating up faggots with nightsticks? Chasing draft dodgers? Look at him now: thick and flabby; he's breathing hard already, and we barely started. Maybe he's scared. Don't worry, old-timer. I'll cover your lard-ass.

The outline of a plan was forming in his mind. If he could just work it out, he'd be the old Billy Mains again. Respected. Feared. Hated a little bit, too, but who gave a shit? That fucking red-headed Maki would tear her pants off for him. The plan was coming, coming slowly, but other thoughts intruded. It was immaterial that the captain was calling the shots. He could always get around that problem; he was a specialist in ignoring orders. Besides, cops could be closely supervised for only so long, and then you were turned loose to perform on your own: unwatched, unjudged. They could burn you with all the station-house chickenshit they wanted, penalties, furloughs, fines, notations in your jacket, but sooner or later they had to let you go single-0 again, and you were the law, dispensing justice with a wave of the hand and the crack of a sap on the head or a club to the ankles or knees. He couldn't wait. He'd be on Gerry Yount like an owl on a rat. Sooner or later . . .

The two men crossed a graveled driveway, leaning over like Cong intruders, the captain leading, their feet crunching lightly. *"Sshhhhh,"* the old man said, turning and holding his finger to his lips. Shit, Billy thought, don't pass out, Cap. The guy don't have sonar down there. He's just another human being. He's four houses away, and he's got to guard a woman and a kid and keep his eye on about ten possible points of entry. A little crunch of pebbles won't set him off, Cap. Relax, stay cool. Just another routine police job. . . .

Clouds of bugs swarmed around as they walked; he figured they were attracted by the stink of death on his uniform. Mosquitoes whined, flies and moths and hard-shelled bugs whirred into his face, and once he swallowed a gnat. The little fuckers loved these hot nights; every goddamn bug in the precinct must be out flying formation. . . .

The two men stepped over a low picket fence and crossed another driveway, this one of warm asphalt that pulled at their feet. Then they threaded their way through a row of chest-high shrubs. They were two houses from the lieutenant's place, and Singletary edged into the shadows. "We'll have to flatten out from here on," he whispered to

Billy. "If that yay-hoo sees us, he'll have a clear field of fire."

My ass, Billy said to himself. What's he gonna shoot at? Two ghosts? Shit, if Yount's that jumpy, he'd of already squeezed off a couple rounds. The captain was acting like the guy was some kind of superman, when the truth was he was barely alive, subhuman, a lousy cop to boot. A fucking altar boy, yellow as puke. He wouldn't be crouched behind the window drawing a bead, he'd be on his knees asking divine guidance. Christ, those holy-roller ideas of his. "Billy, you been born again?" Born again my ass! Once was plenty. He remembered the first night he'd noticed his partner tilting his head over a meal at the drive-in. Saying grace in public, for Chrisakes. In uniform! Didn't that tell you everything about Gerald Fucking Yount?

But that Darlene, she was another story.

Another fucking story, all right, he mumbled to himself as he followed the captain along the front of a fake-brick house bordered by low fir shrubs that poked at his balls. Goddamn cunt. He'd thought he was getting some nice easy cooze, but it turned out to be poison. Might as well stuck his dick in a can of Drāno. . . .

Fat whore must of spilled her guts before Yount snuffed her. Time, date, place, everything. The split of champagne up the old kazoo told the story. She'd confessed to hubby for sure, the dumb bitch, and Yount got even in his own yellowbelly way. Probably waited till she was asleep in bed, defenseless, then killed her and did his number with the bottle. *Sick . . .*

He glanced in the front window of the next house. A newscaster's lips moved silently on the TV. The people must have cleared out fast. The cool blue-white light flickered around the darkened walls.

No wonder Yount had acted so spooky the last couple months. Waiting for his chance, trying to get up the guts. Turned his head away quick when I caught him staring, Billy remembered. Didn't want to make me suspicious. Goddamn, he said to himself, how *do* I get into these fuck-ups? His father's cold voice flitted across his brain: "You're your own worst enemy, boy." Little Billy had broken his wrist climbing. "If there isn't enough trouble around, you'll manage to make some." He had lived his life under that injunction, and now it was happening again. And why? What excuse did he have for getting in this deep with a homicidal maniac and his nympho wife? Why, Christ, he'd almost squared up his private life; he was free of his third wife, the well-known statue Marie; he had a nice little pad and a pool that worked sometimes and a doorman that didn't give a fuck who you brought up to your apartment. Plus he had more tail than he knew what to do with: blow jobs, rim jobs, a couple of broads that liked him to beat their ass till they came. And then, you silly prick, what did you do? You got yourself into this mess, and for what? So you could corn-hole a fat, stupid farm bitch with no tits. A sheep would of made more sense. . . .

Fuck it, he said to himself as he followed the captain's satchel-ass across the final lawn. Quit thinking about it. You're a man of action, kid. Hang in, you'll get your shot.

They reached the house adjoining the Linds' and ducked behind the far side where Yount couldn't see them without a sixteen-foot periscope. Halfway along the stuccoed wall the captain tapped at a window. A dark face appeared and the glass slid up. "Go down a little ways," Willie Bethea called out. "There's a door."

Inside, Willie B led the two men up a stairway, a riot gun crooked in his arm. "This here's the main floor, Cap," Bethea said in a low voice. "Me and Rollie's watching from the living room. You see anything outside?"

"No," the captain answered. "Gimme a minute till my eyes adjust. Jesus Jones, don't these yay-hoos air-condition? Go ahead, Willie, we'll follow you." The old man sounded like a Boy Scout on his first night hike. If somebody said "boo," he'd piss himself.

The silhouette of Rollie Beemer crouched next to a window overlooking the Lind bungalow. "Whattaya see?" the captain asked.

"Not a thing, sir," Beemer replied. "The shades are down, and he's never shown a light. We don't even know what room they're in."

"Probably the front," Singletary said. "I've been inside. There's a living room with windows that give him two different exposures. The only problem he has is the back door, and Packer says there's three locks on it."

They were ignoring a few points, Billy noted. Windows for one. There must be eight or ten on the ground level. One tap with the barrel of a riot gun and they could swarm inside. Jerk-off Yount would collapse at the first sight of uniforms.

The captain crouched down and studied the house across the driveway, Billy in his lee. "We want him alive," the captain whispered, as though he had read Billy's mind. "We want them *all* alive." Billy's thoughts flashed forward, and with chilling clarity he saw what a healthy Gerry Yount could do to him. He saw a sensational murder trial, galleries of reporters, TV, the newspapers, the works. Christ, there'd be somebody there from *Official Detective*. THEY LEFT A TRAIL OF BLOOD. This time it would be Billy's. Everything would come out. *Everything!* This wasn't some piss-ant departmental matter now, it was homicide. *Multiple.* Every fucking detail would be on page ne, repeated on every newscast. His own role would make juicy copy. He would be—finished.

If he'd only kept his private life private. That was the mistake. At his last divorce hearing, she'd given some kinky testimony, and the department had hit him with a two-week furlough for Conduct Unbecoming. Well, he knew the rule: play around all you want, screw a whole goddamn nunnery if you could, but don't embarrass the department! The cornerstone of police ethics everywhere. There were still a few cities where a tin was a license to steal, to shake down and extort and receive stolen goods and break an occasional head for hire, but not if you broke the first rule:

DON'T EMBARRASS THE DEPARTMENT!

This time he would be dismissed outright. Hadn't they already warned him that his next fall would be his last? He'd be lucky they didn't haul out the old statute books and throw a sodomy charge at him. . . .

He tried to imagine life as Citizen Joe Schmuck. He'd have to move to another town, sit out the stink. But he'd never be a cop again, not if Gerald Yount lived to talk. Billy couldn't picture a life without a shield, without a .38 weighting down his belt and a drop weapon strapped to his ankle, without an assortment of saps and clubs and wrist rockets and the power to use them at his own discretion. He'd had the clout for too long to lose it. He'd never be able to adjust. What was he supposed to try next? The ministry? Social work?

He had to be a cop.

But he wouldn't be a cop if Gerald Yount survived. So it was all very simple. "Cap," he said softly, "I got an idea might work."

Singletary had painstakingly raised the window a few inches. Now he was lifting the bell of the bullhorn so it was pointed at the roof of Lind's house.

"Cap, wait!" Billy said, grabbing the older man's arm. "Wait, listen!"

"What?"

"First we got to find out what room they're all in," he said, talking out the side of his mouth. "Cap, if everything breaks down and we gotta take the place, we better hit the right room. If we don't, he'll have all the time he needs to blow 'em away."

"What's your plan?"

"You be ready to get his attention with the bullhorn, Cap. I'll work my way to the back of the driveway, behind that big bush on this side.

See back there? Then while you're occupying him at the front, I'll slip across the driveway and flatten myself against the house. Once I'm in position, there's no way he can see me without opening a window. If he does—you drop him from here with the riot gun."

"And if he doesn't open a window?"

"I'll plot the inside layout for you. There's bound to be a crack someplace between a blind and a window. I'll find out where he's keeping 'em, how he's holding 'em. You take suppose he's in the front room talking to you and the wife and kid're tied up in the back. That gives us a chance to rush him, see what I mean, Cap? I mean if it comes to that, see what I mean?"

"Lemme think—"

"Cap, we're down to the last minutes now. Look, it's safe. There's not much light. I'll get back okay, Cap. You know me." His baby face smiled modestly. "Don't I always get back?"

The captain turned from the window and stabbed a finger into the darkness of the room. "Willie," he said, "what's in the rear of this place?"

"Bedrooms, Cap'n. Two windows look out on the lieutenant's place."

"Cover Mains from there. Mains, if Yount makes you, abort as quick as you can. Don't be proud; just take cover fast. Get me? I won't start with the bullhorn till Willie says you're in place behind the big bush. Then I'll distract him good."

"Right."

"And remember what that crazy yay-hoo said: if anybody comes at him, he'll shoot the hostages. He's psycho enough to do it. So stay down and stay quiet. Don't be a hero, Billy, you hear me? *Don't be a hero!*"

"Right, Cap." Christ, the old fart wanted to talk the idea to death. The seconds were ticking down; every nerve in his body told him to get going, to make his move. Fast, crisp, and—final. He wasn't a fancy strategist, he was a patrol cop. *"Now,* Cap?" he begged.

"Good luck."

He picked his way through the unlit house and slipped down a short flight of wooden steps into the yard. He had to cross about twenty feet of garden between the porch and the bush at the edge of the driveway, and he wriggled across the flowers and vegetables just as he had wriggled across rice fields in Vietnam. "Head down! Ass down!" He could still hear the point man turning and bitching at him in an angry whisper. This job tonight would be a snap next to some of those L.R.R.P. missions. Say what you want about those night-fighting

Commies, they made Gerry Yount look like a pussy.

Gerry Yount! What a laugh! *I'm trembling, I'm trembling!* Billy almost laughed out loud as he slid forward on his belly. Imagine the whole goddamn P.D. shaking in their boots before an asshole like that. Jack the Ripper, saying grace over a cheeseburger. *Sheee-it!*

His hand squashed something soft, and he shook off the remains of a garden slug. Yount was a fucking slug, that's what he was. The whole world would be better off without garbage like him. Scumbag! Never made a solo bust in his life. Yellow bastard used to call for backup on warrant arrests! What possible use was a scumsucker like that?

He climbed to his feet and walked like a man; he didn't stop at the bush, and he didn't wait for the sound of the bullhorn. He drew his revolver with its six gleaming hot-loads and ran across the driveway toward the side of Packer's house. *A misunderstanding, Cap, it was all a misunderstanding.* It would be so easy to explain later. *I thought you said . . . But it worked, didn't it, Cap? Saved the wife and the kid, didn't we? Wasn't that the idea, Cap? We got him good, didn't we? Jeez, I hated to dump him, Cap, honest to Christ. My own partner. I hated to squeeze that trigger, but it was him or the little girl, am I right or wrong?*

He didn't see the fresh-dug hole till it was too late.

The ground dropped out from under him and he slammed face-first against the board and batten siding. Front caps spurted from his mouth like Chiclets.

"Back, get back!" someone called from the window across the drive.

He was stunned, reeling. Where was, where was—"back"?

He staggered to his feet in the half-glow from the streetlight. "Shon of a bish," he mumbled as he circled to get his bearings. "Shon of a bish," he repeated. "Shon of a—"

44

"Shots fired!" the captain barked into his radio. "Maintain your positions! . . . *Mr. Koslo!* Can you hear me? I'm next door. Do you read me now?"

No, of course the yay-hoo couldn't read him. His radio was dead. That's what the bullhorn had been for. He shoved his foot through the window pane and sent his voice blasting across the kill zone: "MR. KOSLO! CAN YOU HEAR ME? *YOUNT!* GODDAMN IT, HOLD YOUR FIRE!"

The radio crackled on his belt-holster: "Were the shots inside or outside?" He recognized the intense voice of Packer Lind.

"Outside, I think," he answered. "I think he fired out a window."

"At who?" Lind asked.

"Stand by. We're checking."

Another voice broke in: "All green, Captain?" It was Elmer Frosch, the SWAT leader, asking for authorization to storm the house with AK-16s and clouds of tear gas and streams of Mace and all the other goodies in his arsenal. Jesus Jones, how those guys loved war! Well, maybe it was time. "Stand by," he repeated, and stuck his head into the warm night air for a look. A cricket chirped from a bush a few feet below his nose.

"Gimme a flash," he said, groping backward till a short Kellite was slapped into his palm like a baton at a track meet. He leaned out as far as he could and bounced the beam off the driveway. Oh, Christ, look! Billy Mains was down, one foot pushing at the gravel like a dreaming dog on a chase. "Cover me!" the captain said over his shoulder. "I gotta get Mains."

"Get away from that window!" Willie Bethea shouted. He yanked the captain backward by the belt as a slug buzzed through the opening like a hornet.

Frosch's voice sounded again from the portable radio; he was more insistent this time: "Green, Captain? *Green?*"

"Negative," he exclaimed from a sitting position. He clambered to his feet and tried to get a fix on the situation. Couldn't those SWAT chargers shut up for a second? He wondered if he should give them the green after all. He'd be more than justified. There'd be no repercussions if he did and maybe plenty if he didn't. . . .

No, he'd be goddamned if he'd turn those hot-blooded assassins loose. They were a last resort. A desperation measure. And he wasn't desperate. Whatever had happened to Billy Mains, there were still helpless civilians in that house, and plenty of ammo in Koslo's—in Yount's—pouches. It might feel good to storm the doors and blow that loony away, and it would produce a few heroes, alive or dead, but what about that helpless woman and her baby? They were depending on him. The Ninth would take care of the Ninth.

He stabbed at the switch on his bullhorn. "MR. KOSLO," he called across the open space, "PLEASE, WILL YOU LISTEN TO REASON? DON'T SHOOT. NO—MORE—SHOOTING! TELL US WHAT YOU WANT. WE'RE STANDING BY TO HELP. PLEASE, I'M ASKING YOU NOT TO FIRE. WE'RE COMING OUT TO ASSIST THE INJURED OFFICER. DO YOU HEAR ME, MR. KOSLO?"

"Come ahead!" a shout came back, high and strained. It seemed to originate from midway in the house, and behind it the captain heard the crying of an infant. At least the baby was still alive. It was Packer's wife the guy had threatened to kill if anyone approached. Was she— dead? "Come on!" the voice called, stronger this time. "I got plenty more for you! Come on! COME ON!"

"MR. KOSLO, PLEASE. NO MORE SHOOTING! WHAT DO YOU WANT US TO DO, SIR?"

"You already lied," the voice returned, calmer now. "You said she'd be here by eleven. It's five after."

"I READ YOU, FRIEND. SHE'S—SHE'S—ON THE WAY."

"Do you think I'm stupid? Huh? *Do you?*" The voice flew into the higher ranges. "DO YOU?"

"NO, WE DON'T. NO, SIR, WE DON'T, MR. KOSLO." The captain wished the bullhorn emitted a softer tone. He didn't want to sound hostile. The slightest edge in his voice might set the guy off. They had promised to produce Darlene Yount as a device to gain time, and the time was up. What now?

"Forget Billy," Willie B called from the darkened door to the back bedroom. "The top of his head's blowed off."

"Two Two Three to Charlie Two," the radio broke in.

"Go, Packer," the captain responded.

"Skip, tell him on the bullhorn we got Darlene. Mrs. Yount. Tell him—she just arrived. She had to come a long way, Cap. Tell him she wants to freshen up a little, but we'll have her there in—a few minutes."

"*What?*"

"Cap, tell him right away!"

The captain's head spun. The way Mains had described Darlene Yount, she was a reeking mound of garbage. They had her clothes, yes, but what good were the clothes without the woman?

"MR. KOSLO, WE'VE GOT DARLENE YOUNT!" he called across on the bullhorn. It was up to his lieutenant now. Not the first time. Maybe Packer was only trying to squeeze out another few minutes. Maybe he had a plan of his own. Just like the guy. He thought like a cop, that one. Once a cop . . . Street sense counted the most. You couldn't learn it.

"SHE JUST ARRIVED, MR. KOSLO," the captain called out, hoping the man wouldn't pick up the uncertainty in his amplified voice. "SHE HAD A LONG TRIP AND SHE WANTS TO FRESHEN UP. DO YOU READ ME, MR. KOSLO?"

"She's—*here?*" the man shouted across the kill zone. He sounded surprised and suspicious, but the captain thought he also heard a note of elation. "His wife is—here? *Where?*"

"SHE'S, UH, WITH THE OFFICERS, MR. KOSLO, JUST DOWN THE STREET. SHE'S GETTING HERSELF TOGETHER BEFORE SHE—BEFORE SHE COMES TO SEE YOU. WANTS TO, UH, LOOK HER BEST. SHE'LL BE HERE IN—IN A FEW MINUTES. YOU HAVE MY WORD, MR. KOSLO, YOU HAVE MY PROMISE. *PLEASE*—DON'T DO ANYTHING RADICAL."

A strained, tremulous voice came back: "Tell her, tell her, come up on the porch. Tell her—he'll be there to meet her."

"I'LL PASS THE MESSAGE, BUDDY. WE'RE WORKING WITH YOU. JUST—NO MORE SHOTS, OKAY? FOR GOD'S SAKE, RELAX! OKAY? SHE'LL BE UP ON THAT PORCH IN A FEW MINUTES."

The man didn't answer. Jesus Jones, who the hell could he be? Wasn't he the third-watch deskman? But why did he refer to Darlene as *"his"* wife," not as *"my"* wife"? Once again the captain had to wonder if two men were inside. One to secure the front and one to secure the back. They'd have their hands full, going up against that kind of fire power. Did two guys ever flip out at the same time? Two *cops?* Well, who was the other one then?

"Charlie Two to Two Two Three," he said into his radio. "I promised him she'd be on the porch in a few minutes."

"She will, Skip." Packer sounded steady and strong. "She will."

45

One thing about this policewoman, Packer said to himself, she knows how to take orders. Even orders that sound crazy. She acted as though she didn't want an explanation, but he intended to give her one anyway, as soon as he cleared the bus. "Fellas, *please!*" he said in a loud voice. "Wait outside! *PLEASE! Everybody!* Turk, you and Artie get a green-and-white."

When the last man had stepped from the command vehicle, he turned to Mary Rob Maki and said, "Okay. Now take it off! Quick!"

The rookie patrolwoman kicked away her forest-green police shoes and began unfastening her Sam Browne belt.

Packer discreetly turned away. "Two Two Three," he said into his radio. "Who's down, Cap?" He mumbled to himself waiting for a response. It couldn't be, uh, *them.* Oh, God, *could it?* The captain had said the guy fired *out* the window. Could they have made a break for it? No, Amnee had better sense. Besides, what kind of a break could you make with a twenty-four-pound baby? Oh, Christ, if he could only get inside to help them. If he could only—

"It was Mains," the captain's voice came back. "Walked right into the kill zone."

"Received." Jesus, Billy Mains had caught one. After all these years. *Please, God, let him just be wounded. And please, God, let this be the end of it.* Sometimes when these wild-eyed hostage-takers drew blood, the anger whistled out of them like a pricked balloon; they turned meek and mild, hands in the air. Could Mains have given his life for Amnee and the baby? Billy Mains, of all people? Well, if he went, he went happy. The kill zone was his place of business.

"Okay, Officer," he said, talking to Maki with his eyes averted. "We're gonna have to put an act together, you and me. Strip to your, uh, your underthings, and—"

"I already have."

"Good. Now put this on." He reached backward and handed her the jumpsuit.

"It's—heavy," she said.

"That's the bulletproofing. Don't worry about fit."

He wondered if Koslo could be fooled so simply. Why do I keep thinking of him as Koslo? he asked himself. *Yount.* That's who he is. That miserable goddamn Yount. Somebody should have seen this coming. Yeah, somebody. *Me.* The way he used to stare into the gumball machine. "Right, Lieutenant." "Yes, Lieutenant." "Sure, Lieutenant." A lunatic under his nose, night after night, and now he was paying the price. *They* were paying. Amnee and—

"I'm in."

Packer turned around. She swam in the jumpsuit, but it would have to do.

"Now the vest," he said, lifting one from the bottom locker. He lowered the soft body armor over her shoulders and his eyes caught the clock over the driver's seat! 11:07 P.M. Seven minutes after the deadline. "Oh, Christ," he said, his throat dry, "we got to hurry. Here!"

He picked up the dead woman's slack suit. "Put this on. I'm—sorry."

He expected her to complain, to gag or show distaste, but she said, "Won't it be too tight?" and started tugging the plum-colored slacks up over the jumpsuit as she spoke.

"She was way bigger than you," he said.

The clock ticked forward to 11:08. Packer cocked his head and listened for shots. All he could hear was the whirring of a mosquito around his ear and the low hum of his radio.

The built-in belt wouldn't snap; the plum pants were big, but not big enough to fit over the jumpsuit. "Kinda hold 'em together with your hand," he said. "Good. Now the top."

The jacket wouldn't stretch around the bulletproof vest. He moved behind and squeezed the dark-purple panels together till she went "Oof!"

"Breathe out!" he ordered, tightening his bear hug while she connected the oversized buttons. "Whew!" she said. "I—can't—"

"It'll be just a few—"

"There!" She waved her hand as though to remind him there was no time for small talk. The clock stood at 11:09. Yount had promised to start shooting at eleven o'clock. Well, he had. But at whom? Billy and who else? God, how he wished he knew! But it wouldn't change the job ahead, even if Amnee and the baby were already—gone. The victims, Packer, *the victims*. No—the subjects.

"Two Two Three to Charlie Two!" he radioed. "Tell, uh, tell Koslo she's on her way. *Emphasize: On her way!* We're bringing her over. Tell him to look out the front window and he'll see a green-and-white with, uh, the lady in the back."

"Received?" The captain sounded incredulous. Let him wonder, Packer thought. Maybe the whole idea's silly, but it's better than sitting around waiting. Yount had proved he would kill: he had nothing to lose by killing more.

"Here," he said, handing over the floppy pink hat.

"Pew!" she said, crinkling her small nose.

"We got a problem," Packer said. "His wife was a brunette." He lifted the reeking hat off her glistening red hair. "Pile it on top," he told her, and clamped the hat back on. Except for a few wisps, nothing showed.

"Your feet," he said. "Christ, I almost forgot."

The pink plastic high-heeled shoes were too wide and too long. "I'll never be able to walk in these," Maki said. She sounded disappointed, as though she had failed him. "He'll know I'm a fake when I take my first step."

Packer stuffed his handkerchief in the loose space behind her heel. He called out the door, "A handkerchief!" He grabbed one from an upraised hand and packed the other shoe.

"Let's go," he said, leading the unsteady policewoman down the pimpled metal steps of the command vehicle and into the green-and-white. As the other men gawked, Packer said, "Artie, you drive. Turk, unlock the shotgun but leave it in the stanchion. Me and, uh, the officer, we'll ride in the back." When they were in place, he said, "Now listen! Flip the roof lights on. Turk, you'll keep moving the spotlight back and forth across the front of my house. Slow! Artie, keep the siren barely spinning. Low enough to get his attention, but not loud enough to spook him."

Siegl eased the car out of the supermarket parking lot and turned left toward the house fifty yards away. "Keep it at walking speed," Packer said. "Whatever we do, we don't want to look threatening. Just drive up nice and easy." It was a relief to be finished planning, to be finished weighing prospects and intangibles. This was what they *had* to do, this wild crazy insane plan, as wild and crazy and insane as anything else that was going on. But it might work, depending on Yount's mental condition, the state of his mixed-up brain, how easily he could be mixed up even more. . . .

And if they failed, what then?

SWAT.

Would Yount have time to kill both—the subjects—before SWAT broke in and mowed him down? Would he have time to kill—just one? *Which one?* Packer covered his eyes with his palms.

"Will I be, uh, getting out?" the woman asked. For the first time, he heard anxiety in her voice.

"We both will," Packer said. He reached across and took her hand.

"How can I walk in these shoes?"

"Shuffle along. Barely lift your feet. The slower you go, the less chance he'll notice you're not walking like her. It'll seem like a dream. He's already dreaming, think of it that way. That's our edge."

The police car crept along the line of parked cars, its roof lights throwing glints of red and blue against the houses and trees. "Dead slow, Artie," Packer ordered. "That's it, pal. Now—tap the siren. *Just tap it!* That's it, that's perfect. Just a low moan. Low and—weird. Let him dream. Turk, a little more action with the spot. Back and forth: that's it. *Don't linger on the windows!* He'll think we're trying to see inside. Good! That's good!"

Packer pushed the microphone button and said, "Two Two Three to Charlie Two. Tell him we're in sight. If he looks out, he'll see us. She's in the back seat. Tell him she's, uh, dying to see him." He looked quickly at Maki; she'd missed his stupid choice of words. She was staring at the house, probably imagining what was behind the curtains. Well, I didn't promise it wouldn't be dangerous, he reminded himself. But by God I'll make it as safe as I can for her. . . . And I'll never forget. . . .

When they were almost under the streetlight in front of the bungalow, Packer said, "Stop the car, but keep the lights and siren going. Low! *Lower!* Turk, if he comes out, crisscross the spot in his face, but not too steady. Just enough to blur his view a little. Light and sound, sound and light. That's it."

The car stopped and vibrated to the idling engine. "Slump down, you guys," Packer said. "Reduce the target." They were twenty-five or thirty feet from his front windows. He pressed the door handle on the curb side and felt it yield. "Ready, uh, Maki?" he asked.

"Y-yes, sir," she said. He could hear her breathing, and her hand trembled under his. A week ago, she'd been in the academy.

"You're bulletproof," he said gently, "except above the neck. He's a cop; he's trained to aim for the body. Break off if there's any firing, got that? Jump behind a car and stay there. We're gonna approach slow. *Real* slow. Stay right behind me. Use me as a shield. And keep your head down, okay? *Whatever you do, keep your head down!*"

"O-k-kay," she said, her green eyes wide. A strand of curly copper poked from the side of the floppy hat. He reached up and tucked it in. "Now," he said, and opened the door.

46

"It's—her," the man called Koslo said, turning from the front window with a faint smile on his thin lips. "I told him they'd listen." He stared into an empty corner of the room. "Didn't believe me, did you?" he said. His voice had a surprised prideful quality, as though he had just done the impossible and still wasn't sure of it himself. Amnee remembered sounding like that in the delivery room, after Emmy.

"Now fix yourself up," he was saying. "Don't you want to look good when she sees you?" The conversation sounded so convincing that she searched the gloom for another person. But there was no one in that dark corner of the room, only the spinning wheel and a potted ficus plant that needed water. There wasn't anything big enough to conceal even a child's body.

"Hold it!" he said, looking outside again. *"Hold everything!"* With his back to her, she had a clear shot. But could she hit him? *Could she kill him?* Crouched at the front window, lifting the edge of the curtain, he was only six or eight feet away, but he was moving from side to side for a better look, or was he trying to keep from being a stationary target? She distrusted the little Iver Johnson and her own marksmanship. She had heard that handguns were inaccurate. What if she missed, or the bullet only nicked him? He would whirl and kill them both.

"What is it?" she couldn't help ask.

"They might be forcing her," he said, staggering back in the room where she held the quieting baby. "I know what they're up to. I know how they think. Cops! *Scum!* They're using *her* to get at *him.* Stand up!"

He moved his big blue-steel revolver to within a few inches of her nose. Dried white flecks marked the corners of his mouth; his lower lip wobbled and he huffed like a man doing hard labor. "Stand up!" he repeated. The gun palpitated in front of her eyes. *"Stand—UP!"*

Now he's going to fire, she said to herself. Either on purpose or accidentally: what does it matter? His hand is shaking and he's going to shoot the baby and me. Now I *must* do it. I *must!*

But how?

She raised herself to her feet, cradling the child.

"Follow orders," he said, his eyes glazed, dead. "Nobody can help. Stick out your right hand."

She stood on stiff legs and shifted Emmy to her left arm and raised her right hand with the cuff still attached. With a practiced movement, he snapped the loose cuff over his own left wrist. "Now hold the kid between us. C'mon, *c'mon! Closer!* So I can stick my head against it. *Closer!* That's it. Side by side and heads touching. I know cops. How they think, umh, uh, how they act. Okay, here we go."

She allowed herself a glance to the right. The muzzle of his oversize revolver rested under the baby's chin. She could see his finger on the trigger.

She eased her own head gently against Emily's and lifted her left hand to pass it through the fine-spun blond hair, but the child seemed almost unnaturally quiet after her outbursts of a few minutes before. Did babies go into shock? Somewhere she had read that shock could kill. But—*babies?*

"I'm ready," she said, her mind racing.

They shuffled slowly toward the door.

She realized that something strange was happening to her mind. She was evaluating plans and strategies in split seconds. In instants, she was conceiving complex courses of action. Textbooks of thoughts and ideas flashed across her mind between one slow step toward the door and the next. She felt almost God-like, as though all the wisdom of the world had been programed into her brain, *and was of no use.* Because she was helpless. Powerless. Paralyzed by the muzzle of a gun against her baby's throat.

She tried to remember a word that a female author had used to describe the Nazi mass murders. The word eluded her galloping mind, but she remembered its meaning: ordinary, trite, lacking in glamour or style or originality. Their own deaths, hers and Emmy's—they *couldn't* be like that. They had to mean something, had to stand for something. The two of them couldn't just be shot to death by a man who didn't know his own name.

Banal—that was the word. Unimaginative and common. Just— *blah.* Two bangs and it would be all over. And within a few minutes the traffic would start up again on Orchard, people would go about their ordinary lives, and Packer would be left to mourn.

Unless—

She *could* hold the gun in her apron pocket and fire it sideways into his belly. It *was* possible. But that would give him seconds to live, minutes even, and he could kill them both before she could get off a second shot.

Another word flashed across her brain like a spark. *Gut-shot.* Packer's deer-hunting friends used it all the time. "Damn buck was gut-shot, he run a half a mile before he dropped." She had a picture of her insane captor staggering about the living room with his intestines in both hands and his stomach spewing multicolored organs, maroon for the liver, olive-green for the gall bladder, salmon-pink for the pancreas, all slopped and dripping with rich red blood like the horses she had seen in paintings from the First World War.

Could she put this fellow human through that agony?

She could.

The baby was still quiet, her pale-blue eyes half closed. Worn out, poor thing. She was in her mommy's arms, and that was enough for now. She probably thought they were playing a new kind of night game. Amnee hummed "Go to Sleep" softly, hoping to God it wouldn't aggravate the man.

At the front door, he pulled up hard on their handcuffs and said, "You're gonna open the door. Soon as we take one step outside, we start moving. Front and back, side to side, get it? The kid's head, it's gonna stick to mine like glue, understand?"

He didn't wait for an answer. "I know cops," he rattled on, talking faster than before. "I know how they think, how they plan. They got a sharpshooter, they got a SWAT unit, they're just waiting for me to stick my head out. But we're not giving them any target. *No target!* If you pull the kid's head an inch away from mine, I'll drop you both."

"Yes, yes, I understand," she said sweetly, as though they had the same objective. "We're all together. We'll do it right. Don't worry."

"Don't *you* worry," he said, sounding offended. "You're the one ought to worry." You're right, she wanted to say, but I did all my worrying in advance. Before there was anything to worry about. My worrying's all used up. . . .

"Undo the locks," he ordered. "Slow. *Slow* . . ."

As she reached up to slide the first bolt, she felt him lean her way, saw his black hair touch Emmy's temple-to-temple. Struggling with her own plans, she had to respect his. No one would dare to shoot at his head, not a rifleman across the street, not even a cop standing square in front. He must have planned carefully. He was crazy, but he wasn't stupid. Artie Siegl had told her a joke like that: "Hey, mister, I'm in here because I'm crazy, not because I'm stupid. . . ." She wondered why she was remembering punch lines, but then she realized she was remembering *everything*. Her mind was leaping forward and backward in time. Maybe it was nature's way of reminding her that her brain was in order, she wouldn't go to pieces: she could *cope*.

"Open the door," he said when the last lock was released.

She held back, her mind discarding option after option. "Open it!" he repeated.

She gripped the knob. She didn't dare anger him; his temper would communicate to the baby, and she wasn't sure how he would behave with a child screaming in his ear. *Stay quiet, Emmy, stay still.*

"She's out there," he said, whispering now. "You understand that? He needs her. *He needs her!*"

She turned the knob, convinced they would walk into a fusillade of police bullets. Her heart should have been running wild, but she felt steady. This must be the way God prepares you for the final moment, she told herself. The last terror seeps away, the hysteria subsides, and what's left is a quiet numbness, a time of peace. This man Yount or Koslo—he seemed on the edge of panic, but she was calmly aware of every action, every transient thought. All her senses were heightened by the danger, and her fear was suppressed, shoved to the back of her mind. Fear had become an indulgence.

"Mommy loves Emmy," she whispered in the tiny ear as she pulled open the door with her free hand.

A beam of light caught her in the face. When she averted her eyes, she saw that Koslo had pressed his cheek against the baby's. He was staring out of his coal-pit eyes into the night. She turned and looked straight ahead. The heat rose from the pavement in shimmering ribbons. Just outside the row of parked cars, she saw a movie-cartoon scene: a wavy green-and-white, double-parked, roof lights spinning, its one visible wheel looking fat as a doughnut. As she watched, the back door of the patrol car opened.

The man yanked her by the handcuff and took a few halting steps across the wooden porch, then led them down the short staircase that Packer had rebuilt. She struggled to keep up as he took a few steps toward the sidewalk, then one to the left and one backward. They moved erratically like a clown horse with two new men inside, and she realized how preposterous they must appear. She also realized that the random two-step completely disarmed the police.

A man got out of the car. A cop. A very tall—

Dear God, she thought, it's Packer. *Packer!* And he's leading—a woman. She wanted to scream his name, but she bit back the impulse. The woman was big and cowlike in a garish purple slack suit and a pink flop-brimmed hat. The two of them moved toward the house like a slow march to the altar at a wedding.

"Mrs. Yount?" Koslo called out. *"Oh, oh, oh . . ."* He sounded close to the breaking point.

For a second he shifted his head away from the baby's, then pressed it back. His pistol wavered against Emmy's throat. As Amnee listened, he began to grunt under his breath: "Ugh! Ugh! *Ugggh!"* She looked out of the corner of her eyes; his chalky face was alive with animal tension.

"Nice Emmy," she said, nuzzling the baby's left cheek. "Nice baby." The man snorted and wrenched them forward.

Somewhere close a siren sang low. She thought she could make out the silhouette of a policeman sitting in the front of the patrol car, but every few seconds the light poked at her face and ruined her focus.

"Kill that spot!" Koslo ordered, pulling the baby's head close and resuming the erratic dance step across the lawn.

The spinning rays from the Visibar poked into the night air, illuminating Packer and the fat woman, throwing a thin surreal wash across the insane man and the drowsy baby and the open space between the two parties, narrowing now as their slow march continued, narrowing till they were only six or eight steps apart.

Koslo jerked her to a stop as though halting a horse.

"Darlene!" he cried in a reverent voice. "Mrs. Yount! Listen, he's inside! Inside—the house! He—he knew you'd be back. He never gave up, Mrs. Yount. Oh, he'll be—so relieved. He's been—waiting." His voice was adoring, obsequious. He sounded almost effeminate.

Packer and the woman stopped just as abruptly, and Amnee watched Koslo's face. All at once his smile faded; his eyes went cold again, then his forehead furrowed into a frown. The muzzle of his gun made a dimple in the baby's milk-white throat.

Dear God, wasn't this fat woman Darlene Yount? Amnee squinted. *No, she wasn't!*

Even with the red and blue lights distorting colors and shades, she could tell this was a bad impersonation. Did he realize it, too?

Slowly she turned her head and looked at his eyes. He stared intently, the tip of his index finger trembling against the trigger.

She dropped her left hand into the apron pocket and groped for the little revolver. The metal lump felt evil, threatening. She was right-handed, and now she was going to have to fire the first and only shot of her life with the wrong hand. *Sinistra,* her Italian neighbor used to call it. "Sinister," for left. God, her mind wouldn't stop racing.

Painstakingly, she managed to turn the Iver Johnson in the deep pocket and aim it across her body toward his midsection. Her finger touched the cool curve of the trigger.

"Step up, Mrs. Yount," he was saying in a suspicious tone. "Let me see you. Let me—touch you."

The fat woman whispered to Packer, standing in front of her and slightly to one side. As she spoke, a curl of hair slipped from her floppy hat. The curl was blond or red. Koslo jerked as though he'd been hit. Monosyllables popped from his mouth: "You—you're—*not*— It—it's—*not*—"

Amnee felt the sideways pressure as he forced her back into their eccentric shuffle. Trying not to stumble, she noticed that his gun hand had twisted slightly. The barrel rested against the baby's neck, and the muzzle pointed away. If he fired now, he would miss.

At last the baby's life was not endangered. And she'll never be endangered again, Amnee told herself. *Never!* If that awful man moves his gun back an inch, I'll, I'll—shoot!

Her finger tensed against the trigger as they moved two steps to the left and one to the right and then began retreating. Dear God, she realized, we'll trip over something and everybody will fire at once.

The scene took on a dreamlike quality: fuzzy, seen through gauze. She was both acting in the dream and observing the action. She knew they were backing toward the porch, but everything seemed to be in slow motion, pressurized, as she followed the stumbling lead of the crazed dance master.

His gun hand was still turned. She glared at the muzzle as they moved in fits and starts.

If that hand moves . . .

"Gerry," the overweight woman called out. "Gerry! It's me!"

"You—*you're*—YOU'RE NOT YOU!" he exclaimed. His pistol lowered and then bobbed up toward the baby's throat.

Amnee jerked the trigger at point-blank range.

She heard nothing, felt nothing. Time stopped, and it was all a dream, and she had a flash memory of one of the police wives telling how her husband had shot someone and never heard a sound.

The man's face was locked in an uncomprehending stare. Was he—dead? Did people stay on their feet after they were—gut-shot? But where was the blood? Where was the hole? *Why didn't he fall?*

His knees buckled and he pitched forward, dragging the two of them down.

Amnee tucked the infant's head tight to her shoulder and stretched out her left hand to cushion the impact. But the wounded man only slipped to his knees in a position of prayer, staring at the woman in pink and plum. Still staring, he dropped his wavering pistol on the lawn and began to shake. Then his mouth opened wide and he slumped over on his side.

Packer was atop all three so fast that Amnee saw him as a large blur.

He kicked at the gun and sent it skidding.

He picked up the baby, squalling now, hugged and kissed her into silence, and handed her gently to the plump woman. He pulled off his own key ring and opened the cuffs, lifted Amnee to her feet, and squeezed her so hard she grunted. "It's okay, honey," he said softly. "It's okay." She had used the same words to comfort the baby. He patted her between the shoulder blades and squeezed her even harder and said in a choked voice, "It's over, honey. Oh, Amnee Amnee Amnee *Amnee* . . ."

"Packer," she said into his rebuilt ear. "Oh, sweetheart." She hugged as hard as she could with her tired arms.

Uniformed men rushed in from every direction. She recognized Turk Molnar, Artie Siegl, the rookie Mills, Willie Bethea and Rollie Beemer, and more men from the Ninth, and a crew of chattering strangers in jumpsuits. The captain puffed and snorted and wiped at his face.

"Packer!" she said, wrenching away. "Packer, *wait!* Help him! He's—*bleeding!*"

Willie Bethea leaned over the man who called himself Koslo. She saw the cop reach into a first-aid kit and pull out a glass capsule and break it under the poor man's nose. Smelling salts. What good could smelling salts do?

"My baby!" Amnee said, suddenly panicked. *"Where's my baby?"*

God, why was she so afraid? Her heart slammed against her rib cage, and the hair rose on the back of her neck. Amnee, Amnee, she told herself, it's over now. But where is my baby? *Did he hurt my baby?* She breathed deeply and closed her eyes with relief when the fat woman handed Emmy over.

"Mommy," the child said sleepily. "Dah okay?"

"Yes, angel, Dah's okay. You okay?"

"Emmy—'pleepy."

The baby rested heavily against her shoulder, and Amnee watched as the fallen man blinked his wasted eyes and tried to raise himself on an elbow. "Packer, *Packer!*" she called out, starting to cry. "He's hurt! I—I shot him."

"Shot him?" Packer said. He looked surprised. "Hon, you, you didn't—just take it easy."

"I shot him, Packer! I shot him with the gun you gave me. *Here!*" She lifted it from her apron pocket like a live rat and handed it over with quaking fingers.

He jerked the thing and the insides popped open. "I thought so," he said. "Five rounds, hon. All intact."

"But I pulled the trigger!"

"You sure?"

"Yes, *yes!* I did! I aimed it across my body and I, I—tried to kill him."

"It misfired, honey. Don't worry." He took her and the baby in his arms.

The man sat quietly, unresisting, a cop holding each wrist. "Darlene," he murmured, then called out, "Darlene! Over here, angel. Over here, *Darlene!*" His voice was entirely different from Koslo's; he was the deskman again. "Hey, fellas," he said, peering out of the purplish black holes that held his eyes, "let me up, will ya? She, she—came back." His head wobbled on his neck like a broken jack-in-the-box; his pasty smiling face looked like a hurry-up job by a cheap embalmer.

"Let him loose," Packer said, kneeling down.

He placed his big hands on the fallen man's shoulders and looked into his eyes. "What's your name?" he asked gently.

"My name? It's *me*, Lieutenant!" He laughed, a dry rattle. "Is this, is this—*what is this?*"

"Where you been tonight, Gerry?"

The deskman's head flopped backward and Packer reached around and supported it in his big hand. "I went—out," he said, the sweat gleaming on his parchment-colored face. "For a walk, Just—a walk. To meet—Darlene. She's right over there. See Darlene? *Don't you see her?"*

"Sure, Gerry," Packer said. He looked across at Mary Rob Maki and rolled his blue eyes almost imperceptibly. "I see her, pal." He reached around the man's thin shoulders. "Listen, Gerry, some people are on the way. Nice people. They're, uh, they're gonna take care of you for a while."

"Will she come with me?" he asked weakly.

Oh, Packer, Amnee thought, *don't deceive him anymore.*

"She'll come with you."

The deskman stared as the fat woman teetered toward him on her pink pumps. His lips barely moved as he said, "I love you, Darlene."

"You look tired, Gerry," Packer said, shifting his position to block the deskman's view. "They'll give you something to sleep."

"Tired," Gerald Yount repeated without moving his lips. "Tired." His pale mouth hung slack, and his head slumped forward on his bony chest.

In the distance, Amnee heard the wail of an ambulance.